Doctor Pascal

Doctor Pascal

EMILE ZOLA

Translated By
MARY J. SERRANO

ÆGYPAN PRESS

Doctor Pascal
A publication of
ÆGYPAN PRESS

www.aegypan.com

I

*I*n the heat of the glowing July afternoon, the room, with blinds carefully closed, was full of a great calm. From the three windows, through the cracks of the old wooden shutters, came only a few scattered sunbeams which, in the midst of the obscurity, made a soft brightness that bathed surrounding objects in a diffused and tender light. It was cool here in comparison with the overpowering heat that was felt outside, under the fierce rays of the sun that blazed upon the front of the house.

Standing before the press which faced the windows, Dr. Pascal was looking for a paper that he had come in search of. With doors wide open, this immense press of carved oak, adorned with strong and handsome mountings of metal, dating from the last century, displayed within its capacious depths an extraordinary collection of papers and manuscripts of all sorts, piled up in confusion and filling every shelf to overflowing. For more than thirty years the doctor had thrown into it every page he wrote, from brief notes to the complete texts of his great works on heredity. Thus it was that his searches here were not always easy. He rummaged patiently among the papers, and when he at last found the one he was looking for, he smiled.

For an instant longer he remained near the bookcase, reading the note by a golden sunbeam that came to him from the middle window. He himself, in this dawnlike light, appeared, with his snow-white hair and beard, strong and vigorous; although he was near sixty, his color was so fresh, his features were so finely cut, his eyes were still so clear, and he had so youthful an air that one might have taken him, in his close-fitting, maroon velvet jacket, for a young man with powdered hair.

"Here, Clotilde," he said at last, "you will copy this note. Ramond would never be able to decipher my diabolical writing."

And he crossed the room and laid the paper beside the young girl, who stood working at a high desk in the embrasure of the window to the right.

"Very well, master," she answered.

She did not even turn round, so engrossed was her attention with the pastel which she was at the moment rapidly sketching in with broad strokes of the crayon. Near her in a vase bloomed a stalk of hollyhocks of a singular shade of violet, striped with yellow. But the profile of her small round head, with its short, fair hair, was clearly distinguishable; an exquisite and serious profile, the straight forehead contracted in a frown of attention, the eyes of an azure blue, the nose delicately molded, the chin firm. Her bent neck, especially, of a milky whiteness, looked adorably youthful under the gold of the clustering curls. In her long black blouse she seemed very tall, with her slight figure, slender throat, and flexible form, the flexible slenderness of the divine figures of the Renaissance. In spite of her twenty-five years, she still retained a childlike air and looked hardly eighteen.

"And," resumed the doctor, "you will arrange the press a little. Nothing can be found there any longer."

"Very well, master," she repeated, without raising her head; "presently."

Pascal had turned round to seat himself at his desk, at the other end of the room, before the window to the left. It was a plain black wooden table, and was littered also with papers and pamphlets of all sorts. And silence again reigned in the peaceful semi-obscurity, contrasting with the overpowering glare outside. The vast apartment, a dozen meters long and six wide, had, in addition to the press, only two bookcases, filled with books. Antique chairs of various kinds stood around in disorder, while for sole adornment, along the walls, hung with an old *salon* Empire paper of a rose pattern, were nailed pastels of flowers of strange coloring dimly visible. The woodwork of three folding-doors, the door opening on the hall and two others at opposite ends of the apartment, the one leading to the doctor's room, the other to that of the young girl, as well as the cornice of the smoke-darkened ceiling, dated from the time of Louis XV.

An hour passed without a sound, without a breath. Then Pascal, who, as a diversion from his work, had opened a newspaper — *Le Temps* — which had lain forgotten on the table, uttered a slight exclamation:

"Why! your father has been appointed editor of the *Epoque,* the prosperous republican journal which has the publishing of the papers of the Tuileries."

This news must have been unexpected by him, for he laughed frankly, at once pleased and saddened, and in an undertone he continued:

"My word! If things had been invented, they could not have been finer. Life is a strange thing. This is a very interesting article."

Clotilde made no answer, as if her thoughts were a hundred leagues away from what her uncle was saying. And he did not speak again, but taking his scissors after he had read the article, he cut it out and pasted it on a sheet of paper, on which he made some marginal notes in his large, irregular handwriting. Then he went back to the press to classify this new document in it. But he was obliged to take a chair, the shelf being so high that he could not reach it notwithstanding his tall stature.

On this high shelf a whole series of enormous bundles of papers were arranged in order, methodically classified. Here were papers of all sorts: sheets of manuscript, documents on stamped paper, articles cut out of newspapers, arranged in envelopes of strong blue paper, each of which bore on the outside a name written in large characters. One felt that these documents were tenderly kept in view, taken out continually, and carefully replaced; for of the whole press, this corner was the only one kept in order.

When Pascal, mounted on the chair, had found the package he was looking for, one of the bulkiest of the envelopes, on which was written the name "Saccard," he added to it the new document, and then replaced the whole under its corresponding alphabetical letter. A moment later he had forgotten the subject, and was complacently straightening a pile of papers that were falling down. And when he at last jumped down off the chair, he said:

"When you are arranging the press, Clotilde, don't touch the packages at the top; do you hear?"

"Very well, master," she responded, for the third time, docilely.

He laughed again, with the gaiety that was natural to him.

"That is forbidden."

"I know it, master."

And he closed the press with a vigorous turn of the key, which he then threw into a drawer of his writing table. The young girl was sufficiently acquainted with his researches to keep his manuscripts in some degree of order; and he gladly employed her as his secretary; he made her copy his notes when some *confrere* and friend, like Dr. Ramond asked him to send him some document. But she was not a *savante*; he simply forbade her to read what he deemed it useless that she should know.

At last, perceiving her so completely absorbed in her work, his attention was aroused.

"What is the matter with you, that you don't open your lips?" he said. "Are you so taken up with the copying of those flowers that you can't speak?"

This was another of the labors which he often entrusted to her — to make drawings, aquarelles, and pastels, which he afterward used in his works as plates. Thus, for the past five years he had been making some curious experiments on a collection of hollyhocks; he had obtained a whole series of new colorings by artificial fecundations. She made these sorts of copies with extraordinary minuteness, an exactitude of design and of coloring so extreme that he marveled unceasingly at the conscientiousness of her work, and he often told her that she had a "good, round, strong, clear little headpiece."

But, this time, when he approached her to look over her shoulder, he uttered a cry of comic fury.

"There you are at your nonsense! Now you are off in the clouds again! Will you do me the favor to tear that up at once?"

She straightened herself, her cheeks flushed, her eyes aglow with the delight she took in her work, her slender fingers stained with the red and blue crayon that she had crushed.

"Oh, master!"

And in this "master," so tender, so caressingly submissive, this term of complete abandonment by which she called him, in order to avoid using the words godfather or uncle, which she thought silly, there was, for the first time, a passionate accent of revolt, the revindication of a being recovering possession of and asserting itself.

For nearly two hours she had been zealously striving to produce an exact and faithful copy of the hollyhocks, and she had just thrown on another sheet a whole bunch of imaginary flowers, of dream-flowers, extravagant and superb. She had, at times, these abrupt shiftings, a need of breaking away in wild fancies in the midst of the most precise of reproductions. She satisfied it at once, falling always into this extraordinary efflorescence of such spirit and fancy that it never repeated itself; creating roses, with bleeding hearts, weeping tears of sulfur, lilies like crystal urns, flowers without any known form, even, spreading out starry rays, with corollas floating like clouds. Today, on a groundwork dashed in with a few bold strokes of black crayon, it was a rain of pale stars, a whole shower of infinitely soft petals; while, in a corner, an unknown bloom, a bud, chastely veiled, was opening.

"Another to nail there!" resumed the doctor, pointing to the wall, on which there was already a row of strangely curious pastels. "But what may that represent, I ask you?"

She remained very grave, drawing back a step, the better to contemplate her work.

"I know nothing about it; it is beautiful."

At this moment appeared Martine, the only servant, become the real mistress of the house, after nearly thirty years of service with the doctor. Although she had passed her sixtieth year, she, too, still retained a youthful air as she went about, silent and active, in her eternal black gown and white cap that gave her the look of a nun, with her small, white, calm face, and lusterless eyes, the light in which seemed to have been extinguished.

Without speaking, she went and sat down on the floor before an easy chair, through a rent in the old covering of which the hair was escaping, and drawing from her pocket a needle and a skein of worsted, she set to work to mend it. For three days past she had been waiting for an hour's time to do this piece of mending, which haunted her.

"While you are about it, Martine," said Pascal jestingly, taking between both his hands the mutinous head of Clotilde, "sew me fast, too, this little noodle, which sometimes wanders off into the clouds."

Martine raised her pale eyes, and looked at her master with her habitual air of adoration.

"Why does monsieur say that?"

"Because, my good girl, in very truth, I believe it is you who have stuffed this good little round, clear, strong headpiece full of notions of the other world, with all your devoutness."

The two women exchanged a glance of intelligence.

"Oh, monsieur! religion has never done any harm to anyone. And when people have not the same ideas, it is certainly better not to talk about them."

An embarrassed silence followed; this was the one difference of opinion which, at times, brought about disagreements among these three united beings who led so restricted a life. Martine was only twenty-nine, a year older than the doctor, when she entered his house, at the time when he made his *debut* as a physician at Plassans, in a bright little house of the new town. And thirteen years later, when Saccard, a brother of Pascal, sent him his daughter Clotilde, aged seven, after his wife's death and at the moment when he was about to marry again, it was she who brought up the child, taking it to church, and communicating to it a little of the devout flame with which she had always burned; while the doctor, who had a broad mind, left them to their joy of believing, for he did not feel that he had the right to interdict to anyone the happiness of faith; he contented himself later on with watching over the young girl's education and giving her clear and sound ideas about everything. For thirteen years, during which the three had lived this retired life at La Souleiade, a small property situated in the outskirts of the town, a quarter of an hour's walk from St. Saturnin, the cathedral, his life had flowed happily along, occupied in secret great works, a little troubled, however, by an ever increasing uneasiness — the collision, more and more violent, every day, between their beliefs.

Pascal took a few turns gloomily up and down the room. Then, like a man who did not mince his words, he said:

"See, my dear, all this phantasmagoria of mystery has turned your pretty head. Your good God had no need of you; I should have kept you for myself alone; and you would have been all the better for it."

But Clotilde, trembling with excitement, her clear eyes fixed boldly upon his, held her ground.

"It is you, master, who would be all the better, if you did not shut yourself up in your eyes of flesh. That is another thing, why do you not wish to see?"

And Martine came to her assistance, in her own style.

"Indeed, it is true, monsieur, that you, who are a saint, as I say everywhere, should accompany us to church. Assuredly, God will save you. But at the bare idea that you should not go straight to paradise, I tremble all over."

He paused, for he had before him, in open revolt, those two whom he had been accustomed to see submissive at his feet, with the tenderness of women won over by his gaiety and his goodness. Already he opened his mouth, and was going to answer roughly, when the uselessness of the discussion became apparent to him.

"There! Let us have peace. I would do better to go and work. And above all, let no one interrupt me!"

With hasty steps he gained his chamber, where he had installed a sort of laboratory, and shut himself up in it. The prohibition to enter it was formal. It was here that he gave himself up to special preparations, of which he spoke to no one. Almost immediately the slow and regular sound of a pestle grinding in a mortar was heard.

"Come," said Clotilde, smiling, "there he is, at his devil's cookery, as grandmother says."

And she tranquilly resumed her copying of the hollyhocks. She completed the drawing with mathematical precision, she found the exact tone of the violet petals, striped with yellow, even to the most delicate discoloration of the shades.

"Ah!" murmured Martine, after a moment, again seated on the ground, and occupied in mending the chair, "what a misfortune for a good man like that to lose his soul willfully. For there is no denying it; I have known him now for thirty years, and in all that time he has never so much as spoken an unkind word to anyone. A real heart of gold, who would take the bit from his own mouth. And handsome, too, and always well, and always gay, a real blessing! It is a murder that he does not wish to make his peace with the good God. We will force him to do it, mademoiselle, will we not?"

Clotilde, surprised at hearing her speak so long at one time on the subject, gave her word with a grave air.

"Certainly, Martine, it is a promise. We will force him."

Silence reigned again, broken a moment afterward by the ringing of the bell attached to the street door below. It had been attached to the door so that they might have notice when anyone entered the house, too vast for the three persons who inhabited it. The servant appeared surprised, and grumbled a few words under her breath. Who could have come in such heat as this? She rose, opened the door, and went and leaned over the balustrade; then she returned, saying:

"It is Mme. Felicite."

Old Mme. Rougon entered briskly. In spite of her eighty years, she had mounted the stairs with the activity of a young girl; she was still the brown, lean, shrill grasshopper of old. Dressed elegantly now in black silk, she might still be taken, seen from behind, thanks to the slenderness of her figure, for some coquette, or some ambitious woman following her favorite pursuit. Seen in front, her eyes still lighted up her withered visage with their fires, and she smiled with an engaging smile when she so desired.

"What! is it you, grandmother?" cried Clotilde, going to meet her. "Why, this sun is enough to bake one."

Felicite, kissing her on the forehead, laughed, saying:

"Oh, the sun is my friend!"

Then, moving with short, quick steps, she crossed the room, and turned the fastening of one of the shutters.

"Open the shutters a little! It is too gloomy to live in the dark in this way. At my house I let the sun come in."

Through the opening a jet of hot light, a flood of dancing sparks entered. And under the sky, of the violet blue of a conflagration, the parched plain could be seen, stretching away in the distance, as if asleep or dead in the overpowering, furnacelike heat, while to the right, above the pink roofs, rose the belfry of St. Saturnin, a gilded tower with arises that, in the blinding light, looked like whitened bones.

"Yes," continued Felicite, "I think of going shortly to the Tulettes, and I wished to know if Charles were here, to take him with me. He is not here I see that — I will take him another day."

But while she gave this pretext for her visit, her ferretlike eyes were making the tour of the apartment. Besides, she did not insist, speaking immediately afterward of her son Pascal, on hearing the rhythmical noise of the pestle, which had not ceased in the adjoining chamber.

"Ah! he is still at his devil's cookery! Don't disturb him, I have nothing to say to him."

Martine, who had resumed her work on the chair, shook her head, as if to say that she had no mind to disturb her master, and there was silence again, while Clotilde wiped her fingers, stained with crayon, on a cloth, and Felicite began to walk about the room with short steps, looking around inquisitively.

Old Mme. Rougon would soon be two years a widow. Her husband who had grown so corpulent that he could no longer move, had succumbed to an attack of indigestion on the 3d of September, 1870, on the night of the day on which he had learned of the catastrophe of Sedan. The ruin of the government of which he flattered himself with being one of the founders, seemed to have crushed him. Thus, Felicite affected to occupy herself no longer with politics, living, thenceforward, like a dethroned queen, the only surviving power of a vanished world. No one was unaware that the Rougons, in 1851, had saved Plassans from anarchy, by causing the *coup d'etat* of the 2d of December to triumph there, and that, a few years later, they had won it again from the legitimist and republican candidates, to give it to a Bonapartist deputy. Up to the time of the war, the Empire had continued all-powerful in the town, so popular that it had obtained there at the plebiscite an overwhelming majority. But since the disasters the town had become republican, the quarter St. Marc had returned to its secret royalist intrigues, while the old quarter and the new town had sent to the chamber a liberal representative, slightly tinged with Orleanism, and ready to take sides with the republic, if it should triumph. And, therefore, it was that Felicite, like the intelligent woman she was, had withdrawn her attention from politics, and consented to be nothing more than the dethroned queen of a fallen government.

But this was still an exalted position, surrounded by a melancholy poetry. For sixteen years she had reigned. The tradition of her two *salons,* the yellow *salon,* in which the *coup d'etat* had matured, and the green *salon,* later the neutral ground on which the conquest of Plassans was completed, embellished itself with the reflection of the vanished past, and was for her a glorious history. And besides, she was very rich. Then, too, she had shown herself dignified in her fall, never uttering a regret or a complaint, parading, with her eighty years, so long a succession of fierce appetites, of abominable maneuvers, of inordinate gratifications, that she became august through them. Her only happiness, now, was to enjoy in peace her large fortune and her past royalty, and she had but one passion left — to defend her past, to extend its fame, suppressing everything that might tarnish it later. Her pride, which lived on the double exploit of which the inhabitants still spoke, watched with jealous care, resolved to leave in existence only creditable documents, those traditions which caused her to be saluted like a fallen queen when she walked through the town.

She went to the door of the chamber and listened to the persistent noise of the pestle, which did not cease. Then, with an anxious brow, she returned to Clotilde.

"Good Heavens! What is he making? You know that he is doing himself the greatest harm with his new drug. I was told, the other day, that he came near killing one of his patients."

"Oh, grandmother!" cried the young girl.

But she was now launched.

"Yes, exactly. The good wives say many other things, besides! Why, go question them, in the faubourg! They will tell you that he grinds dead men's bones in infants' blood."

This time, while even Martine protested, Clotilde, wounded in her affection, grew angry.

"Oh, grandmother, do not repeat such abominations! Master has so great a heart that he thinks only of making everyone happy!"

Then, when she saw that they were both angry, Felicite, comprehending that she had gone too far, resumed her coaxing manner.

"But, my kitten, it is not I who say those frightful things. I repeat to you the stupid reports they spread, so that you may comprehend that Pascal is wrong to pay no heed to public opinion. He thinks he has found a new remedy — nothing could be better! and I will even admit that he will be able to cure everybody, as he hopes. Only, why affect these mysterious ways; why not speak of the matter openly; why, above all, try it only on the rabble of the old quarter and of the country, instead of, attempting among the well-to-do people of the town, striking cures which would do him honor? No, my child, you see your uncle has never been able to act like other people."

She had assumed a grieved tone, lowering her voice, to display the secret wound of her heart.

"God be thanked! it is not men of worth who are wanting in our family; my other sons have given me satisfaction enough. Is it not so? Your Uncle Eugene rose high enough, minister for twelve years, almost emperor! And your father himself handled many a million, and had a part in many a one of the great works which have made Paris a new city. Not to speak at all of your brother, Maxime, so rich, so distinguished, nor of your cousin, Octave Mouret, one of the kings of the new commerce, nor of our dear Abbé Mouret, who is a saint! Well, then, why does Pascal, who might have followed in the footsteps of them all, persist in living in his hole, like an eccentric old fool?"

And as the young girl was again going to protest, she closed her mouth, with a caressing gesture of her hand.

"No, no, let me finish. I know very well that Pascal is not a fool, that he has written remarkable works, that his communications to the Academy of Medicine have even won for him a reputation among *savants*. But what does that count for, compared to what I have dreamed of for him? Yes, all the best practice of the town, a large fortune, the decoration — honors, in short, and a position worthy of the family. My word! I used to say to him when he was a child: 'But where do you come from? You are not one of us!' As for me, I have sacrificed everything for the family; I would let myself be hacked to pieces, that the family might always be great and glorious!"

She straightened her small figure, she seemed to grow tall with the one passion that had formed the joy and pride of her life. But as she resumed her walk, she was startled by suddenly perceiving on the floor the copy of the *Temps*, which the doctor had thrown there, after cutting out the article, to add it to the Saccard papers, and the light from the open window, falling full upon the sheet, enlightened her, no doubt, for she suddenly stopped walking, and threw herself into a chair, as if she at last knew what she had come to learn.

"Your father has been appointed editor of the *Epoque*," she said abruptly.

"Yes," answered Clotilde tranquilly, "master told me so; it was in the paper."

With an anxious and attentive expression, Felicite looked at her, for this appointment of Saccard, this rallying to the republic, was something of vast significance. After the fall of the empire he had dared return to France, notwithstanding his condemnation as director of the Banque Universelle, the colossal fall of which had preceded that of the government. New influences, some incredible intrigue must have placed him on his feet again, for not only had he received his pardon, but he was once more in a position to undertake affairs of considerable importance, launched into journalism, having his share again of all the good things going. And the recollection came to her of the quarrels of other days between him and his brother Eugene Rougon, whom he had so often compromised, and whom, by an ironical turn of events, he was perhaps going to protect, now that the former minister of the Empire was only a simple deputy, resigned to the single role of standing by his fallen master with the obstinacy with which his mother stood by her family.

She still obeyed docilely the orders of her eldest son, the genius, fallen though he was; but Saccard, whatever he might do, had also a part in her heart, from his indomitable determination to succeed, and she was also proud of Maxime, Clotilde's brother, who had taken up his quarters again, after the war, in his mansion in the Avenue of the Bois de Boulogne, where he was consuming the fortune left him by his wife, Louise de Mareuil, become prudent, with the wisdom of a man struck in a vital part, and trying to cheat the paralysis which threatened him.

"Editor of the *Epoque*," she repeated; "it is really the position of a minister which your father has won. And I forgot to tell you, I have written again to your brother, to persuade him to come and see us. That would divert him, it would do him good. Then, there is that child, that poor Charles —"

She did not continue. This was another of the wounds from which her pride bled; a son whom Maxime had had when seventeen by a servant, and who now, at the age of fifteen, weak of intellect, a half-idiot, lived at Plassans, going from the house of one to that of another, a burden to all.

She remained silent a moment longer, waiting for some remark from Clotilde, some transition by which she might come to the subject she wished to touch upon. When she saw that the young girl, occupied in arranging the papers on her desk, was no longer listening, she came to a sudden decision, after casting a glance at Martine, who continued mending the chair, as if she were deaf and dumb.

"Your uncle cut the article out of the *Temps*, then?"

Clotilde smiled calmly.

"Yes, master put it away among his papers. Ah! how many notes he buries in there! Births, deaths, the smallest event in life, everything goes in there. And the genealogical tree is there also, our famous genealogical tree, which he keeps up to date!"

The eyes of old Mme. Rougon flamed. She looked fixedly at the young girl.

"You know them, those papers?"

"Oh, no, grandmother; master has never spoken to me of them; and he has forbidden me to touch them."

But she did not believe her.

"Come! you have them under your hands, you must have read them."

Very simple, with her calm rectitude, Clotilde answered, smilingly again.

"No, when master forbids me to do anything, it is because he has his reasons, and I do not do it."

"Well, my child," cried Felicite vehemently, dominated by her passion, "you, whom Pascal loves tenderly, and whom he would listen to, perhaps, you ought to entreat him to burn all that, for if he should chance to die, and those frightful things which he has in there were to be found, we should all be dishonored!"

Ah, those abominable papers! she saw them at night, in her nightmares, revealing in letters of fire, the true histories, the physiological blemishes of the family, all that wrong side of her glory which she would have wished to bury forever with the ancestors already dead! She knew how it was that the doctor had conceived the idea of collecting these documents at the beginning of his great studies on heredity; how he had found himself led to take his own family as an example, struck by the typical cases which he saw in it, and which helped to support laws discovered by him. Was it not a perfectly natural field of observation, close at hand and with which he was thoroughly familiar? And with the fine, careless justness of the scientist, he had been accumulating for the last thirty years the most private data, collecting and classifying everything, raising this genealogical tree of the Rougon-Macquarts, of which the voluminous papers, crammed full of proofs, were only the commentary.

"Ah, yes," continued Mme. Rougon hotly, "to the fire, to the fire with all those papers that would tarnish our name!"

And as the servant rose to leave the room, seeing the turn the conversation was taking, she stopped her by a quick gesture.

"No, no, Martine; stay! You are not in the way, since you are now one of the family."

Then, in a hissing voice:

"A collection of falsehoods, of gossip, all the lies that our enemies, enraged by our triumph, hurled against us in former days! Think a little of that, my child. Against all of us, against your father, against your mother, against your brother, all those horrors!"

"But how do you know they are horrors, grandmother?"

She was disconcerted for a moment.

"Oh, well; I suspect it! Where is the family that has not had misfortunes which might be injuriously interpreted? Thus, the mother of us all, that dear and venerable Aunt Dide, your great-grandmother, has she not been for the past twenty-one years in the madhouse at the Tulettes? If God has granted her the grace of allowing her to live to the age of one hundred and four years, he has also cruelly afflicted her in depriving her of her reason. Certainly, there is no shame in that; only, what exasperates me — what must not be — is that they should say afterward that we are all mad. And, then, regarding your grand-uncle Macquart, too, deplorable rumors have been spread. Macquart had his faults in past days, I do not seek to defend him. But today, is he not living very reputably on his little property at the Tulettes, two steps away from our unhappy mother, over whom he watches like a good son? And listen! one last example. Your brother, Maxime, committed a great fault when he had by a servant that poor little Charles, and it is certain, besides, that the unhappy child is of unsound mind. No matter. Will it please you if they tell you that your nephew is degenerate; that he reproduces from four generations back, his great-great-grandmother the dear woman to whom we sometimes take him, and with whom he likes so much to be? No! there is no longer any family possible, if people begin to lay bare everything — the nerves of this one, the muscles of that. It is enough to disgust one with living!"

Clotilde, standing in her long black blouse, had listened to her grandmother attentively. She had grown very serious; her arms hung by her sides, her eyes were fixed upon the ground. There was silence for a moment; then she said slowly:

"It is science, grandmother."

"Science!" cried Felicite, trotting about again. "A fine thing, their science, that goes against all that is most sacred in the world! When they shall have demolished everything they will have advanced greatly! They kill respect, they kill the family, they kill the good God!"

"Oh! don't say that, madame!" interrupted Martine, in a grieved voice, her narrow devoutness wounded. "Do not say that M. Pascal kills the good God!"

"Yes, my poor girl, he kills him. And look you, it is a crime, from the religious point of view, to let one's self be damned in that way. You do not love him, on my word of honor! No, you do not love him, you two who have the happiness of believing, since you do nothing to bring him back to the right path. Ah! if I were in your place, I would split that press open with a hatchet. I would make a famous bonfire with all the insults to the good God which it contains!"

She had planted herself before the immense press and was measuring it with her fiery glance, as if to take it by assault, to sack it, to destroy it, in spite of the withered and fragile thinness of her eighty years. Then, with a gesture of ironical disdain:

"If, even with his science, he could know everything!"

Clotilde remained for a moment absorbed in thought, her gaze lost in vacancy. Then she said in an undertone, as if speaking to herself:

"It is true, he cannot know everything. There is always something else below. That is what irritates me; that is what makes us quarrel: for I cannot, like him, put the mystery aside. I am troubled by it, so much so that I suffer cruelly. Below, what wills and acts in the shuddering darkness, all the unknown forces —"

Her voice had gradually become lower and now dropped to an indistinct murmur.

Then Martine, whose face for a moment past had worn a somber expression, interrupted in her turn:

"If it was true, however, mademoiselle, that monsieur would be damned on account of those villainous papers, tell me, ought we to let it happen? For my part, look you, if he were to tell me to throw myself down from the terrace, I would shut my eyes and throw myself, because I know that he is always right. But for his salvation! Oh! if I could, I would work for that, in spite of him. In every way, yes! I would force him; it is too cruel to me to think that he will not be in heaven with us."

"You are quite right, my girl," said Felicite approvingly. "You, at least, love your master in an intelligent fashion."

Between the two, Clotilde still seemed irresolute. In her, belief did not bend to the strict rule of dogma; the religious sentiment did not materialize in the hope of a paradise, of a place of delights, where she was to meet her own again. It was in her simply a need of a beyond, a certainty that the vast world does not stop short at sensation, that there is a whole unknown world, besides, which must be taken into account. But her grandmother, who was so old, this servant, who was so devoted, shook her in her uneasy affection for her uncle. Did they not love him better, in a more enlightened and more upright fashion, they who desired him to be without a stain, freed from his manias as a scientist, pure enough to be among the elect? Phrases of devotional books recurred to her; the continual battle waged against the spirit of evil; the glory of conversions effected after a violent struggle. What if she set herself to this holy task; what if, after all, in spite of himself, she should be able to save him! And an exaltation gradually gained her spirit, naturally inclined to adventurous enterprises.

"Certainly," she said at last, "I should be very happy if he would not persist in his notion of heaping up all those scraps of paper, and if he would come to church with us."

Seeing her about to yield, Mme. Rougon cried out that it was necessary to act, and Martine herself added the weight of all her real authority. They both approached the young girl, and began to instruct her, lowering their voices as if they were engaged in a conspiracy, whence was to result a miraculous benefit, a divine joy with which the whole house would be perfumed. What a triumph if they reconciled the doctor with God! and what sweetness, afterward, to live altogether in the celestial communion of the same faith!

"Well, then, what must I do?" asked Clotilde, vanquished, won over.

But at this moment the doctor's pestle was heard in the silence, with its continued rhythm. And the victorious Felicite, who was about to speak, turned her head uneasily, and looked for a moment at the door of the adjoining chamber. Then, in an undertone, she said:

"Do you know where the key of the press is?"

Clotilde answered only with an artless gesture, that expressed all her repugnance to betray her master in this way.

"What a child you are! I swear to you that I will take nothing; I will not even disturb anything. Only as we are alone and as Pascal never reappears before dinner, we might assure ourselves of what there is in there, might we not? Oh! nothing but a glance, on my word of honor."

The young girl stood motionless, unwilling, still, to give her consent.

"And then, it may be that I am mistaken; no doubt there are none of those bad things there that I have told you of."

This was decisive; she ran to take the key from the drawer, and she herself opened wide the press.

"There, grandmother, the papers are up there."

Martine had gone, without a word, to station herself at the door of the doctor's chamber, her ear on the alert, listening to the pestle, while Felicite, as if riveted to the spot by emotion, regarded the papers. At last, there they were, those terrible documents, the nightmare that had poisoned her life! She saw them, she was going to touch them, to carry them away! And she reached up, straining her little legs, in the eagerness of her desire.

"It is too high, my kitten," she said. "Help me; give them to me!"

"Oh! not that, grandmother! Take a chair!"

Felicite took a chair, and mounted slowly upon it. But she was still too short. By an extraordinary effort she raised herself, lengthening her stature until she was able to touch the envelopes of strong blue paper with the tips of her fingers; and her fingers traveled over them, contracting nervously, scratching like claws. Suddenly there was a crash — it was a geological specimen, a fragment of marble that had been on a lower shelf, and that she had just thrown down.

Instantly the pestle stopped, and Martine said in a stifled voice:

"Take care; here he comes!"

But Felicite, grown desperate, did not hear, did not let go her hold when Pascal entered hastily. He had supposed that some accident had happened, that someone had fallen, and he stood stupefied at what he saw — his mother on the chair, her arm still in the air, while Martine had withdrawn to one side, and Clotilde, very pale, stood waiting, without turning her head. When he comprehended the scene, he himself became as white as a sheet. A terrible anger arose within him.

Old Mme. Rougon, however, troubled herself in no wise. When she saw that the opportunity was lost, she descended from the chair, without making any illusion whatever to the task at which he had surprised her.

"Oh, it is you! I do not wish to disturb you. I came to embrace Clotilde. But here I have been talking for nearly two hours, and I must run away at once. They will be expecting me at home; they won't know what has become of me at this hour. Good-bye until Sunday."

She went away quite at her ease, after smiling at her son, who stood before her silent and respectful. It was an attitude that he had long since adopted, to avoid an explanation which he felt must be cruel, and which he had always feared. He knew her, he was willing to pardon her everything, in his broad tolerance as a scientist, who made allowance for heredity, environment, and circumstances. And, then, was she not his mother? That ought to have sufficed, for, in spite of the frightful blows which his researches inflicted upon the family, he preserved a great affection for those belonging to him.

When his mother was no longer there, his anger burst forth, and fell upon Clotilde. He had turned his eyes away from Martine, and fixed them on the young girl, who did not turn hers away, however, with a courage which accepted the responsibility of her act.

"You! you!" he said at last.

He seized her arm, and pressed it until she cried. But she continued to look him full in the face, without quailing before him, with the indomitable will of her individuality, of her selfhood. She was beautiful and provoking, with her tall, slender figure, robed in its black blouse; and her exquisite, youthful fairness, her straight forehead, her finely cut nose, her firm chin, took on something of a warlike charm in her rebellion.

"You, whom I have made, you who are my pupil, my friend, my other mind, to whom I have given a part of my heart and of my brain! Ah, yes! I should have kept you entirely for myself, and not have allowed your stupid good God to take the best part of you!"

"Oh, monsieur, you blaspheme!" cried Martine, who had approached him, in order to draw upon herself a part of his anger.

But he did not even see her. Only Clotilde existed for him. And he was as if transfigured, stirred up by so great a passion that his handsome face, crowned by his white hair, framed by his white beard, flamed with youthful passion, with an immense tenderness that had been wounded and exasperated.

"You, you!" he repeated in a trembling voice.

"Yes, I! Why then, master, should I not love you better than you love me? And why, if I believe you to be in peril, should I not try to save you? You are greatly concerned about what I think; you would like well to make me think as you do!"

She had never before defied him in this way.

"But you are a little girl; you know nothing!"

"No, I am a soul, and you know no more about souls than I do!"

He released her arm, and waved his hand vaguely toward heaven, and then a great silence fell — a silence full of grave meaning, of the uselessness of the discussion which he did not wish to enter upon. Thrusting her aside rudely, he crossed over to the middle window and opened the blinds, for the sun was declining, and the room was growing dark. Then he returned.

But she, feeling a need of air and space, went to the open window. The burning rain of sparks had ceased, and there fell now, from on high, only the last shiver of the overheated and paling sky; and from the still burning earth ascended warm odors, with the freer respiration of evening. At the foot of the terrace was the railroad, with the outlying dependencies of the station, of which the buildings were to be seen in the distance; then, crossing the vast arid plain, a line of trees marked the course of the Viorne, beyond which rose the hills of Sainte-Marthe, red fields planted with olive trees, supported on terraces by walls of uncemented stones and crowned by somber pine woods — broad amphitheaters, bare and desolate, corroded by the heats of summer, of the color of old baked brick, which this fringe of dark verdure, standing out against the background of the sky, bordered above. To the left opened the gorges of the Seille, great yellow stones that had broken away from the soil, and lay in the midst of blood-colored fields, dominated by an immense band of rocks like the wall of a gigantic fortress; while to the right, at the very entrance to the valley through which flowed the Viorne, rose, one above another, the discolored pink-tiled roofs of the town of Plassans, the compact and confused mass of an old town, pierced by the tops of ancient elms, and dominated by the high tower of St. Saturnin, solitary and serene at this hour in the limpid gold of sunset.

"Ah, my God!" said Clotilde slowly, "one must be arrogant, indeed, to imagine that one can take everything in one's hand and know everything!"

Pascal had just mounted on the chair to assure himself that not one of his packages was missing. Then he took up the fragment of marble, and replaced it on the shelf, and when he had again locked the press with a vigorous turn of the hand, he put the key into his pocket.

"Yes," he replied; "try not to know everything, and above all, try not to bewilder your brain about what we do not know, what we shall doubtless never know!"

Martine again approached Clotilde, to lend her her support, to show her that they both had a common cause. And now the doctor perceived her, also, and felt that they were both united in the same desire for conquest. After years of secret attempts, it was at last open war; the *savant* saw his household turn against his opinions, and menace them with destruction. There is no worse torture than to have treason in one's own home, around one; to be trapped, dispossessed, crushed, by those whom you love, and who love you!

Suddenly this frightful idea presented itself to him.

"And yet both of you love me!" he cried.

He saw their eyes grow dim with tears; he was filled with an infinite sadness, on this tranquil close of a beautiful day. All his gaiety, all his kindness of heart, which came from his intense love of life, were shaken by it.

"Ah, my dear! and you, my poor girl," he said, "you are doing this for my happiness, are you not? But, alas, how unhappy we are going to be!"

II

On the following morning Clotilde was awake at six o'clock. She had gone to bed angry with Pascal; they were at variance with each other. And her first feeling was one of uneasiness, of secret distress, an instant need of making her peace, so that she might no longer have upon her heart the heavy weight that lay there now.

Springing quickly out of bed, she went and half opened the shutters of both windows. The sun, already high, sent his light across the chamber in two golden bars. Into this drowsy room that exhaled a sweet odor of youth, the bright morning brought with it fresh, cheerful air; but the young girl went back and sat down on the edge of the bed in a thoughtful attitude, clad only in her scant nightdress, which made her look still more slender, with her long tapering limbs, her strong, slender body, with its round throat, round neck, round and supple arms; and her adorable neck and throat, of a milky whiteness, had the exquisite softness and smoothness of white satin. For a long time, at the ungrace-ful age between twelve and eighteen, she had looked awkwardly tall, climbing trees like a boy. Then, from the ungainly hoyden had been evolved this charming, delicate and lovely creature.

With absent gaze she sat looking at the walls of the chamber. Al-though La Souleiade dated from the last century, it must have been refurnished under the First Empire, for it was hung with an old-fash-ioned printed calico, with a pattern representing busts of the Sphinx, and garlands of oak leaves. Originally of a bright red, this calico had faded to a pink — an undecided pink, inclining to orange. The curtains of the two windows and of the bed were still in existence, but it had been necessary to clean them, and this had made them still paler. And this faded purple, this dawnlike tint, so delicately soft, was in truth exquisite. As for the bed, covered with the same stuff, it had come down from so remote an antiquity that it had been replaced by another bed found in an adjoining room; another Empire bed, low and very broad, of massive mahogany, ornamented with brasses, its four square pillars adorned also with busts of the Sphinx, like those on the wall. The rest of the furniture matched, however — a press, with whole doors and pillars; a chest of drawers with a marble top, surrounded by a railing; a tall and massive cheval-glass, a large lounge with straight feet, and seats with straight, lyre-shaped backs. But a coverlet made of an old Louis XV. silk skirt brightened the majestic bed, that occupied the middle of the wall fronting the windows; a heap of cushions made the lounge soft; and there were, besides, two *etageres* and a table also covered with old flowered silk, at the further end of the room.

Clotilde at last put on her stockings and slipped on a morning gown of white *pique,* and thrusting the tips of her feet into her grey canvas slippers, she ran into her dressing-room, a back room looking out on the rear of the house. She had had it hung plainly with an *ecru* drill with blue stripes, and it contained only furniture of varnished pine — the toilette table, two presses, and two chairs. It revealed, however, a natural and delicate coquetry which was very feminine. This had grown with her at the same time with her beauty. Headstrong and boyish though she still was at times, she had become a submissive and affectionate woman, desiring to be loved, above everything. The truth was that she had grown up in freedom, without having learned anything more than to read and write, having acquired by herself, later, while assisting her uncle, a vast fund of information. But there had been no plan settled upon between them. He had not wished to make her a prodigy; she had merely conceived a passion for natural history, which revealed to her the mysteries of life. And she had kept her innocence unsullied like a fruit which no hand has touched, thanks, no doubt, to her unconscious and religious waiting for the coming of love — that profound feminine feeling which made her reserve the gift of her whole being for the man whom she should love.

She pushed back her hair and bathed her face; then, yielding to her impatience, she again softly opened the door of her chamber and ventured to cross the vast workroom, noiselessly and on tiptoe. The shutters were still closed, but she could see clearly enough not to stumble against the furniture. When she was at the other end before the door of the doctor's room, she bent forward, holding her breath. Was he already up? What could he be doing? She heard him plainly, walking about with short steps, dressing himself, no doubt. She never entered this chamber in which he chose to hide certain labors; and which thus remained closed, like a tabernacle. One fear had taken possession of her; that of being discovered here by him if he should open the door; and the agitation produced by the struggle between her rebellious pride and a desire to show her submission caused her to grow hot and cold by turns, with sensations until now unknown to her. For an instant her desire for reconciliation was so strong that she was on the point of knocking. Then, as footsteps approached, she ran precipitately away.

Until eight o'clock Clotilde was agitated by an ever-increasing impatience. At every instant she looked at the clock on the mantelpiece of her room; an Empire clock of gilded bronze, representing Love leaning against a pillar, contemplating Time asleep.

Eight was the hour at which she generally descended to the dining room to breakfast with the doctor. And while waiting she made a careful toilette, arranged her hair, and put on another morning gown of white muslin with red spots. Then, having still a quarter of an hour on her hands, she satisfied an old desire and sat down to sew a piece of narrow lace, an imitation of Chantilly, on her working blouse, that black blouse which she had begun to find too boyish, not feminine enough. But on the stroke of eight she laid down her work, and went downstairs quickly.

"You are going to breakfast entirely alone," said Martine tranquilly to her, when she entered the dining room.

"How is that?"

"Yes, the doctor called me, and I passed him in his egg through the half-open door. There he is again, at his mortar and his filter. We won't see him now before noon."

Clotilde turned pale with disappointment. She drank her milk standing, took her roll in her hand, and followed the servant into the kitchen. There were on the ground floor, besides this kitchen and the dining room, only an uninhabited room in which the potatoes were stored, and which had formerly been used as an office by the doctor, when he received his patients in his house — the desk and the armchair had years ago been taken up to his chamber — and another small room, which opened into the kitchen; the old servant's room, scrupulously clean, and furnished with a walnut chest of drawers and a bed like a nun's with white hangings.

"Do you think he has begun to make his liquor again?" asked Clotilde.

"Well, it can be only that. You know that he thinks of neither eating nor drinking when that takes possession of him!"

Then all the young girl's vexation was exhaled in a low plaint:

"Ah, my God! my God!"

And while Martine went to make up her room, she took an umbrella from the hall stand and went disconsolately to eat her roll in the garden, not knowing now how she should occupy her time until midday.

It was now almost seventeen years since Dr. Pascal, having resolved to leave his little house in the new town, had bought La Souleiade for twenty thousand francs, in order to live there in seclusion, and also to give more space and more happiness to the little girl sent him by his brother Saccard from Paris. This Souleiade, situated outside the town gates on a plateau dominating the plain, was part of a large estate whose once vast grounds were reduced to less than two hectares in consequence of successive sales, without counting that the construction of the railroad had taken away the last arable fields. The house itself had been half destroyed by a conflagration and only one of the two buildings remained — a quadrangular wing "of four walls," as they say in Provençe, with five front windows and roofed with large pink tiles. And the doctor, who had bought it completely furnished, had contented himself with repairing it and finishing the boundary walls, so as to be undisturbed in his house.

Generally Clotilde loved this solitude passionately; this narrow kingdom which she could go over in ten minutes, and which still retained remnants of its past grandeur. But this morning she brought there something like a nervous disquietude. She walked for a few moments along the terrace, at the two extremities of which stood two secular cypresses like two enormous funeral tapers, which could be seen three leagues off. The slope then descended to the railroad, walls of uncemented stones supporting the red earth, in which the last vines were dead; and on these giant steps grew only rows of olive and almond trees, with sickly foliage. The heat was already overpowering; she saw the little lizards running about on the disjointed flags, among the hairy tufts of caper bushes.

Then, as if irritated by the vast horizon, she crossed the orchard and the kitchen garden, which Martine still persisted in cultivating in spite of her age, calling in a man only twice a week for the heavier labors; and she ascended to a little pine wood on the right, all that remained of the superb pines which had formerly covered the plateau; but, here, too, she was ill at ease; the pine needles crackled under her feet, a resinous, stifling odor descended from the branches. And walking along the boundary wall past the entrance gate, which opened on the road to Les Fenouilleres, three hundred meters from the first houses of Plassans, she emerged at last on the threshing-yard; an immense yard, fifteen meters in radius, which would of itself have sufficed to prove the former importance of the domain. Ah! this antique area, paved with small round stones, as in the days of the Romans; this species of vast esplanade, covered with short dry grass of the color of gold as with a thick woolen carpet; how joyously she had played there in other days, running about, rolling on the grass, lying for hours on her back, watching the stars coming out one by one in the depths of the illimitable sky!

She opened her umbrella again, and crossed the yard with slower steps. Now she was on the left of the terrace. She had made the tour of the estate, so that she had returned by the back of the house, through the clump of enormous plane trees that on this side cast a thick shade. This was the side on which opened the two windows of the doctor's room. And she raised her eyes to them, for she had approached only in the sudden hope of at last seeing him. But the windows remained closed, and she was wounded by this as by an unkindness to herself. Then only did she perceive that she still held in her hand her roll, which she had forgotten to eat; and she plunged among the trees, biting it impatiently with her fine young teeth.

It was a delicious retreat, this old quincunx of plane trees, another remnant of the past splendor of La Souleiade. Under these giant trees, with their monstrous trunks, there was only a dim light, a greenish light, exquisitely cool, even on the hottest days of summer. Formerly a French garden had been laid out here, of which only the box borders remained; bushes which had habituated themselves to the shade, no doubt, for they grew vigorously, as tall as trees. And the charm of this shady nook was a fountain, a simple leaden pipe fixed in the shaft of a column; whence flowed perpetually, even in the greatest drought, a thread of water as thick as the little finger, which supplied a large mossy basin, the greenish stones of which were cleaned only once in three or four years. When all the wells of the neighborhood were dry, La Souleiade still kept its spring, of which the great plane trees were assuredly the secular children. Night and day for centuries past this slender thread of water, unvarying and continuous, had sung the same pure song with crystal sound.

Clotilde, after wandering awhile among the bushes of box, which reached to her shoulder, went back to the house for a piece of embroidery, and returning with it, sat down at a stone table beside the fountain. Some garden chairs had been placed around it, and they often took coffee here. And after this she affected not to look up again from her work, as if she was completely absorbed in it. Now and then, while seeming to look between the trunks of trees toward the sultry distance, toward the yard, on which the sun blazed fiercely and which glowed like a brazier, she stole a glance from under her long lashes up to the doctor's windows. Nothing appeared, not a shadow. And a feeling of sadness, of resentment, arose within her at this neglect, this contempt in which he seemed to hold her after their quarrel of the day before. She who had got up with so great a desire to make peace at once! He was in no hurry, however; he did not love her then, since he could be satisfied to live at variance with her. And gradually a feeling of gloom took possession of her, her rebellious thoughts returned, and she resolved anew to yield in nothing.

At eleven o'clock, before setting her breakfast on the fire, Martine came to her for a moment, the eternal stocking in her hand which she was always knitting even while walking, when she was not occupied in the affairs of the house.

"Do you know that he is still shut up there like a wolf in his hole, at his villainous cookery?"

Clotilde shrugged her shoulders, without lifting her eyes from her embroidery.

"And then, mademoiselle, if you only knew what they say! Mme. Felicite was right yesterday when she said that it was really enough to make one blush. They threw it in my face that he had killed old Boutin, that poor old man, you know, who had the falling sickness and who died on the road. To believe those women of the faubourg, everyone into whom he injects his remedy gets the true cholera from it, without counting that they accuse him of having taken the devil into partnership."

A short silence followed. Then, as the young girl became more gloomy than before, the servant resumed, moving her fingers still more rapidly:

"As for me, I know nothing about the matter, but what he is making there enrages me. And you, mademoiselle, do you approve of that cookery?"

At last Clotilde raised her head quickly, yielding to the flood of passion that swept over her.

"Listen; I wish to know no more about it than you do, but I think that he is on a very dangerous path. He no longer loves us."

"Oh, yes, mademoiselle; he loves us."

"No, no; not as we love him. If he loved us, he would be here with us, instead of endangering his soul and his happiness and ours, up there, in his desire to save everybody."

And the two women looked at each other for a moment with eyes burning with affection, in their jealous anger. Then they resumed their work in silence, enveloped in shadow.

Above, in his room, Dr. Pascal was working with the serenity of perfect joy. He had practiced his profession for only about a dozen years, from his return to Paris up to the time when he had retired to La Souleiade. Satisfied with the hundred and odd thousand francs which he had earned and which he had invested prudently, he devoted himself almost exclusively to his favorite studies, retaining only a practice among friends, never refusing to go to the bedside of a patient but never sending in his account. When he was paid he threw the money into a drawer in his writing desk, regarding this as pocket-money for his experiments and caprices, apart from his income which sufficed for his wants. And he laughed at the bad reputation for eccentricity which his way of life had gained him; he was happy only when in the midst of his researches on the subjects for which he had a passion. It was matter for surprise to many that this scientist, whose intellectual gifts had been spoiled by a too lively imagination, should have remained at Plassans, this out-of-the-way town where it seemed as if every requirement for his studies must be wanting. But he explained very well the advantages which he had discovered here; in the first place, an utterly peaceful retreat in which he might live the secluded life he desired; then, an unsuspected field for continuous research in the light of the facts of heredity, which was his passion, in this little town where he knew every family and where he could follow the phenomena kept most secret, through two or three generations. And then he was near the seashore; he went there almost every summer, to study the swarming life that is born and propagates itself in the depths of the vast waters. And there was finally, at the hospital in Plassans, a dissecting room to which he was almost the only visitor; a large, bright, quiet room, in which for more than twenty years every unclaimed body had passed under his scalpel. A modest man besides, of a timidity that had long since become shyness, it had been sufficient for him to maintain a correspondence with his old professors and his new friends, concerning the very remarkable papers which he from time to time sent to the Academy of Medicine. He was altogether wanting in militant ambition.

Ah, this heredity! what a subject of endless meditation it was for him! The strangest, the most wonderful part of it all, was it not that the resemblance between parents and children should not be perfect, mathematically exact? He had in the beginning made a genealogical tree of his family, logically traced, in which the influences from generation to generation were distributed equally — the father's part and the mother's part. But the living reality contradicted the theory almost at every point. Heredity, instead of being resemblance, was an effort toward resemblance thwarted by circumstances and environment. And he had arrived at what he called the hypothesis of the abortion of cells. Life is only motion, and heredity being a communicated motion, it happened that the cells in their multiplication from one another jostled one another, pressed one another, made room for themselves, putting forth, each one, the hereditary effort; so that if during this struggle the weaker cells succumbed, considerable disturbances took place, with the final result of organs totally different. Did not variation, the constant invention of nature, which clashed with his theories, come from this? Did not he himself differ from his parents only in consequence of similar accidents, or even as the effect of larvated heredity, in which he had for a time believed? For every genealogical tree has roots which extend as far back into humanity as the first man; one cannot proceed from a single ancestor; one may always resemble a still older, unknown ancestor. He doubted atavism, however; it seemed to him, in spite of a remarkable example taken from his own family, that resemblance at the end of two or three generations must disappear by reason of accidents, of interferences, of a thousand possible combinations. There was then a perpetual becoming, a constant transformation in this communicated effort, this transmitted power, this shock which breathes into matter the breath of life, and which is life itself. And a multiplicity of questions presented themselves to him. Was there a physical and intellectual progress through the ages? Did the brain grow with the growth of the sciences with which it occupied itself? Might one hope, in time, for a larger sum of reason and of happiness? Then there were special problems; one among others, the mystery of which had for a long time irritated him, that of sex; would science never be able to predict, or at least to explain the sex of the embryo being? He had written a very curious paper crammed full of facts on this subject, but which left it in the end in the complete ignorance in which the most exhaustive researches had left it. Doubtless the question of heredity fascinated him as it did only because it remained obscure, vast, and unfathomable, like all the infant sciences where imagination holds sway. Finally, a long study which he had made on the heredity of phthisis revived in him the wavering faith of the healer, arousing in him the noble and wild hope of regenerating humanity.

In short, Dr. Pascal had only one belief — the belief in life. Life was the only divine manifestation. Life was God, the grand motor, the soul of the universe. And life had no other instrument than heredity; heredity made the world; so that if its laws could be known and directed, the world could be made to one's will. In him, to whom sickness, suffering, and death had been a familiar sight, the militant pity of the physician awoke. Ah! to have no more sickness, no more suffering, as little death as possible! His dream ended in this thought — that universal happiness, the future community of perfection and of felicity, could be hastened by intervention, by giving health to all. When all should be healthy, strong, and intelligent, there would be only a superior race, infinitely wise and happy. In India, was not a Brahmin developed from a Soudra in seven generations, thus raising, experimentally, the lowest of beings to the highest type of humanity? And as in his study of consumption he had arrived at the conclusion that it was not hereditary, but that every child of a consumptive carried within him a degenerate soil in which consumption developed with extraordinary facility at the slightest contagion, he had come to think only of invigorating this soil impoverished by heredity; to give it the strength to resist the parasites, or rather the destructive leaven, which he had suspected to exist in the organism, long before the microbe theory. To give strength — the whole problem was there; and to give strength was also to give will, to enlarge the brain by fortifying the other organs.

About this time the doctor, reading an old medical book of the fifteenth century, was greatly struck by a method of treating disease called signature. To cure a diseased organ, it was only necessary to take from a sheep or an ox the corresponding organ in sound condition, boil it, and give the soup to the patient to drink. The theory was to cure like by like, and in diseases of the liver, especially, the old work stated that the cures were numberless. This set the doctor's vivid imagination working. Why not make the trial? If he wished to regenerate those enfeebled by hereditary influences, he had only to give them the normal and healthy nerve substance. The method of the soup, however, seemed to him childish, and he invented in its stead that of grinding in a mortar the brain of a sheep, moistening it with distilled water, and then decanting and filtering the liquor thus obtained. He tried this liquor then mixed with Malaga wine, on his patients, without obtaining any appreciable result. Suddenly, as he was beginning to grow discouraged, he had an inspiration one day, when he was giving a lady suffering from hepatic colics an injection of morphine with the little syringe of Pravaz. What if he were to try hypodermic injections with his liquor? And as soon as he returned home he tried the experiment on himself, making an injection in his side, which he repeated night and morning. The first doses, of a gram only, were without effect. But having doubled, and then tripled the dose, he was enchanted, one morning on getting up, to find that his limbs had all the vigor of twenty. He went on increasing the dose up to five grams, and then his respiration became deeper, and above all he worked with a clearness of mind, an ease, which he had not known for years. A great flood of happiness, of joy in living, inundated his being. From this time, after he had had a syringe made at Paris capable of containing five grams, he was surprised at the happy results which he obtained with his patients, whom he had on their feet again in a few days, full of energy and activity, as if endowed with new life. His method was still tentative and rude, and he divined in it all sorts of dangers, and especially, that of inducing embolism, if the liquor was not perfectly pure. Then he suspected that the strength of his patients came in part from the fever his treatment produced in them. But he was only a pioneer; the method would improve later. Was it not already a miracle to make the ataxic walk, to bring consumptives back to life, as it were; even to give hours of lucidity to the insane? And at the thought of this discovery of the alchemy of the twentieth century, an immense hope opened up before him; he believed he had discovered the universal panacea, the elixir of life, which was to combat human debility, the one real cause of every ill; a veritable scientific Fountain of Youth, which, in giving vigor, health, and will would create an altogether new and superior humanity.

This particular morning in his chamber, a room with a northern aspect and somewhat dark owing to the vicinity of the plane trees, furnished simply with an iron bedstead, a mahogany writing desk, and a large writing table, on which were a mortar and a microscope, he was completing with infinite care the preparation of a vial of his liquor. Since the day before, after pounding the nerve substance of a sheep in distilled water, he had been decanting and filtering it. And he had at last obtained a small bottle of a turbid, opaline liquid, irised by bluish gleams, which he regarded for a long time in the light as if he held in his hand the regenerating blood and symbol of the world.

But a few light knocks at the door and an urgent voice drew him from his dream.

"Why, what is the matter, monsieur? It is a quarter-past twelve; don't you intend to come to breakfast?"

For downstairs breakfast had been waiting for some time past in the large, cool dining room. The blinds were closed, with the exception of one which had just been half opened. It was a cheerful room, with pearl grey panels relieved by blue moldings. The table, the sideboard, and the chairs must have formed part of the set of Empire furniture in the bedrooms; and the old mahogany, of a deep red, stood out in strong relief against the light background. A hanging lamp of polished brass, always shining, gleamed like a sun; while on the four walls bloomed four large bouquets in pastel, of gillyflowers, carnations, hyacinths, and roses.

Joyous, radiant, Dr. Pascal entered.

"Ah, the deuce! I had forgotten! I wanted to finish. Look at this, quite fresh, and perfectly pure this time; something to work miracles with!"

And he showed the vial, which he had brought down in his enthusiasm. But his eye fell on Clotilde standing erect and silent, with a serious air. The secret vexation caused by waiting had brought back all her hostility, and she, who had burned to throw herself on his neck in the morning, remained motionless as if chilled and repelled by him.

"Good!" he resumed, without losing anything of his gaiety, "we are still at odds, it seems. That is something very ugly. So you don't admire my sorcerer's liquor, which resuscitates the dead?"

He seated himself at the table, and the young girl, sitting down opposite him, was obliged at last to answer:

"You know well, master, that I admire everything belonging to you. Only, my most ardent desire is that others also should admire you. And there is the death of poor old Boutin —"

"Oh!" he cried, without letting her finish, "an epileptic, who succumbed to a congestive attack! See! since you are in a bad humor, let us talk no more about that — you would grieve me, and that would spoil my day."

There were soft boiled eggs, cutlets, and cream. Silence reigned for a few moments, during which in spite of her ill-humor she ate heartily, with a good appetite which she had not the coquetry to conceal. Then he resumed, laughing:

"What reassures me is to see that your stomach is in good order. Martine, hand mademoiselle the bread."

The servant waited on them as she was accustomed to do, watching them eat, with her quiet air of familiarity.

Sometimes she even chatted with them.

"Monsieur," she said, when she had cut the bread, "the butcher has brought his bill. Is he to be paid?"

He looked up at her in surprise.

"Why do you ask me that?" he said. "Do you not always pay him without consulting me?"

It was, in effect, Martine who kept the purse. The amount deposited with M. Grandguillot, notary at Plassans, produced a round sum of six thousand francs income. Every three months the fifteen hundred francs were remitted to the servant, and she disposed of them to the best interests of the house; bought and paid for everything with the strictest economy, for she was of so saving a disposition that they bantered her about it continually. Clotilde, who spent very little, had never thought of asking a separate purse for herself. As for the doctor, he took what he required for his experiments and his pocket money from the three or four thousand francs which he still earned every year, and which he kept lying in the drawer of his writing desk; so that there was quite a little treasure there in gold and bank bills, of which he never knew the exact amount.

"Undoubtedly, monsieur, I pay, when it is I who have bought the things; but this time the bill is so large on account of the brains which the butcher has furnished you —"

The doctor interrupted her brusquely:

"Ah, come! so you, too, are going to set yourself against me, are you? No, no; both of you — that would be too much! Yesterday you pained me greatly, and I was angry. But this must cease. I will not have the house turned into a hell. Two women against me, and they the only ones who love me at all? Do you know, I would sooner quit the house at once!"

He did not speak angrily, he even smiled; but the disquietude of his heart was perceptible in the trembling of his voice. And he added with his indulgent, cheerful air:

"If you are afraid for the end of the month, my girl, tell the butcher to send my bill apart. And don't fear; you are not going to be asked for any of your money to settle it with; your sous may lie sleeping."

This was an allusion to Martine's little personal fortune. In thirty years, with four hundred francs wages she had earned twelve thousand francs, from which she had taken only what was strictly necessary for her wants; and increased, almost trebled, by the interest, her savings amounted now to thirty thousand francs, which through a caprice, a desire to have her money apart, she had not chosen to place with M. Grandguillot. They were elsewhere, safely invested in the funds.

"Sous that lie sleeping are honest sous," she said gravely. "But monsieur is right; I will tell the butcher to send a bill apart, as all the brains are for monsieur's cookery and not for mine."

This explanation brought a smile to the face of Clotilde, who was always amused by the jests about Martine's avarice; and the breakfast ended more cheerfully. The doctor desired to take the coffee under the plane trees, saying that he felt the need of air after being shut up all the morning. The coffee was served then on the stone table beside the fountain; and how pleasant it was there in the shade, listening to the cool murmur of the water, while around, the pine wood, the court, the whole place, were glowing in the early afternoon sun.

The doctor had complacently brought with him the vial of nerve substance, which he looked at as it stood on the table.

"So, then, mademoiselle," he resumed, with an air of brusque pleasantry, "you do not believe in my elixir of resurrection, and you believe in miracles!"

"Master," responded Clotilde, "I believe that we do not know everything."

He made a gesture of impatience.

"But we must know everything. Understand then, obstinate little girl, that not a single deviation from the invariable laws which govern the universe has ever been scientifically proved. Up to this day there has been no proof of the existence of any intelligence other than the human. I defy you to find any real will, any reasoning force, outside of life. And everything is there; there is in the world no other will than this force which impels everything to life, to a life ever broader and higher."

He rose with a wave of the hand, animated by so firm a faith that she regarded him in surprise, noticing how youthful he looked in spite of his white hair.

"Do you wish me to repeat my 'Credo' for you, since you accuse me of not wanting yours? I believe that the future of humanity is in the progress of reason through science. I believe that the pursuit of truth, through science, is the divine ideal which man should propose to himself. I believe that all is illusion and vanity outside the treasure of truths slowly accumulated, and which will never again be lost. I believe that the sum of these truths, always increasing, will at last confer on man incalculable power and peace, if not happiness. Yes, I believe in the final triumph of life."

And with a broader sweep of the hand that took in the vast horizon, as if calling on these burning plains in which fermented the saps of all existences to bear him witness, he added:

"But the continual miracle, my child, is life. Only open your eyes, and look."

She shook her head.

"It is in vain that I open my eyes; I cannot see everything. It is you, master, who are blind, since you do not wish to admit that there is beyond an unknown realm which you will never enter. Oh, I know you are too intelligent to be ignorant of that! Only you do not wish to take it into account; you put the unknown aside, because it would embarrass you in your researches. It is in vain that you tell me to put aside the mysterious; to start from the known for the conquest of the unknown. I cannot; the mysterious at once calls me back and disturbs me."

He listened to her, smiling, glad to see her become animated, while he smoothed her fair curls with his hand.

"Yes, yes, I know you are like the rest; you do not wish to live without illusions and without lies. Well, there, there; we understand each other still, even so. Keep well; that is the half of wisdom and of happiness."

Then, changing the conversation:

"Come, you will accompany me, notwithstanding, and help me in my round of miracles. This is Thursday, my visiting day. When the heat shall have abated a little, we will go out together."

She refused at first, in order not to seem to yield; but she at last consented, seeing the pain she gave him. She was accustomed to accompany him on his round of visits. They remained for some time longer under the plane trees, until the doctor went upstairs to dress. When he came down again, correctly attired in a close-fitting coat and wearing a broad-brimmed silk hat, he spoke of harnessing Bonhomme, the horse that for a quarter of a century had taken him on his visits through the streets and the environs of Plassans. But the poor old beast was growing blind, and through gratitude for his past services and affection for himself they now rarely disturbed him. On this afternoon he was very drowsy, his gaze wandered, his legs were stiff with rheumatism. So that the doctor and the young girl, when they went to the stable to see him, gave him a hearty kiss on either side of his nose, telling him to rest on a bundle of fresh hay which the servant had brought. And they decided to walk.

Clotilde, keeping on her spotted white muslin, merely tied on over her curls a large straw hat adorned with a bunch of lilacs; and she looked charming, with her large eyes and her complexion of milk-and-roses under the shadow of its broad brim. When she went out thus on Pascal's arm, she tall, slender, and youthful, he radiant, his face illuminated, so to say, by the whiteness of his beard, with a vigor that made him still lift her across the rivulets, people smiled as they passed, and turned around to look at them again, they seemed so innocent and so happy. On this day, as they left the road to Les Fenouilleres to enter Plassans, a group of gossips stopped short in their talk. It reminded one of one of those ancient kings one sees in pictures; one of those powerful and gentle kings who never grew old, resting his hand on the shoulder of a girl beautiful as the day, whose docile and dazzling youth lends him its support.

They were turning into the Cours Sauvair to gain the Rue de la Banne, when a tall, dark young man of about thirty stopped them.

"Ah, master, you have forgotten me. I am still waiting for your notes on consumption."

It was Dr. Ramond, a young physician, who had settled two years before at Plassans, where he was building up a fine practice. With a superb head, in the brilliant prime of a gracious manhood, he was adored by the women, but he had fortunately a great deal of good sense and a great deal of prudence.

"Why, Ramond, good day! Not at all, my dear friend; I have not forgotten you. It is this little girl, to whom I gave the notes yesterday to copy, and who has not touched them yet."

The two young people shook hands with an air of cordial intimacy.

"Good day, Mlle. Clotilde."

"Good day, M. Ramond."

During a gastric fever, happily mild, which the young girl had had the preceding year, Dr. Pascal had lost his head to the extent of distrusting his own skill, and he had asked his young colleague to assist him — to reassure him. Thus it was that an intimacy, a sort of comradeship, had sprung up among the three.

"You shall have your notes tomorrow, I promise you," she said, smiling.

Ramond walked on with them, however, until they reached the end of the Rue de la Banne, at the entrance of the old quarter whither they were going. And there was in the manner in which he leaned, smiling, toward Clotilde, the revelation of a secret love that had grown slowly, awaiting patiently the hour fixed for the most reasonable of *denouements*. Besides, he listened with deference to Dr. Pascal, whose works he admired greatly.

"And it just happens, my dear friend, that I am going to Guiraude's, that woman, you know, whose husband, a tanner, died of consumption five years ago. She has two children living — Sophie, a girl now going on sixteen, whom I fortunately succeeded in having sent four years before her father's death to a neighboring village, to one of her aunts; and a son, Valentin, who has just completed his twenty-first year, and whom his mother insisted on keeping with her through a blind affection, notwithstanding that I warned her of the dreadful results that might ensue. Well, see if I am right in asserting that consumption is not hereditary, but only that consumptive parents transmit to their children a degenerate soil, in which the disease develops at the slightest contagion. Now, Valentin, who lived in daily contact with his father, is consumptive, while Sophie, who grew up in the open air, has superb health."

He added with a triumphant smile:

"But that will not prevent me, perhaps, from saving Valentin, for he is visibly improved, and is growing fat since I have used my injections with him. Ah, Ramond, you will come to them yet; you will come to my injections!"

The young physician shook hands with both of them, saying:

"I don't say no. You know that I am always with you."

When they were alone they quickened their steps and were soon in the Rue Canquoin, one of the narrowest and darkest streets of the old quarter. Hot as was the sun, there reigned here the semi-obscurity and the coolness of a cave. Here it was, on a ground floor, that Guiraude lived with her son Valentin. She opened the door herself. She was a thin, wasted-looking woman, who was herself affected with a slow decomposition of the blood. From morning till night she crushed almonds with the end of an ox-bone on a large paving stone, which she held between her knees. This work was their only means of living, the son having been obliged to give up all labor. She smiled, however, today on seeing the doctor, for Valentin had just eaten a cutlet with a good appetite, a thing which he had not done for months. Valentin, a sickly-looking young man, with scanty hair and beard and prominent cheekbones, on each of which was a bright red spot, while the rest of his face was of a waxen hue, rose quickly to show how much more sprightly he felt! And Clotilde was touched by the reception given to Pascal as a savior, the awaited Messiah. These poor people pressed his hands — they would like to have kissed his feet; looking at him with eyes shining with gratitude. True, the disease was not yet cured: perhaps this was only the effect of the stimulus, perhaps what he felt was only the excitement of fever. But was it not something to gain time? He gave him another injection while Clotilde, standing before the window, turned her back to them; and when they were leaving she saw him lay twenty francs upon the table.

This often happened to him, to pay his patients instead of being paid by them.

He made three other visits in the old quarter, and then went to see a lady in the new town. When they found themselves in the street again, he said:

"Do you know that, if you were a courageous girl, we should walk to Seguiranne, to see Sophie at her aunt's. That would give me pleasure."

The distance was scarcely three kilometers; that would be only a pleasant walk in this delightful weather. And she agreed gaily, not sulky now, but pressing close to him, happy to hang on his arm. It was five o'clock. The setting sun spread over the fields a great sheet of gold. But as soon as they left Plassans they were obliged to cross the corner of the vast, arid plain, which extended to the right of the Viorne. The new canal, whose irrigating waters were soon to transform the face of the country parched with thirst, did not yet water this quarter, and red fields and yellow fields stretched away into the distance under the melancholy and blighting glare of the sun, planted only with puny almond trees and dwarf olives, constantly cut down and pruned, whose branches twisted and writhed in attitudes of suffering and revolt. In the distance, on the bare hillsides, were to be seen only like pale patches the country houses, flanked by the regulation cypress. The vast, barren expanse, however, with broad belts of desolate fields of hard and distinct coloring, had classic lines of a severe grandeur. And on the road the dust lay twenty centimeters thick, a dust like snow, that the slightest breath of wind raised in broad, flying clouds, and that covered with white powder the fig trees and the brambles on either side.

Clotilde, who amused herself like a child, listening to this dust crackling under her little feet, wished to hold her parasol over Pascal.

"You have the sun in your eyes. Lean a little this way."

But at last he took possession of the parasol, to hold it himself.

"It is you who do not hold it right; and then it tires you. Besides, we are almost there now."

In the parched plain they could already perceive an island of verdure, an enormous clump of trees. This was La Seguiranne, the farm on which Sophie had grown up in the house of her Aunt Dieudonne, the wife of the cross old man. Wherever there was a spring, wherever there was a rivulet, this ardent soil broke out in rich vegetation; and then there were walks bordered by trees, whose luxuriant foliage afforded a delightful coolness and shade. Plane trees, chestnut trees, and young elms grew vigorously. They entered an avenue of magnificent green oaks.

As they approached the farm, a girl who was making hay in the meadow dropped her fork and ran toward them. It was Sophie, who had recognized the doctor and the young lady, as she called Clotilde. She adored them, but she stood looking at them in confusion, unable to express the glad greeting with which her heart overflowed. She resembled her brother Valentin; she had his small stature, his prominent cheek-bones, his pale hair; but in the country, far from the contagion of the paternal environment, she had, it seemed, gained flesh; acquired with her robust limbs a firm step; her cheeks had filled out, her hair had grown luxuriant. And she had fine eyes, which shone with health and gratitude. Her Aunt Dieudonne, who was making hay with her, had come toward them also, crying from afar jestingly, with something of Provençal rudeness:

"Ah, M. Pascal, we have no need of you here! There is no one sick!"

The doctor, who had simply come in search of this fine spectacle of health, answered in the same tone:

"I hope so, indeed. But that does not prevent this little girl here from owing you and me a fine taper!"

"Well, that is the pure truth! And she knows it, M. Pascal. There is not a day that she does not say that but for you she would be at this time like her brother Valentin."

"Bah! We will save him, too. He is getting better, Valentin is. I have just been to see him."

Sophie seized the doctor's hands; large tears stood in her eyes, and she could only stammer:

"Oh, M. Pascal!"

How they loved him! And Clotilde felt her affection for him increase, seeing the affection of all these people for him. They remained chatting there for a few moments longer, in the salubrious shade of the green oaks. Then they took the road back to Plassans, having still another visit to make.

This was to a tavern, that stood at the crossing of two roads and was white with the flying dust. A steam mill had recently been established opposite, utilizing the old buildings of Le Paradou, an estate dating from the last century, and Lafouasse, the tavern keeper, still carried on his little business, thanks to the workmen at the mill and to the peasants who brought their corn to it. He had still for customers on Sundays the few inhabitants of Les Artauds, a neighboring hamlet. But misfortune had struck him; for the last three years he had been dragging himself about groaning with rheumatism, in which the doctor had finally recognized the beginning of ataxia. But he had obstinately refused to take a servant, persisting in waiting on his customers himself, holding on by the furniture. So that once more firm on his feet, after a dozen punctures, he already proclaimed his cure everywhere.

He chanced to be just then at his door, and looked strong and vigorous, with his tall figure, fiery face, and fiery red hair.

"I was waiting for you, M. Pascal. Do you know that I have been able to bottle two casks of wine without being tired!"

Clotilde remained outside, sitting on a stone bench; while Pascal entered the room to give Lafouasse the injection. She could hear them speaking, and the latter, who in spite of his stoutness was very cowardly in regard to pain, complained that the puncture hurt, adding, however, that after all a little suffering was a small price to pay for good health. Then he declared he would be offended if the doctor did not take a glass of something. The young lady would not affront him by refusing to take some syrup. He carried a table outside, and there was nothing for it but they must touch glasses with him.

"To your health, M. Pascal, and to the health of all the poor devils to whom you give back a relish for their victuals!"

Clotilde thought with a smile of the gossip of which Martine had spoken to her, of Father Boutin, whom they accused the doctor of having killed. He did not kill all his patients, then; his remedy worked real miracles, since he brought back to life the consumptive and the ataxic. And her faith in her master returned with the warm affection for him which welled up in her heart. When they left Lafouasse, she was once more completely his; he could do what he willed with her.

But a few moments before, sitting on the stone bench looking at the steam mill, a confused story had recurred to her mind; was it not here in these smoke-blackened buildings, today white with flour, that a drama of love had once been enacted? And the story came back to her; details given by Martine; allusions made by the doctor himself; the whole tragic love adventure of her cousin the Abbé Serge Mouret, then rector of Les Artauds, with an adorable young girl of a wild and passionate nature who lived at Le Paradou.

Returning by the same road Clotilde stopped, and pointing to the vast, melancholy expanse of stubble fields, cultivated plains, and fallow land, said:

"Master, was there not once there a large garden? Did you not tell me some story about it?"

"Yes, yes; Le Paradou, an immense garden — woods, meadows, orchards, parterres, fountains, and brooks that flowed into the Viorne. A garden abandoned for an age; the garden of the Sleeping Beauty, returned to Nature's rule. And as you see they have cut down the woods, and cleared and leveled the ground, to divide it into lots, and sell it by auction. The springs themselves have dried up. There is nothing there now but that fever-breeding marsh. Ah, when I pass by here, it makes my heart ache!"

She ventured to question him further:

"But was it not in Le Paradou that my cousin Serge and your great friend Albine fell in love with each other?"

He had forgotten her presence. He went on talking, his gaze fixed on space, lost in recollections of the past.

"Albine, my God! I can see her now, in the sunny garden, like a great, fragrant bouquet, her head thrown back, her bosom swelling with joy, happy in her flowers, with wild flowers braided among her blond tresses, fastened at her throat, on her corsage, around her slender, bare brown arms. And I can see her again, after she had asphyxiated herself; dead in the midst of her flowers; very white, sleeping with folded hands, and a smile on her lips, on her couch of hyacinths and tuberoses. Dead for love; and how passionately Albine and Serge loved each other, in the great garden their tempter, in the bosom of Nature their accomplice! And what a flood of life swept away all false bonds, and what a triumph of life!"

Clotilde, she too troubled by this passionate flow of murmured words, gazed at him intently. She had never ventured to speak to him of another story that she had heard — the story of the one love of his life — a love which he had cherished in secret for a lady now dead. It was said that he had attended her for a long time without ever so much as venturing to kiss the tips of her fingers. Up to the present, up to near sixty, study and his natural timidity had made him shun women. But, notwithstanding, one felt that he was reserved for some great passion, with his feelings still fresh and ardent, in spite of his white hair.

"And the girl that died, the girl they mourned," she resumed, her voice trembling, her cheeks scarlet, without knowing why. "Serge did not love her, then, since he let her die?"

Pascal started as though awakening from a dream, seeing her beside him in her youthful beauty, with her large, clear eyes shining under the shadow of her broad-brimmed hat. Something had happened; the same breath of life had passed through them both; they did not take each other's arms again. They walked side by side.

"Ah, my dear, the world would be too beautiful, if men did not spoil it all! Albine is dead, and Serge is now rector of St. Eutrope, where he lives with his sister Desiree, a worthy creature who has the good fortune to be half an idiot. He is a holy man; I have never said the contrary. One may be an assassin and serve God."

And he went on speaking of the hard things of life, of the blackness and execrableness of humanity, without losing his gentle smile. He loved life; and the continuous work of life was a continual joy to him in spite of all the evil, all the misery, that it might contain. It mattered not how dreadful life might appear, it must be great and good, since it was lived with so tenacious a will, for the purpose no doubt of this will itself, and of the great work which it unconsciously accomplished. True, he was a scientist, a clear-sighted man; he did not believe in any idyllic humanity living in a world of perpetual peace; he saw, on the contrary, its woes and its vices; he had laid them bare; he had examined them; he had catalogued them for thirty years past, but his passion for life, his admiration for the forces of life, sufficed to produce in him a perpetual gaiety, whence seemed to flow naturally his love for others, a fraternal compassion, a sympathy, which were felt under the roughness of the anatomist and under the affected impersonality of his studies.

"Bah!" he ended, taking a last glance at the vast, melancholy plains. "Le Paradou is no more. They have sacked it, defiled it, destroyed it; but what does that matter! Vines will be planted, corn will spring up, a whole growth of new crops; and people will still fall in love in vintages and harvests yet to come. Life is eternal; it is a perpetual renewal of birth and growth."

He took her arm again and they returned to the town thus, arm in arm like good friends, while the glow of the sunset was slowly fading away in a tranquil sea of violets and roses. And seeing them both pass again, the ancient king, powerful and gentle, leaning against the shoulder of a charming and docile girl, supported by her youth, the women of the faubourg, sitting at their doors, looked after them with a smile of tender emotion.

At La Souleiade Martine was watching for them. She waved her hand to them from afar. What! Were they not going to dine today? Then, when they were near, she said:

"Ah! you will have to wait a little while. I did not venture to put on my leg of mutton yet."

They remained outside to enjoy the charm of the closing day. The pine grove, wrapped in shadow, exhaled a balsamic resinous odor, and from the yard, still heated, in which a last red gleam was dying away, a chillness arose. It was like an assuagement, a sigh of relief, a resting of surrounding Nature, of the puny almond trees, the twisted olives, under the paling sky, cloudless and serene; while at the back of the house the clump of plane trees was a mass of black and impenetrable shadows, where the fountain was heard singing its eternal crystal song.

"Look!" said the doctor, "M. Bellombre has already dined, and he is taking the air."

He pointed to a bench, on which a tall, thin old man of seventy was sitting, with a long face, furrowed with wrinkles, and large, staring eyes, and very correctly attired in a close-fitting coat and cravat.

"He is a wise man," murmured Clotilde. "He is happy."

"He!" cried Pascal. "I should hope not!"

He hated no one, and M. Bellombre, the old college professor, now retired, and living in his little house without any other company than that of a gardener who was deaf and dumb and older than himself, was the only person who had the power to exasperate him.

"A fellow who has been afraid of life; think of that! afraid of life! Yes, a hard and avaricious egotist! If he banished woman from his existence, it was only through fear of having to pay for her shoes. And he has known only the children of others, who have made him suffer — hence his hatred of the child — that flesh made to be flogged. The fear of life, the fear of burdens and of duties, of annoyances and of catastrophes! The fear of life, which makes us through dread of its sufferings refuse its joys. Ah! I tell you, this cowardliness enrages me; I cannot forgive it. We must live — live a complete life — live all our life. Better even suffering, suffering only, than such renunciation — the death of all there is in us that is living and human!"

M. Bellombre had risen, and was walking along one of the walks with slow, tranquil steps. Then, Clotilde, who had been watching him in silence, at last said:

"There is, however, the joy of renunciation. To renounce, not to live; to keep one's self for the spiritual, has not this always been the great happiness of the saints?"

"If they had not lived," cried Pascal, "they could not now be saints. Let suffering come, and I will bless it, for it is perhaps the only great happiness!"

But he felt that she rebelled against this; that he was going to lose her again. At the bottom of our anxiety about the beyond is the secret fear and hatred of life. So that he hastily assumed again his pleasant smile, so affectionate and conciliating.

"No, no! Enough for today; let us dispute no more; let us love each other dearly. And see! Martine is calling us, let us go in to dinner."

III

*F*or a month this unpleasant state of affairs continued, every day growing worse, and Clotilde suffered especially at seeing that Pascal now locked up everything. He had no longer the same tranquil confidence in her as before, and this wounded her so deeply that, if she had at any time found the press open, she would have thrown the papers into the fire as her grandmother Felicite had urged her to do. And the disagreements began again, so that they often remained without speaking to each other for two days together.

One morning, after one of these misunderstandings which had lasted since the day before, Martine said as she was serving the breakfast:

"Just now as I was crossing the Place de la Sous-Prefecture, I saw a stranger whom I thought I recognized going into Mme. Felicite's house. Yes, mademoiselle, I should not be surprised if it were your brother."

On the impulse of the moment, Pascal and Clotilde spoke.

"Your brother! Did your grandmother expect him, then?"

"No, I don't think so, though she has been expecting him at any time for the past six months, I know that she wrote to him again a week ago."

They questioned Martine.

"Indeed, monsieur, I cannot say; since I last saw M. Maxime four years ago, when he stayed two hours with us on his way to Italy, he may perhaps have changed greatly — I thought, however, that I recognized his back."

The conversation continued, Clotilde seeming to be glad of this event, which broke at last the oppressive silence between them, and Pascal ended:

"Well, if it is he, he will come to see us."

It was indeed Maxime. He had yielded, after months of refusal, to the urgent solicitations of old Mme. Rougon, who had still in this quarter an open family wound to heal. The trouble was an old one, and it grew worse every day.

Fifteen years before, when he was seventeen, Maxime had had a child by a servant whom he had seduced. His father Saccard, and his step-mother Renee — the latter vexed more especially at his unworthy choice — had acted in the matter with indulgence. The servant, Justine Megot, belonged to one of the neighboring villages, and was a fair-haired girl, also seventeen, gentle and docile; and they had sent her back to Plassans, with an allowance of twelve hundred francs a year, to bring up little Charles. Three years later she had married there a harness-maker of the faubourg, Frederic Thomas by name, a good workman and a sensible fellow, who was tempted by the allowance. For the rest her conduct was now most exemplary, she had grown fat, and she appeared to be cured of a cough that had threatened a hereditary malady due to the alcoholic propensities of a long line of progenitors. And two other children born of her marriage, a boy who was now ten and a girl who was seven, both plump and rosy, enjoyed perfect health; so that she would have been the most respected and the happiest of women, if it had not been for the trouble which Charles caused in the household. Thomas, notwithstanding the allowance, execrated this son of another man and gave him no peace, which made the mother suffer in secret, being an uncomplaining and submissive wife. So that, although she adored him, she would willingly have given him up to his father's family.

Charles, at fifteen, seemed scarcely twelve, and he had the infantine intelligence of a child of five, resembling in an extraordinary degree his great-great-grandmother, Aunt Dide, the madwoman at the Tulettes. He had the slender and delicate grace of one of those bloodless little kings with whom a race ends, crowned with their long, fair locks, light as spun silk. His large, clear eyes were expressionless, and on his disquieting beauty lay the shadow of death. And he had neither brain nor heart — he was nothing but a vicious little dog, who rubbed himself against people to be fondled. His great-grandmother Felicite, won by this beauty, in which she affected to recognize her blood, had at first put him in a boarding school, taking charge of him, but he had been expelled from it at the end of six months for misconduct. Three times she had changed his boarding school, and each time he had been expelled in disgrace. Then, as he neither would nor could learn anything, and as his health was declining rapidly, they kept him at home, sending him from one to another of the family. Dr. Pascal, moved to pity, had tried to cure him, and had abandoned the hopeless task only after he had kept him with him for nearly a year, fearing the companionship for Clotilde. And now, when Charles was not at his mother's, where he scarcely ever lived at present, he was to be found at the house of Felicite, or that of some other relative, prettily dressed, laden with toys, living like the effeminate little dauphin of an ancient and fallen race.

Old Mme. Rougon, however, suffered because of this bastard, and she had planned to get him away from the gossiping tongues of Plassans, by persuading Maxime to take him and keep him with him in Paris. It would still be an ugly story of the fallen family. But Maxime had for a long time turned a deaf ear to her solicitations, in the fear which continually haunted him of spoiling his life. After the war, enriched by the death of his wife, he had come back to live prudently on his fortune in his mansion on the avenue of the Bois de Boulogne, tormented by the hereditary malady of which he was to die young, having gained from his precocious debauchery a salutary fear of pleasure, resolved above all to shun emotions and responsibilities, so that he might last as long as possible. Acute pains in the limbs, rheumatic he thought them, had been alarming him for some time past; he saw himself in fancy already an invalid tied down to an easy chair; and his father's sudden return to France, the fresh activity which Saccard was putting forth, completed his disquietude. He knew well this devourer of millions; he trembled at finding him again bustling about him with his good-humored, malicious laugh. He felt that he was being watched, and he had the conviction that he would be cut up and devoured if he should be for a single day at his mercy, rendered helpless by the pains which were invading his limbs. And so great a fear of solitude had taken possession of him that he had now yielded to the idea of seeing his son again. If he found the boy gentle, intelligent, and healthy, why should he not take him to live with him? He would thus have a companion, an heir, who would protect him against the machinations of his father. Gradually he came to see himself, in his selfish forethought, loved, petted, and protected; yet for all that he might not have risked such a journey, if his physician had not just at that time sent him to the waters of St. Gervais. Thus, having to go only a few leagues out of his way, he had dropped in unexpectedly that morning on old Mme. Rougon, firmly resolved to take the train again in the evening, after having questioned her and seen the boy.

At two o'clock Pascal and Clotilde were still beside the fountain under the plane trees where they had taken their coffee, when Felicite arrived with Maxime.

"My dear, here's a surprise! I have brought you your brother."

Startled, the young girl had risen, seeing this thin and sallow stranger, whom she scarcely recognized. Since their parting in 1854 she had seen him only twice, once at Paris and again at Plassans. Yet his image, refined, elegant, and vivacious, had remained engraven on her mind; his face had grown hollow, his hair was streaked with silver threads. But notwithstanding, she found in him still, with his delicately handsome head, a languid grace, like that of a girl, even in his premature decrepitude.

"How well you look!" he said simply, as he embraced his sister.

"But," she responded, "to be well one must live in the sunshine. Ah, how happy it makes me to see you again!"

Pascal, with the eye of the physician, had examined his nephew critically. He embraced him in his turn.

"Good day, my boy. And she is right, mind you; one can be well only out in the sunshine — like the trees."

Felicite had gone hastily to the house. She returned, crying:

"Charles is not here, then?"

"No," said Clotilde. "We went to see him yesterday. Uncle Macquart has taken him, and he is to remain for a few days at the Tulettes."

Felicite was in despair. She had come only in the certainty of finding the boy at Pascal's. What was to be done now? The doctor, with his tranquil air, proposed to write to Uncle Macquart, who would bring him back in the morning. But when he learned that Maxime wished positively to go away again by the nine o'clock train, without remaining over night, another idea occurred to him. He would send to the livery stable for a landau, and all four would go to see Charles at Uncle Macquart's. It would even be a delightful drive. It was not quite three leagues from Plassans to the Tulettes — an hour to go, and an hour to return, and they would still have almost two hours to remain there, if they wished to be back by seven. Martine would get dinner, and Maxime would have time enough to dine and catch his train.

But Felicite objected, visibly disquieted by this visit to Macquart.

"Oh, no, indeed! If you think I am going down there in this frightful weather, you are mistaken. It is much simpler to send someone to bring Charles to us."

Pascal shook his head. Charles was not always to be brought back when one wished. He was a boy without reason, who sometimes, if the whim seized him, would gallop off like an untamed animal. And old Mme. Rougon, overruled and furious at having been unable to make any preparation, was at last obliged to yield, in the necessity in which she found herself of leaving the matter to chance.

"Well, be it as you wish, then! Good Heavens, how unfortunately things have turned out!"

Martine hurried away to order the landau, and before three o'clock had struck the horses were on the Nice road, descending the declivity which slopes down to the bridge over the Viorne. Then they turned to the left, and followed the wooded banks of the river for about two miles. After this the road entered the gorges of the Seille, a narrow pass between two giant walls of rock scorched by the ardent rays of the summer sun. Pine trees pushed their way through the clefts; clumps of trees, scarcely thicker at the roots than tufts of grass, fringed the crests and hung over the abyss. It was a chaos; a blasted landscape, a mouth of hell, with its wild turns, its droppings of blood-colored earth sliding down from every cut, its desolate solitude invaded only by the eagles' flight.

Felicite did not open her lips; her brain was at work, and she seemed completely absorbed in her thoughts. The atmosphere was oppressive, the sun sent his burning rays from behind a veil of great livid clouds. Pascal was almost the only one who talked, in his passionate love for this scorched land — a love which he endeavored to make his nephew share. But it was in vain that he uttered enthusiastic exclamations, in vain that he called his attention to the persistence of the olives, the fig trees, and the thorn bushes in pushing through the rock; the life of the rock itself, that colossal and puissant frame of the earth, from which they could almost fancy they heard a sound of breathing arise. Maxime remained cold, filled with a secret anguish in presence of those blocks of savage majesty, whose mass seemed to crush him. And he preferred to turn his eyes toward his sister, who was seated in front of him. He was becoming more and more charmed with her. She looked so healthy and so happy, with her pretty round head, with its straight, well-molded forehead. Now and then their glances met, and she gave him an affectionate smile which consoled him.

But the wildness of the gorge was beginning to soften, the two walls of rock to grow lower; they passed between two peaceful hills, with gentle slopes covered with thyme and lavender. It was the desert still, there were still bare spaces, green or violet hued, from which the faintest breeze brought a pungent perfume.

Then abruptly, after a last turn they descended to the valley of the Tulettes, which was refreshed by springs. In the distance stretched meadows dotted by large trees. The village was seated midway on the slope, among olive trees, and the country house of Uncle Macquart stood a little apart on the left, full in view. The landau turned into the road which led to the insane asylum, whose white walls they could see before them in the distance.

Felicite's silence had grown somber, for she was not fond of exhibiting Uncle Macquart. Another whom the family would be well rid of the day when he should take his departure. For the credit of everyone he ought to have been sleeping long ago under the sod. But he persisted in living, he carried his eighty-three years well, like an old drunkard saturated with liquor, whom the alcohol seemed to preserve. At Plassans he had left a terrible reputation as a do-nothing and a scoundrel, and the old men whispered the execrable story of the corpses that lay between him and the Rougons, an act of treachery in the troublous days of December, 1851, an ambuscade in which he had left comrades with their bellies ripped open, lying on the bloody pavement. Later, when he had returned to France, he had preferred to the good place of which he had obtained the promise this little domain of the Tulettes, which Felicite had bought for him. And he had lived comfortably here ever since; he had no longer any other ambition than that of enlarging it, looking out once more for the good chances, and he had even found the means of obtaining a field which he had long coveted, by making himself useful to his sister-in-law at the time when the latter again reconquered Plassans from the legitimists — another frightful story that was whispered also, of a madman secretly let loose from the asylum, running in the night to avenge himself, setting fire to his house in which four persons were burned. But these were old stories and Macquart, settled down now, was no longer the redoubtable scoundrel who had made all the family tremble. He led a perfectly correct life; he was a wily diplomat, and he had retained nothing of his air of jeering at the world but his bantering smile.

"Uncle is at home," said Pascal, as they approached the house.

This was one of those Provençal structures of a single story, with discolored tiles and four walls washed with a bright yellow. Before the façade extended a narrow terrace shaded by ancient mulberry trees, whose thick, gnarled branches drooped down, forming an arbor. It was here that Uncle Macquart smoked his pipe in the cool shade, in summer. And on hearing the sound of the carriage, he came and stood at the edge of the terrace, straightening his tall form neatly clad in blue cloth, his head covered with the eternal fur cap which he wore from one year's end to the other.

As soon as he recognized his visitors, he called out with a sneer:

"Oh, here come some fine company! How kind of you; you are out for an airing."

But the presence of Maxime puzzled him. Who was he? Whom had he come to see? They mentioned his name to him, and he immediately cut short the explanations they were adding, to enable him to straighten out the tangled skein of relationship.

"The father of Charles — I know, I know! The son of my nephew Saccard, *pardi!* the one who made a fine marriage, and whose wife died —"

He stared at Maxime, seeming happy to find him already wrinkled at thirty-two, with his hair and beard sprinkled with snow.

"Ah, well!" he added, "we are all growing old. But I, at least, have no great reason to complain. I am solid."

And he planted himself firmly on his legs with his air of ferocious mockery, while his fiery red face seemed to flame and burn. For a long time past ordinary brandy had seemed to him like pure water; only spirits of 36 degrees tickled his blunted palate; and he took such drafts of it that he was full of it — his flesh saturated with it — like a sponge. He perspired alcohol. At the slightest breath whenever he spoke, he exhaled from his mouth a vapor of alcohol.

"Yes, truly; you are solid, uncle!" said Pascal, amazed. "And you have done nothing to make you so; you have good reason to ridicule us. Only there is one thing I am afraid of, look you, that some day in lighting your pipe, you may set yourself on fire — like a bowl of punch."

Macquart, flattered, gave a sneering laugh.

"Have your jest, have your jest, my boy! A glass of cognac is worth more than all your filthy drugs. And you will all touch glasses with me, hey? So that it may be said truly that your uncle is a credit to you all. As for me, I laugh at evil tongues. I have corn and olive trees, I have almond trees and vines and land, like any *bourgeois*. In summer I smoke my pipe under the shade of my mulberry trees; in winter I go to smoke it against my wall, there in the sunshine. One has no need to blush for an uncle like that, hey? Clotilde, I have syrup, if you would like some. And you, Felicite, my dear, I know that you prefer anisette. There is everything here, I tell you, there is everything here!"

He waved his arm as if to take possession of the comforts he enjoyed, now that from an old sinner he had become a hermit, while Felicite, whom he had disturbed a moment before by the enumeration of his riches, did not take her eyes from his face, waiting to interrupt him.

"Thank you, Macquart, we will take nothing; we are in a hurry. Where is Charles?"

"Charles? Very good, presently! I understand, papa has come to see his boy. But that is not going to prevent you taking a glass."

And as they positively refused he became offended, and said, with his malicious laugh:

"Charles is not here; he is at the asylum with the old woman."

Then, taking Maxime to the end of the terrace, he pointed out to him the great white buildings, whose inner gardens resembled prison yards.

"Look, nephew, you see those three trees in front of you? Well, beyond the one to the left, there is a fountain in a court. Follow the ground floor, and the fifth window to the right is Aunt Dide's. And that is where the boy is. Yes, I took him there a little while ago."

This was an indulgence of the directors. In the twenty years that she had been in the asylum the old woman had not given a moment's uneasiness to her keeper. Very quiet, very gentle, she passed the days motionless in her easy chair, looking straight before her; and as the boy liked to be with her, and as she herself seemed to take an interest in him, they shut their eyes to this infraction of the rules and left him there sometimes for two or three hours at a time, busily occupied in cutting out pictures.

But this new disappointment put the finishing stroke to Felicite's ill-humor; she grew angry when Macquart proposed that all five should go in a body in search of the boy.

"What an idea! Go you alone, and come back quickly. We have no time to lose."

Her suppressed rage seemed to amuse Uncle Macquart, and perceiving how disagreeable his proposition was to her, he insisted, with his sneering laugh:

"But, my children, we should at the same time have an opportunity of seeing the old mother; the mother of us all. There is no use in talking; you know that we are all descended from her, and it would hardly be polite not to go wish her a good-day, when my grandnephew, who has come from such a distance, has perhaps never before had a good look at her. I'll not disown her, may the devil take me if I do. To be sure she is mad, but all the same, old mothers who have passed their hundredth year are not often to be seen, and she well deserves that we should show ourselves a little kind to her."

There was silence for a moment. A little shiver had run through everyone. And it was Clotilde, silent until now, who first declared in a voice full of feeling:

"You are right, uncle; we will all go."

Felicite herself was obliged to consent. They reentered the landau, Macquart taking the seat beside the coachman. A feeling of disquietude had given a sallow look to Maxime's worn face; and during the short drive he questioned Pascal concerning Charles with an air of paternal interest, which concealed a growing anxiety. The doctor constrained by his mother's imperious glances, softened the truth. Well, the boy's health was certainly not very robust; it was on that account, indeed, that they were glad to leave him for weeks together in the country with his uncle: but he had no definite disease. Pascal did not add that he had for a moment cherished the dream of giving him a brain and muscles by treating him with his hypodermic injections of nerve substance, but that he had always been met by the same difficulty; the slightest puncture brought on a hemorrhage which it was found necessary to stop by compresses; there was a laxness of the tissues, due to degeneracy; a bloody dew which exuded from the skin; he had especially, bleedings at the nose so sudden and so violent that they did not dare to leave him alone, fearing lest all the blood in his veins should flow out. And the doctor ended by saying that although the boy's intelligence had been sluggish, he still hoped that it would develop in an environment of quicker mental activity.

They arrived at the asylum and Macquart, who had been listening to the doctor, descended from his seat, saying:

"He is a gentle little fellow, a very gentle little fellow! And then, he is so beautiful — an angel!"

Maxime, who was still pale, and who shivered in spite of the stifling heat, put no more questions. He looked at the vast buildings of the asylum, the wings of the various quarters separated by gardens, the men's quarters from those of the women, those of the harmless insane from those of the violent insane. A scrupulous cleanliness reigned everywhere, a gloomy silence — broken from time to time by footsteps and the noise of keys. Old Macquart knew all the keepers. Besides, the doors were always to open to Dr. Pascal, who had been authorized to attend certain of the inmates. They followed a passage and entered a court; it was here — one of the chambers on the ground floor, a room covered with a light carpet, furnished with a bed, a press, a table, an armchair, and two chairs. The nurse, who had orders never to quit her charge, happened just now to be absent, and the only occupants of the room were the madwoman, sitting rigid in her armchair at one side of the table, and the boy, sitting on a chair on the opposite side, absorbed in cutting out his pictures.

"Go in, go in!" Macquart repeated. "Oh, there is no danger, she is very gentle!"

The grandmother, Adelaide Fouque, whom her grandchildren, a whole swarm of descendants, called by the pet name of Aunt Dide, did not even turn her head at the noise. In her youth hysterical troubles had unbalanced her mind. Of an ardent and passionate nature and subject to nervous attacks, she had yet reached the great age of eighty-three when a dreadful grief, a terrible moral shock, destroyed her reason. At that time, twenty-one years before, her mind had ceased to act; it had become suddenly weakened without the possibility of recovery. And now, at the age of 104 years, she lived here as if forgotten by the world, a quiet madwoman with an ossified brain, with whom insanity might remain stationary for an indefinite length of time without causing death. Old age had come, however, and had gradually atrophied her muscles. Her flesh was as if eaten away by age. The skin only remained on her bones, so that she had to be carried from her chair to her bed, for it had become impossible for her to walk or even to move. And yet she held herself erect against the back of her chair, a yellow, dried-up skeleton — like an ancient tree of which the bark only remains — with only her eyes still living in her thin, long visage, in which the wrinkles had been, so to say, worn away. She was looking fixedly at Charles.

Clotilde approached her a little tremblingly.

"Aunt Dide, it is we; we have come to see you. Don't you know me, then? Your little girl who comes sometimes to kiss you."

But the madwoman did not seem to hear. Her eyes remained fixed upon the boy, who was finishing cutting out a picture — a purple king in a golden mantle.

"Come, mamma," said Macquart, "don't pretend to be stupid. You may very well look at us. Here is a gentleman, a grandson of yours, who has come from Paris expressly to see you."

At this voice Aunt Dide at last turned her head. Her clear, expressionless eyes wandered slowly from one to another, then rested again on Charles with the same fixed look as before.

They all shivered, and no one spoke again.

"Since the terrible shock she received," explained Pascal in a low voice, "she has been that way; all intelligence, all memory seem extinguished in her. For the most part she is silent; at times she pours forth a flood of stammering and indistinct words. She laughs and cries without cause, she is a thing that nothing affects. And yet I should not venture to say that the darkness of her mind is complete, that no memories remain stored up in its depths. Ah! the poor old mother, how I pity her, if the light has not yet been finally extinguished. What can her thoughts have been for the last twenty-one years, if she still remembers?"

With a gesture he put this dreadful past which he knew from him. He saw her again young, a tall, pale, slender girl with frightened eyes, a widow, after fifteen months of married life with Rougon, the clumsy gardener whom she had chosen for a husband, throwing herself immediately afterwards into the arms of the smuggler Macquart, whom she loved with a wolfish love, and whom she did not even marry. She had lived thus for fifteen years, with her three children, one the child of her marriage, the other two illegitimate, a capricious and tumultuous existence, disappearing for weeks at a time, and returning all bruised, her arms black and blue. Then Macquart had been killed, shot down like a dog by a *gendarme*; and the first shock had paralyzed her, so that even then she retained nothing living but her water-clear eyes in her livid face; and she shut herself up from the world in the hut which her lover had left her, leading there for forty years the dead existence of a nun, broken by terrible nervous attacks. But the other shock was to finish her, to overthrow her reason, and Pascal recalled the atrocious scene, for he had witnessed it — a poor child whom the grandmother had taken to live with her, her grandson Silvere, the victim of family hatred and strife, whose head another *gendarme* shattered with a pistol shot, at the suppression of the insurrectionary movement of 1851. She was always to be bespattered with blood.

Felicite, meanwhile, had approached Charles, who was so engrossed with his pictures that all these people did not disturb him.

"My darling, this gentleman is your father. Kiss him," she said.

And then they all occupied themselves with Charles. He was very prettily dressed in a jacket and short trousers of black velvet, braided with gold cord. Pale as a lily, he resembled in truth one of those king's sons whose pictures he was cutting out, with his large, light eyes and his shower of fair curls. But what especially struck the attention at this moment was his resemblance to Aunt Dide; this resemblance which had overleaped three generations, which had passed from this withered centenarian's countenance, from these dead features wasted by life, to this delicate child's face that was also as if worn, aged, and wasted, through the wear of the race. Fronting each other, the imbecile child of a deathlike beauty seemed the last of the race of which she, forgotten by the world, was the ancestress.

Maxime bent over to press a kiss on the boy's forehead; and a chill struck to his heart — this very beauty disquieted him; his uneasiness grew in this chamber of madness, whence, it seemed to him, breathed a secret horror come from the far-off past.

"How beautiful you are, my pet! Don't you love me a little?"

Charles looked at him without comprehending, and went back to his play.

But all were chilled. Without the set expression of her countenance changing Aunt Dide wept, a flood of tears rolled from her living eyes over her dead cheeks. Her gaze fixed immovably upon the boy, she wept slowly, endlessly. A great thing had happened.

And now an extraordinary emotion took possession of Pascal. He caught Clotilde by the arm and pressed it hard, trying to make her understand. Before his eyes appeared the whole line, the legitimate branch and the bastard branch, which had sprung from this trunk already vitiated by neurosis. Five generations were there present — the Rougons and the Macquarts, Adelaide Fouque at the root, then the scoundrelly old uncle, then himself, then Clotilde and Maxime, and lastly, Charles. Felicite occupied the place of her dead husband. There was no link wanting; the chain of heredity, logical and implacable, was unbroken. And what a world was evoked from the depths of the tragic cabin which breathed this horror that came from the far-off past in such appalling shape that everyone, notwithstanding the oppressive heat, shivered.

"What is it, master?" whispered Clotilde, trembling.

"No, no, nothing!" murmured the doctor. "I will tell you later."

Macquart, who alone continued to sneer, scolded the old mother. What an idea was hers, to receive people with tears when they put themselves out to come and make her a visit. It was scarcely polite. And then he turned to Maxime and Charles.

"Well, nephew, you have seen your boy at last. Is it not true that he is pretty, and that he is a credit to you, after all?"

Felicite hastened to interfere. Greatly dissatisfied with the turn which affairs were taking, she was now anxious only to get away.

"He is certainly a handsome boy, and less backward than people think. Just see how skillful he is with his hands. And you will see when you have brightened him up in Paris, in a different way from what we have been able to do at Plassans, eh?"

"No doubt," murmured Maxime. "I do not say no; I will think about it."

He seemed embarrassed for a moment, and then added:

"You know I came only to see him. I cannot take him with me now as I am to spend a month at St. Gervais. But as soon as I return to Paris I will think of it, I will write to you."

Then, taking out his watch, he cried:

"The devil! Half-past five. You know that I would not miss the nine o'clock train for anything in the world."

"Yes, yes, let us go," said Felicite brusquely. "We have nothing more to do here."

Macquart, whom his sister-in-law's anger seemed still to divert, endeavored to delay them with all sorts of stories. He told of the days when Aunt Dide talked, and he affirmed that he had found her one morning singing a romance of her youth. And then he had no need of the carriage, he would take the boy back on foot, since they left him to him.

"Kiss your papa, my boy, for you know now that you see him, but you don't know whether you shall ever see him again or not."

With the same surprised and indifferent movement Charles raised his head, and Maxime, troubled, pressed another kiss on his forehead.

"Be very good and very pretty, my pet. And love me a little."

"Come, come, we have no time to lose," repeated Felicite.

But the keeper here reentered the room. She was a stout, vigorous girl, attached especially to the service of the madwoman. She carried her to and from her bed, night and morning; she fed her and took care of her like a child. And she at once entered into conversation with Dr. Pascal, who questioned her. One of the doctor's most cherished dreams was to cure the mad by his treatment of hypodermic injections. Since in their case it was the brain that was in danger, why should not hypodermic injections of nerve substance give them strength and will, repairing the breaches made in the organ? So that for a moment he had dreamed of trying the treatment with the old mother; then he began to have scruples, he felt a sort of awe, without counting that madness at that age was total, irreparable ruin. So that he had chosen another subject — a hatter named Sarteur, who had been for a year past in the asylum, to which he had come himself to beg them to shut him up to prevent him from committing a crime. In his paroxysms, so strong an impulse to kill seized him that he would have thrown himself upon the first passer-by. He was of small stature, very dark, with a retreating forehead, an aquiline face with a large nose and a very short chin, and his left cheek was noticeably larger than his right. And the doctor had obtained miraculous results with this victim of emotional insanity, who for a month past had had no attack. The nurse, indeed being questioned, answered that Sarteur had become quiet and was growing better every day.

"Do you hear, Clotilde?" cried Pascal, enchanted. "I have not the time to see him this evening, but I will come again tomorrow. It is my visiting day. Ah, if I only dared; if she were young still —"

His eyes turned toward Aunt Dide. But Clotilde, whom his enthusiasm made smile, said gently:

"No, no, master, you cannot make life anew. There, come. We are the last."

It was true; the others had already gone. Macquart, on the threshold, followed Felicite and Maxime with his mocking glance as they went away. Aunt Dide, the forgotten one, sat motionless, appalling in her leanness, her eyes again fixed upon Charles with his white, worn face framed in his royal locks.

The drive back was full of constraint. In the heat which exhaled from the earth, the landau rolled on heavily to the measured trot of the horses. The stormy sky took on an ashen, copper-colored hue in the deepening twilight. At first a few indifferent words were exchanged; but from the moment in which they entered the gorges of the Seille all conversation ceased, as if they felt oppressed by the menacing walls of giant rock that seemed closing in upon them. Was not this the end of the earth, and were they not going to roll into the unknown, over the edge of some abyss? An eagle soared by, uttering a shrill cry.

Willows appeared again, and the carriage was rolling lightly along the bank of the Viorne, when Felicite began without transition, as if she were resuming a conversation already commenced.

"You have no refusal to fear from the mother. She loves Charles dearly, but she is a very sensible woman, and she understands perfectly that it is to the boy's advantage that you should take him with you. And I must tell you, too, that the poor boy is not very happy with her, since, naturally, the husband prefers his own son and daughter. For you ought to know everything."

And she went on in this strain, hoping, no doubt, to persuade Maxime and draw a formal promise from him. She talked until they reached Plassans. Then, suddenly, as the landau rolled over the pavement of the faubourg, she said:

"But look! there is his mother. That stout blond at the door there."

At the threshold of a harness-maker's shop hung round with horse trappings and halters, Justine sat, knitting a stocking, taking the air, while the little girl and boy were playing on the ground at her feet. And behind them in the shadow of the shop was to be seen Thomas, a stout, dark man, occupied in repairing a saddle.

Maxime leaned forward without emotion, simply curious. He was greatly surprised at sight of this robust woman of thirty-two, with so sensible and so commonplace an air, in whom there was not a trace of the wild little girl with whom he had been in love when both of the same age were entering their seventeenth year. Perhaps a pang shot through his heart to see her plump and tranquil and blooming, while he was ill and already aged.

"I should never have recognized her," he said.

And the landau, still rolling on, turned into the Rue de Rome. Justine had disappeared; this vision of the past — a past so different from the present — had sunk into the shadowy twilight, with Thomas, the children, and the shop.

At La Souleiade the table was set; Martine had an eel from the Viorne, a *sautéed* rabbit, and a leg of mutton. Seven o'clock was striking, and they had plenty of time to dine quietly.

"Don't be uneasy," said Dr. Pascal to his nephew. "We will accompany you to the station; it is not ten minutes' walk from here. As you left your trunk, you have nothing to do but to get your ticket and jump on board the train."

Then, meeting Clotilde in the vestibule, where she was hanging up her hat and her umbrella, he said to her in an undertone:

"Do you know that I am uneasy about your brother?"

"Why so?"

"I have observed him attentively. I don't like the way in which he walks; and have you noticed what an anxious look he has at times? That has never deceived me. In short, your brother is threatened with ataxia."

"Ataxia!" she repeated turning very pale.

A cruel image rose before her, that of a neighbor, a man still young, whom for the past ten years she had seen driven about in a little carriage by a servant. Was not this infirmity the worst of all ills, the ax stroke that separates a living being from social and active life?

"But," she murmured, "he complains only of rheumatism."

Pascal shrugged his shoulders; and putting a finger to his lip he went into the dining room, where Felicite and Maxime were seated.

The dinner was very friendly. The sudden disquietude which had sprung up in Clotilde's heart made her still more affectionate to her brother, who sat beside her. She attended to his wants gaily, forcing him to take the most delicate morsels. Twice she called back Martine, who was passing the dishes too quickly. And Maxime was more and more enchanted by this sister, who was so good, so healthy, so sensible, whose charm enveloped him like a caress. So greatly was he captivated by her that gradually a project, vague at first, took definite shape within him. Since little Charles, his son, terrified him so greatly with his deathlike beauty, his royal air of sickly imbecility, why should he not take his sister Clotilde to live with him? The idea of having a woman in his house alarmed him, indeed, for he was afraid of all women, having had too much experience of them in his youth; but this one seemed to him truly maternal. And then, too, a good woman in his house would make a change in it, which would be a desirable thing. He would at least be left no longer at the mercy of his father, whom he suspected of desiring his death so that he might get possession of his money at once. His hatred and terror of his father decided him.

"Don't you think of marrying, then?" he asked, wishing to try the ground.

The young girl laughed.

"Oh, there is no hurry," she answered.

Then, suddenly, looking at Pascal, who had raised his head, she added: "How can I tell? Oh, I shall never marry."

But Felicite protested. When she saw her so attached to the doctor, she often wished for a marriage that would separate her from him, that would leave her son alone in a deserted home, where she herself might become all powerful, mistress of everything. Therefore she appealed to him. Was it not true that a woman ought to marry, that it was against nature to remain an old maid?

And he gravely assented, without taking his eyes from Clotilde's face.

"Yes, yes, she must marry. She is too sensible not to marry."

"Bah!" interrupted Maxime, "would it be really sensible in her to marry? In order to be unhappy, perhaps; there are so many ill-assorted marriages!"

And coming to a resolution, he added:

"Don't you know what you ought to do? Well, you ought to come and live with me in Paris. I have thought the matter over. The idea of taking charge of a child in my state of health terrifies me. Am I not a child myself, an invalid who needs to be taken care of? You will take care of me; you will be with me, if I should end by losing the use of my limbs."

There was a sound of tears in his voice, so great a pity did he feel for himself. He saw himself, in fancy, sick; he saw his sister at his bedside, like a Sister of Charity; if she consented to remain unmarried he would willingly leave her his fortune, so that his father might not have it. The dread which he had of solitude, the need in which he should perhaps stand of having a sick-nurse, made him very pathetic.

"It would be very kind on your part, and you should have no cause to repent it."

Martine, who was serving the mutton, stopped short in surprise; and the proposition caused the same surprise at the table. Felicite was the first to approve, feeling that the girl's departure would further her plans. She looked at Clotilde, who was still silent and stunned, as it were; while Dr. Pascal waited with a pale face.

"Oh, brother, brother," stammered the young girl, unable at first to think of anything else to say.

Then her grandmother cried:

"Is that all you have to say? Why, the proposition your brother has just made you is a very advantageous one. If he is afraid of taking Charles now, why, you can go with him, and later on you can send for the child. Come, come, that can be very well arranged. Your brother makes an appeal to your heart. Is it not true, Pascal, that she owes him a favorable answer?"

The doctor, by an effort, recovered his self-possession. The chill that had seized him made itself felt, however, in the slowness with which he spoke.

"The offer, in effect, is very kind. Clotilde, as I said before, is very sensible and she will accept it, if it is right that she should do so."

The young girl, greatly agitated, rebelled at this.

"Do you wish to send me away, then, master? Maxime is very good, and I thank him from the bottom of my heart. But to leave everything, my God! To leave all that love me, all that I have loved until now!"

She made a despairing gesture, indicating the place and the people, taking in all La Souleiade.

"But," responded Pascal, looking at her fixedly, "what if Maxime should need you, what if you had a duty to fulfill toward him?"

Her eyes grew moist, and she remained for a moment trembling and desperate; for she alone understood. The cruel vision again arose before her — Maxime, helpless, driven, about in a little carriage by a servant, like the neighbor whom she used to pity. Had she indeed any duty toward a brother who for fifteen years had been a stranger to her? Did not her duty lie where her heart was? Nevertheless, her distress of mind continued; she still suffered in the struggle.

"Listen, Maxime," she said at last, "give me also time to reflect. I will see. Be assured that I am very grateful to you. And if you should one day really have need of me, well, I should no doubt decide to go."

This was all they could make her promise. Felicite, with her usual vehemence, exhausted all her efforts in vain, while the doctor now affected to say that she had given her word. Martine brought a cream, without thinking of hiding her joy. To take away mademoiselle! what an idea, in order that monsieur might die of grief at finding himself all alone. And the dinner was delayed, too, by this unexpected incident. They were still at the dessert when half-past eight struck.

Then Maxime grew restless, tapped the floor with his foot, and declared that he must go.

At the station, whither they all accompanied him he kissed his sister a last time, saying:

"Remember!"

"Don't be afraid," declared Felicite, "we are here to remind her of her promise."

The doctor smiled, and all three, as soon as the train was in motion, waved their handkerchiefs.

On this day, after accompanying the grandmother to her door, Dr. Pascal and Clotilde returned peacefully to La Souleiade, and spent a delightful evening there. The constraint of the past few weeks, the secret antagonism which had separated them, seemed to have vanished. Never had it seemed so sweet to them to feel so united, inseparable. Doubtless it was only this first pang of uneasiness suffered by their affection, this threatened separation, the postponement of which delighted them. It was for them like a return to health after an illness, a new hope of life. They remained for long time in the warm night, under the plane trees, listening to the crystal murmur of the fountain. And they did not even speak, so profoundly did they enjoy the happiness of being together.

IV

Ten days later the household had fallen back into its former state of unhappiness. Pascal and Clotilde remained entire afternoons without exchanging a word; and there were continual outbursts of ill-humor. Even Martine was constantly out of temper. The home of these three had again become a hell.

Then suddenly the condition of affairs was still further aggravated. A Capuchin monk of great sanctity, such as often pass through the towns of the South, came to Plassans to conduct a mission. The pulpit of St. Saturnin resounded with his bursts of eloquence. He was a sort of apostle, a popular and fiery orator, a florid speaker, much given to the use of metaphors. And he preached on the nothingness of modern science with an extraordinary mystical exaltation, denying the reality of this world, and disclosing the unknown, the mysteries of the Beyond. All the devout women of the town were full of excitement about his preaching.

On the very first evening on which Clotilde, accompanied by Martine, attended the sermon, Pascal noticed her feverish excitement when she returned. On the following day her excitement increased, and she returned home later, having remained to pray for an hour in a dark corner of a chapel. From this time she was never absent from the services, returning languid, and with the luminous eyes of a seer; and the Capuchin's burning words haunted her; certain of his images stirred her to ecstasy. She grew irritable, and she seemed to have conceived a feeling of anger and contempt for everyone and everything around her.

Pascal, filled with uneasiness, determined to have an explanation with Martine. He came down early one morning as she was sweeping the dining room.

"You know that I leave you and Clotilde free to go to church, if that pleases you," he said. "I do not believe in oppressing anyone's conscience. But I do not wish that you should make her sick."

The servant, without stopping in her work, said in a low voice:

"Perhaps the sick people are those who don't think that they are sick."

She said this with such an air of conviction that he smiled.

"Yes," he returned; "I am the sick soul whose conversion you pray for; while both of you are in possession of health and of perfect wisdom. Martine, if you continue to torment me and to torment yourselves, as you are doing, I shall grow angry."

He spoke in so furious and so harsh a voice that the servant stopped suddenly in her sweeping, and looked him full in the face. An infinite tenderness, an immense desolation passed over the face of the old maid cloistered in his service. And tears filled her eyes and she hurried out of the room stammering:

"Ah, monsieur, you do not love us."

Then Pascal, filled with an overwhelming sadness, gave up the contest. His remorse increased for having shown so much tolerance, for not having exercised his authority as master, in directing Clotilde's education and bringing up. In his belief that trees grew straight if they were not interfered with, he had allowed her to grow up in her own way, after teaching her merely to read and write. It was without any preconceived plan, while aiding him in making his researches and correcting his manuscripts, and simply by the force of circumstances, that she had read everything and acquired a fondness for the natural sciences. How bitterly he now regretted his indifference! What a powerful impulse he might have given to this clear mind, so eager for knowledge, instead of allowing it to go astray, and waste itself in that desire for the Beyond, which Grandmother Felicite and the good Martine favored. While he had occupied himself with facts, endeavoring to keep from going beyond the phenomenon, and succeeding in doing so, through his scientific discipline, he had seen her give all her thoughts to the unknown, the mysterious. It was with her an obsession, an instinctive curiosity which amounted to torture when she could not satisfy it. There was in her a longing which nothing could appease, an irresistible call toward the unattainable, the unknowable. Even when she was a child, and still more, later, when she grew up, she went straight to the why and the how of things, she demanded ultimate causes. If he showed her a flower, she asked why this flower produced a seed, why this seed would germinate. Then, it would be the mystery of birth and death, and the unknown forces, and God, and all things. In half a dozen questions she would drive him into a corner, obliging him each time to acknowledge his fatal ignorance; and when he no longer knew what to answer her, when he would get rid of her with a gesture of comic fury, she would give a gay laugh of triumph, and go to lose herself again in her dreams, in the limitless vision of all that we do not know, and all that we may believe. Often she astounded him by her explanations. Her mind, nourished on science, started from proved truths, but with such an impetus that she bounded at once straight into the heaven of the legends. All sorts of mediators passed there, angels and saints and supernatural inspirations, modifying matter, endowing it with life; or, again, it was only one single force, the soul of the world, working to fuse things and beings in a final kiss of love in fifty centuries more. She had calculated the number of them, she said.

For the rest, Pascal had never before seen her so excited. For the past week, during which she had attended the Capuchin's mission in the cathedral, she had spent the days visibly in the expectation of the sermon of the evening; and she went to hear it with the rapt exaltation of a girl who is going to her first rendezvous of love. Then, on the following day, everything about her declared her detachment from the exterior life, from her accustomed existence, as if the visible world, the necessary actions of every moment, were but a snare and a folly. She retired within herself in the vision of what was not. Thus she had almost completely given up her habitual occupations, abandoning herself to a sort of unconquerable indolence, remaining for hours at a time with her hands in her lap, her gaze lost in vacancy, rapt in the contemplation of some far-off vision. Now she, who had been so active, so early a riser, rose late, appearing barely in time for the second breakfast, and it could not have been at her toilet that she spent these long hours, for she forgot her feminine coquetry, and would come down with her hair scarcely combed, negligently attired in a gown buttoned awry, but even thus adorable, thanks to her triumphant youth. The morning walks through La Souleiade that she had been so fond of, the races from the top to the bottom of the terraces planted with olive and almond trees, the visits to the pine grove balmy with the odor of resin, the long sun baths in the hot threshing yard, she indulged in no more; she preferred to remain shut up in her darkened room, from which not a movement was to be heard. Then, in the afternoon, in the work room, she would drag herself about languidly from chair to chair, doing nothing, tired and disgusted with everything that had formerly interested her.

Pascal was obliged to renounce her assistance; a paper which he gave her to copy remained three days untouched on her desk. She no longer classified anything; she would not have stooped down to pick up a paper from the floor. More than all, she abandoned the pastels, copies of flowers from nature that she had been making, to serve as plates to a work on artificial fecundations. Some large red mallows, of a new and singular coloring, faded in their vase before she had finished copying them. And yet for a whole afternoon she worked enthusiastically at a fantastic design of dream flowers, an extraordinary efflorescence blooming in the light of a miraculous sun, a burst of golden spike-shaped rays in the center of large purple corollas, resembling open hearts, whence shot, for pistils, a shower of stars, myriads of worlds streaming into the sky, like a milky way.

"Ah, my poor girl," said the doctor to her on this day, "how can you lose your time in such conceits! And I waiting for the copy of those mallows that you have left to die there. And you will make yourself ill. There is no health, nor beauty, even, possible outside reality."

Often now she did not answer, entrenching herself behind her fierce convictions, not wishing to dispute. But doubtless he had this time touched her beliefs to the quick.

"There is no reality," she answered sharply.

The doctor, amused by this bold philosophy from this big child, laughed.

"Yes, I know," he said; "our senses are fallible. We know this world only through our senses, consequently it is possible that the world does not exist. Let us open the door to madness, then; let us accept as possible the most absurd chimeras, let us live in the realm of nightmare, outside of laws and facts. For do you not see that there is no longer any law if you suppress nature, and that the only thing that gives life any interest is to believe in life, to love it, and to put all the forces of our intelligence to the better understanding of it?"

She made a gesture of mingled indifference and bravado, and the conversation dropped. Now she was laying large strokes of blue crayon on the pastel, bringing out its flaming splendor in strong relief on the background of a clear summer night.

But two days later, in consequence of a fresh discussion, matters went still further amiss. In the evening, on leaving the table, Pascal went up to the study to write, while she remained out of doors, sitting on the terrace. Hours passed by, and he was surprised and uneasy, when midnight struck, that he had not yet heard her return to her room. She would have had to pass through the study, and he was very certain that she had not passed unnoticed by him. Going downstairs, he found that Martine was asleep; the vestibule door was not locked, and Clotilde must have remained outside, oblivious of the flight of time. This often happened to her on these warm nights, but she had never before remained out so late.

The doctor's uneasiness increased when he perceived on the terrace the chair, now vacant, in which the young girl had been sitting. He had expected to find her asleep in it. Since she was not there, why had she not come in. Where could she have gone at such an hour? The night was beautiful: a September night, still warm, with a wide sky whose dark, velvety expanse was studded with stars; and from the depths of this moonless sky the stars shone so large and bright that they lighted the earth with a pale, mysterious radiance. He leaned over the balustrade of the terrace, and examined the slope and the stone steps which led down to the railroad; but there was not a movement. He saw nothing but the round motionless tops of the little olive trees. The idea then occurred to him that she must certainly be under the plane trees beside the fountain, whose murmuring waters made perpetual coolness around. He hurried there, and found himself enveloped in such thick darkness that he, who knew every tree, was obliged to walk with outstretched hands to avoid stumbling. Then he groped his way through the dark pine grove, still without meeting anyone. And at last he called in a muffled voice:

"Clotilde! Clotilde!"

The darkness remained silent and impenetrable.

"Clotilde! Clotilde!" he cried again, in a louder voice. Not a sound, not a breath. The very echoes seemed asleep. His cry was drowned in the infinitely soft lake of blue shadows. And then he called her with all the force of his lungs. He returned to the plane trees. He went back to the pine grove, beside himself with fright, scouring the entire domain. Then, suddenly, he found himself in the threshing yard.

At this cool and tranquil hour, the immense yard, the vast circular paved court, slept too. It was so many years since grain had been threshed here that grass had sprung up among the stones, quickly scorched a russet brown by the sun, resembling the long threads of a woolen carpet. And, under the tufts of this feeble vegetation, the ancient pavement did not cool during the whole summer, smoking from sunset, exhaling in the night the heat stored up from so many sultry noons.

The yard stretched around, bare and deserted, in the cooling atmosphere, under the infinite calm of the sky, and Pascal was crossing it to hurry to the orchard, when he almost fell over a form that he had not before observed, extended at full length upon the ground. He uttered a frightened cry.

"What! Are you here?"

Clotilde did not deign even to answer. She was lying on her back, her hands clasped under the back of her neck, her face turned toward the sky; and in her pale countenance, only her large shining eyes were visible.

"And here I have been tormenting myself and calling you for an hour past! Did you not hear me shouting?"

She at last unclosed her lips.

"Yes."

"Then that is very senseless! Why did you not answer me?"

But she fell back into her former silence, refusing all explanation, and with a stubborn brow kept her gaze fixed steadily on the sky.

"There, come in and go to bed, naughty child. You will tell me tomorrow."

She did not stir, however; he begged her ten times over to go into the house, but she would not move. He ended by sitting down beside her on the short grass, through which penetrated the warmth of the pavement beneath.

"But you cannot sleep out of doors. At least answer me. What are you doing here?"

"I am looking."

And from her large eyes, fixed and motionless, her gaze seemed to mount up among the stars. She seemed wholly absorbed in the contemplation of the pure starry depths of the summer sky.

"Ah, master!" she continued, in a low monotone; "how narrow and limited is all that you know compared to what there is surely up there. Yes, if I did not answer you it was because I was thinking of you, and I was filled with grief. You must not think me bad."

In her voice there was a thrill of such tenderness that it moved him profoundly. He stretched himself on the grass beside her, so that their elbows touched, and they went on talking.

"I greatly fear, my dear, that your griefs are not rational. It gives you pain to think of me. Why so?"

"Oh, because of things that I should find it hard to explain to you; I am not a *savante*. You have taught me much, however, and I have learned more myself, being with you. Besides, they are things that I feel. Perhaps I might try to tell them to you, as we are all alone here, and the night is so beautiful."

Her full heart overflowed, after hours of meditation, in the peaceful confidence of the beautiful night. He did not speak, fearing to disturb her, but awaited her confidences in silence.

"When I was a little girl and you used to talk to me about science, it seemed to me that you were speaking to me of God, your words burned so with faith and hope. Nothing seemed impossible to you. With science you were going to penetrate the secret of the world, and make the perfect happiness of humanity a reality. According to you, we were progressing with giant strides. Each day brought its discovery, its certainty. Ten, fifty, a hundred years more, perhaps, and the heavens would open and we should see truth face to face. Well, the years pass, and nothing opens, and truth recedes."

"You are an impatient girl," he answered simply. "If ten centuries more be necessary we must only wait for them to pass."

"It is true. I cannot wait. I need to know; I need to be happy at once, and to know everything at once, and to be perfectly and forever happy. Oh, that is what makes me suffer, not to be able to reach at a bound complete knowledge, not to be able to rest in perfect felicity, freed from scruples and doubts. Is it living to advance with tortoiselike pace in the darkness, not to be able to enjoy an hour's tranquility, without trembling at the thought of the coming anguish? No, no! All knowledge and all happiness in a single day? Science has promised them to us, and if she does not give them to us, then she fails in her engagements."

Then he, too, began to grow heated.

"But what you are saying is folly, little girl. Science is not revelation. It marches at its human pace, its very effort is its glory. And then it is not true that science has promised happiness."

She interrupted him hastily.

"How, not true! Open your books up there, then. You know that I have read them. Do they not overflow with promises? To read them one would think we were marching on to the conquest of earth and heaven. They demolish everything, and they swear to replace everything — and that by pure reason, with stability and wisdom. Doubtless I am like the children. When I am promised anything I wish that it shall be given me at once. My imagination sets to work, and the object must be very beautiful to satisfy me. But it would have been easy not to have promised anything. And above all, at this hour, in view of my eager and painful longing, it would be very ill done to tell me that nothing has been promised me."

He made a gesture, a simple gesture of protestation and impatience, in the serene and silent night.

"In any case," she continued, "science has swept away all our past beliefs. The earth is bare, the heavens are empty, and what do you wish that I should become, even if you acquit science of having inspired the hopes I have conceived? For I cannot live without belief and without happiness. On what solid ground shall I build my house when science shall have demolished the old world, and while she is waiting to construct the new? All the ancient city has fallen to pieces in this catastrophe of examination and analysis; and all that remains of it is a mad population vainly seeking a shelter among its ruins, while anxiously looking for a solid and permanent refuge where they may begin life anew. You must not be surprised, then, at our discouragement and our impatience. We can wait no longer. Since tardy science has failed in her promises, we prefer to fall back on the old beliefs, which for centuries have sufficed for the happiness of the world."

"Ah! that is just it," he responded in a low voice; "we are just at the turning point, at the end of the century, fatigued and exhausted with the appalling accumulation of knowledge which it has set moving. And it is the eternal need for falsehood, the eternal need for illusion which distracts humanity, and throws it back upon the delusive charm of the unknown. Since we can never know all, what is the use of trying to know more than we know already? Since the truth, when we have attained it, does not confer immediate and certain happiness, why not be satisfied with ignorance, the darkened cradle in which humanity slept the deep sleep of infancy? Yes, this is the aggressive return of the mysterious, it is the reaction against a century of experimental research. And this had to be; desertions were to be expected, since every need could not be satisfied at once. But this is only a halt; the onward march will continue, up there, beyond our view, in the illimitable fields of space."

For a moment they remained silent, still motionless on their backs, their gaze lost among the myriads of worlds shining in the dark sky. A falling star shot across the constellation of Cassiopeia, like a flaming arrow. And the luminous universe above turned slowly on its axis, in solemn splendor, while from the dark earth around them arose only a faint breath, like the soft, warm breath of a sleeping woman.

"Tell me," he said, in his good-natured voice, "did your Capuchin turn your head this evening, then?"

"Yes," she answered frankly; "he says from the pulpit things that disturb me. He preaches against everything you have taught me, and it is as if the knowledge which I owe to you, transformed into a poison, were consuming me. My God! What is going to become of me?"

"My poor child! It is terrible that you should torture yourself in this way! And yet I had been quite tranquil about you, for you have a well-balanced mind — you have a good, little, round, clear, solid head-piece, as I have often told you. You will soon calm down. But what confusion in the brains of others, at the end of the century, if you, who are so sane, are troubled! Have you not faith, then?"

She answered only by a heavy sigh.

"Assuredly, viewed from the standpoint of happiness, faith is a strong staff for the traveler to lean upon, and the march becomes easy and tranquil when one is fortunate enough to possess it."

"Oh, I no longer know whether I believe or not!" she cried. "There are days when I believe, and there are other days when I side with you and with your books. It is you who have disturbed me; it is through you I suffer. And perhaps all my suffering springs from this, from my revolt against you whom I love. No, no! tell me nothing; do not tell me that I shall soon calm down. At this moment that would only irritate me still more. I know well that you deny the supernatural. The mysterious for you is only the inexplicable. Even you concede that we shall never know all; and therefore you consider that the only interest life can have is the continual conquest over the unknown, the eternal effort to know more. Ah, I know too much already to believe. You have already succeeded but too well in shaking my faith, and there are times when it seems to me that this will kill me."

He took her hand that lay on the still warm grass, and pressed it hard.

"No, no; it is life that frightens you, little girl. And how right you are in saying that happiness consists in continual effort. For from this time forward tranquil ignorance is impossible. There is no halt to be looked for, no tranquility in renunciation and willful blindness. We must go on, go on in any case with life, which goes on always. Everything that is proposed, a return to the past, to dead religions, patched up religions arranged to suit new wants, is a snare. Learn to know life, then; to love it, live it as it ought to be lived — that is the only wisdom."

But she shook off his hand angrily. And her voice trembled with vexation.

"Life is horrible. How do you wish me to live it tranquil and happy? It is a terrible light that your science throws upon the world. Your analysis opens up all the wounds of humanity to display their horror. You tell everything; you speak too plainly; you leave us nothing but disgust for people and for things, without any possible consolation."

He interrupted her with a cry of ardent conviction.

"We tell everything. Ah, yes; in order to know everything and to remedy everything!"

Her anger rose, and she sat erect.

"If even equality and justice existed in your nature — but you acknowledge it yourself, life is for the strongest, the weak infallibly perishes because he is weak — there are no two beings equal, either in health, in beauty, or intelligence; everything is left to haphazard meeting, to the chance of selection. And everything falls into ruin, when grand and sacred justice ceases to exist."

"It is true," he said, in an undertone, as if speaking to himself, "there is no such thing as equality. No society based upon it could continue to exist. For centuries, men thought to remedy evil by character. But that idea is being exploded, and now they propose justice. Is nature just?

I think her logical, rather. Logic is perhaps a natural and higher justice, going straight to the sum of the common labor, to the grand final labor."

"Then it is justice," she cried, "that crushes the individual for the happiness of the race, that destroys an enfeebled species to fatten the victorious species. No, no; that is crime. There is in that only foulness and murder. He was right this evening in the church. The earth is corrupt, science only serves to show its rottenness. It is on high that we must all seek a refuge. Oh, master, I entreat you, let me save myself, let me save you!"

She burst into tears, and the sound of her sobs rose despairingly on the stillness of the night. He tried in vain to soothe her, her voice dominated his.

"Listen to me, master. You know that I love you, for you are everything to me. And it is you who are the cause of all my suffering. I can scarcely endure it when I think that we are not in accord, that we should be separated forever if we were both to die tomorrow. Why will you not believe?"

He still tried to reason with her.

"Come, don't be foolish, my dear —"

But she threw herself on her knees, she seized him by the hands, she clung to him with a feverish force. And she sobbed louder and louder, in such a clamor of despair that the dark fields afar off were startled by it.

"Listen to me, he said it in the church. You must change your life and do penance; you must burn everything belonging to your past errors — your books, your papers, your manuscripts. Make this sacrifice, master, I entreat it of you on my knees. And you will see the delightful existence we shall lead together."

At last he rebelled.

"No, this is too much. Be silent!"

"If you listen to me, master, you will do what I wish. I assure you that I am horribly unhappy, even in loving you as I love you. There is something wanting in our affection. So far it has been profound but unavailing, and I have an irresistible longing to fill it, oh, with all that is divine and eternal. What can be wanting to us but God? Kneel down and pray with me!"

With an abrupt movement he released himself, angry in his turn.

"Be silent; you are talking nonsense. I have left you free, leave me free."

"Master, master! it is our happiness that I desire! I will take you far, far away. We will go to some solitude to live there in God!"

"Be silent! No, never!"

Then they remained for a moment confronting each other, mute and menacing. Around them stretched La Souleiade in the deep silence of the night, with the light shadows of its olive trees, the darkness of its pine and plane trees, in which the saddened voice of the fountain was singing, and above their heads it seemed as if the spacious sky, studded with stars, shuddered and grew pale, although the dawn was still far off.

Clotilde raised her arm as if to point to this infinite, shuddering sky; but with a quick gesture Pascal seized her hand and drew it down toward the earth in his. And no word further was spoken; they were beside themselves with rage and hate. The quarrel was fierce and bitter.

She drew her hand away abruptly, and sprang backward, like some proud, untamable animal, rearing; then she rushed quickly through the darkness toward the house. He heard the patter of her little boots on the stones of the yard, deadened afterward by the sand of the walk. He, on his side, already grieved and uneasy, called her back in urgent tones. But she ran on without answering, without hearing. Alarmed, and with a heavy heart, he hurried after her, and rounded the clump of plane trees just in time to see her rush into the house like a whirlwind. He darted in after her, ran up the stairs, and struck against the door of her room, which she violently bolted. And here he stopped and grew calm, by a strong effort resisting the desire to cry out, to call her again, to break in the door so as to see her once more, to convince her, to have her all to himself. For a moment he remained motionless, chilled by the deathlike silence of the room, from which not the faintest sound issued. Doubtless she had thrown herself on the bed, and was stifling her cries and her sobs in the pillow. He determined at last to go downstairs again and close the hall door, and then he returned softly and listened, waiting for some sound of moaning. And day was breaking when he went disconsolately to bed, choking back his tears.

Thenceforward it was war without mercy. Pascal felt himself spied upon, trapped, menaced. He was no longer master of his house; he had no longer any home. The enemy was always there, forcing him to be constantly on his guard, to lock up everything. One after the other, two vials of nerve-substance which he had compounded were found in fragments, and he was obliged to barricade himself in his room, where he could be heard pounding for days together, without showing himself even at mealtime. He no longer took Clotilde with him on his visiting days, because she discouraged his patients by her attitude of aggressive incredulity. But from the moment he left the house, the doctor had only one desire — to return to it quickly, for he trembled lest he should find his locks forced, and his drawers rifled on his return. He no longer employed the young girl to classify and copy his notes, for several of them had disappeared, as if they had been carried away by the wind. He did not even venture to employ her to correct his proofs, having ascertained that she had cut out of an article an entire passage, the sentiment of which offended her Catholic belief. And thus she remained idle, prowling about the rooms, and having an abundance of time to watch for an occasion which would put in her possession the key of the large press. This was her dream, the plan which she revolved in her mind during her long silence, while her eyes shone and her hands burned with fever — to have the key, to open the press, to take and burn everything in an *auto-da-fe* which would be pleasing to God. A few pages of manuscript, forgotten by him on a corner of the table, while he went to wash his hands and put on his coat, had disappeared, leaving behind only a little heap of ashes in the fireplace. He could no longer leave a scrap of paper about. He carried away everything; he hid everything. One evening, when he had remained late with a patient, as he was returning home in the dusk a wild terror seized him at the faubourg, at sight of a thick black smoke rising up in clouds that darkened the heavens. Was it not La Souleiade that was burning down, set on fire by the bonfire made with his papers? He ran toward the house, and was reassured only on seeing in a neighboring field a fire of roots burning slowly.

But how terrible are the tortures of the scientist who feels himself menaced in this way in the labors of his intellect! The discoveries which he has made, the writings which he has counted upon leaving behind him, these are his pride, they are creatures of his blood — his children — and whoever destroys, whoever burns them, burns a part of himself. Especially, in this perpetual lying in wait for the creatures of his brain, was Pascal tortured by the thought that the enemy was in his house, installed in his very heart, and that he loved her in spite of everything, this creature whom he had made what she was. He was left disarmed, without possible defense; not wishing to act, and having no other resources than to watch with vigilance. On all sides the investment was closing around him. He fancied he felt the little pilfering hands stealing into his pockets. He had no longer any tranquility, even with the doors closed, for he feared that he was being robbed through the crevices.

"But, unhappy child," he cried one day, "I love but you in the world, and you are killing me! And yet you love me, too; you act in this way because you love me, and it is abominable. It would be better to have done with it all at once, and throw ourselves into the river with a stone tied around our necks."

She did not answer, but her dauntless eyes said ardently that she would willingly die on the instant, if it were with him.

"And if I should suddenly die tonight, what would happen tomorrow? You would empty the press, you would empty the drawers, you would make a great heap of all my works and burn them! You would, would you not? Do you know that that would be a real murder, as much as if you assassinated someone? And what abominable cowardice, to kill the thoughts!"

"No," she said at last, in a low voice; "to kill evil, to prevent it from spreading and springing up again!"

All their explanations only served to kindle anew their anger. And they had terrible ones. And one evening, when old Mme. Rougon had chanced in on one of these quarrels, she remained alone with Pascal, after Clotilde had fled to hide herself in her room. There was silence for a moment. In spite of the heartbroken air which she had assumed, a wicked joy shone in the depths of her sparkling eyes.

"But your unhappy house is a hell!" she cried at last.

The doctor avoided an answer by a gesture. He had always felt that his mother backed the young girl, inflaming her religious faith, utilizing this ferment of revolt to bring trouble into his house. He was not deceived. He knew perfectly well that the two women had seen each other during the day, and that he owed to this meeting, to a skillful embittering of Clotilde's mind, the frightful scene at which he still trembled. Doubtless his mother had come to learn what mischief had been wrought, and to see if the *denouement* was not at last at hand.

"Things cannot go on in this way," she resumed. "Why do you not separate since you can no longer agree. You ought to send her to her brother Maxime. He wrote to me not long since asking her again."

He straightened himself, pale and determined.

"To part angry with each other? Ah, no, no! that would be an eternal remorse, an incurable wound. If she must one day go away, I wish that we may be able to love each other at a distance. But why go away? Neither of us complains of the other."

Felicite felt that she had been too hasty. Therefore she assumed her hypocritical, conciliating air.

"Of course, if it pleases you both to quarrel, no one has anything to say in the matter. Only, my poor friend, permit me, in that case, to say that I think Clotilde is not altogether in the wrong. You force me to confess that I saw her a little while ago; yes, it is better that you should know, notwithstanding my promise to be silent. Well, she is not happy; she makes a great many complaints, and you may imagine that I scolded her and preached complete submission to her. But that does not prevent me from being unable to understand you myself, and from thinking that you do everything you can to make yourself unhappy."

She sat down in a corner of the room, and obliged him to sit down with her, seeming delighted to have him here alone, at her mercy. She had already, more than once before, tried to force him to an explanation in this way, but he had always avoided it. Although she had tortured him for years past, and he knew her thoroughly, he yet remained a deferential son, he had sworn never to abandon this stubbornly respectful attitude. Thus, the moment she touched certain subjects, he took refuge in absolute silence.

"Come," she continued; "I can understand that you should not wish to yield to Clotilde; but to me? How if I were to entreat you to make me the sacrifice of all those abominable papers which are there in the press! Consider for an instant if you should die suddenly, and those papers should fall into strange hands. We should all be disgraced. You would not wish that, would you? What is your object, then? Why do you persist in so dangerous a game? Promise me that you will burn them."

He remained silent for a time, but at last he answered:

"Mother, I have already begged of you never to speak on that subject. I cannot do what you ask."

"But at least," she cried, "give me a reason. Anyone would think our family was as indifferent to you as that drove of oxen passing below there. Yet you belong to it. Oh, I know you do all you can not to belong to it! I myself am sometimes astonished at you. I ask myself where you can have come from. But for all that, it is very wicked of you to run this risk, without stopping to think of the grief you are causing to me, your mother. It is simply wicked."

He grew still paler, and yielding for an instant to his desire to defend himself, in spite of his determination to keep silent, he said:

"You are hard; you are wrong. I have always believed in the necessity, the absolute efficacy of truth. It is true that I tell the truth about others and about myself, and it is because I believe firmly that in telling the truth I do the only good possible. In the first place, those papers are not intended for the public; they are only personal notes which it would be painful to me to part with. And then, I know well that you would not burn only them — all my other works would also be thrown into the fire. Would they not? And that is what I do not wish; do you understand? Never, while I live, shall a line of my writing be destroyed here."

But he already regretted having said so much, for he saw that she was urging him, leading him on to the cruel explanation she desired.

"Then finish, and tell me what it is that you reproach us with. Yes, me, for instance; what do you reproach me with? Not with having brought you up with so much difficulty. Ah, fortune was slow to win! If we enjoy a little happiness now, we have earned it hard. Since you have seen everything, and since you put down everything in your papers, you can testify with truth that the family has rendered greater services to others than it has ever received. On two occasions, but for us, Plassans would have been in a fine pickle. And it is perfectly natural that we should have reaped only ingratitude and envy, to the extent that even today the whole town would be enchanted with a scandal that should bespatter us with mud. You cannot wish that, and I am sure that you will do justice to the dignity of my attitude since the fall of the Empire, and the misfortunes from which France will no doubt never recover."

"Let France rest, mother," he said, speaking again, for she had touched the spot where she knew he was most sensitive. "France is tenacious of life, and I think she is going to astonish the world by the rapidity of her convalescence. True, she has many elements of corruption. I have not sought to hide them, I have rather, perhaps, exposed them to view. But you greatly misunderstand me if you imagine that I believe in her final dissolution, because I point out her wounds and her lesions. I believe in the life which ceaselessly eliminates hurtful substances, which makes new flesh to fill the holes eaten away by gangrene, which infallibly advances toward health, toward constant renovation, amid impurities and death."

He was growing excited, and he was conscious of it, and making an angry gesture, he spoke no more. His mother had recourse to tears, a few little tears which came with difficulty, and which were quickly dried. And the fears which saddened her old age returned to her, and she entreated him to make his peace with God, if only out of regard for the family. Had she not given an example of courage ever since the downfall of the Empire? Did not all Plassans, the quarter of St. Marc, the old quarter and the new town, render homage to the noble attitude she maintained in her fall? All she asked was to be helped; she demanded from all her children an effort like her own. Thus she cited the example of Eugene, the great man who had fallen from so lofty a height, and who resigned himself to being a simple deputy, defending until his latest breath the fallen government from which he had derived his glory. She was also full of eulogies of Aristide, who had never lost hope, who had reconquered, under the new government, an exalted position, in spite of the terrible and unjust catastrophe which had for a moment buried him under the ruins of the Union Universelle. And would he, Pascal, hold himself aloof, would he do nothing that she might die in peace, in the joy of the final triumph of the Rougons, he who was so intelligent, so affectionate, so good? He would go to mass, would he not, next

Sunday? and he would burn all those vile papers, only to think of which made her ill. She entreated, commanded, threatened. But he no longer answered her, calm and invincible in his attitude of perfect deference. He wished to have no discussion. He knew her too well either to hope to convince her or to venture to discuss the past with her.

"Why!" she cried, when she saw that he was not to be moved, "you do not belong to us. I have always said so. You are a disgrace to us."

He bent his head and said:

"Mother, when you reflect you will forgive me."

On this day Felicite was beside herself with rage when she went away; and when she met Martine at the door of the house, in front of the plane trees, she unburdened her mind to her, without knowing that Pascal, who had just gone into his room, heard all. She gave vent to her resentment, vowing, in spite of everything, that she would in the end succeed in obtaining possession of the papers and destroying them, since he did not wish to make the sacrifice. But what turned the doctor cold was the manner in which Martine, in a subdued voice, soothed her. She was evidently her accomplice. She repeated that it was necessary to wait; not to do anything hastily; that mademoiselle and she had taken a vow to get the better of monsieur, by not leaving him an hour's peace. They had sworn it. They would reconcile him with the good God, because it was not possible that an upright man like monsieur should remain without religion. And the voices of the two women became lower and lower, until they finally sank to a whisper, an indistinct murmur of gossiping and plotting, of which he caught only a word here and there; orders given, measures to be taken, an invasion of his personal liberty. When his mother at last departed, with her light step and slender, youthful figure, he saw that she went away very well satisfied.

Then came a moment of weakness, of utter despair. Pascal dropped into a chair, and asked himself what was the use of struggling, since the only beings he loved allied themselves against him. Martine, who would have thrown herself into the fire at a word from him, betraying him in this way for his good! And Clotilde leagued with this servant, plotting with her against him in holes and corners, seeking her aid to set traps for him! Now he was indeed alone; he had around him only traitresses, who poisoned the very air he breathed. But these two still loved him. He might perhaps have succeeded in softening them, but when he knew that his mother urged them on, he understood their fierce persistence, and he gave up the hope of winning them back. With the timidity of a man who had spent his life in study, aloof from women, notwithstanding his secret passion, the thought that they were there to oppose him, to attempt to bend him to their will, overwhelmed him. He felt that someone of them was always behind him. Even when he shut himself up in his room, he fancied that they were on the other side of the wall; and he was constantly haunted by the idea that they would rob him of his thought, if they could perceive it in his brain, before he should have formulated it.

This was assuredly the period in his life in which Dr. Pascal was most unhappy. To live constantly on the defensive, as he was obliged to do, crushed him, and it seemed to him as if the ground on which his house stood was no longer his, as if it was receding from beneath his feet. He now regretted keenly that he had not married, and that he had no children. Had not he himself been afraid of life? And had he not been well punished for his selfishness? This regret for not having children now never left him. His eyes now filled with tears whenever he met on the road bright-eyed little girls who smiled at him. True, Clotilde was there, but his affection for her was of a different kind — crossed at present by storms — not a calm, infinitely sweet affection, like that for a child with which he might have soothed his lacerated heart. And then, no doubt what he desired in his isolation, feeling that his days were drawing to an end, was above all, continuance; in a child he would survive, he would live forever. The more he suffered, the greater the consolation he would have found in bequeathing this suffering, in the faith which he still had in life. He considered himself indemnified for the physiological defects of his family. But even the thought that heredity sometimes passes over a generation, and that the disorders of his ancestors might reappear in a child of his did not deter him; and this unknown child, in spite of the old corrupt stock, in spite of the long succession of execrable relations, he desired ardently at certain times: as one desires unexpected gain, rare happiness, the stroke of fortune which is to console and enrich forever. In the shock which his other affections had received, his heart bled because it was too late.

One sultry night toward the end of September, Pascal found himself unable to sleep. He opened one of the windows of his room; the sky was dark, some storm must be passing in the distance, for there was a continuous rumbling of thunder. He could distinguish vaguely the dark mass of the plane trees, which occasional flashes of lightning detached, in a dull green, from the darkness. His soul was full of anguish; he lived over again the last unhappy days, days of fresh quarrels, of torture caused by acts of treachery, by suspicions, which grew stronger every day, when a sudden recollection made him start. In his fear of being robbed, he had finally adopted the plan of carrying the key of the large press in his pocket. But this afternoon, oppressed by the heat, he had taken off his jacket, and he remembered having seen Clotilde hang it up on a nail in

the study. A sudden pang of terror shot through him, sharp and cold
as a steel point; if she had felt the key in the pocket she had stolen it.
He hastened to search the jacket which he had a little before thrown
upon a chair; the key was not here. At this very moment he was being
robbed; he had the clear conviction of it. Two o'clock struck. He did
not again dress himself, but, remaining in his trousers only, with his
bare feet thrust into slippers, his chest bare under his unfastened
nightshirt, he hastily pushed open the door, and rushed into the
workroom, his candle in his hand.

"Ah! I knew it," he cried. "Thief! Assassin!"

It was true; Clotilde was there, undressed like himself, her bare feet
covered by canvas slippers, her legs bare, her arms bare, her shoulders
bare, clad only in her chemise and a short skirt. Through caution, she
had not brought a candle. She had contented herself with opening one
of the window shutters, and the continual lightning flashes of the storm
which was passing southward in the dark sky, sufficed her, bathing
everything in a livid phosphorescence. The old press, with its broad
sides, was wide open. Already she had emptied the top shelf, taking
down the papers in armfuls, and throwing them on the long table in
the middle of the room, where they lay in a confused heap. And with
feverish haste, fearing lest she should not have the time to burn them,
she was making them up into bundles, intending to hide them, and
send them afterward to her grandmother, when the sudden flare of the
candle, lighting up the room, caused her to stop short in an attitude of
surprise and resistance.

"You rob me; you assassinate me!" repeated Pascal furiously.

She still held one of the bundles in her bare arms. He wished to take
it away from her, but she pressed it to her with all her strength,
obstinately resolved upon her work of destruction, without showing
confusion or repentance, like a combatant who has right upon his side.
Then, madly, blindly, he threw himself upon her, and they struggled
together. He clutched her bare flesh so that he hurt her.

"Kill me!" she gasped. "Kill me, or I shall destroy everything!"

He held her close to him, with so rough a grasp that she could scarcely
breathe, crying:

"When a child steals, it is punished!"

A few drops of blood appeared and trickled down her rounded
shoulder, where an abrasion had cut the delicate satin skin. And, on the
instant, seeing her so breathless, so divine, in her virginal slender height,
with her tapering limbs, her supple arms, her slim body with its slender,
firm throat, he released her. By a last effort he tore the package from
her.

"And you shall help me to put them all up there again, by Heaven! Come here: begin by arranging them on the table. Obey me, do you hear?"

"Yes, master!"

She approached, and helped him to arrange the papers, subjugated, crushed by this masculine grasp, which had entered into her flesh, as it were. The candle which flared up in the heavy night air, lighted them; and the distant rolling of the thunder still continued, the window facing the storm seeming on fire.

V

*F*or an instant Pascal looked at the papers, the heap of which seemed enormous, lying thus in disorder on the long table that stood in the middle of the room. In the confusion several of the blue paper envelopes had burst open, and their contents had fallen out — letters, newspaper clippings, documents on stamped paper, and manuscript notes.

He was already mechanically beginning to seek out the names written on the envelopes in large characters, to classify the packages again, when, with an abrupt gesture, he emerged from the somber meditation into which he had fallen. And turning to Clotilde who stood waiting, pale, silent, and erect, he said:

"Listen to me; I have always forbidden you to read these papers, and I know that you have obeyed me. Yes, I had scruples of delicacy. It is not that you are an ignorant girl, like so many others, for I have allowed you to learn everything concerning man and woman, which is assuredly bad only for bad natures. But to what end disclose to you too early these terrible truths of human life? I have therefore spared you the history of our family, which is the history of every family, of all humanity; a great deal of evil and a great deal of good."

He paused as if to confirm himself in his resolution and then resumed quite calmly and with supreme energy:

"You are twenty-five years old; you ought to know. And then the life we are leading is no longer possible. You live and you make me live in a constant nightmare, with your ecstatic dreams. I prefer to show you the reality, however execrable it may be. Perhaps the blow which it will inflict upon you will make of you the woman you ought to be. We will classify these papers again together, and read them, and learn from them a terrible lesson of life!"

Then, as she still continued motionless, he resumed:

"Come, we must be able to see well. Light those other two candles there."

He was seized by a desire for light, a flood of light; he would have desired the blinding light of the sun; and thinking that the light of the three candles was not sufficient, he went into his room for a pair of three-branched candelabra which were there. The nine candles were blazing, yet neither of them, in their disorder — he with his chest bare, she with her left shoulder stained with blood, her throat and arms bare — saw the other. It was past two o'clock, but neither of them had any consciousness of the hour; they were going to spend the night in this eager desire for knowledge, without feeling the need of sleep, outside time and space. The mutterings of the storm, which, through the open window, they could see gathering, grew louder and louder.

Clotilde had never before seen in Pascal's eyes the feverish light which burned in them now. He had been overworking himself for some time past, and his mental sufferings made him at times abrupt, in spite of his good-natured complacency. But it seemed as if an infinite tenderness, trembling with fraternal pity, awoke within him, now that he was about to plunge into the painful truths of existence; and it was something emanating from himself, something very great and very good which was to render innocuous the terrible avalanche of facts which was impending. He was determined that he would reveal everything, since it was necessary that he should do so in order to remedy everything. Was not this an unanswerable, a final argument for evolution, the story of these beings who were so near to them? Such was life, and it must be lived. Doubtless she would emerge from it like the steel tempered by the fire, full of tolerance and courage.

"They are setting you against me," he resumed; "they are making you commit abominable acts, and I wish to restore your conscience to you. When you know, you will judge and you will act. Come here, and read with me."

She obeyed. But these papers, about which her grandmother had spoken so angrily, frightened her a little; while a curiosity that grew with every moment awoke within her. And then, dominated though she was by the virile authority which had just constrained and subjugated her, she did not yet yield. But might she not listen to him, read with him? Did she not retain the right to refuse or to give herself afterward? He spoke at last.

"Will you come?"

"Yes, master, I will."

He showed her first the genealogical tree of the Rougon-Macquarts. He did not usually lock it in the press, but kept it in the desk in his room, from which he had taken it when he went there for the candelabra. For more than twenty years past he had kept it up to date, inscribing the births, deaths, marriages, and other important events that had taken place in the family, making brief notes in each case, in accordance with his theory of heredity.

It was a large sheet of paper, yellow with age, with folds cut by wear, on which was drawn boldly a symbolical tree, whose branches spread and subdivided into five rows of broad leaves; and each leaf bore a name, and contained, in minute handwriting, a biography, a hereditary case.

A scientist's joy took possession of the doctor at sight of this labor of twenty years, in which the laws of heredity established by him were so clearly and so completely applied.

"Look, child! You know enough about the matter, you have copied enough of my notes to understand. Is it not beautiful? A document so complete, so conclusive, in which there is not a gap? It is like an experiment made in the laboratory, a problem stated and solved on the blackboard. You see below, the trunk, the common stock, Aunt Dide; then the three branches issuing from it, the legitimate branch, Pierre Rougon, and the two illegitimate branches, Ursule Macquart and Antoine Macquart; then, new branches arise, and ramify, on one side, Maxime, Clotilde, and Victor, the three children of Saccard, and Angelique, the daughter of Sidonie Rougon; on the other, Pauline, the daughter of Lisa Macquart, and Claude, Jacques, Etienne, and Anna, the four children of Gervaise, her sister; there, at the extremity, is Jean, their brother, and here in the middle, you see what I call the knot, the legitimate issue and the illegitimate issue, uniting in Marthe Rougon and her cousin Francois Mouret, to give rise to three new branches, Octave, Serge, and Desiree Mouret; while there is also the issue of Ursule and the hatter Mouret; Silvere, whose tragic death you know; Helene and her daughter Jean; finally, at the top are the latest offshoots, our poor Charles, your brother Maxime's son, and two other children, who are dead, Jacques Louis, the son of Claude Lantier, and Louiset, the son of Anna Coupeau. In all five generations, a human tree which, for five springs already, five springtides of humanity, has sent forth shoots, at the impulse of the sap of eternal life."

He became more and more animated, pointing out each case on the sheet of old yellow paper, as if it were an anatomical chart.

"And as I have already said, everything is here. You see in direct heredity, the differentiations, that of the mother, Silvere, Lisa, Desiree, Jacques, Louiset, yourself; that of the father, Sidonie, Francois, Gervaise, Octave, Jacques, Louis. Then there are the three cases of crossing: by conjugation, Ursule, Aristide, Anna, Victor; by dissemination, Maxime, Serge, Etienne; by fusion, Antoine, Eugene, Claude. I even noted a fourth case, a very remarkable one, an even cross, Pierre and Pauline; and varieties are established, the differentiation of the mother, for example, often accords with the physical resemblance of the father; or, it is the contrary which takes place, so that, in the crossing, the physical and mental predominance remains with one parent or the other, according to circumstances. Then here is indirect heredity, that of the collateral branches. I have but one well established example of this, the striking personal resemblance of Octave Mouret to his uncle Eugene Rougon. I have also but one example of transmission by influence, Anna, the daughter of Gervaise and Coupeau, who bore a striking resemblance, especially in her childhood, to Lantier, her mother's first lover. But what I am very rich in is in examples of reversion to the original stock — the three finest cases, Marthe, Jeanne, and Charles, resembling Aunt Dide; the resemblance thus passing over one, two, and three generations. This is certainly exceptional, for I scarcely believe in atavism; it seems to me that the new elements brought by the partners, accidents, and the infinite variety of crossings must rapidly efface particular characteristics, so as to bring back the individual to the general type. And there remains variation — Helene, Jean, Angelique. This is the combination, the chemical mixture in which the physical and mental characteristics of the parents are blended, without any of their traits seeming to reappear in the new being."

There was silence for a moment. Clotilde had listened to him with profound attention, wishing to understand. And he remained absorbed in thought, his eyes still fixed on the tree, in the desire to judge his work impartially. He then continued in a low tone, as if speaking to himself:

"Yes, that is as scientific as possible. I have placed there only the members of the family, and I had to give an equal part to the partners, to the fathers and mothers come from outside, whose blood has mingled with ours, and therefore modified it. I had indeed made a mathematically exact tree, the father and the mother bequeathing themselves, by halves, to the child, from generation to generation, so that in Charles, for example, Aunt Dide's part would have been only a twelfth — which would be absurd, since the physical resemblance is there complete. I have therefore thought it sufficient to indicate the elements come from elsewhere, taking into account marriages and the new factor which each introduced. Ah! these sciences that are yet in their infancy, in which hypothesis speaks stammeringly, and imagination rules, these are the domain of the poet as much as of the scientist. Poets go as pioneers in the advance guard, and they often discover new countries, suggesting solutions. There is there a borderland which belongs to them, between the conquered, the definitive truth, and the unknown, whence the truth of tomorrow will be torn. What an immense fresco there is to be painted, what a stupendous human tragedy, what a comedy there is to be written with heredity, which is the very genesis of families, of societies, and of the world!"

His eyes fixed on vacancy, he remained for a time lost in thought. Then, with an abrupt movement, he came back to the envelopes and, pushing the tree aside, said:

"We will take it up again presently; for, in order that you may understand now, it is necessary that events should pass in review before you, and that you should see in action all these actors ticketed here, each one summed up in a brief note. I will call for the envelopes, you will hand them to me one by one, and I will show you the papers in each, and tell you their contents, before putting it away again up there on the shelf. I will not follow the alphabetical order, but the order of events themselves. I have long wished to make this classification. Come, look for the names on the envelopes; Aunt Dide first."

At this moment the edge of the storm which lighted up the sky caught La Souleiade slantingly, and burst over the house in a deluge of rain. But they did not even close the window. They heard neither the peals of thunder nor the ceaseless beating of the rain upon the roof. She handed him the envelope bearing the name of Aunt Dide in large characters; and he took from it papers of all sorts, notes taken by him long ago, which he proceeded to read.

"Hand me Pierre Rougon. Hand me Ursule Macquart. Hand me Antoine Macquart."

Silently she obeyed him, her heart oppressed by a dreadful anguish at all she was hearing. And the envelopes were passed on, displayed their contents, and were piled up again in the press.

First was the foundress of the family, Adelaide Fouque, the tall, crazy girl, the first nervous lesion giving rise to the legitimate branch, Pierre Rougon, and to the two illegitimate branches, Ursule and Antoine Macquart, all that *bourgeois* and sanguinary tragedy, with the *coup d'etat* of December, 1854, for a background, the Rougons, Pierre and Felicite, preserving order at Plassans, bespattering with the blood of Silvere their rising fortunes, while Adelaide, grown old, the miserable Aunt Dide, was shut up in the Tulettes, like a specter of expiation and of waiting.

Then like a pack of hounds, the appetites were let loose. The supreme appetite of power in Eugene Rougon, the great man, the disdainful genius of the family, free from base interests, loving power for its own sake, conquering Paris in old boots with the adventurers of the coming Empire, rising from the legislative body to the senate, passing from the presidency of the council of state to the portfolio of minister; made by his party, a hungry crowd of followers, who at the same time supported and devoured him; conquered for an instant by a woman, the beautiful Clorinde, with whom he had been imbecile enough to fall in love, but having so strong a will, and burning with so vehement a desire to rule, that he won back power by giving the lie to his whole life, marching to his triumphal sovereignty of vice emperor.

With Aristide Saccard, appetite ran to low pleasures, the whole hot quarry of money, luxury, women — a devouring hunger which left him homeless, at the time when millions were changing hands, when the whirlwind of wild speculation was blowing through the city, tearing down everywhere to construct anew, when princely fortunes were made, squandered, and remade in six months; a greed of gold whose ever increasing fury carried him away, causing him, almost before the body of his wife Angele was cold in death, to sell his name, in order to have the first indispensable thousand francs, by marrying Renee. And it was Saccard, too, who, a few years later, put in motion the immense money-press of the Banque Universelle. Saccard, the never vanquished; Saccard, grown more powerful, risen to be the clever and daring grand financier, comprehending the fierce and civilizing role that money plays, fighting, winning, and losing battles on the Bourse, like Napoleon at Austerlitz and Waterloo; engulfing in disaster a world of miserable people; sending forth into the unknown realms of crime his natural son Victor, who disappeared, fleeing through the dark night, while he himself, under the impassable protection of unjust nature, was loved by the adorable Mme. Caroline, no doubt in recompense of all the evil he had done.

Here a tall, spotless lily had bloomed in this compost, Sidonie Rougon, the sycophant of her brother, the go-between in a hundred suspicious affairs, giving birth to the pure and divine Angelique, the little embroiderer with fairylike fingers who worked into the gold of the chasubles the dream of her Prince Charming, so happy among her companions the saints, so little made for the hard realities of life, that she obtained the grace of dying of love, on the day of her marriage, at the first kiss of Felicien de Hautecoeur, in the triumphant peal of bells ringing for her splendid nuptials.

The union of the two branches, the legitimate and the illegitimate, took place then, Marthe Rougon espousing her cousin Francois Mouret, a peaceful household slowly disunited, ending in the direst catastrophes — a sad and gentle woman taken, made use of, and crushed in the vast machine of war erected for the conquest of a city; her three children torn from her, she herself leaving her heart in the rude grasp of the Abbé Faujas. And the Rougons saved Plassans a second time, while she was dying in the glare of the conflagration in which her husband was being consumed, mad with long pent-up rage and the desire for revenge.

Of the three children, Octave Mouret was the audacious conqueror, the clear intellect, resolved to demand from the women the sovereignty of Paris, fallen at his *debut* into the midst of a corrupt *bourgeois* society, acquiring there a terrible sentimental education, passing from the capricious refusal of one woman to the unresisting abandonment of another, remaining, fortunately, active, laborious, and combative, gradually emerging, and improved even, from the low plotting, the ceaseless ferment of a rotten society that could be heard already cracking to its foundations. And Octave Mouret, victorious, revolutionized commerce; swallowed up the cautious little shops that carried on business in the old-fashioned way; established in the midst of feverish Paris the colossal palace of temptation, blazing with lights, overflowing with velvets, silks, and laces; won fortunes exploiting woman; lived in smiling scorn of woman until the day when a little girl, the avenger of her sex, the innocent and wise Denise, vanquished him and held him captive at her feet, groaning with anguish, until she did him the favor, she who was so poor, to marry him in the midst of the apotheosis of his Louvre, under the golden shower of his receipts.

There remained the two other children, Serge Mouret and Desiree Mouret, the latter innocent and healthy, like some happy young animal; the former refined and mystical, who was thrown into the priesthood by a nervous malady hereditary in his family, and who lived again the story of Adam, in the Eden of Le Paradou. He was born again to love Albine, and to lose her, in the bosom of sublime nature, their accomplice; to be recovered, afterward by the Church, to war eternally with life, striving to kill his manhood, throwing on the body of the dead Albine the handful of earth, as officiating priest, at the very time when Desiree, the sister and friend of animals, was rejoicing in the midst of the swarming life of her poultry yard.

Further on there opened a calm glimpse of gentle and tragic life, Helene Mouret living peacefully with her little girl, Jeanne, on the heights of Passy, overlooking Paris, the bottomless, boundless human sea, in face of which was unrolled this page of love: the sudden passion of Helene for a stranger, a physician, brought one night by chance to the bedside of her daughter; the morbid jealousy of Jeanne — the instinctive jealousy of a loving girl — disputing her mother with love, her mother already so wasted by her unhappy passion that the daughter died because of her fault; terrible price of one hour of desire in the entire cold and discreet life of a woman, poor dead child, lying alone in the silent cemetery, in face of eternal Paris.

With Lisa Macquart began the illegitimate branch; appearing fresh and strong in her, as she displayed her portly, prosperous figure, sitting at the door of her pork shop in a light colored apron, watching the central market, where the hunger of a people muttered, the age-long battle of the Fat and the Lean, the lean Florent, her brother-in-law, execrated, and set upon by the fat fishwomen and the fat shopwomen, and whom even the fat pork-seller herself, honest, but unforgiving, caused to be arrested as a republican who had broken his ban, convinced that she was laboring for the good digestion of all honest people.

From this mother sprang the sanest, the most human of girls, Pauline Quenu, the well-balanced, the reasonable, the virgin; who, knowing everything, accepted the joy of living in so ardent a love for others that, in spite of the revolt of her youthful heart, she resigned to her friend her cousin and betrothed, Lazare, and afterward saved the child of the disunited household, becoming its true mother; always triumphant, always gay, notwithstanding her sacrificed and ruined life, in her monotonous solitude, facing the great sea, in the midst of a little world of sufferers groaning with pain, but who did not wish to die.

Then came Gervaise Macquart with her four children: bandy-legged, pretty, and industrious Gervaise, whom her lover Lantier turned into the street in the faubourg, where she met the zinc worker Coupeau, the skillful, steady workman whom she married, and with whom she lived so happily at first, having three women working in her laundry, but afterward sinking with her husband, as was inevitable, to the degradation of her surroundings. He, gradually conquered by alcohol, brought by it to madness and death; she herself perverted, become a slattern, her moral ruin completed by the return of Lantier, living in the tranquil ignominy of a household of three, thenceforward the wretched victim of want, her accomplice, to which she at last succumbed, dying one night of starvation.

Her eldest son, Claude, had the unhappy genius of a great painter struck with madness, the impotent madness of feeling within him the masterpiece to which his fingers refused to give shape; a giant wrestler always defeated, a crucified martyr to his work, adoring woman, sacrificing his wife Christine, so loving and for a time so beloved, to the increate, divine woman of his visions, but whom his pencil was unable to delineate in her nude perfection, possessed by a devouring passion for producing, an insatiable longing to create, a longing so torturing when it could not be satisfied, that he ended it by hanging himself.

Jacques brought crime, the hereditary taint being transmuted in him into an instinctive appetite for blood, the young and fresh blood from the gashed throat of a woman, the first comer, the passer-by in the street: a horrible malady against which he struggled, but which took possession of him again in the course of his *amour* with the submissive and sensual Severine, whom a tragic story of assassination caused to live in constant terror, and whom he stabbed one evening in an excess of frenzy, maddened by the sight of her white throat. Then this savage human beast rushed among the trains filing past swiftly, and mounted the snorting engine of which he was the engineer, the beloved engine which was one day to crush him to atoms, and then, left without a guide, to rush furiously off into space braving unknown disasters.

Etienne, in his turn driven out, arrived in the black country on a freezing night in March, descended into the voracious pit, fell in love with the melancholy Catherine, of whom a ruffian robbed him; lived with the miners their gloomy life of misery and base promiscuousness, until one day when hunger, prompting rebellion, sent across the barren plain a howling mob of wretches who demanded bread, tearing down and burning as they went, under the menace of the guns of the band that went off of themselves, a terrible convulsion announcing the end of the world. The avenging blood of the Maheus was to rise up later; of Alzire dead of starvation, Maheu killed by a bullet, Zacharie killed by an explosion of firedamp, Catherine under the ground. La Maheude alone survived to weep her dead, descending again into the mine to earn her thirty sons, while Etienne, the beaten chief of the band, haunted by the dread of future demands, went away on a warm April morning, listening to the secret growth of the new world whose germination was soon to dazzle the earth.

Nana then became the avenger; the girl born among the social filth of the faubourgs; the golden fly sprung from the rottenness below, that was tolerated and concealed, carrying in the fluttering of its wings the ferment of destruction, rising and contaminating the aristocracy, poisoning men only by alighting upon them, in the palaces through whose windows it entered; the unconscious instrument of ruin and death — fierce flame of Vandeuvres, the melancholy fate of Foucarmont, lost in the Chinese waters, the disaster of Steiner, reduced to live as an honest man, the imbecility of La Faloise and the tragic ruin of the Muffats, and the white corpse of Georges, watched by Philippe, come out of prison the day before, when the air of the epoch was so contaminated that she herself was infected, and died of malignant smallpox, caught at the deathbed of her son Louiset, while Paris passed beneath her windows, intoxicated, possessed by the frenzy of war, rushing to general ruin.

Lastly comes Jean Macquart, the workman and soldier become again a peasant, fighting with the hard earth, which exacts that every grain of corn shall be purchased with a drop of sweat, fighting, above all, with the country people, whom covetousness and the long and difficult battle with the soil cause to burn with the desire, incessantly stimulated, of possession. Witness the Fouans, grown old, parting with their fields as if they were parting with their flesh; the Buteaus in their eager greed committing parricide, to hasten the inheritance of a field of lucern; the stubborn Francoise dying from the stroke of a scythe, without speaking, rather than that a sod should go out of the family — all this drama of simple natures governed by instinct, scarcely emerged from primitive barbarism — all this human filth on the great earth, which alone remains immortal, the mother from whom they issue and to whom they return again, she whom they love even to crime, who continually remakes life, for its unknown end, even with the misery and the abomination of the beings she nourishes. And it was Jean, too, who, become a widower and having enlisted again at the first rumor of war, brought the inexhaustible reserve, the stock of eternal rejuvenation which the earth keeps; Jean, the humblest, the staunchest soldier at the final downfall, swept along in the terrible and fatal storm which, from the frontier to Sedan, in sweeping away the Empire, threatened to sweep away the country; always wise, circumspect, firm in his hope, loving with fraternal affection his comrade Maurice, the demented child of the people, the holocaust doomed to expiation, weeping tears of blood when inexorable destiny chose himself to hew off this rotten limb, and after all had ended — the continual defeats, the frightful civil war, the lost provinces, the thousands of millions of francs to pay — taking up the march again, notwithstanding, returning to the land which awaited him, to the great and difficult task of making a new France.

Pascal paused; Clotilde had handed him all the packages, one by one, and he had gone over them all, laid bare the contents of all, classified them anew, and placed them again on the top shelf of the press. He was out of breath, exhausted by his swift course through all this humanity, while, without voice, without movement, the young girl, stunned by this overflowing torrent of life, waited still, incapable of thought or judgment. The rain still beat furiously upon the dark fields. The lightning had just struck a tree in the neighborhood, that had split with a terrible crash. The candles flared up in the wind that came in from the open window.

"Ah!" he resumed, pointing to the papers again, "there is a world in itself, a society, a civilization, the whole of life is there, with its manifestations, good and bad, in the heat and labor of the forge which shapes everything. Yes, our family of itself would suffice as an example to science, which will perhaps one day establish with mathematical exactness the laws governing the diseases of the blood and nerves that show themselves in a race, after a first organic lesion, and that determine, according to environment, the sentiments, desires, and passions of each individual of that race, all the human, natural and instinctive manifestations which take the names of virtues and vices. And it is also a historical document, it relates the story of the Second Empire, from the *coup d'etat* to Sedan; for our family spring from the people, they spread themselves through the whole of contemporary society, invaded every place, impelled by their unbridled appetites, by that impulse, essentially modern, that eager desire that urges the lower classes to enjoyment, in their ascent through the social strata. We started, as I have said, from Plassans, and here we are now arrived once more at Plassans."

He paused again, and then resumed in a low, dreamy voice:

"What an appalling mass stirred up! how many passions, how many joys, how many sufferings crammed into this colossal heap of facts! There is pure history: the Empire founded in blood, at first pleasure-loving and despotic, conquering rebellious cities, then gliding to a slow disintegration, dissolving in blood — in such a sea of blood that the entire nation came near being swamped in it. There are social studies: wholesale and retail trade, prostitution, crime, land, money, the *bourgeoisie,* the people — that people who rot in the sewer of the faubourgs, who rebel in the great industrial centers, all that ever-increasing growth of mighty socialism, big with the new century. There are simple human studies: domestic pages, love stories, the struggle of minds and hearts against unjust nature, the destruction of those who cry out under their too difficult task, the cry of virtue immolating itself, victorious over pain, There are fancies, flights of the imagination beyond the real: vast gardens always in bloom, cathedrals with slender, exquisitely wrought spires, marvelous tales come down from paradise, ideal affections remounting to heaven in a kiss. There is everything, the good and the bad, the vulgar and the sublime, flowers, mud, blood, laughter, the torrent of life itself, bearing humanity endlessly on!"

He took up again the genealogical tree which had remained neglected on the table, spread it out and began to go over it once more with his finger, enumerating now the members of the family who were still living: Eugene Rougon, a fallen majesty, who remained in the Chamber, the witness, the impassible defender of the old world swept away at the downfall of the Empire. Aristide Saccard, who, after having changed his principles, had fallen upon his feet a republican, the editor of a great journal, on the way to make new millions, while his natural son Victor, who had never reappeared, was living still in the shade, since he was not in the galleys, cast forth by the world into the future, into the unknown, like a human beast foaming with the hereditary virus, who must communicate his malady with every bite he gives. Sidonie Rougon, who had for a time disappeared, weary of disreputable affairs, had lately retired to a sort of religious house, where she was living in monastic austerity, the treasurer of the Marriage Fund, for aiding in the marriage of girls who were mothers. Octave Mouret, proprietor of the great establishment *Au Bonheur des Dames*, whose colossal fortune still continued increasing, had had, toward the end of the winter, a third child by his wife Denise Baudu, whom he adored, although his mind was beginning to be deranged again. The Abbé Mouret, cure at St. Eutrope, in the heart of a marshy gorge, lived there in great retirement, and very modestly, with his sister Desiree, refusing all advancement from his bishop, and waiting for death like a holy man, rejecting all medicines, although he was already suffering from consumption in its first stage. Helene Mouret was living very happily in seclusion with her second husband, M. Rambaud, on the little estate which they owned near Marseilles, on the seashore; she had had no child by her second husband. Pauline Quenu was still at Bonneville at the other extremity of France, in face of the vast ocean, alone with little Paul, since the death of Uncle Chanteau, having resolved never to marry, in order to devote herself entirely to the son of her cousin Lazare, who had become a widower and had gone to America to make a fortune. Etienne Lantier, returning to Paris after the strike at Montsou, had compromised himself later in the insurrection of the Commune, whose principles he had defended with ardor; he had been condemned to death, but his sentence being commuted was transported and was now at Noumea. It was even said that he had married immediately on his arrival there, and that he had had a child, the sex of which, however, was not known with certainty. Finally, Jean Macquart, who had received his discharge after the Bloody Week, had settled at Valqueyras, near Plassans, where he had had the good fortune to marry a healthy girl, Melanie Vial, the daughter of a well-to-do peasant, whose lands he farmed, and his wife had borne him a son in May.

"Yes, it is true," he resumed, in a low voice; "races degenerate. There is here a veritable exhaustion, rapid deterioration, as if our family, in their fury of enjoyment, in the gluttonous satisfaction of their appetites, had consumed themselves too quickly. Louiset, dead in infancy; Jacques Louis, a half imbecile, carried off by a nervous disease; Victor returned to the savage state, wandering about in who knows what dark places; our poor Charles, so beautiful and so frail; these are the latest branches of the tree, the last pale offshoots into which the puissant sap of the larger branches seems to have been unable to mount. The worm was in the trunk, it has ascended into the fruit, and is devouring it. But one must never despair; families are a continual growth. They go back beyond the common ancestor, into the unfathomable strata of the races that have lived, to the first being; and they will put forth new shoots without end, they will spread and ramify to infinity, through future ages. Look at our tree; it counts only five generations. It has not so much importance as a blade of grass, even, in the human forest, vast and dark, of which the peoples are the great secular oaks. Think only of the immense roots which spread through the soil; think of the continual putting forth of new leaves above, which mingle with other leaves of the ever-rolling sea of treetops, at the fructifying, eternal breath of life. Well, hope lies there, in the daily reconstruction of the race by the new blood which comes from without. Each marriage brings other elements, good or bad, of which the effect is, however, to prevent certain and progressive regeneration. Breaches are repaired, faults effaced, an equilibrium is inevitably re-established at the end of a few generations, and it is the average man that always results; vague humanity, obstinately pursuing its mysterious labor, marching toward its unknown end."

He paused, and heaved a deep sigh.

"Ah! our family, what is it going to become; in what being will it finally end?"

He continued, not now taking into account the survivors whom he had just named; having classified these, he knew what they were capable of, but he was full of keen curiosity regarding the children who were still infants. He had written to a *confrere* in Noumea for precise information regarding the wife whom Etienne had lately married there, and the child which she had had, but he had heard nothing, and he feared greatly that on that side the tree would remain incomplete. He was more fully furnished with documents regarding the two children of Octave Mouret, with whom he continued to correspond; the little girl was growing up puny and delicate, while the little boy, who strongly resembled his mother, had developed superbly, and was perfectly healthy. His strongest hope, besides these, was in Jean's children, the eldest of whom was a magnificent boy, full of the youthful vigor of the races that go back to the soil to regenerate themselves. Pascal occasionally went to Valqueyras, and he returned happy from that fertile spot, where the father, quiet and rational, was always at his plow, the mother cheerful and simple, with her vigorous frame, capable of bearing a world. Who knew what sound branch was to spring from that side? Perhaps the wise and puissant of the future were to germinate there. The worst of it, for the beauty of his tree, was that all these little boys and girls were still so young that he could not classify them. And his voice grew tender as he spoke of this hope of the future, these fair-haired children, in the unavowed regret for his celibacy.

Still contemplating the tree spread out before him, he cried:

"And yet it is complete, it is decisive. Look! I repeat to you that all hereditary cases are to be found there. To establish my theory, I had only to base it on the collection of these facts. And indeed, the marvelous thing is that there you can put your finger on the cause why creatures born of the same stock can appear radically different, although they are only logical modifications of common ancestors. The trunk explains the branches, and these explain the leaves. In your father Saccard and your Uncle Eugene Rougon, so different in their temperaments and their lives, it is the same impulse which made the inordinate appetites of the one and the towering ambition of the other. Angelique, that pure lily, is born from the disreputable Sidonie, in the rapture which makes mystics or lovers, according to the environment. The three children of the Mourets are born of the same breath which makes of the clever Octave the dry goods merchant, a millionaire; of the devout Serge, a poor country priest; of the imbecile Desiree, a beautiful and happy girl. But the example is still more striking in the children of Gervaise; the neurosis passes down, and Nana sells herself; Etienne is a rebel; Jacques, a murderer; Claude, a genius; while Pauline, their cousin german, near by, is victorious virtue — virtue which struggles and immolates itself. It is heredity, life itself which makes imbeciles, madmen, criminals and great men. Cells abort, others take their place, and we have a scoundrel or a madman instead of a man of genius, or simply an honest man. And humanity rolls on, bearing everything on its tide."

Then in a new shifting of his thought, growing still more animated, he continued:

"And animals — the beast that suffers and that loves, which is the rough sketch, as it were, of man — all the animals our brothers, that live our life, yes, I would have put them in the ark, I would give them a place among our family, show them continually mingling with us, completing our existence. I have known cats whose presence was the mysterious charm of the household; dogs that were adored, whose death was mourned, and left in the heart an inconsolable grief. I have known goats, cows, and asses of very great importance, and whose personality played such a part that their history ought to be written. And there is our Bonhomme, our poor old horse, that has served us for a quarter of a century. Do you not think that he has mingled his life with ours, and that henceforth he is one of the family? We have modified him, as he has influenced us a little; we shall end by being made in the same image, and this is so true that now, when I see him, half blind, with wandering gaze, his legs stiff with rheumatism, I kiss him on both cheeks as if he were a poor old relation who had fallen to my charge. Ah, animals, all creeping and crawling things, all creatures that lament, below man, how large a place in our sympathies it would be necessary to give them in a history of life!"

This was a last cry in which Pascal gave utterance to his passionate tenderness for all created beings. He had gradually become more and more excited, and had so come to make this confession of his faith in the continuous and victorious work of animated nature. And Clotilde, who thus far had not spoken, pale from the catastrophe in which her plans had ended, at last opened her lips to ask:

"Well, master, and what am I here?"

She placed one of her slender fingers on the leaf of the tree on which she saw her name written. He had always passed this leaf by. She insisted.

"Yes, I; what am I? Why have you not read me my envelope?"

For a moment he remained silent, as if surprised at the question.

"Why? For no reason. It is true, I have nothing to conceal from you. You see what is written here? 'Clotilde, born in 1847. Selection of the mother. Reversional heredity, with moral and physical predominance of the maternal grandfather.' Nothing can be clearer. Your mother has predominated in you; you have her fine intelligence, and you have also something of her coquetry, at times of her indolence and of her submissiveness. Yes, you are very feminine, like her. Without your being aware of it, I would say that you love to be loved. Besides, your mother was a great novel reader, an imaginative being who loved to spend whole days dreaming over a book; she doted on nursery tales, had her fortune told by cards, consulted clairvoyants; and I have always thought that your concern about spiritual matters, your anxiety about the unknown, came from that source. But what completed your character by giving you a dual nature, was the influence of your grandfather, Commandant Sicardot. I knew him; he was not a genius, but he had at least a great deal of uprightness and energy. Frankly, if it were not for him, I do not believe that you would be worth much, for the other influences are hardly good. He has given you the best part of your nature, combativeness, pride, and frankness."

She had listened to him with attention. She nodded slightly, to signify that it was indeed so, that she was not offended, although her lips trembled visibly at these new details regarding her people and her mother.

"Well," she resumed, "and you, master?"

This time he did not hesitate.

"Oh, I!" he cried, "what is the use of speaking of me? I do not belong to the family. You see what is written here. 'Pascal, born in 1813. Individual variation. Combination in which the physical and moral characters of the parents are blended, without any of their traits seeming to appear in the new being.' My mother has told me often enough that I did not belong to it, that in truth she did not know where I could have come from."

Those words came from him like a cry of relief, of involuntary joy.

"And the people make no mistake in the matter. Have you ever heard me called Pascal Rougon in the town? No; people always say simply Dr. Pascal. It is because I stand apart. And it may not be very affectionate to feel so, but I am delighted at it, for there are in truth inheritances too heavy to bear. It is of no use that I love them all. My heart beats nonetheless joyously when I feel myself another being, different from them, without any community with them. Not to be of them, my God! not to be of them! It is a breath of pure air; it is what gives me the courage to have them all here, to put them, in all their nakedness, in their envelopes, and still to find the courage to live!"

He stopped, and there was silence for a time. The rain had ceased, the storm was passing away, the thunderclaps sounded more and more distant, while from the refreshed fields, still dark, there came in through the open window a delicious odor of moist earth. In the calm air the candles were burning out with a tall, tranquil flame.

"Ah!" said Clotilde simply, with a gesture of discouragement, "what are we to become finally?"

She had declared it to herself one night, in the threshing yard; life was horrible, how could one live peaceful and happy? It was a terrible light that science threw on the world. Analysis searched every wound of humanity, in order to expose its horror. And now he had spoken still more bluntly; he had increased the disgust which she had for persons and things, pitilessly dissecting her family. The muddy torrent had rolled on before her for nearly three hours, and she had heard the most dreadful revelations, the harsh and terrible truth about her people, her people who were so dear to her, whom it was her duty to love; her father grown powerful through pecuniary crimes; her brother dissolute; her grandmother unscrupulous, covered with the blood of the just; the others almost all tainted, drunkards, ruffians, murderers, the monstrous blossoming of the human tree.

The blow had been so rude that she could not yet recover from it, stunned as she was by the revelation of her whole family history, made to her in this way at a stroke. And yet the lesson was rendered innocuous, so to say, by something great and good, a breath of profound humanity which had borne her through it. Nothing bad had come to her from it. She felt herself beaten by a sharp sea wind, the storm wind which strengthens and expands the lungs. He had revealed everything, speaking freely even of his mother, without judging her, continuing to preserve toward her his deferential attitude, as a scientist who does not judge events. To tell everything in order to know everything, in order to remedy everything, was not this the cry which he had uttered on that beautiful summer night?

And by the very excess of what he had just revealed to her, she remained shaken, blinded by this too strong light, but understanding him at last, and confessing to herself that he was attempting in this an immense work. In spite of everything, it was a cry of health, of hope in the future. He spoke as a benefactor who, since heredity made the world, wished to fix its laws, in order to control it, and to make a new and happy world. Was there then only mud in this overflowing stream, whose sluices he had opened? How much gold had passed, mingled with the grass and the flowers on its borders? Hundreds of beings were still flying swiftly before her, and she was haunted by good and charming faces, delicate girlish profiles, by the serene beauty of women. All passion bled there, hearts swelled with every tender rapture. They were numerous, the Jeannes, the Angeliques, the Paulines, the Marthes, the Gervaises, the Helenes. They and others, even those who were least good, even terrible men, the worst of the band, showed a brotherhood with humanity.

And it was precisely this breath which she had felt pass, this broad current of sympathy, that he had introduced naturally into his exact scientific lesson. He did not seem to be moved; he preserved the impersonal and correct attitude of the demonstrator, but within him what tender suffering, what a fever of devotion, what a giving up of his whole being to the happiness of others? His entire work, constructed with such mathematical precision, was steeped in this fraternal suffering, even in its most cruel ironies. Had he not just spoken of the animals, like an elder brother of the wretched living beings that suffer? Suffering exasperated him; his wrath was because of his too lofty dream, and he had become harsh only in his hatred of the factitious and the transitory; dreaming of working, not for the polite society of a time, but for all humanity in the gravest hours of its history. Perhaps, even, it was this revolt against the vulgarity of the time which had made him throw himself, in bold defiance, into theories and their application. And the work remained human, overflowing as it was with an infinite pity for beings and things.

Besides, was it not life? There is no absolute evil. Most often a virtue presents itself side by side with a defect. No man is bad to everyone, each man makes the happiness of someone; so that, when one does not view things from a single standpoint only, one recognizes in the end the utility of every human being. Those who believe in God should say to themselves that if their God does not strike the wicked dead, it is because he sees his work in its totality, and that he cannot descend to the individual. Labor ends to begin anew; the living, as a whole, continue, in spite of everything, admirable in their courage and their industry; and love of life prevails over all.

This giant labor of men, this obstinacy in living, is their excuse, is redemption. And then, from a great height the eye saw only this continual struggle, and a great deal of good, in spite of everything, even though there might be a great deal of evil. One shared the general indulgence, one pardoned, one had only an infinite pity and an ardent charity. The haven was surely there, waiting those who have lost faith in dogmas, who wish to understand the meaning of their lives, in the midst of the apparent iniquity of the world. One must live for the effort of living, for the stone to be carried to the distant and unknown work, and the only possible peace in the world is in the joy of making this effort.

Another hour passed; the entire night had flown by in this terrible lesson of life, without either Pascal or Clotilde being conscious of where they were, or of the flight of time. And he, overworked for some time past, and worn out by the life of suspicion and sadness which he had been leading, started nervously, as if he had suddenly awakened.

"Come, you know all; do you feel your heart strong, tempered by the truth, full of pardon and of hope? Are you with me?"

But, still stunned by the frightful moral shock which she had received, she too, started, bewildered. Her old beliefs had been so completely overthrown, so many new ideas were awakening within her, that she did not dare to question herself, in order to find an answer. She felt herself seized and carried away by the omnipotence of truth. She endured it without being convinced.

"Master," she stammered, "master —"

And they remained for a moment face to face, looking at each other. Day was breaking, a dawn of exquisite purity, far off in the vast, clear sky, washed by the storm. Not a cloud now stained the pale azure tinged with rose color. All the cheerful sounds of awakening life in the rain-drenched fields came in through the window, while the candles, burned down to the socket, paled in the growing light.

"Answer; are you with me, altogether with me?"

For a moment he thought she was going to throw herself on his neck and burst into tears. A sudden impulse seemed to impel her. But they saw each other in their semi-nudity. She, who had not noticed it before, was now conscious that she was only half dressed, that her arms were bare, her shoulders bare, covered only by the scattered locks of her unbound hair, and on her right shoulder, near the armpit, on lowering her eyes, she perceived again the few drops of blood of the bruise which he had given her, when he had grasped her roughly, in struggling to master her. Then an extraordinary confusion took possession of her, a certainty that she was going to be vanquished, as if by this grasp he had become her master, and forever. This sensation was prolonged; she was seized and drawn on, without the consent of her will, by an irresistible impulse to submit.

Abruptly Clotilde straightened herself, struggling with herself, wishing to reflect and to recover herself. She pressed her bare arms against her naked throat. All the blood in her body rushed to her skin in a rosy blush of shame. Then, in her divine and slender grace, she turned to flee.

"Master, master, let me go — I will see —"

With the swiftness of alarmed maidenhood, she took refuge in her chamber, as she had done once before. He heard her lock the door hastily, with a double turn of the key. He remained alone, and he asked himself suddenly, seized by infinite discouragement and sadness, if he had done right in speaking, if the truth would germinate in this dear and adored creature, and bear one day a harvest of happiness.

VI

*T*he days wore on. October began with magnificent weather — a sultry autumn in which the fervid heat of summer was prolonged, with a cloudless sky. Then the weather changed, fierce winds began to blow, and a last storm channeled gullies in the hillsides. And to the melancholy household at La Souleiade the approach of winter seemed to have brought an infinite sadness.

It was a new hell. There were no more violent quarrels between Pascal and Clotilde. The doors were no longer slammed. Voices raised in dispute no longer obliged Martine to go continually upstairs to listen outside the door. They scarcely spoke to each other now; and not a single word had been exchanged between them regarding the midnight scene, although weeks had passed since it had taken place. He, through an inexplicable scruple, a strange delicacy of which he was not himself conscious, did not wish to renew the conversation, and to demand the answer which he expected — a promise of faith in him and of submission. She, after the great moral shock which had completely transformed her, still reflected, hesitated, struggled, fighting against herself, putting off her decision in order not to surrender, in her instinctive rebelliousness. And the misunderstanding continued, in the midst of the mournful silence of the miserable house, where there was no longer any happiness.

During all this time Pascal suffered terribly, without making any complaint. He had sunk into a dull distrust, imagining that he was still being watched, and that if they seemed to leave him at peace it was only in order to concoct in secret the darkest plots. His uneasiness increased, even, and he expected every day some catastrophe to happen — the earth suddenly to open and swallow up his papers, La Souleiade itself to be razed to the ground, carried away bodily, scattered to the winds.

The persecution against his thought, against his moral and intellectual life, in thus hiding itself, and so rendering him helpless to defend himself, became so intolerable to him that he went to bed every night in a fever. He would often start and turn round suddenly, thinking he was going to surprise the enemy behind him engaged in some piece of treachery, to find nothing there but the shadow of his own fears. At other times, seized by some suspicion, he would remain on the watch for hours together, hidden, behind his blinds, or lying in wait in a passage; but not a soul stirred, he heard nothing but the violent beating of his heart. His fears kept him in a state of constant agitation; he never went to bed at night without visiting every room; he no longer slept, or, if he did, he would waken with a start at the slightest noise, ready to defend himself.

And what still further aggravated Pascal's sufferings was the constant, the ever more bitter thought that the wound was inflicted upon him by the only creature he loved in the world, the adored Clotilde, whom for twenty years he had seen grow in beauty and in grace, whose life had hitherto bloomed like a beautiful flower, perfuming his. She, great God! for whom his heart was full of affection, whom he had never analyzed, she, who had become his joy, his courage, his hope, in whose young life he lived over again. When she passed by, with her delicate neck, so round, so fresh, he was invigorated, bathed in health and joy, as at the coming of spring.

His whole life, besides, explained this invasion, this subjugation of his being by the young girl who had entered into his heart while she was still a little child, and who, as she grew up, had gradually taken possession of the whole place. Since he had settled at Plassans, he had led a blest existence, wrapped up in his books, far from women. The only passion he was ever known to have had, was his love for the lady who had died, whose fingertips he had never kissed. He had not lived; he had within him a reserve of youthfulness, of vigor, whose surging flood now clamored rebelliously at the menace of approaching age. He would have become attached to an animal, a stray dog that he had chanced to pick up in the street, and that had licked his hand. And it was this child whom he loved, all at once become an adorable woman, who now distracted him, who tortured him by her hostility.

Pascal, so gay, so kind, now became insupportably gloomy and harsh. He grew angry at the slightest word; he would push aside the astonished Martine, who would look up at him with the submissive eyes of a beaten animal. From morning till night he went about the gloomy house, carrying his misery about with him, with so forbidding a countenance that no one ventured to speak to him.

He never took Clotilde with him now on his visits, but went alone. And thus it was that he returned home one afternoon, his mind distracted because of an accident which had happened; having on his conscience, as a physician, the death of a man.

He had gone to give a hypodermic injection to Lafouasse, the tavern keeper, whose ataxia had within a short time made such rapid progress that he regarded him as doomed. But, notwithstanding, Pascal still fought obstinately against the disease, continuing the treatment, and as ill luck would have it, on this day the little syringe had caught up at the bottom of the vial an impure particle, which had escaped the filter. Immediately a drop of blood appeared; to complete his misfortune, he had punctured a vein. He was at once alarmed, seeing the tavern keeper turn pale and gasp for breath, while large drops of cold perspiration broke out upon his face. Then he understood; death came as if by a stroke of lightning, the lips turning blue, the face black. It was an embolism; he had nothing to blame but the insufficiency of his preparations, his still rude method. No doubt Lafouasse had been doomed. He could not, perhaps, have lived six months longer, and that in the midst of atrocious sufferings, but the brutal fact of this terrible death was nonetheless there, and what despairing regret, what rage against impotent and murderous science, and what a shock to his faith! He returned home, livid, and did not make his appearance again until the following day, after having remained sixteen hours shut up in his room, lying in a semi-stupor on the bed, across which he had thrown himself, dressed as he was.

On the afternoon of this day Clotilde, who was sitting beside him in the study, sewing, ventured to break the oppressive silence. She looked up, and saw him turning over the leaves of a book wearily, searching for some information which he was unable to find.

"Master, are you ill? Why do you not tell me, if you are. I would take care of you."

He kept his eyes bent upon the book, and muttered:

"What does it matter to you whether I am ill or not? I need no one to take care of me."

She resumed, in a conciliating voice:

"If you have troubles, and can tell them to me, it would perhaps be a relief to you to do so. Yesterday you came in looking so sad. You must not allow yourself to be cast down in that way. I have spent a very anxious night. I came to your door three times to listen, tormented by the idea that you were suffering."

Gently as she spoke, her words were like the cut of a whip. In his weak and nervous condition a sudden access of rage made him push away the book and rise up trembling.

"So you spy upon me, then. I cannot even retire to my room without people coming to glue their ears to the walls. Yes, you listen even to the beatings of my heart. You watch for my death, to pillage and burn everything here."

His voice rose and all his unjust suffering vented itself in complaints and threats.

"I forbid you to occupy yourself about me. Is there nothing else that you have to say to me? Have you reflected? Can you put your hand in mine loyally, and say to me that we are in accord?"

She did not answer. She only continued to look at him with her large clear eyes, frankly declaring that she would not surrender yet, while he, exasperated more and more by this attitude, lost all self-control.

"Go away, go away," he stammered, pointing to the door. "I do not wish you to remain near me. I do not wish to have enemies near me. I do not wish you to remain near me to drive me mad!"

She rose, very pale, and went at once out of the room, without looking behind, carrying her work with her.

During the month which followed, Pascal took refuge in furious and incessant work. He now remained obstinately, for whole days at a time, alone in the study, sometimes passing even the nights there, going over old documents, to revise all his works on heredity. It seemed as if a sort of frenzy had seized him to assure himself of the legitimacy of his hopes, to force science to give him the certainty that humanity could be remade — made a higher, a healthy humanity. He no longer left the house, he abandoned his patients even, and lived among his papers, without air or exercise. And after a month of this overwork, which exhausted him without appeasing his domestic torments, he fell into such a state of nervous exhaustion that illness, for some time latent, declared itself at last with alarming violence.

Pascal, when he rose in the morning, felt worn out with fatigue, wearier and less refreshed than he had been on going to bed the night before. He constantly had pains all over his body; his limbs failed him, after five minutes' walk; the slightest exertion tired him; the least movement caused him intense pain. At times the floor seemed suddenly to sway beneath his feet. He had a constant buzzing in his ears, flashes of light dazzled his eyes. He took a loathing for wine, he had no longer any appetite, and his digestion was seriously impaired. Then, in the midst of the apathy of his constantly increasing idleness he would have sudden fits of aimless activity. The equilibrium was destroyed, he had at times outbreaks of nervous irritability, without any cause. The slightest emotion brought tears to his eyes. Finally, he would shut himself up in his room, and give way to paroxysms of despair so violent that he would sob for hours at a time, without any immediate cause of grief, overwhelmed simply by the immense sadness of things.

In the early part of December Pascal had a severe attack of neuralgia. Violent pains in the bones of the skull made him feel at times as if his head must split. Old Mme. Rougon, who had been informed of his illness, came to inquire after her son. But she went straight to the kitchen, wishing to have a talk with Martine first. The latter, with a heart-broken and terrified air, said to her that monsieur must certainly be going mad; and she told her of his singular behavior, the continual tramping about in his room, the locking of all the drawers, the rounds which he made from the top to the bottom of the house, until two o'clock in the morning. Tears filled her eyes and she at last hazarded the opinion that monsieur must be possessed with a devil, and that it would be well to notify the cure of St. Saturnin.

"So good a man," she said, "a man for whom one would let one's self be cut in pieces! How unfortunate it is that one cannot get him to go to church, for that would certainly cure him at once."

Clotilde, who had heard her grandmother's voice, entered at this moment. She, too, wandered through the empty rooms, spending most of her time in the deserted apartment on the ground floor. She did not speak, however, but only listened with her thoughtful and expectant air.

"Ah, good day! It is you, my dear. Martine tells me that Pascal is possessed with a devil. That is indeed my opinion also; only the devil is called pride. He thinks that he knows everything. He is Pope and Emperor in one, and naturally it exasperates him when people don't agree with him."

She shrugged her shoulders with supreme disdain.

"As for me, all that would only make me laugh if it were not so sad. A fellow who knows nothing about anything; who has always been wrapped up in his books; who has not lived. Put him in a drawing room, and he would know as little how to act as a newborn babe. And as for women, he does not even know what they are."

Forgetting to whom she was speaking, a young girl and a servant, she lowered her voice, and said confidentially:

"Well, one pays for being too sensible, too. Neither a wife nor a sweetheart nor anything. That is what has finally turned his brain."

Clotilde did not move. She only lowered her eyelids slowly over her large thoughtful eyes; then she raised them again, maintaining her impenetrable countenance, unwilling, unable, perhaps, to give expression to what was passing within her. This was no doubt all still confused, a complete evolution, a great change which was taking place, and which she herself did not clearly understand.

"He is upstairs, is he not?" resumed Felicite. "I have come to see him, for this must end; it is too stupid."

And she went upstairs, while Martine returned to her saucepans, and Clotilde went to wander again through the empty house.

Upstairs in the study Pascal sat seemingly in a stupor, his face bent over a large open book. He could no longer read, the words danced before his eyes, conveying no meaning to his mind. But he persisted, for it was death to him to lose his faculty for work, hitherto so powerful. His mother at once began to scold him, snatching the book from him, and flinging it upon a distant table, crying that when one was sick one should take care of one's self. He rose with a quick, angry movement, about to order her away as he had ordered Clotilde. Then, by a last effort of the will, he became again deferential.

"Mother, you know that I have never wished to dispute with you. Leave me, I beg of you."

She did not heed him, but began instead to take him to task about his continual distrust. It was he himself who had given himself a fever, always fancying that he was surrounded by enemies who were setting traps for him, and watching him to rob him. Was there any common sense in imagining that people were persecuting him in that way? And then she accused him of allowing his head to be turned by his discovery, his famous remedy for curing every disease. That was as much as to think himself equal to the good God; which only made it all the more cruel when he found out how mistaken he was. And she mentioned Lafouasse, the man whom he had killed — naturally, she could understand that that had not been very pleasant for him; indeed there was cause enough in it to make him take to his bed.

Pascal, still controlling himself, very pale and with eyes cast on the ground, contented himself with repeating:

"Mother, leave me, I beg of you."

"No, I won't leave you," she cried with the impetuosity which was natural to her, and which her great age had in no wise diminished. "I have come precisely to stir you up a little, to rid you of this fever which is consuming you. No, this cannot continue. I don't wish that we should again become the talk of the whole town on your account. I wish you to take care of yourself."

He shrugged his shoulders, and said in a low voice, as if speaking to himself, with an uneasy look, half of conviction, half of doubt:

"I am not ill."

But Felicite, beside herself, burst out, gesticulating violently·

"Not ill! not ill! Truly, there is no one like a physician for not being able to see himself. Why, my poor boy, everyone that comes near you is shocked by your appearance. You are becoming insane through pride and fear!"

This time Pascal raised his head quickly, and looked her straight in the eyes, while she continued:

"This is what I had to tell you, since it seems that no one else would undertake the task. You are old enough to know what you ought to do. You should make an effort to shake off all this; you should think of something else; you should not let a fixed idea take possession of you, especially when you belong to a family like ours. You know it; have sense, and take care of yourself."

He grew paler than before, looking fixedly at her still, as if he were sounding her, to know what there was of her in him. And he contented himself with answering:

"You are right, mother. I thank you."

When he was again alone, he dropped into his seat before the table, and tried once more to read his book. But he could not succeed, anymore than before, in fixing his attention sufficiently to understand the words, whose letters mingled confusedly together before his eyes. And his mother's words buzzed in his ears; a vague terror, which had some time before sprung up within him, grew and took shape, haunting him now as an immediate and clearly defined danger. He who two months before had boasted triumphantly of not belonging to the family, was he about to receive the most terrible of contradictions? Ah, this egotistic joy, this intense joy of not belonging to it, was it to give place to the terrible anguish of being struck in his turn? Was he to have the humiliation of seeing the taint revive in him? Was he to be dragged down to the horror of feeling himself in the clutches of the monster of heredity? The sublime idea, the lofty certitude which he had of abolishing suffering, of strengthening man's will, of making a new and a higher humanity, a healthy humanity, was assuredly only the beginning of the monomania of vanity. And in his bitter complaint of being watched, in his desire to watch the enemies who, he thought, were obstinately bent on his destruction, were easily to be recognized the symptoms of the monomania of suspicion. So then all the diseases of the race were to end in this terrible case — madness within a brief space, then general paralysis, and a dreadful death.

From this day forth Pascal was as if possessed. The state of nervous exhaustion into which overwork and anxiety had thrown him left him an unresisting prey to this haunting fear of madness and death. All the morbid sensations which he felt, his excessive fatigue on rising, the buzzing in his ears, the flashes of light before his eyes, even his attacks of indigestion and his paroxysms of tears, were so many infallible symptoms of the near insanity with which he believed himself threatened. He had completely lost, in his own case, the keen power of diagnosis of the observant physician, and if he still continued to reason about it, it was only to confound and pervert symptoms, under the influence of the moral and physical depression into which he had fallen. He was no longer master of himself; he was mad, so to say, to convince himself hour by hour that he must become so.

All the days of this pale December were spent by him in going deeper and deeper into his malady. Every morning he tried to escape from the haunting subject, but he invariably ended by shutting himself in the study to take up again, in spite of himself, the tangled skein of the day before.

The long study which he had made of heredity, his important researches, his works, completed the poisoning of his peace, furnishing him with ever renewed causes of disquietude. To the question which he put to himself continually as to his own hereditary case, the documents were there to answer it by all possible combinations. They were so numerous that he lost himself among them now. If he had deceived himself, if he could not set himself apart, as a remarkable case of variation, should he place himself under the head of reversional heredity, passing over one, two, or even three generations? Or was his case rather a manifestation of larvated heredity, which would bring anew proof to the support of his theory of the germ plasm, or was it simply a singular case of hereditary resemblance, the sudden apparition of some unknown ancestor at the very decline of life?

From this moment he never rested, giving himself up completely to the investigation of his case, searching his notes, rereading his books. And he studied himself, watching the least of his sensations, to deduce from them the facts on which he might judge himself. On the days when his mind was most sluggish, or when he thought he experienced particular phenomena of vision, he inclined to a predominance of the original nervous lesion; while, if he felt that his limbs were affected, his feet heavy and painful, he imagined he was suffering the indirect influence of some ancestor come from outside. Everything became confused, until at last he could recognize himself no longer, in the midst of the imaginary troubles which agitated his disturbed organism. And every evening the conclusion was the same, the same knell sounded in his brain — heredity, appalling heredity, the fear of becoming mad.

In the early part of January Clotilde was an involuntary spectator of a scene which wrung her heart. She was sitting before one of the windows of the study, reading, concealed by the high back of her chair, when she saw Pascal, who had been shut up in his room since the day before, entering. He held open before his eyes with both hands a sheet of yellow paper, in which she recognized the genealogical tree. He was so completely absorbed, his gaze was so fixed, that she might have come forward without his observing her. He spread the tree upon the table, continuing to look at it for a long time, with the terrified expression of interrogation which had become habitual to him, which gradually changed to one of supplication, the tears coursing down his cheeks.

Why, great God! would not the tree answer him, and tell him what ancestor he resembled, in order that he might inscribe his case on his own leaf, beside the others? If he was to become mad, why did not the tree tell him so clearly, which would have calmed him, for he believed that his suffering came only from his uncertainty? Tears clouded his vision, yet still he looked, he exhausted himself in this longing to know, in which his reason must finally give way.

Clotilde hastily concealed herself as she saw him walk over to the press, which he opened wide. He seized the envelopes, threw them on the table, and searched among them feverishly. It was the scene of the terrible night of the storm that was beginning over again, the gallop of nightmares, the procession of phantoms, rising at his call from this heap of old papers. As they passed by, he addressed to each of them a question, an ardent prayer, demanding the origin of his malady, hoping for a word, a whisper which should set his doubts at rest. First, it was only an indistinct murmur, then came words and fragments of phrases.

"Is it you — is it you — is it you — oh, old mother, the mother of us all — who are to give me your madness? Is it you, inebriate uncle, old scoundrel of an uncle, whose drunkenness I am to pay for? Is it you, ataxic nephew, or you, mystic nephew, or yet you, idiot niece, who are to reveal to me the truth, showing me one of the forms of the lesion from which I suffer? Or is it rather you, second cousin, who hanged yourself; or you, second cousin, who committed murder; or you, second cousin, who died of rottenness, whose tragic ends announce to me mine — death in a cell, the horrible decomposition of being?"

And the gallop continued, they rose and passed by with the speed of the wind. The papers became animate, incarnate, they jostled one another, they trampled on one another, in a wild rush of suffering humanity.

"Ah, who will tell me, who will tell me, who will tell me? — Is it he who died mad? he who was carried off by phthisis? he who was killed by paralysis? she whose constitutional feebleness caused her to die in early youth? — Whose is the poison of which I am to die? What is it, hysteria, alcoholism, tuberculosis, scrofula? And what is it going to make of me, an ataxic or a madman? A madman. Who was it said a madman? They all say it — a madman, a madman, a madman!"

Sobs choked Pascal. He let his dejected head fall among the papers, he wept endlessly, shaken by shuddering sobs. And Clotilde, seized by a sort of awe, feeling the presence of the fate which rules over races, left the room softly, holding her breath; for she knew that it would mortify him exceedingly if he knew that she had been present.

Long periods of prostration followed. January was very cold. But the sky remained wonderfully clear, a brilliant sun shone in the limpid blue; and at La Souleiade, the windows of the study facing south formed a sort of hothouse, preserving there a delightfully mild temperature. They did not even light a fire, for the room was always filled with a flood of sunshine, in which the flies that had survived the winter flew about lazily. The only sound to be heard was the buzzing of their wings. It was a close and drowsy warmth, like a breath of spring that had lingered in the old house baked by the heat of summer.

Pascal, still gloomy, dragged through the days there, and it was there, too, that he overheard one day the closing words of a conversation which aggravated his suffering. As he never left his room now before breakfast, Clotilde had received Dr. Ramond this morning in the study, and they were talking there together in an undertone, sitting beside each other in the bright sunshine.

It was the third visit which Ramond had made during the last week. Personal reasons, the necessity, especially, of establishing definitely his position as a physician at Plassans, made it expedient for him not to defer his marriage much longer: and he wished to obtain from Clotilde a decisive answer. On each of his former visits the presence of a third person had prevented him from speaking. As he desired to receive her answer from herself directly he had resolved to declare himself to her in a frank conversation. Their intimate friendship, and the discretion and good sense of both, justified him in taking this step. And he ended, smiling, looking into her eyes:

"I assure you, Clotilde, that it is the most reasonable of *denouements*. You know that I have loved you for a long time. I have a profound affection and esteem for you. That alone might perhaps not be sufficient, but, in addition, we understand each other perfectly, and we should be very happy together, I am convinced of it."

She did not cast down her eyes; she, too, looked at him frankly, with a friendly smile. He was, in truth, very handsome, in his vigorous young manhood.

"Why do you not marry Mlle. Leveque, the lawyer's daughter?" she asked. "She is prettier and richer than I am, and I know that she would gladly accept you. My dear friend, I fear that you are committing a folly in choosing me."

He did not grow impatient, seeming still convinced of the wisdom of his determination.

"But I do not love Mlle. Leveque, and I do love you. Besides, I have considered everything, and I repeat that I know very well what I am about. Say yes; you can take no better course."

Then she grew very serious, and a shadow passed over her face, the shadow of those reflections, of those almost unconscious inward struggles, which kept her silent for days at a time. She did not see clearly yet, she still struggled against herself, and she wished to wait.

"Well, my friend, since you are really serious, do not ask me to give you an answer today; grant me a few weeks longer. Master is indeed very ill. I am greatly troubled about him; and you would not like to owe my consent to a hasty impulse. I assure you, for my part, that I have a great deal of affection for you, but it would be wrong to decide at this moment; the house is too unhappy. It is agreed, is it not? I will not make you wait long."

And to change the conversation she added:

"Yes, I am uneasy about master. I wished to see you, in order to tell you so. The other day I surprised him weeping violently, and I am certain the fear of becoming mad haunts him. The day before yesterday, when you were talking to him, I saw that you were examining him. Tell me frankly, what do you think of his condition? Is he in any danger?"

"Not the slightest!" exclaimed Dr. Ramond. "His system is a little out of order, that is all. How can a man of his ability, who has made so close a study of nervous diseases, deceive himself to such an extent? It is discouraging, indeed, if the clearest and most vigorous minds can go so far astray. In his case his own discovery of hypodermic injections would be excellent. Why does he not use them with himself?"

And as the young girl replied, with a despairing gesture, that he would not listen to her, that he would not even allow her to speak to him now, Ramond said:

"Well, then, I will speak to him."

It was at this moment that Pascal came out of his room, attracted by the sound of voices. But on seeing them both so close to each other, so animated, so youthful, and so handsome in the sunshine — clothed with sunshine, as it were — he stood still in the doorway. He looked fixedly at them, and his pale face altered.

Ramond had a moment before taken Clotilde's hand, and he was holding it in his.

"It is a promise, is it not? I should like the marriage to take place this summer. You know how much I love you, and I shall eagerly await your answer."

"Very well," she answered. "Before a month all will be settled."

A sudden giddiness made Pascal stagger. Here now was this boy, his friend, his pupil, who had introduced himself into his house to rob him of his treasure! He ought to have expected this *denouement*, yet the sudden news of a possible marriage surprised him, overwhelmed him like an unforeseen catastrophe that had forever ruined his life. This girl whom he had fashioned, whom he had believed his own, she would leave him, then, without regret, she would leave him to die alone in his solitude. Only the day before she had made him suffer so intensely that he had asked himself whether he should not part from her and send her to her brother, who was always writing for her. For an instant he had even decided on this separation, for the good of both. Yet to find her here suddenly, with this man, to hear her promise to give him an answer, to think that she would marry, that she would soon leave him, this stabbed him to the heart.

At the sound of his heavy step as he came forward, the two young people turned round in some embarrassment.

"Why, master, we were just talking about you," said Ramond gaily. "Yes, to be frank with you, we were conspiring. Come, why do you not take care of yourself? There is nothing serious the matter with you; you would be on your feet again in a fortnight if you did."

Pascal, who had dropped into a chair, continued to look at them. He had still the power to control himself, and his countenance gave no evidence of the wound which he had just received. He would assuredly die of it, and no one would suspect the malady which had carried him off. But it was a relief to him to be able to give vent to his feelings, and he declared violently that he would not take even so much as a glass of tisane.

"Take care of myself!" he cried; "what for? Is it not all over with my old carcass?"

Ramond insisted, with a good-tempered smile.

"You are sounder than any of us. This is a trifling disturbance, and you know that you have the remedy in your own hands. Use your hypodermic injection."

Pascal did not allow him to finish. This filled the measure of his rage. He angrily asked if they wished him to kill himself, as he had killed Lafouasse. His injections! A pretty invention, of which he had good reason to be proud. He abjured medicine, and he swore that he would never again go near a patient. When people were no longer good for anything they ought to die; that would be the best thing for everybody. And that was what he was going to try to do, so as to have done with it all.

"Bah! bah!" said Ramond at last, resolving to take his leave, through fear of exciting him still further; "I will leave you with Clotilde; I am not at all uneasy, Clotilde will take care of you."

But Pascal had on this morning received the final blow. He took to his bed toward evening, and remained for two whole days without opening the door of his room. It was in vain that Clotilde, at last becoming alarmed, knocked loudly at the door. There was no answer. Martine went in her turn and begged monsieur, through the keyhole, at least to tell her if he needed anything. A deathlike silence reigned; the room seemed to be empty.

Then, on the morning of the third day, as the young girl by chance turned the knob, the door yielded; perhaps it had been unlocked for hours. And she might enter freely this room in which she had never set foot: a large room, rendered cold by its northern exposure, in which she saw a small iron bed without curtains, a shower bath in a corner, a long black wooden table, a few chairs, and on the table, on the floor, along the walls, an array of chemical apparatus, mortars, furnaces, machines, instrument cases. Pascal, up and dressed, was sitting on the edge of his bed, in trying to arrange which he had exhausted himself.

"Don't you want me to nurse you, then?" she asked with anxious tenderness, without venturing to advance into the room.

"Oh, you can come in," he said with a dejected gesture. "I won't beat you. I have not the strength to do that now."

And from this day on he tolerated her about him, and allowed her to wait on him. But he had caprices still. He would not let her enter the room when he was in bed, possessed by a sort of morbid shame; then he made her send him Martine. But he seldom remained in bed, dragging himself about from chair to chair, in his utter inability to do any kind of work. His malady continued to grow worse, until at last he was reduced to utter despair, tortured by sick headaches, and without the strength, as he said, to put one foot before the other, convinced every morning that he would spend the night at the Tulettes, a raving maniac. He grew thin; his face, under its crown of white hair — which he still cared for through a last remnant of vanity — acquired a look of suffering, of tragic beauty. And although he allowed himself to be waited on, he refused roughly all remedies, in the distrust of medicine into which he had fallen.

Clotilde now devoted herself to him entirely. She gave up everything else; at first she attended low mass, then she left off going to church altogether. In her impatience for some certain happiness, she felt as if she were taking a step toward that end by thus devoting all her moments to the service of a beloved being whom she wished to see once more well and happy. She made a complete sacrifice of herself, she sought to find happiness in the happiness of another; and all this unconsciously, solely at the impulse of her woman's heart, in the midst of the crisis through which she was still passing, and which was modifying her character profoundly, without her knowledge. She remained silent regarding the disagreement which separated them. The idea did not again occur to her to throw herself on his neck, crying that she was his, that he might return to life, since she gave herself to him. In her thoughts she grieved to see him suffer; she was only an affectionate girl, who took care of him, as any female relative would have done. And her attentions were very pure, very delicate, occupying her life so completely that her days now passed swiftly, exempt from tormenting thoughts of the Beyond, filled with the one wish of curing him.

But where she had a hard battle to fight was in prevailing upon him to use his hypodermic injections upon himself. He flew into a passion, disowned his discovery, and called himself an imbecile. She too cried out. It was she now who had faith in science, who grew indignant at seeing him doubt his own genius. He resisted for a long time; then yielding to the empire which she had acquired over him, he consented, simply to avoid the affectionate dispute which she renewed with him every morning. From the very first he experienced great relief from the injections, although he refused to acknowledge it. His mind became clearer, and he gradually gained strength. Then she was exultant, filled with enthusiastic pride in him. She vaunted his treatment, and became indignant because he did not admire himself, as an example of the miracles which he was able to work. He smiled; he was now beginning to see clearly into his own condition. Ramond had spoken truly, his illness had been nothing but nervous exhaustion. Perhaps he would get over it after all.

"Ah, it is you who are curing me, little girl," he would say, not wishing to confess his hopes. "Medicines, you see, act according to the hand that gives them."

The convalescence was slow, lasting through the whole of February. The weather remained clear and cold; there was not a single day in which the study was not flooded with warm, pale sunshine. There were hours of relapse, however, hours of the blackest melancholy, in which all the patient's terrors returned; when his guardian, disconsolate, was obliged to sit at the other end of the room, in order not to irritate him still more. He despaired anew of his recovery. He became again bitter and aggressively ironical.

It was on one of those bad days that Pascal, approaching a window, saw his neighbor, M. Bellombre, the retired professor, making the round of his garden to see if his fruit trees were well covered with blossoms. The sight of the old man, so neat and so erect, with the fine placidity of the egoist, on whom illness had apparently never laid hold, suddenly put Pascal beside himself.

"Ah!" he growled, "there is one who will never overwork himself, who will never endanger his health by worrying!"

And he launched forth into an ironical eulogy on selfishness. To be alone in the world, not to have a friend, to have neither wife nor child, what happiness! That hard-hearted miser, who for forty years had had only other people's children to cuff, who lived aloof from the world, without even a dog, with a deaf and dumb gardener older than himself, was he not an example of the greatest happiness possible on earth? Without a responsibility, without a duty, without an anxiety, other than that of taking care of his dear health! He was a wise man, he would live a hundred years.

"Ah, the fear of life! that is cowardice which is truly the best wisdom. To think that I should ever have regretted not having a child of my own! Has anyone a right to bring miserable creatures into the world? Bad heredity should be ended, life should be ended. The only honest man is that old coward there!"

M. Bellombre continued peacefully making the round of his pear trees in the March sunshine. He did not risk a too hasty movement; he economized his fresh old age. If he met a stone in his path, he pushed it aside with the end of his cane, and then walked tranquilly on.

"Look at him! Is he not well preserved; is he not handsome? Have not all the blessings of heaven been showered down upon him? He is the happiest man I know."

Clotilde, who had listened in silence, suffered from the irony of Pascal, the full bitterness of which she divined. She, who usually took M. Bellombre's part, felt a protest rise up within her. Tears came to her eyes, and she answered simply in a low voice:

"Yes; but he is not loved."

These words put a sudden end to the painful scene. Pascal, as if he had received an electric shock, turned and looked at her. A sudden rush of tenderness brought tears to his eyes also, and he left the room to keep from weeping.

The days wore on in the midst of these alternations of good and bad hours. He recovered his strength but slowly, and what put him in despair was that whenever he attempted to work he was seized by a profuse perspiration. If he had persisted, he would assuredly have fainted. So long as he did not work he felt that his convalescence was making little progress. He began to take an interest again, however, in his accustomed investigations. He read over again the last pages that he had written, and, with this reawakening of the scientist in him, his former anxieties returned. At one time he fell into a state of such depression, that the house and all it contained ceased to exist for him. He might have been robbed, everything he possessed might have been taken and destroyed, without his even being conscious of the disaster. Now he became again watchful, from time to time he would feel his pocket, to assure himself that the key of the press was there.

But one morning when he had overslept himself, and did not leave his room until eleven o'clock, he saw Clotilde in the study, quietly occupied in copying with great exactness in pastel a branch of flowering almond. She looked up, smiling; and taking a key that was lying beside her on the desk, she offered it to him, saying:

"Here, master."

Surprised, not yet comprehending, he looked at the object which she held toward him.

"What is that?" he asked.

"It is the key of the press, which you must have dropped from your pocket yesterday, and which I picked up here this morning."

Pascal took it with extraordinary emotion. He looked at it, and then at Clotilde. Was it ended, then? She would persecute him no more. She was no longer eager to rob everything, to burn everything. And seeing her still smiling, she also looking moved, an immense joy filled his heart.

He caught her in his arms, crying:

"Ah, little girl, if we might only not be too unhappy!"

Then he opened a drawer of his table and threw the key into it, as he used to do formerly.

From this time on he gained strength, and his convalescence progressed more rapidly. Relapses were still possible, for he was still very weak. But he was able to write, and this made the days less heavy. The sun, too, shone more brightly, the study being so warm at times that it became necessary to half close the shutters. He refused to see visitors, barely tolerated Martine, and had his mother told that he was sleeping, when she came at long intervals to inquire for him. He was happy only in this delightful solitude, nursed by the rebel, the enemy of yesterday, the docile pupil of today. They would often sit together in silence for a long time, without feeling any constraint. They meditated, or lost themselves in infinitely sweet reveries.

One day, however, Pascal seemed very grave. He was now convinced that his illness had resulted from purely accidental causes, and that heredity had had no part in it. But this filled him nonetheless with humility.

"My God!" he murmured, "how insignificant we are! I who thought myself so strong, who was so proud of my sane reason! And here have I barely escaped being made insane by a little trouble and overwork!"

He was silent, and sank again into thought. After a time his eyes brightened, he had conquered himself. And in a moment of reason and courage, he came to a resolution.

"If I am getting better," he said, "it is especially for your sake that I am glad."

Clotilde, not understanding, looked up and said:

"How is that?"

"Yes, on account of your marriage. Now you will be able to fix the day."

She still seemed surprised.

"Ah, true — my marriage!"

"Shall we decide at once upon the second week in June?"

"Yes, the second week in June; that will do very well."

They spoke no more; she fixed her eyes again on the piece of sewing on which she was engaged, while he, motionless, and with a grave face, sat looking into space.

VII

On this day, on arriving at La Souleiade, old Mme. Rougon perceived Martine in the kitchen garden, engaged in planting leeks; and, as she sometimes did, she went over to the servant to have a chat with her, and find out from her how things were going on, before entering the house.

For some time past she had been in despair about what she called Clotilde's desertion. She felt truly that she would now never obtain the documents through her. The girl was behaving disgracefully, she was siding with Pascal, after all she had done for her; and she was becoming perverted to such a degree that for a month past she had not been seen in Church. Thus she returned to her first idea, to get Clotilde away and win her son over when, left alone, he should be weakened by solitude. Since she had not been able to persuade the girl to go live with her brother, she eagerly desired the marriage. She would like to throw her into Dr. Ramond's arms tomorrow, in her impatience at so many delays. And she had come this afternoon with a feverish desire to hurry on matters.

"Good-day, Martine. How is everyone here?"

The servant, kneeling down, her hands full of clay, lifted up her pale face, protected against the sun by a handkerchief tied over her cap.

"As usual, madame, pretty well."

They went on talking, Felicite treating her as a confidante, as a devoted daughter, one of the family, to whom she could tell everything. She began by questioning her; she wished to know if Dr. Ramond had come that morning. He had come, but they had talked only about indifferent matters. This put her in despair, for she had seen the doctor on the previous day, and he had unbosomed himself to her, chagrined at not having yet received a decisive answer, and eager now to obtain at least Clotilde's promise. Things could not go on in this way, the young girl must be compelled to engage herself to him.

"He has too much delicacy," she cried. "I have told him so. I knew very well that this morning, even, he would not venture to demand a positive answer. And I have come to interfere in the matter. We shall see if I cannot oblige her to come to a decision."

Then, more calmly:

"My son is on his feet now; he does not need her."

Martine, who was again stooping over the bed, planting her leeks, straightened herself quickly.

"Ah, that for sure!"

And a flush passed over her face, worn by thirty years of service. For a wound bled within her; for some time past the master scarcely tolerated her about him. During the whole time of his illness he had kept her at a distance, accepting her services less and less every day, and finally closing altogether to her the door of his room and of the workroom. She had a vague consciousness of what was taking place, an instinctive jealousy tortured her, in her adoration of the master, whose chattel she had been satisfied to be for so many years.

"For sure, we have no need of mademoiselle. I am quite able to take care of monsieur."

Then she, who was so discreet, spoke of her labors in the garden, saying that she made time to cultivate the vegetables, so as to save a few days' wages of a man. True, the house was large, but when one was not afraid of work, one could manage to do all there was to be done. And then, when mademoiselle should have left them, that would be always one less to wait upon. And her eyes brightened unconsciously at the thought of the great solitude, of the happy peace in which they should live after this departure.

"It would give me pain," she said, lowering her voice, "for it would certainly give monsieur a great deal. I would never have believed that I could be brought to wish for such a separation. Only, madame, I agree with you that it is necessary, for I am greatly afraid that mademoiselle will end by going to ruin here, and that there will be another soul lost to the good God. Ah, it is very sad; my heart is so heavy about it sometimes that it is ready to burst."

"They are both upstairs, are they not?" said Felicite. "I will go up and see them, and I will undertake to oblige them to end the matter."

An hour later, when she came down again, she found Martine still on her knees on the soft earth, finishing her planting. Upstairs, from her first words, when she said that she had been talking with Dr. Ramond, and that he had shown himself anxious to know his fate quickly, she saw that Dr. Pascal approved — he looked grave, he nodded his head as if to say that this wish seemed to him very natural. Clotilde, herself, ceasing to smile, seemed to listen to him with deference. But she manifested some surprise. Why did they press her? Master had fixed the marriage for the second week in June; she had, then, two full months before her. Very soon she would speak about it with Ramond. Marriage was so serious a matter that they might very well give her time to reflect, and let her wait until the last moment to engage herself. And she said all this with her air of good sense, like a person resolved on coming to a decision. And Felicite was obliged to content herself with the evident desire that both had that matters should have the most reasonable conclusion.

"Indeed I believe that it is settled," ended Felicite. "He seems to place no obstacle in the way, and she seems only to wish not to act hastily, like a girl who desires to examine her heart closely, before engaging herself for life. I will give her a week more for reflection."

Martine, sitting on her heels, was looking fixedly on the ground with a clouded face.

"Yes, yes," she murmured, in a low voice, "mademoiselle has been reflecting a great deal of late. I am always meeting her in some corner. You speak to her, and she does not answer you. That is the way people are when they are breeding a disease, or when they have a secret on their mind. There is something going on; she is no longer the same, no longer the same."

And she took the dibble again and planted a leek, in her rage for work; while old Mme. Rougon went away, somewhat tranquilized; certain, she said, that the marriage would take place.

Pascal, in effect, seemed to accept Clotilde's marriage as a thing settled, inevitable. He had not spoken with her about it again, the rare allusions which they made to it between themselves, in their hourly conversations, left them undisturbed; and it was simply as if the two months which they still had to live together were to be without end, an eternity stretching beyond their view.

She, especially, would look at him smiling, putting off to a future day troubles and decisions with a pretty vague gesture, as if to leave everything to beneficent life. He, now well and gaining strength daily, grew melancholy only when he returned to the solitude of his chamber at night, after she had retired. He shuddered and turned cold at the thought that a time would come when he would be always alone. Was it the beginning of old age that made him shiver in this way? He seemed to see it stretching before him, like a shadowy region in which he already began to feel all his energy melting away. And then the regret of having neither wife nor child filled him with rebelliousness, and wrung his heart with intolerable anguish.

Ah, why had he not lived! There were times when he cursed science, accusing it of having taken from him the best part of his manhood. He had let himself be devoured by work; work had consumed his brain, consumed his heart, consumed his flesh. All this solitary, passionate labor had produced only books, blackened paper, that would be scattered to the winds, whose cold leaves chilled his hands as he turned them over. And no living woman's breast to lean upon, no child's warm locks to kiss! He had lived the cold, solitary life of a selfish scientist, and he would die in cold solitude. Was he indeed going to die thus? Would he never taste the happiness enjoyed by even the common porters, by the carters who cracked their whips, passing by under his windows? But he must hasten, if he would; soon, no doubt, it would be too late. All his unemployed youth, all his pent-up desires, surged tumultuously through his veins. He swore that he would yet love, that he would live a new life, that he would drain the cup of every passion that he had not yet tasted, before he should be an old man. He would knock at the doors, he would stop the passers-by, he would scour the fields and town.

On the following day, when he had taken his shower bath and left his room, all his fever was calmed, the burning pictures had faded away, and he fell back into his natural timidity. Then, on the next night, the fear of solitude drove sleep away as before, his blood kindled again, and the same despair, the same rebelliousness, the same longing not to die without having known family joys returned. He suffered a great deal in this crisis.

During these feverish nights, with eyes wide open in the darkness, he dreamed always, over and over again the same dream. A girl would come along the road, a girl of twenty, marvelously beautiful; and she would enter and kneel down before him in an attitude of submissive adoration, and he would marry her. She was one of those pilgrims of love such as we find in ancient story, who have followed a star to come and restore health and strength to some aged king, powerful and covered with glory. He was the aged king, and she adored him, she wrought the miracle, with her twenty years, of bestowing on him a part of her youth. In her love he recovered his courage and his faith in life.

Ah, youth! he hungered fiercely for it. In his declining days this passionate longing for youth was like a revolt against approaching age, a desperate desire to turn back, to be young again, to begin life over again. And in this longing to begin life over again, there was not only regret for the vanished joys of youth, the inestimable treasure of dead hours, to which memory lent its charm; there was also the determined will to enjoy, now, his health and strength, to lose nothing of the joy of loving! Ah, youth! how eagerly he would taste of its every pleasure, how eagerly he would drain every cup, before his teeth should fall out, before his limbs should grow feeble, before the blood should be chilled in his veins. A pang pierced his heart when he remembered himself, a slender youth of twenty, running and leaping agilely, vigorous and hardy as a young oak, his teeth glistening, his hair black and luxuriant. How he would cherish them, these gifts scorned before, if a miracle could restore them to him!

And youthful womanhood, a young girl who might chance to pass by, disturbed him, causing him profound emotion. This was often even altogether apart from the individual: the image, merely, of youth, the perfume and the dazzling freshness which emanated from it, bright eyes, healthy lips, blooming cheeks, a delicate neck, above all, rounded and satin-smooth, shaded on the back with down; and youthful womanhood always presented itself to him tall and slight, divinely slender in its chaste nudeness. His eyes, gazing into vacancy, followed the vision, his heart was steeped in infinite longing. There was nothing good or desirable but youth; it was the flower of the world, the only beauty, the only joy, the only true good, with health, which nature could bestow on man. Ah, to begin life over again, to be young again, to clasp in his embrace youthful womanhood!

Pascal and Clotilde, now that the fine April days had come, covering the fruit trees with blossoms, resumed their morning walks in La Souleiade. It was the first time that he had gone out since his illness, and she led him to the threshing yard, along the paths in the pine wood, and back again to the terrace crossed by the two bars of shadows thrown by the secular cypresses. The sun had already warmed the old flagstones there, and the wide horizon stretched out under a dazzling sky.

One morning when Clotilde had been running, she returned to the house in such exuberant spirits and so full of pleasant excitement that she went up to the workroom without taking off either her garden hat or the lace scarf which she had tied around her neck.

"Oh," she said, "I am so warm! And how stupid I am, not to have taken off my things downstairs. I will go down again at once."

She had thrown the scarf on a chair on entering.

But her feverish fingers became impatient when she tried to untie the strings of her large straw hat.

"There, now! I have fastened the knot. I cannot undo it, and you must come to my assistance."

Pascal, happy and excited too by the pleasure of the walk, rejoiced to see her so beautiful and so merry. He went over and stood in front of her.

"Wait; hold up your chin. Oh, if you keep moving like that, how do you suppose I can do it?"

She laughed aloud. He could see the laughter swelling her throat, like a wave of sound. His fingers became entangled under her chin, that delicious part of the throat whose warm satin he involuntarily touched. She had on a gown cut sloping in the neck, and through the opening he inhaled all the living perfume of the woman, the pure fragrance of her youth, warmed by the sunshine. All at once a vertigo seized him and he thought he was going to faint.

"No, no! I cannot do it," he said, "unless you keep still!"

The blood throbbed in his temples, and his fingers trembled, while she leaned further back, unconsciously offering the temptation of her fresh girlish beauty. It was the vision of royal youth, the bright eyes, the healthy lips, the blooming cheeks, above all, the delicate neck, satin smooth and round, shaded on the back by down. And she seemed to him so delicately graceful, with her slender throat, in her divine bloom!

"There, it is done!" she cried.

Without knowing how, he had untied the strings. The room whirled round, and then he saw her again, bareheaded now, with her starlike face, shaking back her golden curls laughingly. Then he was seized with a fear that he would catch her in his arms and press mad kisses on her bare neck, and arms, and throat. And he fled from the room, taking with him the hat, which he had kept in his hand, saying:

"I will hang it in the hall. Wait for me; I want to speak to Martine."

Once downstairs, he hurried to the abandoned room and locked himself into it, trembling lest she should become uneasy and come down here to seek him. He looked wild and haggard, as if he had just committed a crime. He spoke aloud, and he trembled as he gave utterance for the first time to the cry that he had always loved her madly, passionately. Yes, ever since she had grown into womanhood he had adored her. And he saw her clearly before him, as if a curtain had been suddenly torn aside, as she was when, from an awkward girl, she became a charming and lovely creature, with her long tapering limbs, her strong slender body, with its round throat, round neck, and round and supple arms. And it was monstrous, but it was true — he hungered for all this with a devouring hunger, for this youth, this fresh, blooming, fragrant flesh.

Then Pascal, dropping into a rickety chair, hid his face in his hands, as if to shut out the light of day, and burst into great sobs. Good God! what was to become of him? A girl whom his brother had confided to him, whom he had brought up like a good father, and who was now — this temptress of twenty-five — a woman in her supreme omnipotence! He felt himself more defenseless, weaker than a child.

And above this physical desire, he loved her also with an immense tenderness, enamored of her moral and intellectual being, of her right-mindedness, of her fine intelligence, so fearless and so clear. Even their discord, the disquietude about spiritual things by which she was tortured, made her only all the more precious to him, as if she were a being different from himself, in whom he found a little of the infinity of things. She pleased him in her rebellions, when she held her ground against him, — she was his companion and pupil; he saw her such as he had made her, with her great heart, her passionate frankness, her triumphant reason. And she was always present with him; he did not believe that he could exist where she was not; he had need of her breath; of the flutter of her skirts near him; of her thoughtfulness and affection, by which he felt himself constantly surrounded; of her looks; of her smile; of her whole daily woman's life, which she had given him, which she would not have the cruelty to take back from him again. At the thought that she was going away, that she would not be always here, it seemed to him as if the heavens were about to fall and crush him; as if the end of all things had come; as if he were about to be plunged in icy darkness. She alone existed in the world, she alone was lofty and virtuous, intelligent and beautiful, with a miraculous beauty. Why, then, since he adored her and since he was her master, did he not go upstairs and take her in his arms and kiss her like an idol? They were both free, she was ignorant of nothing, she was a woman in age. This would be happiness.

Pascal, who had ceased to weep, rose, and would have walked to the door. But suddenly he dropped again into his chair, bursting into a fresh passion of sobs. No, no, it was abominable, it could not be! He felt on his head the frost of his white hair; and he had a horror of his age, of his fifty-nine years, when he thought of her twenty-five years. His former chill fear again took possession of him, the certainty that she had subjugated him, that he would be powerless against the daily temptation. And he saw her giving him the strings of her hat to untie; compelling him to lean over her to make some correction in her work; and he saw himself, too, blind, mad, devouring her neck with ardent kisses. His indignation against himself at this was so great that he arose, now courageously, and had the strength to go upstairs to the workroom, determined to conquer himself.

Upstairs Clotilde had tranquilly resumed her drawing. She did not even look around at his entrance, but contented herself with saying:

"How long you have been! I was beginning to think that Martine must have made a mistake of at least ten sous in her accounts."

This customary jest about the servant's miserliness made him laugh. And he went and sat down quietly at his table. They did not speak again until breakfast time. A great sweetness bathed him and calmed him, now that he was near her. He ventured to look at her, and he was touched by her delicate profile, by her serious, womanly air of application. Had he been the prey of a nightmare, downstairs, then? Would he be able to conquer himself so easily?

"Ah!" he cried, when Martine called them, "how hungry I am! You shall see how I am going to make new muscle!"

She went over to him, and took him by the arm, saying:

"That's right, master; you must be gay and strong!"

But that night, when he was in his own room, the agony began again. At the thought of losing her he was obliged to bury his face in the pillow to stifle his cries. He pictured her to himself in the arms of another, and all the tortures of jealousy racked his soul. Never could he find the courage to consent to such a sacrifice. All sorts of plans clasped together in his seething brain; he would turn her from the marriage, and keep her with him, without ever allowing her to suspect his passion; he would take her away, and they would go from city to city, occupying their minds with endless studies, in order to keep up their companionship as master and pupil; or even, if it should be necessary, he would send her to her brother to nurse him, he would lose her forever rather than give her to a husband. And at each of these resolutions he felt his heart, torn asunder, cry out with anguish in the imperious need of possessing her entirely. He was no longer satisfied with her presence, he wished to keep her for himself, with himself, as she appeared to him in her radiant beauty, in the darkness of his chamber, with her unbound hair falling around her.

His arms clasped the empty air, and he sprang out of bed, staggering like a drunken man; and it was only in the darkness and silence of the workroom that he awoke from this sudden fit of madness. Where, then, was he going, great God? To knock at the door of this sleeping child? to break it in, perhaps, with a blow of his shoulder? The soft, pure respiration, which he fancied he heard like a sacred wind in the midst of the profound silence, struck him on the face and turned him back. And he returned to his room and threw himself on his bed, in a passion of shame and wild despair.

On the following day when he arose, Pascal, worn out by want of sleep, had come to a decision. He took his daily shower bath, and he felt himself stronger and saner. The resolution to which he had come was to compel Clotilde to give her word. When she should have formally promised to marry Ramond, it seemed to him that this final solution would calm him, would forbid his indulging in any false hopes. This would be a barrier the more, an insurmountable barrier between her and him. He would be from that moment armed against his desire, and if he still suffered, it would be suffering only, without the horrible fear of becoming a dishonorable man.

On this morning, when he told the young girl that she ought to delay no longer, that she owed a decisive answer to the worthy fellow who had been awaiting it so long, she seemed at first astonished. She looked straight into his eyes, but he had sufficient command over himself not to show confusion; he insisted merely, with a slightly grieved air, as if it distressed him to have to say these things to her. Finally, she smiled faintly and turned her head aside, saying:

"Then, master, you wish me to leave you?"

"My dear," he answered evasively, "I assure you that this is becoming ridiculous. Ramond will have the right to be angry."

She went over to her desk, to arrange some papers which were on it. Then, after a moment's silence, she said:

"It is odd; now you are siding with grandmother and Martine. They, too, are persecuting me to end this matter. I thought I had a few days more. But, in truth, if you all three urge me —"

She did not finish, and he did not press her to explain herself more clearly.

"When do you wish me to tell Ramond to come, then?"

"Why, he may come whenever he wishes; it does not displease me to see him. But don't trouble yourself. I will let him know that we will expect him one of these afternoons."

On the following day the same scene began over again. Clotilde had taken no step yet, and Pascal was now angry. He suffered martyrdom; he had crises of anguish and rebelliousness when she was not present to calm him by her smiling freshness. And he insisted, in emphatic language, that she should behave seriously and not trifle any longer with an honorable man who loved her.

"The devil! Since the thing is decided, let us be done with it. I warn you that I will send word to Ramond, and that he will be here tomorrow at three o'clock."

She listened in silence, her eyes fixed on the ground. Neither seemed to wish to touch upon the question as to whether the marriage had really been decided on or not, and they took the standpoint that there had been a previous decision, which was irrevocable. When she looked up again he trembled, for he felt a breath pass by; he thought she was on the point of saying that she had questioned herself, and that she refused this marriage. What would he have done, what would have become of him, good God! Already he was filled with an immense joy and a wild terror. But she looked at him with the discreet and affectionate smile which never now left her lips, and she answered with a submissive air:

"As you please, master. Send him word to be here tomorrow at three o'clock."

Pascal spent so dreadful a night that he rose late, saying, as an excuse, that he had one of his old headaches. He found relief only under the icy deluge of the shower bath. At ten o'clock he left the house, saying he would go himself to see Ramond; but he had another object in going out — he had seen at a show in Plassans a corsage of old point d'Alencon; a marvel of beauty which lay there awaiting some lover's generous folly, and the thought had come to him in the midst of the tortures of the night, to make a present of it to Clotilde, to adorn her wedding gown. This bitter idea of himself adorning her, of making her beautiful and fair for the gift of herself, touched his heart, exhausted by sacrifice. She knew the corsage, she had admired it with him one day wonderingly, wishing for it only to place it on the shoulders of the Virgin at St. Saturnin, an antique Virgin adored by the faithful. The shopkeeper gave it to him in a little box which he could conceal, and which he hid, on his return to the house, in the bottom of his writing-desk.

At three o'clock Dr. Ramond presented himself, and he found Pascal and Clotilde in the parlor, where they had been awaiting him with secret excitement and a somewhat forced gaiety, avoiding any further allusion to his visit. They received him smilingly with exaggerated cordiality.

"Why, you are perfectly well again, master!" said the young man. "You never looked so strong."

Pascal shook his head.

"Oh, oh, strong, perhaps! only the heart is no longer here."

This involuntary avowal made Clotilde start, and she looked from one to the other, as if, by the force of circumstances, she compared them with each other — Ramond, with his smiling and superb face — the face of the handsome physician adored by the women — his luxuriant black hair and beard, in all the splendor of his young manhood; and Pascal, with his white hair and his white beard. This fleece of snow, still so abundant, retained the tragic beauty of the six months of torture that he had just passed through. His sorrowful face had aged a little, only his eyes remained still youthful; brown eyes, brilliant and limpid. But at this moment all his features expressed so much gentleness, such exalted goodness, that Clotilde ended by letting her gaze rest upon him with profound tenderness. There was silence for a moment and each heart thrilled.

"Well, my children," resumed Pascal heroically, "I think you have something to say to each other. I have something to do, too, downstairs. I will come up again presently."

And he left the room, smiling back at them.

And soon as they were alone, Clotilde went frankly straight over to Ramond, with both hands outstretched. Taking his hands in hers, she held them as she spoke.

"Listen, my dear friend; I am going to give you a great grief. You must not be too angry with me, for I assure you that I have a very profound friendship for you."

He understood at once, and he turned very pale.

"Clotilde give me no answer now, I beg of you; take more time, if you wish to reflect further."

"It is useless, my dear friend, my decision is made."

She looked at him with her fine, loyal look. She had not released his hands, in order that he might know that she was not excited, and that she was his friend. And it was he who resumed, in a low voice:

"Then you say no?"

"I say no, and I assure you that it pains me greatly to say it. Ask me nothing; you will no doubt know later on."

He sat down, crushed by the emotion which he repressed like a strong and self-contained man, whose mental balance the greatest sufferings cannot disturb. Never before had any grief agitated him like this. He remained mute, while she, standing, continued:

"And above all, my friend, do not believe that I have played the coquette with you. If I have allowed you to hope, if I have made you wait so long for my answer, it was because I did not in very truth see clearly myself. You cannot imagine through what a crisis I have just passed — a veritable tempest of emotions, surrounded by darkness from out of which I have but just found my way."

He spoke at last.

"Since it is your wish, I will ask you nothing. Besides, it is sufficient for you to answer one question. You do not love me, Clotilde?"

She did not hesitate, but said gravely, with an emotion which softened the frankness of her answer:

"It is true, I do not love you; I have only a very sincere affection for you."

He rose, and stopped by a gesture the kind words which she would have added.

"It is ended; let us never speak of it again. I wished you to be happy. Do not grieve for me. At this moment I feel as if the house had just fallen about me in ruins. But I must only extricate myself as best I can."

A wave of color passed over his pale face, he gasped for air, he crossed over to the window, then he walked back with a heavy step, seeking to recover his self-possession. He drew a long breath. In the painful silence which had fallen they heard Pascal coming upstairs noisily, to announce his return.

"I entreat you," murmured Clotilde hurriedly, "to say nothing to master. He does not know my decision, and I wish to break it to him myself, for he was bent upon this marriage."

Pascal stood still in the doorway. He was trembling and breathless, as if he had come upstairs too quickly. He still found strength to smile at them, saying:

"Well, children, have you come to an understanding?"

"Yes, undoubtedly," responded Ramond, as agitated as himself.

"Then it is all settled?"

"Quite," said Clotilde, who had been seized by a faintness.

Pascal walked over to his work-table, supporting himself by the furniture, and dropped into the chair beside it.

"Ah, ah! you see the legs are not so strong after all. It is this old carcass of a body. But the heart is strong. And I am very happy, my children, your happiness will make me well again."

But when Ramond, after a few minutes' further conversation, had gone away, he seemed troubled at finding himself alone with the young girl, and he again asked her:

"It is settled, quite settled; you swear it to me?"

"Entirely settled."

After this he did not speak again. He nodded his head, as if to repeat that he was delighted; that nothing could be better; that at last they were all going to live in peace. He closed his eyes, feigning to drop asleep, as he sometimes did in the afternoon. But his heart beat violently, and his closely shut eyelids held back the tears.

That evening, at about ten o'clock, when Clotilde went downstairs for a moment to give an order to Martine before she should have gone to bed, Pascal profited by the opportunity of being left alone, to go and lay the little box containing the lace corsage on the young girl's bed. She came upstairs again, wished him the accustomed good-night, and he had been for at least twenty minutes in his own room, and was already in his shirt sleeves, when a burst of gaiety sounded outside his door. A little hand tapped, and a fresh voice cried, laughing:

"Come, come and look!"

He opened the door, unable to resist this appeal of youth, conquered by his joy.

"Oh, come, come and see what a beautiful little bird has put on my bed!"

And she drew him to her room, taking no refusal. She had lighted the two candles in it, and the antique, pleasant chamber, with its hangings of faded rose color, seemed transformed into a chapel; and on the bed, like a sacred cloth offered to the adoration of the faithful, she had spread the corsage of old point d'Alencon.

"You would not believe it! Imagine, I did not see the box at first. I set things in order a little, as I do every evening. I undressed, and it was only when I was getting into bed that I noticed your present. Ah, what a surprise! I was overwhelmed by it! I felt that I could never wait for the morning, and I put on a skirt and ran to look for you."

It was not until then that he perceived that she was only half dressed, as on the night of the storm, when he had surprised her stealing his papers. And she seemed divine, with her tall, girlish form, her tapering limbs, her supple arms, her slender body, with its small, firm throat.

She took his hands and pressed them caressingly in her little ones.

"How good you are; how I thank you! Such a marvel of beauty, so lovely a present for me, who am nobody! And you remember that I had admired it, this antique relic of art. I said to you that only the Virgin of St. Saturnin was worthy of wearing it on her shoulders. I am so happy! oh, so happy! For it is true, I love beautiful things; I love them so passionately that at times I wish for impossibilities, gowns woven of sunbeams, impalpable veils made of the blue of heaven. How beautiful I am going to look! how beautiful I am going to look!"

Radiant in her ecstatic gratitude, she drew close to him, still looking at the corsage, and compelling him to admire it with her. Then a sudden curiosity seized her.

"But why did you make me this royal present?"

Ever since she had come to seek him in her joyful excitement, Pascal had been walking in a dream. He was moved to tears by this affectionate gratitude; he stood there, not feeling the terror which he had dreaded, but seeming, on the contrary, to be filled with joy, as at the approach of a great and miraculous happiness. This chamber, which he never entered, had the religious sweetness of holy places that satisfy all longings for the unattainable.

His countenance, however, expressed surprise. And he answered:

"Why, this present, my dear, is for your wedding gown."

She, in her turn, looked for a moment surprised as if she had not understood him. Then, with the sweet and singular smile which she had worn of late she said gaily:

"Ah, true, my marriage!"

Then she grew serious again, and said:

"Then you want to get rid of me? It was in order to have me here no longer that you were so bent upon marrying me. Do you still think me your enemy, then?"

He felt his tortures return, and he looked away from her, wishing to retain his courage.

"My enemy, yes. Are you not so? We have suffered so much through each other these last days. It is better in truth that we should separate. And then I do not know what your thoughts are; you have never given me the answer I have been waiting for."

She tried in vain to catch his glance, which he still kept turned away. She began to talk of the terrible night on which they had gone together through the papers. It was true, in the shock which her whole being had suffered, she had not yet told him whether she was with him or against him. He had a right to demand an answer.

She again took his hands in hers, and forced him to look at her.

"And it is because I am your enemy that you are sending me away? I am not your enemy. I am your servant, your chattel, your property. Do you hear? I am with you and for you, for you alone!"

His face grew radiant; an intense joy shone within his eyes.

"Yes, I will wear this lace. It is for my wedding day, for I wish to be beautiful, very beautiful for you. But do you not understand me, then? You are my master; it is you I love."

"No, no! be silent; you will make me mad! You are betrothed to another. You have given your word. All this madness is happily impossible."

"The other! I have compared him with you, and I have chosen you. I have dismissed him. He has gone away, and he will never return. There are only we two now, and it is you I love, and you love me. I know it, and I give myself to you."

He trembled violently. He had ceased to struggle, vanquished by the longing of eternal love.

The spacious chamber, with its antique furniture, warmed by youth, was as if filled with light. There was no longer either fear or suffering; they were free. She gave herself to him knowingly, willingly, and he accepted the supreme gift like a priceless treasure which the strength of his love had won. Suddenly she murmured in his ear, in a caressing voice, lingering tenderly on the words:

"Master, oh, master, master!"

And this word, which she used formerly as a matter of habit, at this hour acquired a profound significance, lengthening out and prolonging itself, as if it expressed the gift of her whole being. She uttered it with grateful fervor, like a woman who accepts, and who surrenders herself. Was not the mystic vanquished, the real acknowledged, life glorified with love at last confessed and shared.

"Master, master, this comes from far back. I must tell you; I must make my confession. It is true that I went to church in order to be happy. But I could not believe. I wished to understand too much; my reason rebelled against their dogmas; their paradise appeared to me an incredible puerility. But I believed that the world does not stop at sensation; that there is a whole unknown world, which must be taken into account; and this, master, I believe still. It is the idea of the Beyond, which not even happiness, found at last upon your neck, will efface. But this longing for happiness, this longing to be happy at once, to have some certainty — how I have suffered from it. If I went to church, it was because I missed something, and I went there to seek it. My anguish consisted in this irresistible need to satisfy my longing. You remember what you used to call my eternal thirst for illusion and falsehood. One night, in the threshing yard, under the great starry sky, do you remember? I burst out against your science, I was indignant because of the ruins with which it strews the earth, I turned my eyes away from the dreadful wounds which it exposes. And I wished, master, to take you to a solitude where we might both live in God, far from the world, forgotten by it. Ah, what torture, to long, to struggle, and not to be satisfied!"

Softly, without speaking, he kissed her on both eyes.

"Then, master, do you remember again, there was the great moral shock on the night of the storm, when you gave me that terrible lesson of life, emptying out your envelopes before me. You had said to me already: 'Know life, love it, live it as it ought to be lived.' But what a vast, what a frightful flood, rolling ever onward toward a human sea, swelling it unceasingly for the unknown future! And, master, the silent work within me began then. There was born, in my heart and in my flesh, the bitter strength of the real. At first I was as if crushed, the blow was so rude. I could not recover myself. I kept silent, because I did not know clearly what to say. Then, gradually, the evolution was effected. I still had struggles, I still rebelled against confessing my defeat. But every day after this the truth grew clearer within me, I knew well that you were my master, and that there was no happiness for me outside of you, of your science and your goodness. You were life itself, broad and tolerant life; saying all, accepting all, solely through the love of energy and effort, believing in the work of the world, placing the meaning of destiny in the labor which we all accomplish with love, in our desperate eagerness to live, to love, to live anew, to live always, in spite of all the abominations and miseries of life. Oh, to live, to live! This is the great task, the work that always goes on, and that will doubtless one day be completed!"

Silent still, he smiled radiantly, and kissed her on the mouth.

"And, master, though I have always loved you, even from my earliest youth, it was, I believe, on that terrible night that you marked me for, and made me your own. You remember how you crushed me in your grasp. It left a bruise, and a few drops of blood on my shoulder. Then your being entered, as it were into mine. We struggled; you were the stronger, and from that time I have felt the need of a support. At first I thought myself humiliated; then I saw that it was but an infinitely sweet submission. I always felt your power within me. A gesture of your hand in the distance thrilled me as though it had touched me. I would have wished that you had seized me again in your grasp, that you had crushed me in it, until my being had mingled with yours forever. And I was not blind; I knew well that your wish was the same as mine, that the violence which had made me yours had made you mine; that you struggled with yourself not to seize me and hold me as I passed by you. To nurse you when you were ill was some slight satisfaction. From that time, light began to break upon me, and I at last understood. I went no more to church, I began to be happy near you, you had become certainty and happiness. Do you remember that I cried to you, in the threshing yard, that something was wanting in our affection. There was a void in it which I longed to fill. What could be wanting to us unless it were God? And it was God — love, and life."

VIII

*T*hen came a period of idyllic happiness. Clotilde was the spring, the tardy rejuvenation that came to Pascal in his declining years. She came, bringing to him, with her love, sunshine and flowers. Their rapture lifted them above the earth; and all this youth she bestowed on him after his thirty years of toil, when he was already weary and worn probing the frightful wounds of humanity. He revived in the light of her great shining eyes, in the fragrance of her pure breath. He had faith again in life, in health, in strength, in the eternal renewal of nature.

On the morning after her avowal it was ten o'clock before Clotilde left her room. In the middle of the workroom she suddenly came upon Martine and, in her radiant happiness, with a burst of joy that carried everything before it, she rushed toward her, crying:

"Martine, I am not going away! Master and I — we love each other."

The old servant staggered under the blow. Her poor worn face, nunlike under its white cap and with its look of renunciation, grew white in the keenness of her anguish. Without a word, she turned and fled for refuge to her kitchen, where, leaning her elbows on her chopping- table, and burying her face in her clasped hands, she burst into a passion of sobs.

Clotilde, grieved and uneasy, followed her. And she tried to comprehend and to console her.

"Come, come, how foolish you are! What possesses you? Master and I will love you all the same; we will always keep you with us. You are not going to be unhappy because we love each other. On the contrary, the house is going to be gay now from morning till night."

But Martine only sobbed all the more desperately.

"Answer me, at least. Tell me why you are angry and why you cry. Does it not please you then to know that master is so happy, so happy! See, I will call master and he will make you answer."

At this threat the old servant suddenly rose and rushed into her own room, which opened out of the kitchen, slamming the door behind her. In vain the young girl called and knocked until she was tired; she could obtain no answer. At last Pascal, attracted by the noise, came downstairs, saying:

"Why, what is the matter?"

"Oh, it is that obstinate Martine! Only fancy, she began to cry when she knew that we loved each other. And she has barricaded herself in there, and she will not stir."

She did not stir, in fact. Pascal, in his turn, called and knocked. He scolded; he entreated. Then, one after the other, they began all over again. Still there was no answer. A deathlike silence reigned in the little room. And he pictured it to himself, this little room, religiously clean, with its walnut bureau, and its monastic bed furnished with white hangings. No doubt the servant had thrown herself across this bed, in which she had slept alone all her woman's life, and was burying her face in the bolster to stifle her sobs.

"Ah, so much the worse for her?" said Clotilde at last, in the egotism of her joy, "let her sulk!"

Then throwing her arms around Pascal, and raising to his her charming face, still glowing with the ardor of self-surrender, she said:

"Master, I will be your servant today."

He kissed her on the eyes with grateful emotion; and she at once set about preparing the breakfast, turning the kitchen upside down. She had put on an enormous white apron, and she looked charming, with her sleeves rolled up, showing her delicate arms, as if for some great undertaking. There chanced to be some cutlets in the kitchen which she cooked to a turn. She added some scrambled eggs, and she even succeeded in frying some potatoes. And they had a delicious breakfast, twenty times interrupted by her getting up in her eager zeal, to run for the bread, the water, a forgotten fork. If he had allowed her, she would have waited upon him on her knees. Ah! to be alone, to be only they two in this large friendly house, and to be free to laugh and to love each other in peace.

They spent the whole afternoon in sweeping and putting things in order. He insisted upon helping her. It was a play; they amused themselves like two merry children. From time to time, however, they went back to knock at Martine's door to remonstrate with her. Come, this was foolish, she was not going to let herself starve! Was there ever seen such a mule, when no one had said or done anything to her! But only the echo of their knocks came back mournfully from the silent room. Not the slightest sound, not a breath responded. Night fell, and they were obliged to make the dinner also, which they ate, sitting beside each other, from the same plate. Before going to bed, they made a last attempt, threatening to break open the door, but their ears, glued to the wood, could not catch the slightest sound. And on the following day, when they went downstairs and found the door still hermetically closed, they began to be seriously uneasy. For twenty- four hours the servant had given no sign of life.

Then, on returning to the kitchen after a moment's absence, Clotilde and Pascal were stupefied to see Martine sitting at her table, picking some sorrel for the breakfast. She had silently resumed her place as servant.

"But what was the matter with you?" cried Clotilde. "Will you speak now?"

She lifted up her sad face, stained by tears. It was very calm, however, and it expressed now only the resigned melancholy of old age. She looked at the young girl with an air of infinite reproach; then she bent her head again without speaking.

"Are you angry with us, then?"

And as she still remained silent, Pascal interposed:

"Are you angry with us, my good Martine?"

Then the old servant looked up at him with her former look of adoration, as if she loved him sufficiently to endure all and to remain in spite of all. At last she spoke.

"No, I am angry with no one. The master is free. It is all right, if he is satisfied."

A new life began from this time. Clotilde, who in spite of her twenty-five years had still remained childlike, now, under the influence of love, suddenly bloomed into exquisite womanhood. Since her heart had awakened, the serious and intelligent boy that she had looked like, with her round head covered with its short curls, had given place to an adorable woman, altogether womanly, submissive and tender, loving to be loved. Her great charm, notwithstanding her learning picked up at random from her reading and her work, was her virginal *naïveté*, as if her unconscious awaiting of love had made her reserve the gift of her whole being to be utterly absorbed in the man whom she should love. No doubt she had given her love as much through gratitude and admiration as through tenderness; happy to make him happy; experiencing a profound joy in being no longer only a little girl to be petted, but something of his very own which he adored, a precious possession, a thing of grace and joy, which he worshiped on bended knees. She still had the religious submissiveness of the former devotee, in the hands of a master mature and strong, from whom she derived consolation and support, retaining, above and beyond affection, the sacred awe of the believer in the spiritual which she still was. But more than all, this woman, so intoxicated with love, was a delightful personification of health and gaiety; eating with a hearty appetite; having something of the valor of her grandfather the soldier; filling the house with her swift and graceful movements, with the bloom of her satin skin, the slender grace of her neck, of all her young form, divinely fresh.

And Pascal, too, had grown handsome again under the influence of love, with the serene beauty of a man who had retained his vigor, notwithstanding his white hairs. His countenance had no longer the sorrowful expression which it had worn during the months of grief and suffering through which he had lately passed; his eyes, youthful still, had recovered their brightness, his features their smiling grace; while his white hair and beard grew thicker, in a leonine abundance which lent him a youthful air. He had kept himself, in his solitary life as a passionate worker, so free from vice and dissipation that he found now within him a reserve of life and vigor eager to expend itself at last. There awoke within him new energy, a youthful impetuosity that broke forth in gestures and exclamations, in a continual need of expansion, of living. Everything wore a new and enchanting aspect to him; the smallest glimpse of sky moved him to wonder; the perfume of a simple flower threw him into an ecstasy; an everyday expression of affection, worn by use, touched him to tears, as if it had sprung fresh from the heart and had not been hackneyed by millions of lips. Clotilde's "I love you," was an infinite caress, whose celestial sweetness no human being had ever before known. And with health and beauty he recovered also his gaiety, that tranquil gaiety which had formerly been inspired by his love of life, and which now threw sunshine over his love, over everything that made life worth living.

They two, blooming youth and vigorous maturity, so healthy, so gay, so happy, made a radiant couple. For a whole month they remained in seclusion, not once leaving La Souleiade. The place where both now liked to be was the spacious workroom, so intimately associated with their habits and their past affection. They would spend whole days there, scarcely working at all, however. The large carved oak press remained with closed doors; so, too, did the bookcases. Books and papers lay undisturbed upon the tables. Like a young married couple they were absorbed in their one passion, oblivious of their former occupations, oblivious of life. The hours seemed all too short to enjoy the charm of being together, often seated in the same large antique easy chair, happy in the depths of this solitude in which they secluded themselves, in the tranquility of this lofty room, in this domain which was altogether theirs, without luxury and without order, full of familiar objects, brightened from morning till night by the returning gaiety of the April sunshine. When, seized with remorse, he would talk about working, she would link her supple arms through his and laughingly hold him prisoner, so that he should not make himself ill again with overwork. And downstairs, they loved, too, the dining room, so gay with its light panels relieved by blue bands, its antique mahogany furniture, its large flower pastels, its brass hanging lamp, always shining. They ate in it with a hearty appetite and they left it, after each meal, only to go upstairs again to their dear solitude.

Then when the house seemed too small, they had the garden, all La Souleiade. Spring advanced with the advancing sun, and at the end of April the roses were beginning to bloom. And what a joy was this domain, walled around, where nothing from the outside world could trouble them! Hours flew by unnoted, as they sat on the terrace facing the vast horizon and the shady banks of the Viorne, and the slopes of Sainte-Marthe, from the rocky bars of the Seille to the valley of Plassans in the dusty distance. There was no shade on the terrace but that of the two secular cypresses planted at its two extremities, like two enormous green tapers, which could be seen three leagues away. At times they descended the slope for the pleasure of ascending the giant steps, and climbing the low walls of uncemented stones which supported the plantations, to see if the stunted olive trees and the puny almonds were budding. More often there were delightful walks under the delicate needles of the pine wood, steeped in sunshine and exhaling a strong odor of resin; endless walks along the wall of enclosure, from behind which the only sound they could hear was, at rare intervals, the grating noise of some cart jolting along the narrow road to Les Fenouilleres; and they spent delightful hours in the old threshing yard, where they could see the whole horizon, and where they loved to stretch themselves, tenderly remembering their former tears, when, loving each other unconsciously to themselves, they had quarreled under the stars. But their favorite retreat, where they always ended by losing themselves, was the quincunx of tall plane trees, whose branches, now of a tender green, looked like lacework. Below, the enormous box trees, the old borders of the French garden, of which now scarcely a trace remained, formed a sort of labyrinth of which they could never find the end. And the slender stream of the fountain, with its eternal crystalline murmur, seemed to sing within their hearts. They would sit hand in hand beside the mossy basin, while the twilight fell around them, their forms gradually fading into the shadow of the trees, while the water which they could no longer see, sang its flutelike song.

Up to the middle of May Pascal and Clotilde secluded themselves in this way, without even crossing the threshold of their retreat. One morning he disappeared and returned an hour later, bringing her a pair of diamond earrings which he had hurried out to buy, remembering this was her birthday. She adored jewels, and the gift astonished and delighted her. From this time not a week passed in which he did not go out once or twice in this way to bring her back some present. The slightest excuse was sufficient for him — a *fête,* a wish, a simple pleasure. He brought her rings, bracelets, a necklace, a slender diadem. He would take out the other jewels and please himself by putting them all upon her in the midst of their laughter. She was like an idol, seated on her chair, covered with gold, — a band of gold on her hair, gold on her bare arms and on her bare throat, all shining with gold and precious stones. Her woman's vanity was delightfully gratified by this. She allowed herself to be adored thus, to be adored on bended knees, like a divinity, knowing well that this was only an exalted form of love. She began at last to scold a little, however; to make prudent remonstrances; for, in truth, it was an absurdity to bring her all these gifts which she must afterward shut up in a drawer, without ever wearing them, as she went nowhere.

They were forgotten after the hour of joy and gratitude which they gave her in their novelty was over. But he would not listen to her, carried away by a veritable mania for giving; unable, from the moment the idea of giving her an article took possession of him, to resist the desire of buying it. It was a munificence of the heart; an imperious desire to prove to her that he thought of her always; a pride in seeing her the most magnificent, the happiest, the most envied of women; a generosity more profound even, which impelled him to despoil himself of everything, of his money, of his life. And then, what a delight, when he saw he had given her a real pleasure, and she threw herself on his neck, blushing, thanking him with kisses. After the jewels, it was gowns, articles of dress, toilet articles. Her room was littered, the drawers were filled to overflowing.

One morning she could not help getting angry. He had brought her another ring.

"Why, I never wear them! And if I did, my fingers would be covered to the tips. Be reasonable, I beg of you."

"Then I have not given you pleasure?" he said with confusion.

She threw her arms about his neck, and assured him with tears in her eyes that she was very happy. He was so good to her! He was so unwearied in his devotion to her! And when, later in the morning, he ventured to speak of making some changes in her room, of covering the walls with tapestry, of putting down a carpet, she again remonstrated.

"Oh! no, no! I beg of you. Do not touch my old room, so full of memories, where I have grown up, where I told you I loved you. I should no longer feel myself at home in it."

Downstairs, Martine's obstinate silence condemned still more strongly these excessive and useless expenses. She had adopted a less familiar attitude, as if, in the new situation, she had fallen from her role of housekeeper and friend to her former station of servant. Toward Clotilde, especially, she changed, treating her like a young lady, like a mistress to whom she was less affectionate but more obedient than formerly. Two or three times, however, she had appeared in the morning with her face discolored and her eyes sunken with weeping, answering evasively when questioned, saying that nothing was the matter, that she had taken cold. And she never made any remark about the gifts with which the drawers were filled. She did not even seem to see them, arranging them without a word either of praise or dispraise. But her whole nature rebelled against this extravagant generosity, of which she could never have conceived the possibility. She protested in her own fashion; exaggerating her economy and reducing still further the expenses of the housekeeping, which she now conducted on so narrow a scale that she retrenched even in the smallest expenses. For instance, she took only two-thirds of the milk which she had been in the habit of taking, and she served sweet dishes only on Sundays. Pascal and Clotilde, without venturing to complain, laughed between themselves at this parsimony, repeating the jests which had amused them for ten years past, saying that after dressing the vegetables she strained them in the colander, in order to save the butter for future use.

But this quarter she insisted upon rendering an account. She was in the habit of going every three months to Master Grandguillot, the notary, to receive the fifteen hundred francs income, of which she disposed afterward according to her judgment, entering the expenses in a book which the doctor had years ago ceased to verify. She brought it to him now and insisted upon his looking over it. He excused himself, saying that it was all right.

"The thing is, monsieur," she said, "that this time I have been able to put some money aside. Yes, three hundred francs. Here they are."

He looked at her in amazement. Generally she just made both ends meet. By what miracle of stinginess had she been able to save such a sum?

"Ah! my poor Martine," he said at last, laughing, "that is the reason, then, that we have been eating so many potatoes of late. You are a pearl of economy, but indeed you must treat us a little better in the future."

This discreet reproach wounded her so profoundly that she allowed herself at last to say:

"Well, monsieur, when there is so much extravagance on the one hand, it is well to be prudent on the other."

He understood the allusion, but instead of being angry, he was amused by the lesson.

"Ah, ah! it is you who are examining my accounts! But you know very well, Martine, that I, too, have my savings laid by."

He alluded to the money which he still received occasionally from his patients, and which he threw into a drawer of his writing-desk. For more than sixteen years past he had put into this drawer every year about four thousand francs, which would have amounted to a little fortune if he had not taken from it, from day to day, without counting them, considerable sums for his experiments and his whims. All the money for the presents came out of this drawer, which he now opened continually. He thought that it would never be empty; he had been so accustomed to take from it whatever he required that it had never occurred to him to fear that he would ever come to the bottom of it.

"One may very well have a little enjoyment out of one's savings," he said gaily. "Since it is you who go to the notary's, Martine, you are not ignorant that I have my income apart."

Then she said, with the colorless voice of the miser who is haunted by the dread of an impending disaster:

"And what would you do if you hadn't it?"

Pascal looked at her in astonishment, and contented himself with answering with a shrug, for the possibility of such a misfortune had never even entered his mind. He fancied that avarice was turning her brain, and he laughed over the incident that evening with Clotilde.

In Plassans, too, the presents were the cause of endless gossip. The rumor of what was going on at La Souleiade, this strange and sudden passion, had spread, no one could tell how, by that force of expansion which sustains curiosity, always on the alert in small towns. The servant certainly had not spoken, but her air was perhaps sufficient; words perhaps had dropped from her involuntarily; the lovers might have been watched over the walls. And then came the buying of the presents, confirming the reports and exaggerating them. When the doctor, in the early morning, scoured the streets and visited the jeweler's and the dressmaker's, eyes spied him from the windows, his smallest purchases were watched, all the town knew in the evening that he had given her a silk bonnet, a bracelet set with sapphires. And all this was turned into a scandal. This uncle in love with his niece, committing a young man's follies for her, adorning her like a holy Virgin. The most extraordinary stories began to circulate, and people pointed to La Souleiade as they passed by.

But old Mme. Rougon was, of all persons, the most bitterly indignant. She had ceased going to her son's house when she learned that Clotilde's marriage with Dr. Ramond had been broken off. They had made sport of her. They did nothing to please her, and she wished to show how deep her displeasure was. Then a full month after the rupture, during which she had understood nothing of the pitying looks, the discreet condolences, the vague smiles which met her everywhere, she learned everything with a suddenness that stunned her. She, who, at the time of Pascal's illness, in her mortification at the idea of again becoming the talk of the town through that ugly story, had raised such a storm! It was far worse this time; the height of scandal, a love affair for people to regale themselves with. The Rougon legend was again in peril; her unhappy son was decidedly doing his best to find some way to destroy the family glory won with so much difficulty. So that in her anger she, who had made herself the guardian of this glory, resolving to purify the legend by every means in her power, put on her hat one morning and hurried to La Souleiade with the youthful vivacity of her eighty years.

Pascal, whom the rupture with his mother enchanted, was fortunately not at home, having gone out an hour before to look for a silver buckle which he had thought of for a belt. And Felicite fell upon Clotilde as the latter was finishing her toilet, her arms bare, her hair loose, looking as fresh and smiling as a rose.

The first shock was rude. The old lady unburdened her mind, grew indignant, spoke of the scandal they were giving. Suddenly her anger vanished. She looked at the young girl, and she thought her adorable. In her heart she was not surprised at what was going on. She laughed at it, all she desired was that it should end in a correct fashion, so as to silence evil tongues. And she cried with a conciliating air:

"Get married then! Why do you not get married?"

Clotilde remained silent for a moment, surprised. She had not thought of marriage. Then she smiled again.

"No doubt we will get married, grandmother. But later on, there is no hurry."

Old Mme. Rougon went away, obliged to be satisfied with this vague promise.

It was at this time that Pascal and Clotilde ceased to seclude themselves. Not through any spirit of bravado, not because they wished to answer ugly rumors by making a display of their happiness, but as a natural amplification of their joy; their love had slowly acquired the need of expansion and of space, at first beyond the house, then beyond the garden, into the town, as far as the whole vast horizon. It filled everything; it took in the whole world.

The doctor then tranquilly resumed his visits, and he took the young girl with him. They walked together along the promenades, along the streets, she on his arm, in a light gown, with flowers in her hat, he buttoned up in his coat with his broad-brimmed hat. He was all white; she all blond. They walked with their heads high, erect and smiling, radiating such happiness that they seemed to walk in a halo. At first the excitement was extraordinary. The shopkeepers came and stood at their doors, the women leaned out of the windows, the passers-by stopped to look after them. People whispered and laughed and pointed to them. Then they were so handsome; he superb and triumphant, she so youthful, so submissive, and so proud, that an involuntary indulgence gradually gained on everyone. People could not help defending them and loving them, and they ended by smiling on them in a delightful contagion of tenderness. A charm emanated from them which brought back all hearts to them. The new town, with its *bourgeois* population of functionaries and townspeople who had grown wealthy, was the last conquest. But the Quartier St. Marc, in spite of its austerity, showed itself at once kind and discreetly tolerant when they walked along its deserted grass-worn sidewalks, beside the antique houses, now closed and silent, which exhaled the evaporated perfume of the loves of other days. But it was the old quarter, more especially, that promptly received them with cordiality, this quarter of which the common people, instinctively touched, felt the grace of the legend, the profound myth of the couple, the beautiful young girl supporting the royal and rejuvenated master. The doctor was adored here for his goodness, and his companion quickly became popular, and was greeted with tokens of admiration and approval as soon as she appeared. They, meantime, if they had seemed ignorant of the former hostility, now divined easily the forgiveness and the indulgent tenderness which surrounded them, and this made them more beautiful; their happiness charmed the entire town.

One afternoon, as Pascal and Clotilde turned the corner of the Rue de la Banne, they perceived Dr. Ramond on the opposite side of the street. It had chanced that they had learned the day before that he had asked and had obtained the hand of Mlle. Leveque, the advocate's daughter. It was certainly the most sensible course he could have taken, for his business interests made it advisable that he should marry, and the young girl, who was very pretty and very rich, loved him. He, too, would certainly love her in time. Therefore Clotilde joyfully smiled her congratulations to him as a sincere friend. Pascal saluted him with an affectionate gesture. For a moment Ramond, a little moved by the meeting, stood perplexed. His first impulse seemed to have been to cross over to them. But a feeling of delicacy must have prevented him, the thought that it would be brutal to interrupt their dream, to break in upon this solitude *a deux*, in which they moved, even amid the elbowings of the street. And he contented himself with a friendly salutation, a smile in which he forgave them their happiness. This was very pleasant for all three.

At this time Clotilde amused herself for several days by painting a large pastel representing the tender scene of old King David and Abishag, the young Shunammite. It was a dream picture, one of those fantastic compositions into which her other self, her romantic self, put her love of the mysterious. Against a background of flowers thrown on the canvas, flowers that looked like a shower of stars, of barbaric richness, the old king stood facing the spectator, his hand resting on the bare shoulder of Abishag. He was attired sumptuously in a robe heavy with precious stones, that fell in straight folds, and he wore the royal fillet on his snowy locks. But she was more sumptuous still, with only the lilylike satin of her skin, her tall, slender figure, her round, slender throat, her supple arms, divinely graceful. He reigned over, he leaned, as a powerful and beloved master, on this subject, chosen from among all others, so proud of having been chosen, so rejoiced to give to her king the rejuvenating gift of her youth. All her pure and triumphant beauty expressed the serenity of her submission, the tranquility with which she gave herself, before the assembled people, in the full light of day. And he was very great and she was very fair, and there radiated from both a starry radiance.

Up to the last moment Clotilde had left the faces of the two figures vaguely outlined in a sort of mist. Pascal, standing behind her, jested with her to hide his emotion, for he fancied he divined her intention. And it was as he thought; she finished the faces with a few strokes of the crayon — old King David was he, and she was Abishag, the Shunam-mite. But they were enveloped in a dreamlike brightness, it was them-selves deified; the one with hair all white, the other with hair all blond, covering them like an imperial mantle, with features lengthened by ecstasy, exalted to the bliss of angels, with the glance and the smile of immortal youth.

"Ah, dear!" he cried, "you have made us too beautiful; you have wandered off again to dreamland — yes, as in the days, do you remember, when I used to scold you for putting there all the fantastic flowers of the Unknown?"

And he pointed to the walls, on which bloomed the fantastic *parterre* of the old pastels, flowers not of the earth, grown in the soil of paradise.

But she protested gaily.

"Too beautiful? We could not be too beautiful! I assure you it is thus that I picture us to myself, thus that I see us; and thus it is that we are. There! see if it is not the pure reality."

She took the old fifteenth century Bible which was beside her, and showed him the simple wood engraving.

"You see it is exactly the same."

He smiled gently at this tranquil and extraordinary affirmation.

"Oh, you laugh, you look only at the details of the picture. It is the spirit which it is necessary to penetrate. And look at the other engrav-ings, it is the same theme in all — Abraham and Hagar, Ruth and Boaz. And you see they are all handsome and happy."

Then they ceased to laugh, leaning over the old Bible whose pages she turned with her white fingers, he standing behind her, his white beard mingling with her blond, youthful tresses.

Suddenly he whispered to her softly:

"But you, so young, do you never regret that you have chosen me — me, who am so old, as old as the world?"

She gave a start of surprise, and turning round looked at him.

"You old! No, you are young, younger than I!"

And she laughed so joyously that he, too, could not help smiling. But he insisted a little tremulously:

"You do not answer me. Do you not sometimes desire a younger lover, you who are so youthful?"

She put up her lips and kissed him, saying in a low voice:

"I have but one desire, to be loved — loved as you love me, above and beyond everything."

The day on which Martine saw the pastel nailed to the wall, she looked at it a moment in silence, then she made the sign of the cross, but whether it was because she had seen God or the devil, no one could say.

A few days before Easter she had asked Clotilde if she would not accompany her to church, and the latter having made a sign in the negative, she departed for an instant from the deferential silence which she now habitually maintained. Of all the new things which astonished her in the house, what most astonished her was the sudden irreligiousness of her young mistress. So she allowed herself to resume her former tone of remonstrance, and to scold her as she used to do when she was a little girl and refused to say her prayers. "Had she no longer the fear of the Lord before her, then? Did she no longer tremble at the idea of going to hell, to burn there forever?"

Clotilde could not suppress a smile.

"Oh, hell! you know that it has never troubled me a great deal. But you are mistaken if you think I am no longer religious. If I have left off going to church it is because I perform my devotions elsewhere, that is all."

Martine looked at her, open-mouthed, not comprehending her. It was all over; mademoiselle was indeed lost. And she never again asked her to accompany her to St. Saturnin. But her own devotion increased until it at last became a mania. She was no longer to be met, as before, with the eternal stocking in her hand which she knitted even when walking, when not occupied in her household duties. Whenever she had a moment to spare, she ran to church and remained there, repeating endless prayers. One day when old Mme. Rougon, always on the alert, found her behind a pillar, an hour after she had seen her there before, Martine excused herself, blushing like a servant who had been caught idling, saying:

"I was praying for monsieur."

Meanwhile Pascal and Clotilde enlarged still more their domain, taking longer and longer walks every day, extending them now outside the town into the open country. One afternoon, as they were going to La Seguiranne, they were deeply moved, passing by the melancholy fields where the enchanted gardens of Le Paradou had formerly extended. The vision of Albine rose before them. Pascal saw her again blooming like the spring, in the rejuvenation which this living flower had brought him too, feeling the pressure of this pure arm against his heart. Never could he have believed, he who had already thought himself very old when he used to enter this garden to give a smile to the little fairy within, that she would have been dead for years when life, the good mother, should bestow upon him the gift of so fresh a spring, sweetening his declining years. And Clotilde, having felt the vision rise before them, lifted up her face to his in a renewed longing for tenderness. She was Albine, the eternal lover. He kissed her on the lips, and though no word had been uttered, the level fields sown with corn and oats, where Le Paradou had once rolled its billows of luxuriant verdure, thrilled in sympathy.

Pascal and Clotilde were now walking along the dusty road, through the bare and arid country. They loved this sun-scorched land, these fields thinly planted with puny almond trees and dwarf olives, these stretches of bare hills dotted with country houses, that showed on them like pale patches accentuated by the dark bars of the secular cypresses. It was like an antique landscape, one of those classic landscapes represented in the paintings of the old schools, with harsh coloring and well balanced and majestic lines. All the ardent sunshine of successive summers that had parched this land flowed through their veins, and lent them a new beauty and animation, as they walked under the sky forever blue, glowing with the clear flame of eternal love. She, protected from the sun by her straw hat, bloomed and luxuriated in this bath of light like a tropical flower, while he, in his renewed youth, felt the burning sap of the soil ascend into his veins in a flood of virile joy.

This walk to La Seguiranne had been an idea of the doctor's, who had learned through Aunt Dieudonne of the approaching marriage of Sophie to a young miller of the neighborhood; and he desired to see if everyone was well and happy in this retired corner. All at once they were refreshed by a delightful coolness as they entered the avenue of tall green oaks. On either side the springs, the mothers of these giant shade trees, flowed on in their eternal course. And when they reached the house of the shrew they came, as chance would have it, upon the two lovers, Sophie and her miller, kissing each other beside the well; for the girl's aunt had just gone down to the lavatory behind the willows of the Viorne. Confused, the couple stood in blushing silence. But the doctor and his companion laughed indulgently, and the lovers, reassured, told them that the marriage was set for St. John's Day, which was a long way off, to be sure, but which would come all the same. Sophie, saved from the hereditary malady, had improved in health and beauty, and was growing as strong as one of the trees that stood with their feet in the moist grass beside the springs, and their heads bare to the sunshine. Ah, the vast, glowing sky, what life it breathed into all created things! She had but one grief, and tears came to her eyes when she spoke of her brother Valentin, who perhaps would not live through the week. She had had news of him the day before; he was past hope. And the doctor was obliged to prevaricate a little to console her, for he himself expected hourly the inevitable termination. When he and his companion left La Seguiranne they returned slowly to Plassans, touched by this happy, healthy love saddened by the chill of death.

In the old quarter a woman whom Pascal was attending informed him that Valentin had just died. Two of the neighbors were obliged to take away La Guiraude, who, half-crazed, clung, shrieking, to her son's body. The doctor entered the house, leaving Clotilde outside. At last, they again took their way to La Souleiade in silence. Since Pascal had resumed his visits he seemed to make them only through professional duty; he no longer became enthusiastic about the miracles wrought by his treatment. But as far as Valentin's death was concerned, he was surprised that it had not occurred before; he was convinced that he had prolonged the patient's life for at least a year. In spite of the extraordinary results which he had obtained at first, he knew well that death was the inevitable end. That he had held it in check for months ought then to have consoled him and soothed his remorse, still unassuaged, for having involuntarily caused the death of Lafouasse, a few weeks sooner than it would otherwise have occurred. But this did not seem to be the case, and his brow was knitted in a frown as they returned to their beloved solitude. But there a new emotion awaited him; sitting under the plane trees, whither Martine had sent him, he saw Sarteur, the hatter, the inmate of the Tulettes whom he had been so long treating by his hypodermic injections, and the experiment so zealously continued seemed to have succeeded. The injections of nerve substance had evidently given strength to his will, since the madman was here, having left the asylum that morning, declaring that he no longer had any attacks, that he was entirely cured of the homicidal mania that impelled him to throw himself upon any passer-by to strangle him. The doctor looked at him as he spoke. He was a small dark man, with a retreating forehead and aquiline features, with one cheek perceptibly larger than the other. He was perfectly quiet and rational, and filled with so lively a gratitude that he kissed his savior's hands. The doctor could not help being greatly affected by all this, and he dismissed the man kindly, advising him to return to his life of labor, which was the best hygiene, physical and moral. Then he recovered his calmness and sat down to table, talking gaily of other matters.

Clotilde looked at him with astonishment and even with a little indignation.

"What is the matter, master?" she said. "You are no longer satisfied with yourself."

"Oh, with myself I am never satisfied!" he answered jestingly. "And with medicine, you know — it is according to the day."

It was on this night that they had their first quarrel. She was angry with him because he no longer had any pride in his profession. She returned to her complaint of the afternoon, reproaching him for not taking more credit to himself for the cure of Sarteur, and even for the prolongation of Valentin's life. It was she who now had a passion for his fame. She reminded him of his cures; had he not cured himself? Could he deny the efficacy of his treatment? A thrill ran through him as he recalled the great dream which he had once cherished — to combat debility, the sole cause of disease; to cure suffering humanity; to make a higher, and healthy humanity; to hasten the coming of happiness, the future kingdom of perfection and felicity, by intervening and giving health to all! And he possessed the liquor of life, the universal panacea which opened up this immense hope!

Pascal was silent for a moment. Then he murmured:

"It is true. I cured myself, I have cured others, and I still think that my injections are efficacious in many cases. I do not deny medicine. Remorse for a deplorable accident, like that of Lafouasse, does not render me unjust. Besides, work has been my passion, it is in work that I have up to this time spent my energies; it was in wishing to prove to myself the possibility of making decrepit humanity one day strong and intelligent that I came near dying lately. Yes, a dream, a beautiful dream!"

"No, no! a reality, the reality of your genius, master."

Then, lowering his voice almost to a whisper, he breathed this confession:

"Listen, I am going to say to you what I would say to no one else in the world, what I would not say to myself aloud. To correct nature, to interfere, in order to modify it and thwart it in its purpose, is this a laudable task? To cure the individual, to retard his death, for his personal pleasure, to prolong his existence, doubtless to the injury of the species, is not this to defeat the aims of nature? And have we the right to desire a stronger, a healthier humanity, modeled after our idea of health and strength? What have we to do in the matter? Why should we interfere in this work of life, neither the means nor the end of which are known to us? Perhaps everything is as it ought to be. Perhaps we should risk killing love, genius, life itself. Remember, I make the confession to you alone; but doubt has taken possession of me, I tremble at the thought of my twentieth century alchemy. I have come to believe that it is greater and wiser to allow evolution to take its course."

He paused; then he added so softly that she could scarcely hear him:

"Do you know that instead of nerve-substance I often use only water with my patients. You no longer hear me grinding for days at a time. I told you that I had some of the liquor in reserve. Water soothes them, this is no doubt simply a mechanical effect. Ah! to soothe, to prevent suffering — that indeed I still desire! It is perhaps my greatest weakness, but I cannot bear to see anyone suffer. Suffering puts me beside myself, it seems a monstrous and useless cruelty of nature. I practice now only to prevent suffering."

"Then, master," she asked, in the same indistinct murmur, "if you no longer desire to cure, do you still think everything must be told? For the frightful necessity of displaying the wounds of humanity had no other excuse than the hope of curing them."

"Yes, yes, it is necessary to know, in every case, and to conceal nothing; to tell everything regarding things and individuals. Happiness is no longer possible in ignorance; certainty alone makes life tranquil. When people know more they will doubtless accept everything. Do you not comprehend that to desire to cure everything, to regenerate everything is a false ambition inspired by our egotism, a revolt against life, which we declare to be bad, because we judge it from the point of view of self-interest? I know that I am more tranquil, that my intellect has broadened and deepened ever since I have held evolution in respect. It is my love of life which triumphs, even to the extent of not questioning its purpose, to the extent of confiding absolutely in it, of losing myself in it, without wishing to remake it according to my own conception of good and evil. Life alone is sovereign, life alone knows its aim and its end. I can only try to know it in order to live it as it should be lived. And this I have understood only since I have possessed your love. Before I possessed it I sought the truth elsewhere, I struggled with the fixed idea of saving the world. You have come, and life is full; the world is saved every hour by love, by the immense and incessant labor of all that live and love throughout space. Impeccable life, omnipotent life, immortal life!"

They continued to talk together in low tones for some time longer, planning an idyllic life, a calm and healthful existence in the country. It was in this simple prescription of an invigorating environment that the experiments of the physician ended. He exclaimed against cities. People could be well and happy only in the country, in the sunshine, on the condition of renouncing money, ambition, even the proud excesses of intellectual labor. They should do nothing but live and love, cultivate the soil, and bring up their children.

IX

*D*r. Pascal then resumed his professional visits in the town and the surrounding country. And he was generally accompanied by Clotilde, who went with him into the houses of the poor, where she, too, brought health and cheerfulness.

But, as he had one night confessed to her in secret, his visits were now only visits of relief and consolation. If he had before practiced with repugnance it was because he had felt how vain was medical science. Empiricism disheartened him. From the moment that medicine ceased to be an experimental science and became an art, he was filled with disquiet at the thought of the infinite variety of diseases and of their remedies, according to the constitution of the patient. Treatment changed with every new hypothesis; how many people, then, must the methods now abandoned have killed! The perspicacity of the physician became everything, the healer was only a happily endowed diviner, himself groping in the dark and effecting cures through his fortunate endowment. And this explained why he had given up his patients almost altogether, after a dozen years of practice, to devote himself entirely to study. Then, when his great labors on heredity had restored to him for a time the hope of intervening and curing disease by his hypodermic injections, he had become again enthusiastic, until the day when his faith in life, after having impelled him, to aid its action in this way, by restoring the vital forces, became still broader and gave him the higher conviction that life was self-sufficing, that it was the only giver of health and strength, in spite of everything. And he continued to visit, with his tranquil smile, only those of his patients who clamored for him loudly, and who found themselves miraculously relieved when he injected into them only pure water.

Clotilde now sometimes allowed herself to jest about these hypodermic injections. She was still at heart, however, a fervent worshiper of his skill; and she said jestingly that if he performed miracles as he did it was because he had in himself the godlike power to do so. Then he would reply jestingly, attributing to her the efficacy of their common visits, saying that he cured no one now when she was absent, that it was she who brought the breath of life, the unknown and necessary force from the Beyond. So that the rich people, the *bourgeois,* whose houses she did not enter, continued to groan without his being able to relieve them. And this affectionate dispute diverted them; they set out each time as if for new discoveries, they exchanged glances of kindly intelligence with the sick. Ah, this wretched suffering which revolted them, and which was now all they went to combat; how happy they were when they thought it vanquished! They were divinely recompensed when they saw the cold sweats disappear, the moaning lips become stilled, the deathlike faces recover animation. It was assuredly the love which they brought to this humble, suffering humanity that produced the alleviation.

"To die is nothing; that is in the natural order of things," Pascal would often say. "But why suffer? It is cruel and unnecessary!"

One afternoon the doctor was going with the young girl to the little village of Sainte-Marthe to see a patient, and at the station, for they were going by train, so as to spare Bonhomme, they had a reencounter. The train which they were waiting for was from the Tulettes. Sainte-Marthe was the first station in the opposite direction, going to Marseilles. When the train arrived, they hurried on board and, opening the door of a compartment which they thought empty, they saw old Mme. Rougon about to leave it. She did not speak to them, but passing them by, sprang down quickly in spite of her age, and walked away with a stiff and haughty air.

"It is the 1st of July," said Clotilde when the train had started. "Grandmother is returning from the Tulettes, after making her monthly visit to Aunt Dide. Did you see the glance she cast at me?"

Pascal was at heart glad of the quarrel with his mother, which freed him from the continual annoyance of her visits.

"Bah!" he said simply, "when people cannot agree it is better for them not to see each other."

But the young girl remained troubled and thoughtful. After a few moments she said in an undertone:

"I thought her changed — looking paler. And did you notice? she who is usually so carefully dressed had only one glove on — a yellow glove, on the right hand. I don't know why it was, but she made me feel sick at heart."

Pascal, who was also disturbed, made a vague gesture. His mother would no doubt grow old at last, like everybody else. But she was very active, very full of fire still. She was thinking, he said, of bequeathing her fortune to the town of Plassans, to build a house of refuge, which should bear the name of Rougon. Both had recovered their gaiety when he cried suddenly:

"Why, it is tomorrow that you and I are to go to the Tulettes to see our patients. And you know that I promised to take Charles to Uncle Macquart's."

Felicite was in fact returning from the Tulettes, where she went regularly on the first of every month to inquire after Aunt Dide. For many years past she had taken a keen interest in the madwoman's health, amazed to see her lasting so long, and furious with her for persisting in living so far beyond the common term of life, until she had become a very prodigy of longevity. What a relief, the fine morning on which they should put underground this troublesome witness of the past, this specter of expiation and of waiting, who brought living before her the abominations of the family! When so many others had been taken she, who was demented and who had only a spark of life left in her eyes, seemed forgotten. On this day she had found her as usual, skeletonlike, stiff and erect in her armchair. As the keeper said, there was now no reason why she should ever die. She was a hundred and five years old.

When she left the asylum Felicite was furious. She thought of Uncle Macquart. Another who troubled her, who persisted in living with exasperating obstinacy! Although he was only eighty-four years old, three years older than herself, she thought him ridiculously aged, past the allotted term of life. And a man who led so dissipated a life, who had gone to bed dead drunk every night for the last sixty years! The good and the sober were taken away; he flourished in spite of everything, blooming with health and gaiety. In days past, just after he had settled at the Tulettes, she had made him presents of wines, liqueurs and brandy, in the unavowed hope of ridding the family of a fellow who was really disreputable, and from whom they had nothing to expect but annoyance and shame. But she had soon perceived that all this liquor served, on the contrary, to keep up his health and spirits and his sarcastic humor, and she had left off making him presents, seeing that he throve on what she had hoped would prove a poison to him. She had cherished a deadly hatred toward him since then. She would have killed him if she had dared, every time she saw him, standing firmly on his drunken legs, and laughing at her to her face, knowing well that she was watching for his death, and triumphant because he did not give her the pleasure of burying with him all the old dirty linen of the family, the blood and mud of the two conquests of Plassans.

"You see, Felicite," he would often say to her with his air of wicked mockery, "I am here to take care of the old mother, and the day on which we both make up our minds to die it would be through compliment to you — yes, simply to spare you the trouble of running to see us so good-naturedly, in this way, every month."

Generally she did not now give herself the disappointment of going to Macquart's, but inquired for him at the asylum. But on this occasion, having learned there that he was passing through an extraordinary attack of drunkenness, not having drawn a sober breath for a fortnight, and so intoxicated that he was probably unable to leave the house, she was seized with the curiosity to learn for herself what his condition really was. And as she was going back to the station, she went out of her way in order to stop at Macquart's house.

The day was superb — a warm and brilliant summer day. On either side of the path which she had taken, she saw the fields that she had given him in former days — all this fertile land, the price of his secrecy and his good behavior. Before her appeared the house, with its pink tiles and its bright yellow walls, looking gay in the sunshine. Under the ancient mulberry trees on the terrace she enjoyed the delightful coolness and the beautiful view. What a pleasant and safe retreat, what a happy solitude was this for an old man to end in joy and peace a long and well-spent life!

But she did not see him, she did not hear him. The silence was profound. The only sound to be heard was the humming of the bees circling around the tall marshmallows. And on the terrace there was nothing to be seen but a little yellow dog, stretched at full length on the bare ground, seeking the coolness of the shade. He raised his head growling, about to bark, but, recognizing the visitor, he lay down again quietly.

Then, in this peaceful and sunny solitude she was seized with a strange chill, and she called:

"Macquart! Macquart!"

The door of the house under the mulberry trees stood wide open. But she did not dare to go in; this empty house with its wide open door gave her a vague uneasiness. And she called again:

"Macquart! Macquart!"

Not a sound, not a breath. Profound silence reigned again, but the humming of the bees circling around the tall marshmallows sounded louder than before.

At last Felicite, ashamed of her fears, summoned courage to enter. The door on the left of the hall, opening into the kitchen, where Uncle Macquart generally sat, was closed. She pushed it open, but she could distinguish nothing at first, as the blinds had been closed, probably in order to shut out the heat. Her first sensation was one of choking, caused by an overpowering odor of alcohol which filled the room; every article of furniture seemed to exude this odor, the whole house was impregnated with it. At last, when her eyes had become accustomed to the semi-obscurity, she perceived Macquart. He was seated at the table, on which were a glass and a bottle of spirits of thirty-six degrees, completely empty. Settled in his chair, he was sleeping profoundly, dead drunk. This spectacle revived her anger and contempt.

"Come, Macquart," she cried, "is it not vile and senseless to put one's self in such a state! Wake up, I say, this is shameful!"

His sleep was so profound that she could not even hear him breathing. In vain she raised her voice, and slapped him smartly on the hands.

"Macquart! Macquart! Macquart! Ah, faugh! You are disgusting, my dear!"

Then she left him, troubling herself no further about him, and walked around the room, evidently seeking something. Coming down the dusky road from the asylum she had been seized with a consuming thirst, and she wished to get a glass of water. Her gloves embarrassed her, and she took them off and put them on a corner of the table. Then she succeeded in finding the jug, and she washed a glass and filled it to the brim, and was about to empty it when she saw an extraordinary sight — a sight which agitated her so greatly that she set the glass down again beside her gloves, without drinking.

By degrees she had begun to see objects more clearly in the room, which was lighted dimly by a few stray sunbeams that filtered through the cracks of the old shutters. She now saw Uncle Macquart distinctly, neatly dressed in a blue cloth suit, as usual, and on his head the eternal fur cap which he wore from one year's end to the other. He had grown stout during the last five or six years, and he looked like a veritable mountain of flesh overlaid with rolls of fat. And she noticed that he must have fallen asleep while smoking, for his pipe — a short black pipe — had fallen into his lap. Then she stood still, stupefied with amazement — the burning tobacco had been scattered in the fall, and the cloth of the trousers had caught fire, and through a hole in the stuff, as large already as a hundred-sous piece, she saw the bare thigh, whence issued a little blue flame.

At first Felicite had thought that it was linen — the drawers or the shirt — that was burning. But soon doubt was no longer possible, she saw distinctly the bare flesh and the little blue flame issuing from it, lightly dancing, like a flame wandering over the surface of a vessel of lighted alcohol. It was as yet scarcely higher than the flame of a night light, pale and soft, and so unstable that the slightest breath of air caused it to change its place. But it increased and spread rapidly, and the skin cracked and the fat began to melt.

An involuntary cry escaped from Felicite's throat.

"Macquart! Macquart!"

But still he did not stir. His insensibility must have been complete; intoxication must have produced a sort of coma, in which there was an absolute paralysis of sensation, for he was living, his breast could be seen rising and falling, in slow and even respiration.

"Macquart! Macquart!"

Now the fat was running through the cracks of the skin, feeding the flame, which was invading the abdomen. And Felicite comprehended vaguely that Uncle Macquart was burning before her like a sponge soaked with brandy. He had, indeed, been saturated with it for years past, and of the strongest and most inflammable kind. He would no doubt soon be blazing from head to foot, like a bowl of punch.

Then she ceased to try to awaken him, since he was sleeping so soundly. For a full minute she had the courage to look at him, awe-stricken, but gradually coming to a determination. Her hands, however, began to tremble, with a little shiver which she could not control. She was choking, and taking up the glass of water again with both hands, she emptied it at a draft. And she was going away on tiptoe, when she remembered her gloves. She went back, groped for them anxiously on the table and, as she thought, picked them both up. Then she left the room, closing the door behind her carefully, and as gently as if she were afraid of disturbing someone.

When she found herself once more on the terrace, in the cheerful sunshine and the pure air, in face of the vast horizon bathed in light, she heaved a sigh of relief. The country was deserted; no one could have seen her entering or leaving the house. Only the yellow dog was still stretched there, and he did not even deign to look up. And she went away with her quick, short step, her youthful figure lightly swaying. A hundred steps away, an irresistible impulse compelled her to turn round to give a last look at the house, so tranquil and so cheerful on the hillside, in the declining light of the beautiful day.

Only when she was in the train and went to put on her gloves did she perceive that one of them was missing. But she supposed that it had fallen on the platform at the station as she was getting into the car. She believed herself to be quite calm, but she remained with one hand gloved and one hand bare, which, with her, could only be the result of great agitation.

On the following day Pascal and Clotilde took the three o'clock train to go to the Tulettes. The mother of Charles, the harness-maker's wife, had brought the boy to them, as they had offered to take him to Uncle Macquart's, where he was to remain for the rest of the week. Fresh quarrels had disturbed the peace of the household, the husband having resolved to tolerate no longer in his house another man's child, that do-nothing, imbecile prince's son. As it was Grandmother Rougon who had dressed him, he was, indeed, dressed on this day, again, in black velvet trimmed with gold braid, like a young lord, a page of former times going to court. And during the quarter of an hour which the journey lasted, Clotilde amused herself in the compartment, in which they were alone, by taking off his cap and smoothing his beautiful blond locks, his royal hair that fell in curls over his shoulders. She had a ring on her finger, and as she passed her hand over his neck she was startled to perceive that her caress had left behind it a trace of blood. One could not touch the boy's skin without the red dew exuding from it; the tissues had become so lax through extreme degeneration that the slightest scratch brought on a hemorrhage. The doctor became at once uneasy, and asked him if he still bled at the nose as frequently as formerly. Charles hardly knew what to answer; first saying no, then, recollecting himself, he said that he had bled a great deal the other day. He seemed, indeed, weaker; he grew more childish as he grew older; his intelligence, which had never developed, had become clouded. This tall boy of fifteen, so beautiful, so girlish-looking, with the color of a flower that had grown in the shade, did not look ten.

At the Tulettes Pascal decided that they would first take the boy to Uncle Macquart's. They ascended the steep road. In the distance the little house looked gay in the sunshine, as it had looked on the day before, with its yellow walls and its green mulberry trees extending their twisted branches and covering the terrace with a thick, leafy roof. A delightful sense of peace pervaded this solitary spot, this sage's retreat, where the only sound to be heard was the humming of the bees, circling round the tall marshmallows.

"Ah, that rascal of an uncle!" said Pascal, smiling, "how I envy him!"

But he was surprised not to have already seen him standing at the edge of the terrace. And as Charles had run off dragging Clotilde with him to see the rabbits, as he said, the doctor continued the ascent alone, and was astonished when he reached the top to see no one. The blinds were closed, the hill door yawned wide open. Only the yellow dog was at the threshold, his legs stiff, his hair bristling, howling with a low and continuous moan. When he saw the visitor, whom he no doubt recognized, approaching, he stopped howling for an instant and went and stood further off, then he began again to whine softly.

Pascal, filled with apprehension, could not keep back the uneasy cry that rose to his lips:

"Macquart! Macquart!"

No one answered; a deathlike silence reigned over the house, with its door yawning wide open, like the mouth of a cavern. The dog continued to howl.

Then Pascal grew impatient, and cried more loudly.

"Macquart! Macquart!"

There was not a stir; the bees hummed, the sky looked down serenely on the peaceful scene. Then he hesitated no longer. Perhaps Macquart was asleep. But the instant he pushed open the door of the kitchen on the left of the hall, a horrible odor escaped from it, an odor of burned flesh and bones. When he entered the room he could hardly breathe, so filled was it by a thick vapor, a stagnant and nauseous cloud, which choked and blinded him. The sunbeams that filtered through the cracks made only a dim light. He hurried to the fireplace, thinking that perhaps there had been a fire, but the fireplace was empty, and the articles of furniture around appeared to be uninjured. Bewildered, and feeling himself growing faint in the poisoned atmosphere, he ran to the window and threw the shutters wide open. A flood of light entered.

Then the scene presented to the doctor's view filled him with amazement. Everything was in its place; the glass and the empty bottle of spirits were on the table; only the chair in which Uncle Macquart must have been sitting bore traces of fire, the front legs were blackened and the straw was partially consumed. What had become of Macquart? Where could he have disappeared? In front of the chair, on the brick floor, which was saturated with grease, there was a little heap of ashes, beside which lay the pipe — a black pipe, which had not even broken in falling. All of Uncle Macquart was there, in this handful of fine ashes; and he was in the red cloud, also, which floated through the open window; in the layer of soot which carpeted the entire kitchen; the horrible grease of burned flesh, enveloping everything, sticky and foul to the touch.

It was the finest case of spontaneous combustion physician had ever seen. The doctor had, indeed, read in medical papers of surprising cases, among others that of a shoemaker's wife, a drunken woman who had fallen asleep over her foot warmer, and of whom they had found only a hand and foot. He had, until now, put little faith in these cases, unwilling to admit, like the ancients, that a body impregnated with alcohol could disengage an unknown gas, capable of taking fire spontaneously and consuming the flesh and the bones. But he denied the truth of them no longer; besides, everything became clear to him as he reconstructed the scene — the coma of drunkenness producing absolute insensibility; the pipe falling on the clothes, which had taken fire; the flesh, saturated with liquor, burning and cracking; the fat melting, part of it running over the ground and part of it aiding the combustion, and all, at last — muscles, organs, and bones — consumed in a general blaze. Uncle Macquart was all there, with his blue cloth suit, and his fur cap, which he wore from one year's end to the other. Doubtless, as soon as he had begun to burn like a bonfire he had fallen forward, which would account for the chair being only blackened; and nothing of him was left, not a bone, not a tooth, not a nail, nothing but this little heap of grey dust which the draft of air from the door threatened at every moment to sweep away.

Clotilde had meanwhile entered, Charles remaining outside, his attention attracted by the continued howling of the dog.

"Good Heavens, what a smell!" she cried. "What is the matter?"

When Pascal explained to her the extraordinary catastrophe that had taken place, she shuddered. She took up the bottle to examine it, but she put it down again with horror, feeling it moist and sticky with Uncle Macquart's flesh. Nothing could be touched, the smallest objects were coated, as it were, with this yellowish grease which stuck to the hands.

A shudder of mingled awe and disgust passed through her, and she burst into tears, faltering:

"What a sad death! What a horrible death!"

Pascal had recovered from his first shock, and he was almost smiling.

"Why horrible? He was eighty-four years old; he did not suffer. As for me, I think it a superb death for that old rascal of an uncle, who, it may be now said, did not lead a very exemplary life. You remember his envelope; he had some very terrible and vile things upon his conscience, which did not prevent him, however, from settling down later and growing old, surrounded by every comfort, like an old humbug, receiving the recompense of virtues which he did not possess. And here he lies like the prince of drunkards, burning up of himself, consumed on the burning funeral pile of his own body!"

And the doctor waved his hand in admiration.

"Just think of it. To be drunk to the point of not feeling that one is on fire; to set one's self aflame, like a bonfire on St. John's day; to disappear in smoke to the last bone. Think of Uncle Macquart starting on his journey through space; first diffused through the four corners of the room, dissolved in air and floating about, bathing all that belonged to him; then escaping in a cloud of dust through the window, when I opened it for him, soaring up into the sky, filling the horizon. Why, that is an admirable death! To disappear, to leave nothing of himself behind but a little heap of ashes and a pipe beside it!"

And he picked up the pipe to keep it, as he said, as a relic of Uncle Macquart; while Clotilde, who thought she perceived a touch of bitter mockery in his eulogistic rhapsody, shuddered anew with horror and disgust. But suddenly she perceived something under the table — part of the remains, perhaps.

"Look at that fragment there."

He stooped down and picked up with surprise a woman's glove, a yellow glove.

"Why!" she cried, "it is grandmother's glove; the glove that was missing last evening."

They looked at each other; by a common impulse the same explanation rose to their lips, Felicite was certainly there yesterday; and a sudden conviction forced itself on the doctor's mind — the conviction that his mother had seen Uncle Macquart burning and that she had not quenched him. Various indications pointed to this — the state of complete coolness in which he found the room, the number of hours which he calculated to have been necessary for the combustion of the body. He saw clearly the same thought dawning in the terrified eyes of his companion. But as it seemed impossible that they should ever know the truth, he fabricated aloud the simplest explanation:

"No doubt your grandmother came in yesterday on her way back from the asylum, to say good day to Uncle Macquart, before he had begun drinking."

"Let us go away! let us go away!" cried Clotilde. "I am stifling here; I cannot remain here!"

Pascal, too, wished to go and give information of the death. He went out after her, shut up the house, and put the key in his pocket. Outside, they heard the little yellow dog still howling. He had taken refuge between Charles' legs, and the boy amused himself pushing him with his foot and listening to him whining, without comprehending.

The doctor went at once to the house of M. Maurin, the notary at the Tulettes, who was also mayor of the commune. A widower for ten years past, and living with his daughter, who was a childless widow, he had maintained neighborly relations with old Macquart, and had occasionally kept little Charles with him for several days at a time, his daughter having become interested in the boy who was so handsome and so much to be pitied. M. Maurin, horrified at the news, went at once with the doctor to draw up a statement of the accident, and promised to make out the death certificate in due form. As for religious ceremonies, funeral obsequies, they seemed scarcely possible. When they entered the kitchen the draft from the door scattered the ashes about, and when they piously attempted to collect them again they succeeded only in gathering together the scrapings of the flags, a collection of accumulated dirt, in which there could be but little of Uncle Macquart.

What, then, could they bury? It was better to give up the idea. So they gave it up. Besides, Uncle Macquart had been hardly a devout Catholic, and the family contented themselves with causing masses to be said later on for the repose of his soul.

The notary, meantime, had immediately declared that there existed a will, which had been deposited with him, and he asked Pascal to meet him at his house on the next day but one for the reading; for he thought he might tell the doctor at once that Uncle Macquart had chosen him as his executor. And he ended by offering, like a kindhearted man, to keep Charles with him until then, comprehending how greatly the boy, who was so unwelcome at his mother's, would be in the way in the midst of all these occurrences. Charles seemed enchanted, and he remained at the Tulettes.

It was not until very late, until seven o'clock, that Clotilde and Pascal were able to take the train to return to Plassans, after the doctor had at last visited the two patients whom he had to see. But when they returned together to the notary's on the day appointed for the meeting, they had the disagreeable surprise of finding old Mme. Rougon installed there. She had naturally learned of Macquart's death, and had hurried there on the following day, full of excitement, and making a great show of grief; and she had just made her appearance again today, having heard the famous testament spoken of. The reading of the will, however, was a simple matter, unmarked by any incident. Macquart had left all the fortune that he could dispose of for the purpose of erecting a superb marble monument to himself, with two angels with folded wings, weeping. It was his own idea, a reminiscence of a similar tomb which he had seen abroad — in Germany, perhaps — when he was a soldier. And he had charged his nephew Pascal to superintend the erection of the monument, as he was the only one of the family, he said, who had any taste.

During the reading of the will Clotilde had remained in the notary's garden, sitting on a bench under the shade of an ancient chestnut tree. When Pascal and Felicite again appeared, there was a moment of great embarrassment, for they had not spoken to one another for some months past. The old lady, however, affected to be perfectly at her ease, making no allusion whatever to the new situation, and giving it to be understood that they might very well meet and appear united before the world, without for that reason entering into an explanation or becoming reconciled. But she committed the mistake of laying too much stress on the great grief which Macquart's death had caused her. Pascal, who suspected the overflowing joy, the unbounded delight which it gave her to think that this family ulcer was to be at last healed, that this abominable uncle was at last out of the way, became gradually possessed by an impatience, an indignation, which he could not control. His eyes fastened themselves involuntarily on his mother's gloves, which were black.

Just then she was expressing her grief in lowered tones:

"But how imprudent it was, at his age, to persist in living alone — like a wolf in his lair! If he had only had a servant in the house with him!"

Then the doctor, hardly conscious of what he was saying, terrified at hearing himself say the words, but impelled by an irresistible force, said:

"But, mother, since you were there, why did you not quench him?"

Old Mme. Rougon turned frightfully pale. How could her son have known? She looked at him for an instant in open-mouthed amazement; while Clotilde grew as pale as she, in the certainty of the crime, which was now evident. It was an avowal, this terrified silence which had fallen between the mother, the son, and the granddaughter — the shuddering silence in which families bury their domestic tragedies. The doctor, in despair at having spoken, he who avoided so carefully all disagreeable and useless explanations, was trying desperately to retract his words, when a new catastrophe extricated him from his terrible embarrassment.

Felicite desired to take Charles away with her, in order not to trespass on the notary's kind hospitality; and as the latter had sent the boy after breakfast to spend an hour or two with Aunt Dide, he had sent the maid servant to the asylum with orders to bring him back immediately. It was at this juncture that the servant, whom they were waiting for in the garden, made her appearance, covered with perspiration, out of breath, and greatly excited, crying from a distance:

"My God! My God! come quickly. Master Charles is bathed in blood."

Filled with consternation, all three set off for the asylum. This day chanced to be one of Aunt Dide's good days; very calm and gentle she sat erect in the armchair in which she had spent the hours, the long hours for twenty-two years past, looking straight before her into vacancy. She seemed to have grown still thinner, all the flesh had disappeared, her limbs were now only bones covered with parchmentlike skin; and her keeper, the stout fair-haired girl, carried her, fed her, took her up and laid her down as if she had been a bundle. The ancestress, the forgotten one, tall, bony, ghastly, remained motionless, her eyes, only seeming to have life, her eyes shining clear as spring water in her thin withered face. But on this morning, again a sudden rush of tears had streamed down her cheeks, and she had begun to stammer words without any connection; which seemed to prove that in the midst of

her senile exhaustion and the incurable torpor of madness, the slow
induration of the brain and the limbs was not yet complete; there still
were memories stored away, gleams of intelligence still were possible.
Then her face had resumed its vacant expression. She seemed indifferent
to everyone and everything, laughing, sometimes, at an accident, at a
fall, but most often seeing nothing and hearing nothing, gazing fixedly
into vacancy.

When Charles had been brought to her the keeper had immediately
installed him before the little table, in front of his great-great- grandmother. The girl kept a package of pictures for him — soldiers, captains,
kings clad in purple and gold, and she gave them to him with a pair of
scissors, saying:

"There, amuse yourself quietly, and behave well. You see that today
grandmother is very good. You must be good, too."

The boy raised his eyes to the madwoman's face, and both looked at
each other. At this moment the resemblance between them was extraordinary. Their eyes, especially, their vacant and limpid eyes, seemed to
lose themselves in one another, to be identical. Then it was the physi-
ognomy, the whole face, the worn features of the centenarian, that
passed over three generations to this delicate child's face, it, too, worn
already, as it were, and aged by the wear of the race. Neither smiled, they
regarded each other intently, with an air of grave imbecility.

"Well!" continued the keeper, who had acquired the habit of talking
to herself to cheer herself when with her mad charge, "you cannot deny
each other. The same hand made you both. You are the very spit-down
of each other. Come, laugh a bit, amuse yourselves, since you like to be
together."

But to fix his attention for any length of time fatigued Charles, and
he was the first to lower his eyes; he seemed to be interested in his
pictures, while Aunt Dide, who had an astonishing power of fixing her
attention, as if she had been turned into stone, continued to look at
him fixedly, without even winking an eyelid.

The keeper busied herself for a few moments in the little sunny room,
made gay by its light, blue-flowered paper. She made the bed which she
had been airing, she arranged the linen on the shelves of the press. But
she generally profited by the presence of the boy to take a little relaxa-
tion. She had orders never to leave her charge alone, and now that he
was here she ventured to trust her with him.

"Listen to me well," she went on, "I have to go out for a little, and
if she stirs, if she should need me, ring for me, call me at once; do you
hear? You understand, you are a big enough boy to be able to call one."

He had looked up again, and made a sign that he had understood and that he would call her. And when he found himself alone with Aunt Dide he returned to his pictures quietly. This lasted for a quarter of an hour amid the profound silence of the asylum, broken only at intervals by some prison sound — a stealthy step, the jingling of a bunch of keys, and occasionally a loud cry, immediately silenced. But the boy must have been tired by the excessive heat of the day, for sleep gradually stole over him. Soon his head, fair as a lily, drooped, and as if weighed down by the too heavy casque of his royal locks, he let it sink gently on the pictures and fell asleep, with his cheek resting on the gold and purple kings. The lashes of his closed eyelids cast a shadow on his delicate skin, with its small blue veins, through which life pulsed feebly. He was beautiful as an angel, but with the indefinable corruption of a whole race spread over his countenance. And Aunt Dide looked at him with her vacant stare in which there was neither pleasure nor pain, the stare of eternity contemplating things earthly.

At the end of a few moments, however, an expression of interest seemed to dawn in the clear eyes. Something had just happened, a drop of blood was forming on the edge of the left nostril of the boy. This drop fell and another formed and followed it. It was the blood, the dew of blood, exuding this time, without a scratch, without a bruise, which issued and flowed of itself in the laxity of the degenerate tissues. The drops became a slender thread which flowed over the gold of the pictures. A little pool covered them, and made its way to a corner of the table; then the drops began again, splashing dully one by one upon the floor. And he still slept, with the divinely calm look of a cherub, not even conscious of the life that was escaping from him; and the madwoman continued to look at him, with an air of increasing interest, but without terror, amused, rather, her attention engaged by this, as by the flight of the big flies, which her gaze often followed for hours.

Several minutes more passed, the slender thread had grown larger, the drops followed one another more rapidly, falling on the floor with a monotonous and persistent drip. And Charles, at one moment, stirred, opened his eyes, and perceived that he was covered with blood. But he was not frightened; he was accustomed to this bloody spring, which issued from him at the slightest cause. He merely gave a sigh of weariness. Instinct, however, must have warned him, for he moaned more loudly than before, and called confusedly in stammering accents:

"Mamma! mamma!"

His weakness was no doubt already excessive, for an irresistible stupor once more took possession of him, his head dropped, his eyes closed, and he seemed to fall asleep again, continuing his plaint, as if in a dream, moaning in fainter and fainter accents:

"Mamma! mamma!"

Now the pictures were inundated; the black velvet jacket and trousers, braided with gold, were stained with long streaks of blood, and the little red stream began again to flow persistently from his left nostril, without stopping, crossed the red pool on the table and fell upon the ground, where it at last formed a veritable lake. A loud cry from the madwoman, a terrified call would have sufficed. But she did not cry, she did not call; motionless, rigid, emaciated, sitting there forgotten of the world, she gazed with the fixed look of the ancestress who sees the destinies of her race being accomplished. She sat there as if dried up, bound; her limbs and her tongue tied by her hundred years, her brain ossified by madness, incapable of willing or of acting. And yet the sight of the little red stream began to stir some feeling in her. A tremor passed over her deathlike countenance, a flush mounted to her cheeks. Finally, a last plaint roused her completely:

"Mamma! mamma!"

Then it was evident that a terrible struggle was taking place in Aunt Dide. She carried her skeletonlike hand to her forehead as if she felt her brain bursting. Her mouth was wide open, but no sound issued from it; the dreadful tumult that had arisen within her had no doubt paralyzed her tongue. She tried to rise, to run, but she had no longer any muscles; she remained fastened to her seat. All her poor body trembled in the superhuman effort which she was making to cry for help, without being able to break the bonds of old age and madness which held her prisoner. Her face was distorted with terror; memory gradually awakening, she must have comprehended everything.

And it was a slow and gentle agony, of which the spectacle lasted for several minutes more. Charles, silent now, as if he had again fallen asleep, was losing the last drops of blood that had remained in his veins, which were emptying themselves softly. His lilylike whiteness increased until it became a deathlike pallor. His lips lost their rosy color, became a pale pink, then white. And, as he was about to expire, he opened his large eyes and fixed them on his great-great- grandmother, who watched the light dying in them. All the waxen face was already dead, the eyes only were still living. They still kept their limpidity, their brightness. All at once they became vacant, the light in them was extinguished. This was the end — the death of the eyes, and Charles had died, without a struggle, exhausted, like a fountain from which all the water has run out. Life no longer pulsed through the veins of his delicate skin, there was now only the shadow of its wings on his white face. But he remained divinely beautiful, his face lying in blood, surrounded by his royal blond locks, like one of those little bloodless dauphins who, unable to bear the execrable heritage of their race, die of decrepitude and imbecility at sixteen.

The boy exhaled his latest breath as Dr. Pascal entered the room, followed by Felicite and Clotilde. And when he saw the quantity of blood that inundated the floor, he cried:

"Ah, my God! it is as I feared, a hemorrhage from the nose! The poor darling, no one was with him, and it is all over!"

But all three were struck with terror at the extraordinary spectacle that now met their gaze. Aunt Dide, who seemed to have grown taller, in the superhuman effort she was making, had almost succeeded in raising herself up, and her eyes, fixed on the dead boy, so fair and so gentle, and on the red sea of blood, beginning to congeal, that was lying around him, kindled with a thought, after a long sleep of twenty-two years. This final lesion of madness, this irremediable darkness of the mind, was evidently not so complete but that some memory of the past, lying hidden there, might awaken suddenly under the terrible blow which had struck her. And the ancestress, the forgotten one, lived again, emerged from her oblivion, rigid and wasted, like a specter of terror and grief.

For an instant she remained panting. Then with a shudder, which made her teeth chatter, she stammered a single phrase:

"The *gendarme!* the *gendarme!*"

Pascal and Felicite and Clotilde understood. They looked at one another involuntarily, turning very pale. The whole dreadful history of the old mother — of the mother of them all — rose before them, the ardent love of her youth, the long suffering of her mature age. Already two moral shocks had shaken her terribly — the first, when she was in her ardent prime, when a *gendarme* shot down her lover Macquart, the smuggler, like a dog; the second, years ago, when another *gendarme* shattered with a pistol shot the skull of her grandson Silvere, the insurgent, the victim of the hatred and the sanguinary strife of the family. Blood had always bespattered her. And a third moral shock finished her; blood bespattered her again, the impoverished blood of her race, which she had just beheld flowing slowly, and which lay upon the ground, while the fair royal child, his veins and his heart empty, slept.

Three times — face to face with her past life, her life red with passion and suffering, haunted by the image of expiation — she stammered:

"The *gendarme!* the *gendarme!* the *gendarme!*"

Then she sank back into her armchair. They thought she was dead, killed by the shock.

But the keeper at this moment at last appeared, endeavoring to excuse herself, fearing that she would be dismissed. When, aided by her, Dr. Pascal had placed Aunt Dide on the bed, he found that the old mother was still alive. She was not to die until the following day, at the age of one hundred and five years, three months, and seven days, of congestion of the brain, caused by the last shock she had received.

Pascal, turning to his mother, said:

"She will not live twenty-four hours; tomorrow she will be dead. Ah! Uncle Macquart, then she, and this poor boy, one after another. How much misery and grief!"

He paused and added in a lower tone:

"The family is thinning out; the old trees fall and the young die standing."

Felicite must have thought this another allusion. She was sincerely shocked by the tragic death of little Charles. But, notwithstanding, above the horror which she felt there arose a sense of immense relief. Next week, when they should have ceased to weep, what a rest to be able to say to herself that all this abomination of the Tulettes was at an end, that the family might at last rise, and shine in history!

Then she remembered that she had not answered the involuntary accusation made against her by her son at the notary's; and she spoke again of Macquart, through bravado:

"You see now that servants are of no use. There was one here, and yet she prevented nothing; it would have been useless for Uncle Macquart to have had one to take care of him; he would be in ashes now, all the same."

She sighed, and then continued in a broken voice:

"Well, well, neither our own fate nor that of others is in our hands; things happen as they will. These are great blows that have fallen upon us. We must only trust to God for the preservation and the prosperity of our family."

Dr. Pascal bowed with his habitual air of deference and said:

"You are right, mother."

Clotilde knelt down. Her former fervent Catholic faith had revived in this chamber of blood, of madness, and of death. Tears streamed down her cheeks, and with clasped hands she was praying fervently for the dear ones who were no more. She prayed that God would grant that their sufferings might indeed be ended, their faults pardoned, and that they might live again in another life, a life of unending happiness. And she prayed with the utmost fervor, in her terror of a hell, which after this miserable life would make suffering eternal.

From this day Pascal and Clotilde went to visit their sick side by side, filled with greater pity than ever. Perhaps, with Pascal, the feeling of his powerlessness against inevitable disease was even stronger than before. The only wisdom was to let nature take its course, to eliminate dangerous elements, and to labor only in the supreme work of giving health and strength. But the suffering and the death of those who are dear to us awaken in us a hatred of disease, an irresistible desire to combat and to vanquish it. And the doctor never tasted so great a joy as when he succeeded, with his hypodermic injections, in soothing a paroxysm of pain, in seeing the groaning patient grow tranquil and fall asleep. Clotilde, in return, adored him, proud of their love, as if it were a consolation which they carried, like the viaticum, to the poor.

X

Martine one morning obtained from Dr. Pascal, as she did every three months, his receipt for fifteen hundred francs, to take it to the notary Grandguillot, to get from him what she called their "income." The doctor seemed surprised that the payment should have fallen due again so soon; he had never been so indifferent as he was now about money matters, leaving to Martine the care of settling everything. And he and Clotilde were under the plane trees, absorbed in the joy that filled their life, lulled by the ceaseless song of the fountain, when the servant returned with a frightened face, and in a state of extraordinary agitation. She was so breathless with excitement that for a moment she could not speak.

"Oh, my God! Oh, my God!" she cried at last. "M. Grandguillot has gone away!"

Pascal did not at first comprehend.

"Well, my girl, there is no hurry," he said; "you can go back another day."

"No, no! He has gone away; don't you hear? He has gone away forever —"

And as the waters rush forth in the bursting of a dam, her emotion vented itself in a torrent of words.

"I reached the street, and I saw from a distance a crowd gathered before the door. A chill ran through me; I felt that some misfortune had happened. The door closed, and not a blind open, as if there was somebody dead in the house. They told me when I got there that he had run away; that he had not left a sou behind him; that many families would be ruined."

She laid the receipt on the stone table.

"There! There is your paper! It is all over with us, we have not a sou left, we are going to die of starvation!" And she sobbed aloud in the anguish of her miserly heart, distracted by this loss of a fortune, and trembling at the prospect of impending want.

Clotilde sat stunned and speechless, her eyes fixed on Pascal, whose predominating feeling at first seemed to be one of incredulity. He endeavored to calm Martine. Why! why! it would not do to give up in this way. If all she knew of the affair was what she had heard from the people in the street, it might be only gossip, after all, which always exaggerates everything. M. Grandguillot a fugitive; M. Grandguillot a thief; that was monstrous, impossible! A man of such probity, a house liked and respected by all Plassans for more than a century past. Why people thought money safer there than in the Bank of France.

"Consider, Martine, this would not have come all of a sudden, like a thunderclap; there would have been some rumors of it beforehand. The deuce! an old reputation does not fall to pieces in that way, in a night."

At this she made a gesture of despair.

"Ah, monsieur, that is what most afflicts me, because, you see, it throws some of the responsibility on me. For weeks past I have been hearing stories on all sides. As for you two, naturally you hear nothing; you don't even know whether you are alive or dead."

Neither Pascal nor Clotilde could refrain from smiling; for it was indeed true that their love lifted them so far above the earth that none of the common sounds of existence reached them.

"But the stories I heard were so ugly that I didn't like to worry you with them. I thought they were lies."

She was silent for a moment, and then added that while some people merely accused M. Grandguillot of having speculated on the Bourse, there were others who accused him of still worse practices. And she burst into fresh sobs.

"My God! My God! what is going to become of us? We are all going to die of starvation!"

Shaken, then, moved by seeing Clotilde's eyes, too, filled with tears, Pascal made an effort to remember, to see clearly into the past. Years ago, when he had been practicing in Plassans, he had deposited at different times, with M. Grandguillot, the twenty thousand francs on the interest of which he had lived comfortably for the past sixteen years, and on each occasion the notary had given him a receipt for the sum deposited. This would no doubt enable him to establish his position as a personal creditor. Then a vague recollection awoke in his memory; he remembered, without being able to fix the date, that at the request of the notary, and in consequence of certain representations made by him, which Pascal had forgotten, he had given the lawyer a power of attorney for the purpose of investing the whole or a part of his money, in mortgages, and he was even certain that in this power the name of the attorney had been left in blank. But he was ignorant as to whether this document had ever been used or not; he had never taken the trouble to inquire how his money had been invested. A fresh pang of miserly anguish made Martine cry out:

"Ah, monsieur, you are well punished for your sin. Was that a way to abandon one's money? For my part, I know almost to a sou how my account stands every quarter; I have every figure and every document at my fingers' ends."

In the midst of her distress an unconscious smile broke over her face, lighting it all up. Her long cherished passion had been gratified; her four hundred francs wages, saved almost intact, put out at interest for thirty years, at last amounted to the enormous sum of twenty thousand francs. And this treasure was put away in a safe place which no one knew. She beamed with delight at the recollection, and she said no more.

"But who says that our money is lost?" cried Pascal.

"M. Grandguillot had a private fortune; he has not taken away with him his house and his lands, I suppose. They will look into the affair; they will make an investigation. I cannot make up my mind to believe him a common thief. The only trouble is the delay: a liquidation drags on so long."

He spoke in this way in order to reassure Clotilde, whose growing anxiety he observed. She looked at him, and she looked around her at La Souleiade; her only care his happiness; her most ardent desire to live here always, as she had lived in the past, to love him always in this beloved solitude. And he, wishing to tranquilize her, recovered his fine indifference; never having lived for money, he did not imagine that one could suffer from the want of it.

"But I have some money!" he cried, at last. "What does Martine mean by saying that we have not a sou left, and that we are going to die of starvation!"

And he rose gaily, and made them both follow him saying:

"Come, come, I am going to show you some money. And I will give some of it to Martine that she may make us a good dinner this evening."

Upstairs in his room he triumphantly opened his desk before them. It was in a drawer of this desk that for years past he had thrown the money which his later patients had brought him of their own accord, for he had never sent them an account. Nor had he ever known the exact amount of his little treasure, of the gold and bank bills mingled together in confusion, from which he took the sums he required for his pocket money, his experiments, his presents, and his alms. During the last few months he had made frequent visits to his desk, making deep inroads into its contents. But he had been so accustomed to find there the sums he required, after years of economy during which he had spent scarcely anything, that he had come to believe his savings inexhaustible.

He gave a satisfied laugh, then, as he opened the drawer, crying:

"Now you shall see! Now you shall see!"

And he was confounded, when, after searching among the heap of notes and bills, he succeeded in collecting only a sum of 615 francs — two notes of 100 francs each, 400 francs in gold, and 15 francs in change. He shook out the papers, he felt in every corner of the drawer, crying:

"But it cannot be! There was always money here before, there was a heap of money here a few days ago. It must have been all those old bills that misled me. I assure you that last week I saw a great deal of money. I had it in my hand."

He spoke with such amusing good faith, his childlike surprise was so sincere, that Clotilde could not keep from smiling. Ah, the poor master, what a wretched business man he was! Then, as she observed Martine's look of anguish, her utter despair at sight of this insignificant sum, which was now all there was for the maintenance of all three, she was seized with a feeling of despair; her eyes filled with tears, and she murmured:

"My God, it is for me that you have spent everything; if we have nothing now, if we are ruined, it is I who am the cause of it!"

Pascal had already forgotten the money he had taken for the presents. Evidently that was where it had gone. The explanation tranquilized him And as she began to speak in her grief of returning everything to the dealers, he grew angry.

"Give back what I have given you! You would give a piece of my heart with it, then! No, I would rather die of hunger, I tell you!"

Then his confidence already restored, seeing a future of unlimited possibilities opening out before him, he said:

"Besides, we are not going to die of hunger tonight, are we, Martine? There is enough here to keep us for a long time."

Martine shook her head. She would undertake to manage with it for two months, for two and a half, perhaps, if people had sense, but not longer. Formerly the drawer was replenished; there was always some money coming in; but now that monsieur had given up his patients, they had absolutely no income. They must not count on any help from outside, then. And she ended by saying:

"Give me the two one-hundred-franc bills. I'll try and make them last for a month. Then we shall see. But be very prudent; don't touch the four hundred francs in gold; lock the drawer and don't open it again."

"Oh, as to that," cried the doctor, "you may make your mind easy. I would rather cut off my right hand."

And thus it was settled. Martine was to have entire control of this last purse; and they might trust to her economy, they were sure that she would save the centimes. As for Clotilde, who had never had a private purse, she would not even feel the want of money. Pascal only would suffer from no longer having his inexhaustible treasure to draw upon, but he had given his promise to allow the servant to buy everything.

"There! That is a good piece of work!" he said, relieved, as happy as if he had just settled some important affair which would assure them a living for a long time to come.

A week passed during which nothing seemed to have changed at La Souleiade. In the midst of their tender raptures neither Pascal nor Clotilde thought anymore of the want which was impending. And one morning during the absence of the latter, who had gone with Martine to market, the doctor received a visit which filled him at first with a sort of terror. It was from the woman who had sold him the beautiful corsage of old point d'Alencon, his first present to Clotilde. He felt himself so weak against a possible temptation that he trembled. Even before the woman had uttered a word he had already begun to defend himself — no, no, he neither could nor would buy anything. And with outstretched hands he prevented her from taking anything out of her little bag, declaring to himself that he would look at nothing. The dealer, however, a fat, amiable woman, smiled, certain of victory. In an insinuating voice she began to tell him a long story of how a lady, whom she was not at liberty to name, one of the most distinguished ladies in Plassans, who had suddenly met with a reverse of fortune, had been obliged to part with one of her jewels; and she then enlarged on the splendid chance — a piece of jewelry that had cost twelve hundred francs, and she was willing to let it go for five hundred. She opened her bag slowly, in spite of the terrified and ever-louder protestations of the doctor, and took from it a slender gold necklace set simply with seven pearls in front; but the pearls were of wonderful brilliancy — flawless, and perfect in shape. The ornament was simple, chaste, and of exquisite delicacy. And instantly he saw in fancy the necklace on Clotilde's beautiful neck, as its natural adornment. Any other jewel would have been a useless ornament, these pearls would be the fitting symbol of her youth. And he took the necklace in his trembling fingers, experiencing a mortal anguish at the idea of returning it. He defended himself still, however; he declared that he had not five hundred francs, while the dealer continued, in her smooth voice, to push the advantage she had gained. After another quarter an hour, when she thought she had him secure, she suddenly offered him the necklace for three hundred francs, and he yielded; his mania for giving, his desire to please his idol, to adorn her, conquered. When he went to the desk to take the fifteen gold pieces to count them out to the dealer, he felt convinced that the notary's affairs would be arranged, and that they would soon have plenty of money.

When Pascal found himself once more alone, with the ornament in his pocket, he was seized with a childish delight, and he planned his little surprise, while waiting, excited and impatient, for Clotilde's return. The moment she made her appearance his heart began to beat violently. She was very warm, for an August sun was blazing in the sky, and she laid aside her things quickly, pleased with her walk, telling him, laughing, of the good bargain Martine had made — two pigeons for eighteen sous. While she was speaking he pretended to notice something on her neck.

"Why, what have you on your neck? Let me see."

He had the necklace in his hand, and he succeeded in putting it around her neck, while feigning to pass his fingers over it, to assure himself that there was nothing there. But she resisted, saying gaily:

"Don't! There is nothing on my neck. Here, what are you doing? What have you in your hand that is tickling me?"

He caught hold of her, and drew her before the long mirror, in which she had a full view of herself. On her neck the slender chain showed like a thread of gold, and the seven pearls, like seven milky stars, shone with soft luster against her satin skin. She looked charmingly childlike. Suddenly she gave a delighted laugh, like the cooing of a dove swelling out its throat proudly.

"Oh, master, master, how good you are! Do you think of nothing but me, then? How happy you make me!"

And the joy which shone in her eyes, the joy of the woman and the lover, happy to be beautiful and to be adored, recompensed him divinely for his folly.

She drew back her head, radiant, and held up her mouth to him. He bent over and kissed her.

"Are you happy?"

"Oh, yes, master, happy, happy! Pearls are so sweet, so pure! And these are so becoming to me!"

For an instant longer she admired herself in the glass, innocently vain of her fair flowerlike skin, under the nacre drops of the pearls. Then, yielding to a desire to show herself, hearing the servant moving about outside, she ran out, crying:

"Martine, Martine! See what master has just given me! Say, am I not beautiful!"

But all at once, seeing the old maid's severe face, that had suddenly turned an ashen hue, she became confused, and all her pleasure was spoiled. Perhaps she had a consciousness of the jealous pang which her brilliant youth caused this poor creature, worn out in the dumb resignation of her servitude, in adoration of her master. This, however, was only a momentary feeling, unconscious in the one, hardly suspected by the other, and what remained was the evident disapprobation of the economical servant, condemning the present with her sidelong glance.

Clotilde was seized with a little chill.

"Only," she murmured, "master has rummaged his desk again. Pearls are very dear, are they not?"

Pascal, embarrassed, too, protested volubly, telling them of the splendid opportunity presented by the dealer's visit. An incredibly good stroke of business — it was impossible to avoid buying the necklace.

"How much?" asked the young girl with real anxiety.

"Three hundred francs."

Martine, who had not yet opened her lips, but who looked terrible in her silence, could not restrain a cry.

"Good God! enough to live upon for six weeks, and we have not bread!"

Large tears welled from Clotilde's eyes. She would have torn the necklace from her neck if Pascal had not prevented her. She wished to give it to him on the instant, and she faltered in heart-broken tones:

"It is true, Martine is right. Master is mad, and I am mad, too, to keep this for an instant, in the situation in which we are. It would burn my flesh. Let me take it back, I beg of you."

Never would he consent to this, he said. Now his eyes, too, were moist, he joined in their grief, crying that he was incorrigible, that they ought to have taken all the money away from him. And running to the desk he took the hundred francs that were left, and forced Martine to take them, saying:

"I tell you that I will not keep another sou. I should spend this, too. Take it, Martine; you are the only one of us who has any sense. You will make the money last, I am very certain, until our affairs are settled. And you, dear, keep that; do not grieve me."

Nothing more was said about this incident. But Clotilde kept the necklace, wearing it under her gown; and there was a sort of delightful mystery in feeling on her neck, unknown to everyone, this simple, pretty ornament. Sometimes, when they were alone, she would smile at Pascal and draw the pearls from her dress quickly, and show them to him without a word; and as quickly she would replace them again on her warm neck, filled with delightful emotion. It was their fond folly which she thus recalled to him, with a confused gratitude, a vivid and radiant joy — a joy which nevermore left her.

A straitened existence, sweet in spite of everything, now began for them. Martine made an exact inventory of the resources of the house, and it was not reassuring. The provision of potatoes only promised to be of any importance. As ill luck would have it, the jar of oil was almost out, and the last cask of wine was also nearly empty. La Souleiade, having neither vines nor olive trees, produced only a few vegetables and some fruits — pears, not yet ripe, and trellis grapes, which were to be their only delicacies. And meat and bread had to be bought every day. So that from the first day the servant put Pascal and Clotilde on rations, suppressing the former sweets, creams, and pastry, and reducing the food to the quantity barely necessary to sustain life. She resumed all her former authority, treating them like children who were not to be consulted, even with regard to their wishes or their tastes. It was she who arranged the menus, who knew better than themselves what they wanted; but all this like a mother, surrounding them with unceasing care, performing the miracle of enabling them to live still with comfort on their scanty resources; occasionally severe with them, for their own good, as one is severe with a child when it refuses to eat its food. And it seemed as if this maternal care, this last immolation, the illusory peace with which she surrounded their love, gave her, too, a little happiness, and drew her out of the dumb despair into which she had fallen. Since she had thus watched over them she had begun to look like her old self, with her little white face, the face of a nun vowed to chastity; her calm ash-colored eyes, which expressed the resignation of her thirty years of servitude. When, after the eternal potatoes and the little cutlet at four sous, undistinguishable among the vegetables, she was able, on certain days, without compromising her budget, to give them pancakes, she was triumphant, she laughed to see them laugh.

Pascal and Clotilde thought everything she did was right, which did not prevent them, however, from jesting about her when she was not present. The old jests about her avarice were repeated over and over again. They said that she counted the grains of pepper, so many grains for each dish, in her passion for economy. When the potatoes had too little oil, when the cutlets were reduced to a mouthful, they would exchange a quick glance, stifling their laughter in their napkins, until she had left the room. Everything was a source of amusement to them, and they laughed innocently at their misery.

At the end of the first month Pascal thought of Martine's wages. Usually she took her forty francs herself from the common purse which she kept.

"My poor girl," he said to her one evening, "what are you going to do for your wages, now that we have no more money?"

She remained for a moment with her eyes fixed on the ground, with an air of consternation, then she said:

"Well, monsieur, I must only wait."

But he saw that she had not said all that was in her mind, that she had thought of some arrangement which she did not know how to propose to him, so he encouraged her.

"Well, then, if monsieur would consent to it, I should like monsieur to sign me a paper."

"How, a paper?"

"Yes, a paper, in which monsieur should say, every month, that he owes me forty francs."

Pascal at once made out the paper for her, and this made her quite happy. She put it away as carefully as if it had been real money. This evidently tranquilized her. But the paper became a new subject of wondering amusement to the doctor and his companion. In what did the extraordinary power consist which money has on certain natures? This old maid, who would serve him on bended knees, who adored him above everything, to the extent of having devoted to him her whole life, to ask for this silly guarantee, this scrap of paper which was of no value, if he should be unable to pay her.

So far neither Pascal nor Clotilde had any great merit in preserving their serenity in misfortune, for they did not feel it. They lived high above it, in the rich and happy realm of their love. At table they did not know what they were eating; they might fancy they were partaking of a princely banquet, served on silver dishes. They were unconscious of the increasing destitution around them, of the hunger of the servant who lived upon the crumbs from their table; and they walked through the empty house as through a palace hung with silk and filled with riches. This was undoubtedly the happiest period of their love. The workroom had pleasant memories of the past, and they spent whole days there, wrapped luxuriously in the joy of having lived so long in it together. Then, out of doors, in every corner of La Souleiade, royal summer had set up his blue tent, dazzling with gold. In the morning, in the embalsamed walks on the pine grove; at noon under the dark shadow of the plane trees, lulled by the murmur of the fountain; in the evening on the cool terrace, or in the still warm threshing yard bathed in the faint blue radiance of the first stars, they lived with rapture their straitened life, their only ambition to live always together, indifferent to all else. The earth was theirs, with all its riches, its pomps, and its dominions, since they loved each other.

Toward the end of August however, matters grew bad again. At times they had rude awakenings, in the midst of this life without ties, without duties, without work; this life which was so sweet, but which it would be impossible, hurtful, they knew, to lead always. One evening Martine told them that she had only fifty francs left, and that they would have difficulty in managing for two weeks longer, even giving up wine. In addition to this the news was very serious; the notary Grandguillot was beyond a doubt insolvent, so that not even the personal creditors would receive anything. In the beginning they had relied on the house and the two farms which the fugitive notary had left perforce behind him, but it was now certain that this property was in his wife's name and, while he was enjoying in Switzerland, as it was said, the beauty of the mountains, she lived on one of the farms, which she cultivated quietly, away from the annoyances of the liquidation. In short, it was infamous — a hundred families ruined; left without bread. An assignee had indeed been appointed, but he had served only to confirm the disaster, since not a centime of assets had been discovered. And Pascal, with his usual indifference, neglected even to go and see him to speak to him about his own case, thinking that he already knew all that there was to be known about it, and that it was useless to stir up this ugly business, since there was neither honor nor profit to be derived from it.

Then, indeed, the future looked threatening at La Souleiade. Black want stared them in the face. And Clotilde, who, in reality, had a great deal of good sense, was the first to take alarm. She maintained her cheerfulness while Pascal was present, but, more prescient than he, in her womanly tenderness, she fell into a state of absolute terror if he left her for an instant, asking herself what was to become of him at his age with so heavy a burden upon his shoulders. For several days she cher-

ished in secret a project — to work and earn money, a great deal of money,
with her pastels. People had so often praised her extraordinary and
original talent that, taking Martine into her confidence, she sent her
one fine morning to offer some of her fantastic bouquets to the color
dealer of the Cours Sauvaire, who was a relation, it was said, of a Parisian
artist. It was with the express condition that nothing was to be exhibited
in Plassans, that everything was to be sent to a distance. But the result
was disastrous; the merchant was frightened by the strangeness of the
design, and by the fantastic boldness of the execution, and he declared
that they would never sell. This threw her into despair; great tears welled
her eyes. Of what use was she? It was a grief and a humiliation to be
good for nothing. And the servant was obliged to console her, saying
that no doubt all women were not born for work; that some grew like
the flowers in the gardens, for the sake of their fragrance; while others
were the wheat of the fields that is ground up and used for food.

Martine, meantime, cherished another project; it was to urge the
doctor to resume his practice. At last she mentioned it to Clotilde, who
at once pointed out to her the difficulty, the impossibility almost, of
such an attempt. She and Pascal had been talking about his doing so
only the day before. He, too, was anxious, and had thought of work as
the only chance of salvation. The idea of opening an office again was
naturally the first that had presented itself to him. But he had been for
so long a time the physician of the poor! How could he venture now
to ask payment when it was so many years since he had left off doing
so? Besides, was it not too late, at his age, to recommence a career? not
to speak of the absurd rumors that had been circulating about him, the
name which they had given him of a crack-brained genius. He would
not find a single patient now, it would be a useless cruelty to force him
to make an attempt which would assuredly result only in a lacerated
heart and empty hands. Clotilde, on the contrary, had used all her
influence to turn him from the idea. Martine comprehended the rea-
sonableness of these objections, and she too declared that he must be
prevented from running the risk of so great a chagrin. But while she was
speaking a new idea occurred to her, as she suddenly remembered an
old register, which she had met with in a press, and in which she had
in former times entered the doctor's visits. For a long time it was she
who had kept the accounts. There were so many patients who had never
paid that a list of them filled three of the large pages of the register.
Why, then, now that they had fallen into misfortune, should they not
ask from these people the money which they justly owed? It might be
done without saying anything to monsieur, who had never been willing
to appeal to the law. And this time Clotilde approved of her idea. It was

a perfect conspiracy. Clotilde consulted the register, and made out the bills, and the servant presented them. But nowhere did she receive a sou; they told her at every door that they would look over the account; that they would stop in and see the doctor himself. Ten days passed, no one came, and there were now only six francs in the house, barely enough to live upon for two or three days longer.

Martine, when she returned with empty hands on the following day from a new application to an old patient, took Clotilde aside and told her that she had just been talking with Mme. Felicite at the corner of the Rue de la Banne. The latter had undoubtedly been watching for her. She had not again set foot in La Souleiade. Not even the misfortune which had befallen her son — the sudden loss of his money, of which the whole town was talking — had brought her to him; she still continued stern and indignant. But she waited in trembling excitement, she maintained her attitude as an offended mother only in the certainty that she would at last have Pascal at her feet, shrewdly calculating that he would sooner or later be compelled to appeal to her for assistance. When he had not a sou left, when he knocked at her door, then she would dictate her terms; he should marry Clotilde, or, better still, she would demand the departure of the latter. But the days passed, and he did not come. And this was why she had stopped Martine, assuming a pitying air, asking what news there was, and seeming to be surprised that they had not had recourse to her purse, while giving it to be understood that her dignity forbade her to take the first step.

"You should speak to monsieur, and persuade him," ended the servant. And indeed, why should he not appeal to his mother? That would be entirely natural.

"Oh! never would I undertake such a commission," cried Clotilde. "Master would be angry, and with reason. I truly believe he would die of starvation before he would eat grandmother's bread."

But on the evening of the second day after this, at dinner, as Martine was putting on the table a piece of boiled beef left over from the day before, she gave them notice.

"I have no more money, monsieur, and tomorrow there will be only potatoes, without oil or butter. It is three weeks now that you have had only water to drink; now you will have to do without meat."

They were still cheerful, they could still jest.

"Have you salt, my good girl?"

"Oh, that; yes, monsieur, there is still a little left."

"Well, potatoes and salt are very good when one is hungry."

That night, however, Pascal noticed that Clotilde was feverish; this was the hour in which they exchanged confidences, and she ventured to tell him of her anxiety on his account, on her own, on that of the whole house. What was going to become of them when all their resources should be exhausted? For a moment she thought of speaking to him of his mother. But she was afraid, and she contented herself with confessing to him what she and Martine had done — the old register examined, the bills made out and sent, the money asked everywhere in vain. In other circumstances he would have been greatly annoyed and very angry at this confession; offended that they should have acted without his knowledge, and contrary to the attitude he had maintained during his whole professional life. He remained for a long tine silent, strongly agitated, and this would have sufficed to prove how great must be his secret anguish at times, under his apparent indifference to poverty. Then he forgave Clotilde, clasping her wildly to his breast, and finally he said that she had done right, that they could not continue to live much longer as they were living, in a destitution which increased every day. Then they fell into silence, each trying to think of a means of procuring the money necessary for their daily wants, each suffering keenly; she, desperate at the thought of the tortures that awaited him; he unable to accustom himself to the idea of seeing her wanting bread. Was their happiness forever ended, then? Was poverty going to blight their spring with its chill breath?

At breakfast, on the following day, they ate only fruit. The doctor was very silent during the morning, a prey to a visible struggle. And it was not until three o'clock that he took a resolution.

"Come, we must stir ourselves," he said to his companion. "I do not wish you to fast this evening again; so put on your hat, we will go out together."

She looked at him, waiting for an explanation.

"Yes, since they owe us money, and have refused to give it to you, I will see whether they will also refuse to give it to me."

His hands trembled; the thought of demanding payment in this way, after so many years, evidently made him suffer terribly; but he forced a smile, he affected to be very brave. And she, who knew from the trembling of his voice the extent of his sacrifice, had tears in her eyes.

"No, no, master; don't go if it makes you suffer so much. Martine can go again."

But the servant, who was present, approved highly of monsieur's intention.

"And why should not monsieur go? There's no shame in asking what is owed to one, is there? Everyone should have his own; for my part, I think it quite right that monsieur should show at last that he is a man."

Then, as before, in their hours of happiness, old King David, as Pascal jestingly called himself, left the house, leaning on Abishag's arm. Neither of them was yet in rags; he still wore his tightly buttoned overcoat; she had on her pretty linen gown with red spots, but doubtless the consciousness of their poverty lowered them in their own estimation, making them feel that they were now only two poor people who occupied a very insignificant place in the world, for they walked along by the houses, shunning observation. The sunny streets were almost deserted. A few curious glances embarrassed them. They did not hasten their steps, however; only their hearts were oppressed at the thought of the visits they were about to make.

Pascal resolved to begin with an old magistrate whom he had treated for an affection of the liver. He entered the house, leaving Clotilde sitting on the bench in the Cours Sauvaire. But he was greatly relieved when the magistrate, anticipating his demand, told him that he did not receive his rents until October, and that he would pay him then. At the house of an old lady of seventy, a paralytic, the rebuff was of a different kind. She was offended because her account had been sent to her through a servant who had been impolite; so that he hastened to offer her his excuses, giving her all the time she desired. Then he climbed up three flights of stairs to the apartment of a clerk in the tax collector's office, whom he found still ill, and so poor that he did not even venture to make his demand. Then followed a mercer, a lawyer's wife, an oil merchant, a baker — all well-to-do people; and all turned him away, some with excuses, others by denying him admittance; a few even pretended not to know what he meant. There remained the Marquise de Valqueyras, the sole representative of a very ancient family, a widow with a girl of ten, who was very rich, and whose avarice was notorious. He had left her for the last, for he was greatly afraid of her. Finally he knocked at the door of her ancient mansion, at the foot of the Cours Sauvaire, a massive structure of the time of Mazarin. He remained so long in the house that Clotilde, who was walking under the trees, at last became uneasy.

When he finally made his appearance, at the end of a full half hour, she said jestingly, greatly relieved:

"Why, what was the matter? Had she no money?"

But here, too, he had been unsuccessful; she complained that her tenants did not pay her.

"Imagine," he continued, in explanation of his long absence, "the little girl is ill. I am afraid that it is the beginning of a gastric fever. So she wished me to see the child, and I examined her."

A smile which she could not suppress came to Clotilde's lips.

"And you prescribed for her?"

"Of course; could I do otherwise?"

She took his arm again, deeply affected, and he felt her press it against her heart. For a time they walked on aimlessly. It was all over; they had knocked at every debtor's door, and nothing now remained for them to do but to return home with empty hands. But this Pascal refused to do, determined that Clotilde should have something more than the potatoes and water which awaited them. When they ascended the Cours Sauvaire, they turned to the left, to the new town; drifting now whither cruel fate led them.

"Listen," said Pascal at last; "I have an idea. If I were to speak to Ramond he would willingly lend us a thousand francs, which we could return to him when our affairs are arranged."

She did not answer at once. Ramond, whom she had rejected, who was now married and settled in a house in the new town, in a fair way to become the fashionable physician of the place, and to make a fortune! She knew, indeed, that he had a magnanimous soul and a kind heart. If he had not visited them again it had been undoubtedly through delicacy. Whenever they chanced to meet, he saluted them with so admiring an air, he seemed so pleased to see their happiness.

"Would that be disagreeable to you?" asked Pascal ingenuously. For his part, he would have thrown open to the young physician his house, his purse, and his heart.

"No, no," she answered quickly. "There has never been anything between us but affection and frankness. I think I gave him a great deal of pain, but he has forgiven me. You are right; we have no other friend. It is to Ramond that we must apply."

Ill luck pursued them, however. Ramond was absent from home, attending a consultation at Marseilles, and he would not be back until the following evening. And it young Mme. Ramond, an old friend of Clotilde's, some three years her junior, who received them. She seemed a little embarrassed, but she was very amiable, notwithstanding. But the doctor, naturally, did not prefer his request, and contented himself with saying, in explanation of his visit, that he had missed Ramond. When they were in the street again, Pascal and Clotilde felt themselves once more abandoned and alone. Where now should they turn? What new effort should they make? And they walked on again aimlessly.

"I did not tell you, master," Clotilde at last ventured to murmur, "but it seems that Martine met grandmother the other day. Yes, grandmother has been uneasy about us. She asked Martine why we did not go to her, if we were in want. And see, here is her house."

They were in fact, in the Rue de la Banne. They could see the corner of the Place de la Sous-Prefecture. But he at once silenced her.

"Never, do you hear! Nor shall you go either. You say that because it grieves you to see me in this poverty. My heart, too, is heavy, to think that you also are in want, that you also suffer. But it is better to suffer than to do a thing that would leave one an eternal remorse. I will not. I cannot."

They emerged from the Rue de la Banne, and entered the old quarter.

"I would a thousand times rather apply to a stranger. Perhaps we still have friends, even if they are only among the poor."

And resolved to beg, David continued his walk, leaning on the arm of Abishag; the old mendicant king went from door to door, leaning on the shoulder of the loving subject whose youth was now his only support. It was almost six o'clock; the heat had abated; the narrow streets were filling with people; and in this populous quarter where they were loved, they were everywhere greeted with smiles. Something of pity was mingled with the admiration they awakened, for everyone knew of their ruin. But they seemed of a nobler beauty than before, he all white, she all blond, pressing close to each other in their misfortune. They seemed more united, more one with each other than ever; holding their heads erect, proud of their glorious love, though touched by misfortune; he shaken, while she, with a courageous heart, sustained him. And in spite of the poverty that had so suddenly overtaken them they walked without shame, very poor and very great, with the sorrowful smile under which they concealed the desolation of their souls. Workmen in dirty blouses passed them by, who had more money in their pockets than they. No one ventured to offer them the sou which is not refused to those who are hungry. At the Rue Canoquin they stopped at the house of Gulraude. She had died the week before. Two other attempts which they made failed. They were reduced now to consider where they could borrow ten francs. They had been walking about the town for three hours, but they could not resolve to go home empty-handed.

Ah, this Plassans, with its Cours Sauvaire, its Rue de Rome, and its Rue de la Banne, dividing it into three quarters; this Plassans; with its windows always closed, this sun-baked town, dead in appearance, but which concealed under this sleeping surface a whole nocturnal life of the clubhouse and the gaming table. They walked through it three times more with slackened pace, on this clear, calm close of a glowing August day. In the yard of the coach office a few old stage-coaches, which still plied between the town and the mountain villages, were standing un-harnessed; and under the thick shade of the plane trees at the doors of the cafés, the customers, who were to be seen from seven o'clock in the

morning, looked after them smiling. In the new town, too, the servants
came and stood at the doors of the wealthy houses; they met with less
sympathy here than in the deserted streets of the Quartier St. Marc,
whose antique houses maintained a friendly silence. They returned to
the heart of the old quarter where they were most liked; they went as far
as St. Saturnin, the cathedral, whose apse was shaded by the garden of
the chapter, a sweet and peaceful solitude, from which a beggar drove
them by himself asking an alms from them. They were building rapidly
in the neighborhood of the railway station; a new quarter was growing
up there, and they bent their steps in that direction. Then they returned
a last time to the Place de la Sous-Prefecture, with a sudden reawakening
of hope, thinking that they might meet someone who would offer them
money. But they were followed only by the indulgent smile of the town,
at seeing them so united and so beautiful. Only one woman had tears
in her eyes, foreseeing, perhaps, the sufferings that awaited them. The
stones of the Viorne, the little sharp paving stones, wounded their feet.
And they had at last to return to La Souleiade, without having succeeded
in obtaining anything, the old mendicant king and his submissive
subject; Abishag, in the flower of her youth, leading back David, old
and despoiled of his wealth, and weary from having walked the streets
in vain.

It was eight o'clock, and Martine, who was waiting for them, comprehended that she would have no cooking to do this evening. She
pretended that she had dined, and as she looked ill Pascal sent her at
once to bed.

"We do not need you," said Clotilde. "As the potatoes are on the fire
we can take them up very well ourselves."

The servant, who was feverish and out of humor, yielded. She muttered some indistinct words — when people had eaten up everything
what was the use of sitting down to table? Then, before shutting herself
into her room, she added:

"Monsieur, there is no more hay for Bonhomme. I thought he was
looking badly a little while ago; monsieur ought to go and see him."

Pascal and Clotilde, filled with uneasiness, went to the stable. The
old horse was, in fact, lying on the straw in the somnolence of expiring
old age. They had not taken him out for six months past, for his legs,
stiff with rheumatism, refused to support him, and he had become
completely blind. No one could understand why the doctor kept the
old beast. Even Martine had at last said that he ought to be slaughtered,
if only through pity. But Pascal and Clotilde cried out at this, as much
excited as if it had been proposed to them to put an end to some aged
relative who was not dying fast enough. No, no, he had served them for

more than a quarter of a century; he should die comfortably with them, like the worthy fellow he had always been. And tonight the doctor did not scorn to examine him, as if he had never attended any other patients than animals. He lifted up his hoofs, looked at his gums, and listened to the beating of his heart.

"No, there is nothing the matter with him," he said at last. "It is simply old age. Ah, my poor old fellow, I think, indeed, we shall never again travel the roads together."

The idea that there was no more hay distressed Clotilde. But Pascal reassured her — an animal of that age, that no longer moved about, needed so little. She stooped down and took a few handfuls of grass from a heap which the servant had left there, and both were rejoiced when Bonhomme deigned, solely and simply through friendship, as it seemed, to eat the grass out of her hand.

"Oh," she said, laughing, "so you still have an appetite! You cannot be very sick, then; you must not try to work upon our feelings. Good night, and sleep well."

And they left him to his slumbers after having each given him, as usual, a hearty kiss on either side of his nose.

Night fell, and an idea occurred to them, in order not to remain downstairs in the empty house — to close up everything and eat their dinner upstairs. Clotilde quickly took up the dish of potatoes, the salt-cellar, and a fine decanter of water; while Pascal took charge of a basket of grapes, the first which they had yet gathered from an early vine at the foot of the terrace. They closed the door, and laid the cloth on a little table, putting the potatoes in the middle between the salt-cellar and the decanter, and the basket of grapes on a chair beside them. And it was a wonderful feast, which reminded them of the delicious breakfast they had made on the morning on which Martine had obstinately shut herself up in her room, and refused to answer them. They experienced the same delight as then at being alone, at waiting upon themselves, at eating from the same plate, sitting close beside each other. This evening, which they had anticipated with so much dread, had in store for them the most delightful hours of their existence. As soon as they found themselves at home in the large friendly room, as far removed from the town which they had just been scouring as if they had been a hundred leagues away from it, all uneasiness and all sadness vanished — even to the recollection of the wretched afternoon wasted in useless wanderings. They were once more indifferent to all that was not their affection; they no longer remembered that they had lost their fortune; that they might have to hunt up a friend on the morrow in order to be able to dine in the evening. Why torture themselves with fears of coming want, when all they required to enjoy the greatest possible happiness was to be together?

But Pascal felt a sudden terror.

"My God! and we dreaded this evening so greatly! Is it wise to be happy in this way? Who knows what tomorrow may have in store for us?"

But she put her little hand over his mouth; she desired that he should have one more evening of perfect happiness.

"No, no; tomorrow we shall love each other as we love each other today. Love me with all your strength, as I love you."

And never had they eaten with more relish. She displayed the appetite of a healthy young girl with a good digestion; she ate the potatoes with a hearty appetite, laughing, thinking them delicious, better than the most vaunted delicacies. He, too, recovered the appetite of his youthful days. They drank with delight deep drafts of pure water. Then the grapes for dessert filled them with admiration; these grapes so fresh, this blood of the earth which the sun had touched with gold. They ate to excess; they became drunk on water and fruit, and more than all on gaiety. They did not remember ever before to have enjoyed such a feast together; even the famous breakfast they had made, with its luxuries of cutlets and bread and wine, had not given them this intoxication, this joy in living, when to be together was happiness enough, changing the china to dishes of gold, and the miserable food to celestial fare such as not even the gods enjoyed.

It was now quite dark, but they did not light the lamp. Through the wide open windows they could see the vast summer sky. The night breeze entered, still warm and laden with a faint odor of lavender. The moon had just risen above the horizon, large and round, flooding the room with a silvery light, in which they saw each other as in a dream light infinitely bright and sweet.

XI

But on the following day their disquietude all returned. They were now obliged to go in debt. Martine obtained on credit bread, wine, and a little meat, much to her shame, be it said, forced as she was to maneuver and tell lies, for no one was ignorant of the ruin that had overtaken the house. The doctor had indeed thought of mortgaging La Souleiade, but only as a last resource. All he now possessed was this property, which was worth twenty thousand francs, but for which he would perhaps not get fifteen thousand, if he should sell it; and when these should be spent black want would be before them, the street, without even a stone of their own on which to lay their heads. Clotilde therefore begged Pascal to wait and not to take any irrevocable step so long as things were not utterly desperate.

Three or four days passed. It was the beginning of September, and the weather unfortunately changed; terrible storms ravaged the entire country; a part of the garden wall was blown down, and as Pascal was unable to rebuild it, the yawning breach remained. Already they were beginning to be rude at the baker's. And one morning the old servant came home with the meat from the butcher's in tears, saying that he had given her the refuse. A few days more and they would be unable to obtain anything on credit. It had become absolutely necessary to consider how they should find the money for their small daily expenses.

One Monday morning, the beginning of another week of torture, Clotilde was very restless. A struggle seemed to be going on within her, and it was only when she saw Pascal refuse at breakfast his share of a piece of beef which had been left over from the day before that she at last came to a decision. Then with a calm and resolute air, she went out after breakfast with Martine, after quietly putting into the basket of the latter a little package — some articles of dress which she was giving her, she said.

When she returned two hours later she was very pale. But her large eyes, so clear and frank, were shining. She went up to the doctor at once and made her confession.

"I must ask your forgiveness, master, for I have just been disobeying you, and I know that I am going to pain you greatly."

"Why, what have you been doing?" he asked uneasily, not understanding what she meant.

Slowly, without removing her eyes from him, she drew from her pocket an envelope, from which she took some bank-notes. A sudden intuition enlightened him, and he cried:

"Ah, my God! the jewels, the presents I gave you!"

And he, who was usually so good-tempered and gentle, was convulsed with grief and anger. He seized her hands in his, crushing with almost brutal force the fingers which held the notes.

"My God! what have you done, unhappy girl? It is my heart that you have sold, both our hearts, that had entered into those jewels, which you have given with them for money! The jewels which I gave you, the souvenirs of our divinest hours, your property, yours only, how can you wish me to take them back, to turn them to my profit? Can it be possible — have you thought of the anguish that this would give me?"

"And you, master," she answered gently, "do you think that I could consent to our remaining in the unhappy situation in which we are, in want of everything, while I had these rings and necklaces and earrings laid away in the bottom of a drawer? Why, my whole being would rise in protest. I should think myself a miser, a selfish wretch, if I had kept them any longer. And, although it was a grief for me to part with them — ah, yes, I confess it, so great a grief that I could hardly find the courage to do it — I am certain that I have only done what I ought to have done as an obedient and loving woman."

And as he still grasped her hands, tears came to her eyes, and she added in the same gentle voice and with a faint smile:

"Don't press so hard; you hurt me."

Then repentant and deeply moved, Pascal, too, wept.

"I am a brute to get angry in this way. You acted rightly; you could not do otherwise. But forgive me; it was hard for me to see you despoil yourself. Give me your hands, your poor hands, and let me kiss away the marks of my stupid violence."

He took her hands again in his tenderly; he covered them with kisses; he thought them inestimably precious, so delicate and bare, thus stripped of their rings. Consoled now, and joyous, she told him of her escapade — how she had taken Martine into her confidence, and how both had gone to the dealer who had sold him the corsage of point d'Alencon, and how after interminable examining and bargaining the woman had given six thousand francs for all the jewels. Again he repressed a gesture of despair — six thousand francs! when the jewels had cost him more than three times that amount — twenty thousand francs at the very least.

"Listen," he said to her at last; "I will take this money, since, in the goodness of your heart, you have brought it to me. But it is clearly understood that it is yours. I swear to you that I will, for the future, be more miserly than Martine herself. I will give her only the few sous that are absolutely necessary for our maintenance, and you will find in the desk all that may be left of this sum, if I should never be able to complete it and give it back to you entire."

He clasped her in an embrace that still trembled with emotion. Presently, lowering his voice to a whisper, he said:

"And did you sell everything, absolutely everything?"

Without speaking, she disengaged herself a little from his embrace, and put her fingers to her throat, with her pretty gesture, smiling and blushing. Finally, she drew out the slender chain on which shone the seven pearls, like milky stars. Then she put it back again out of sight.

He, too, blushed, and a great joy filled his heart. He embraced her passionately.

"Ah!" he cried, "how good you are, and how I love you!"

But from this time forth the recollection of the jewels which had been sold rested like a weight upon his heart; and he could not look at the money in his desk without pain. He was haunted by the thought of approaching want, inevitable want, and by a still more bitter thought — the thought of his age, of his sixty years which rendered him useless, incapable of earning a comfortable living for a wife; he had been suddenly and rudely awakened from his illusory dream of eternal love to the disquieting reality. He had fallen unexpectedly into poverty, and he felt himself very old — this terrified him and filled him with a sort of remorse, of desperate rage against himself, as if he had been guilty of a crime. And this embittered his every hour; if through momentary forgetfulness he permitted himself to indulge in a little gaiety his distress soon returned with greater poignancy than ever, bringing with it a sudden and inexplicable sadness. He did not dare to question himself, and his dissatisfaction with himself and his suffering increased every day.

Then a frightful revelation came to him. One morning, when he was alone, he received a letter bearing the Plassans postmark, the superscription on which he examined with surprise, not recognizing the writing. This letter was not signed; and after reading a few lines he made an angry movement as if to tear it up and throw it away; but he sat down trembling instead, and read it to the end. The style was perfectly courteous; the long phrases rolled on, measured and carefully worded,

like diplomatic phrases, whose only aim is to convince. It was demonstrated to him with a superabundance of arguments that the scandal of
La Souleiade had lasted too long already. If passion, up to a certain
point, explained the fault, yet a man of his age and in his situation was
rendering himself contemptible by persisting in wrecking the happiness
of the young relative whose trustfulness he abused. No one was ignorant
of the ascendancy which he had acquired over her; it was admitted that
she gloried in sacrificing herself for him; but ought he not, on his side,
to comprehend that it was impossible that she should love an old man,
that what she felt was merely pity and gratitude, and that it was high
time to deliver her from this senile love, which would finally leave her
with a dishonored name! Since he could not even assure her a small
fortune, the writer hoped he would act like an honorable man, and have
the strength to separate from her, through consideration for her happiness, if it were not yet too late. And the letter concluded with the
reflection that evil conduct was always punished in the end.

From the first sentence Pascal felt that this anonymous letter came
from his mother. Old Mme. Rougon must have dictated it; he could
hear in it the very inflections of her voice. But after having begun the
letter angry and indignant, he finished it pale and trembling, seized by
the shiver which now passed through him continually and without
apparent cause. The letter was right, it enlightened him cruelly regarding
the source of his mental distress, showing him that it was remorse for
keeping Clotilde with him, old and poor as he was. He got up and
walked over to a mirror, before which he stood for a long time, his eyes
gradually filling with tears of despair at sight of his wrinkles and his
white beard. The feeling of terror which arose within him, the mortal
chill which invaded his heart, was caused by the thought that separation
had become necessary, inevitable. He repelled the thought, he felt that
he would never have the strength for a separation, but it still returned;
he would never now pass a single day without being assailed by it,
without being torn by the struggle between his love and his reason until
the terrible day when he should become resigned, his strength and his
tears exhausted. In his present weakness, he trembled merely at the
thought of one day having this courage. And all was indeed over, the
irrevocable had begun; he was filled with fear for Clotilde, so young
and so beautiful, and all there was left him now was the duty of saving
her from himself.

Then, haunted by every word, by every phrase of the letter, he tortured
himself at first by trying to persuade himself that she did not love him,
that all she felt for him was pity and gratitude. It would make the rupture
more easy to him, he thought, if he were once convinced that she

sacrificed herself, and that in keeping her with him longer he was only gratifying his monstrous selfishness. But it was in vain that he studied her, that he subjected her to proofs, she remained as tender and devoted as ever, making the dreaded decision still more difficult. Then he pondered over all the causes that vaguely, but ceaselessly urged their separation. The life which they had been leading for months past, this life without ties or duties, without work of any sort, was not good. He thought no longer of himself, he considered himself good for nothing now but to go away and bury himself out of sight in some remote corner; but for her was it not an injurious life, a life which would deteriorate her character and weaken her will? And suddenly he saw himself in fancy dying, leaving her alone to perish of hunger in the streets. No, no! this would be a crime; he could not, for the sake of the happiness of his few remaining days, bequeath to her this heritage of shame and misery.

One morning Clotilde went for a walk in the neighborhood, from which she returned greatly agitated, pale and trembling, and as soon as she was upstairs in the workroom, she almost fainted in Pascal's arms, faltering:

"Oh, my God! oh, my God! those women!"

Terrified, he pressed her with questions.

"Come, tell me! What has happened?"

A flush mounted to her face. She flung her arms around his neck and hid her head on his shoulder.

"It was those women! Reaching a shady spot, I was closing my parasol, and I had the misfortune to throw down a child. And they all rose against me, crying out such things, oh, such things — things that I cannot repeat, that I could not understand!"

She burst into sobs. He was livid; he could find nothing to say to her; he kissed her wildly, weeping like herself. He pictured to himself the whole scene; he saw her pursued, hooted at, reviled. Presently he faltered:

"It is my fault, it is through me you suffer. Listen, we will go away from here, far, far away, where we shall not be known, where you will be honored, where you will be happy."

But seeing him weep, she recovered her calmness by a violent effort. And drying her tears, she said:

"Ah! I have behaved like a coward in telling you all this. After promising myself that I would say nothing of it to you. But when I found myself at home again, my anguish was so great that it all came out. But you see now it is all over, don't grieve about it. I love you."

She smiled, and putting her arms about him she kissed him in her turn, trying to soothe his despair.

"I love you. I love you so dearly that it will console me for everything. There is only you in the world, what matters anything that is not you? You are so good; you make me so happy!"

But he continued to weep, and she, too, began to weep again, and there was a moment of infinite sadness, of anguish, in which they mingled their kisses and their tears.

Pascal, when she left him alone for an instant, thought himself a wretch. He could no longer be the cause of misfortune to this child, whom he adored. And on the evening of the same day an event took place which brought about the solution hitherto sought in vain, with the fear of finding it. After dinner Martine beckoned him aside, and gave him a letter, with all sorts of precautions, saying:

"I met Mme. Felicite, and she charged me to give you this letter, monsieur, and she told me to tell you that she would have brought it to you herself, only that regard for her reputation prevented her from returning here. She begs you to send her back M. Maxime's letter, letting her know mademoiselle's answer."

It was, in fact, a letter from Maxime, and Mme. Felicite, glad to have received it, used it as a new means of conquering her son, after having waited in vain for misery to deliver him up to her, repentant and imploring. As neither Pascal nor Clotilde had come to demand aid or succor from her, she had once more changed her plan, returning to her old idea of separating them; and, this time, the opportunity seemed to her decisive. Maxime's letter was a pressing one; he urged his grandmother to plead his cause with his sister. Ataxia had declared itself; he was able to walk now only leaning on his servant's arm. His solitude terrified him, and he urgently entreated his sister to come to him. He wished to have her with him as a rampart against his father's abominable designs; as a sweet and upright woman after all, who would take care of him. The letter gave it to be understood that if she conducted herself well toward him she would have no reason to repent it; and ended by reminding the young girl of the promise she had made him, at the time of his visit to Plassans, to come to him, if the day ever arrived when he really needed her.

Pascal turned cold. He read the four pages over again. Here an opportunity to separate presented itself, acceptable to him and advantageous for Clotilde, so easy and so natural that they ought to accept it at once; yet, in spite of all his reasoning he felt so weak, so irresolute still that his limbs trembled under him, and he was obliged to sit down for a moment. But he wished to be heroic, and controlling himself, he called to his companion.

"Here!" he said, "read this letter which your grandmother has sent me."

Clotilde read the letter attentively to the end without a word, without a sign. Then she said simply:

"Well, you are going to answer it, are you not? I refuse."

He was obliged to exercise a strong effort of self-control to avoid uttering a great cry of joy, as he pressed her to his heart. As if it were another person who spoke, he heard himself saying quietly:

"You refuse — impossible! You must reflect. Let us wait till tomorrow to give an answer; and let us talk it over, shall we?"

Surprised, she cried excitedly:

"Part from each other! and why? And would you really consent to it? What folly! we love each other, and you would have me leave you and go away where no one cares for me! How could you think of such a thing? It would be stupid."

He avoided touching on this side of the question, and hastened to speak of promises made — of duty.

"Remember, my dear, how greatly affected you were when I told you that Maxime was in danger. And think of him now, struck down by disease, helpless and alone, calling you to his side. Can you abandon him in that situation? You have a duty to fulfill toward him."

"A duty?" she cried. "Have I any duties toward a brother who has never occupied himself with me? My only duty is where my heart is."

"But you have promised. I have promised for you. I have said that you were rational, and you are not going to belie my words."

"Rational? It is you who are not rational. It is not rational to separate when to do so would make us both die of grief."

And with an angry gesture she closed the discussion, saying:

"Besides, what is the use of talking about it? There is nothing simpler; it is only necessary to say a single word. Answer me. Are you tired of me? Do you wish to send me away?"

He uttered a cry.

"Send you away! I! Great God!"

"Then it is all settled. If you do not send me away I shall remain."

She laughed now, and, running to her desk, wrote in red pencil across her brother's letter two words — "I refuse;" then she called Martine and insisted upon her taking the letter back at once. Pascal was radiant; a wave of happiness so intense inundated his being that he let her have her way. The joy of keeping her with him deprived him even of his power of reasoning.

But that very night, what remorse did he not feel for having been so cowardly! He had again yielded to his longing for happiness. A deathlike sweat broke out upon him when he saw her in imagination far away; himself alone, without her, without that caressing and subtle essence that pervaded the atmosphere when she was near; her breath, her brightness, her courageous rectitude, and the dear presence, physical and mental, which had now become as necessary to his life as the light of day itself. She must leave him, and he must find the strength to die of it. He despised himself for his want of courage, he judged the situation with terrible clear-sightedness. All was ended. An honorable existence and a fortune awaited her with her brother; he could not carry his senile selfishness so far as to keep her any longer in the misery in which he was, to be scorned and despised. And fainting at the thought of all he was losing, he swore to himself that he would be strong, that he would not accept the sacrifice of this child, that he would restore her to happiness and to life, in her own despite.

And now the struggle of self-abnegation began. Some days passed; he had demonstrated to her so clearly the rudeness of her "I refuse," on Maxime's letter, that she had written a long letter to her grandmother, explaining to her the reasons for her refusal. But still she would not leave La Souleiade. As Pascal had grown extremely parsimonious, in his desire to trench as little as possible on the money obtained by the sale of the jewels, she surpassed herself, eating her dry bread with merry laughter. One morning he surprised her giving lessons of economy to Martine. Twenty times a day she would look at him intently and then throw herself on his neck and cover his face with kisses, to combat the dreadful idea of a separation, which she saw always in his eyes. Then she had another argument. One evening after dinner he was seized with a palpitation of the heart, and almost fainted. This surprised him; he had never suffered from the heart, and he believed it to be simply a return of his old nervous trouble. Since his great happiness he had felt less strong, with an odd sensation, as if some delicate hidden spring had snapped within him. Greatly alarmed, she hurried to his assistance. Well! now he would no doubt never speak again of her going away. When one loved people, and they were ill, one stayed with them to take care of them.

The struggle thus became a daily, an hourly one. It was a continual assault made by affection, by devotion, by self-abnegation, in the one desire for another's happiness. But while her kindness and tenderness made the thought of her departure only the more cruel for Pascal, he felt every day more and more strongly the necessity for it. His resolution was now taken. But he remained at bay, trembling and hesitating as to the means of persuading her. He pictured to himself her despair, her tears; what should he do? how should he tell her? how could they bring themselves to give each other a last embrace, never to see each other again? And the days passed, and he could think of nothing, and he began once more to accuse himself of cowardice.

Sometimes she would say jestingly, with a touch of affectionate malice:

"Master, you are too kind-hearted not to keep me."

But this vexed him; he grew excited, and with gloomy despair answered:

"No, no! don't talk of my kindness. If I were really kind you would have been long ago with your brother, leading an easy and honorable life, with a bright and tranquil future before you, instead of obstinately remaining here, despised, poor, and without any prospect, to be the sad companion of an old fool like me! No, I am nothing but a coward and a dishonorable man!"

She hastily stopped him. And it was in truth his kindness of heart, above all, that bled, that immense kindness of heart which sprang from his love of life, which he diffused over persons and things, in his continual care for the happiness of everyone and everything. To be kind, was not this to love her, to make her happy, at the price of his own happiness? This was the kindness which it was necessary for him to exercise, and which he felt that he would one day exercise, heroic and decisive. But like the wretch who has resolved upon suicide, he waited for the opportunity, the hour, and the means, to carry out his design. Early one morning, on going into the workroom, Clotilde was surprised to see Dr. Pascal seated at his table. It was many weeks since he had either opened a book or touched a pen.

"Why! you are working?" she said.

Without raising his head he answered absently:

"Yes; this is the genealogical tree that I had not even brought up to date."

She stood behind him for a few moments, looking at him writing. He was completing the notices of Aunt Dide, of Uncle Macquart, and of little Charles, writing the dates of their death. Then, as he did not stir, seeming not to know that she was there, waiting for the kisses and the smiles of other mornings, she walked idly over to the window and back again.

"So you are in earnest," she said, "you are really working?"

"Certainly; you see I ought to have noted down these deaths last month. And I have a heap of work waiting there for me."

She looked at him fixedly, with that steady inquiring gaze with which she sought to read his thoughts.

"Very well, let us work. If you have papers to examine, or notes to copy, give them to me."

And from this day forth he affected to give himself up entirely to work. Besides, it was one of his theories that absolute rest was unprofitable, that it should never be prescribed, even to the overworked. As the fish lives in the water, so a man lives only in the external medium which surrounds him, the sensations which he receives from it transforming themselves in him into impulses, thoughts, and acts; so that if there were absolute rest, if he continued to receive sensations without giving them out again, digested and transformed, an engorgement would result, a *malaise*, an inevitable loss of equilibrium. For himself he had always found work to be the best regulator of his existence. Even on the mornings when he felt ill, if he set to work he recovered his equipoise. He never felt better than when he was engaged on some long work, methodically planned out beforehand, so many pages to so many hours every morning, and he compared this work to a balancing-pole, which enabled him to maintain his equilibrium in the midst of daily miseries, weaknesses, and mistakes. So that he attributed entirely to the idleness in which he had been living for some weeks past, the palpitation which at times made him feel as if he were going to suffocate. If he wished to recover his health he had only to take up again his great work.

And Pascal spent hours developing and explaining these theories to Clotilde, with a feverish and exaggerated enthusiasm. He seemed to be once more possessed by the love of knowledge and study in which, up to the time of his sudden passion for her, he had spent his life exclusively. He repeated to her that he could not leave his work unfinished, that he had still a great deal to do, if he desired to leave a lasting monument behind him. His anxiety about the envelopes seemed to have taken possession of him again; he opened the large press twenty times a day, taking them down from the upper shelf and enriching them by new notes. His ideas on heredity were already undergoing a transformation; he would have liked to review the whole, to recast the whole, to deduce from the family history, natural and social, a vast synthesis, a resume, in broad strokes, of all humanity. Then, besides, he reviewed his method of treatment by hypodermic injections, with the purpose of amplifying it — a confused vision of a new therapeutics; a vague and remote theory based on his convictions and his personal experience of the beneficent dynamic influence of work.

Now every morning, when he seated himself at his table, he would lament:

"I shall not live long enough; life is too short."

He seemed to feel that he must not lose another hour. And one morning he looked up abruptly and said to his companion, who was copying a manuscript at his side:

"Listen well, Clotilde. If I should die —"

"What an idea!" she protested, terrified.

"If I should die," he resumed, "listen to me well — close all the doors immediately. You are to keep the envelopes, you, you only. And when you have collected all my other manuscripts, send them to Ramond. These are my last wishes, do you hear?"

But she refused to listen to him.

"No, no!" she cried hastily, "you talk nonsense!"

"Clotilde, swear to me that you will keep the envelopes, and that you will send all my other papers to Ramond."

At last, now very serious, and her eyes filled with tears, she gave him the promise he desired. He caught her in his arms, he, too, deeply moved, and lavished caresses upon her, as if his heart had all at once reopened to her. Presently he recovered his calmness, and spoke of his fears. Since he had been trying to work they seemed to have returned. He kept constant watch upon the press, pretending to have observed Martine prowling about it. Might they not work upon the fanaticism of this girl, and urge her to a bad action, persuading her that she was securing her master's eternal welfare? He had suffered so much from suspicion! In the dread of approaching solitude his former tortures returned — the tortures of the scientist, who is menaced and persecuted by his own, at his own fireside, in his very flesh, in the work of his brain.

One evening, when he was again discussing this subject with Clotilde, he said unthinkingly:

"You know that when you are no longer here —"

She turned very pale and, as he stopped with a start, she cried:

"Oh, master, master, you have not given up that dreadful idea, then? I can see in your eyes that you are hiding something from me, that you have a thought which you no longer share with me. But if I go away and you should die, who will be here then to protect your work?"

Thinking that she had become reconciled, to the idea of her departure, he had the strength to answer gaily:

"Do you suppose that I would allow myself to die without seeing you once more. I will write to you, of course. You must come back to close my eyes."

Now she burst out sobbing, and sank into a chair.

"My God! Can it be! You wish that tomorrow we should be together no longer, we who have never been separated!"

From this day forth Pascal seemed more engrossed than ever in his work. He would sit for four or five hours at a time, whole mornings and afternoons, without once raising his head. He overacted his zeal. He would allow no one to disturb him, by so much as a word. And when Clotilde would leave the room on tiptoe to give an order downstairs or to go on some errand, he would assure himself by a furtive glance that she was gone, and then let his head drop on the table, with an air of profound dejection. It was a painful relief from the extraordinary effort which he compelled himself to make when she was present; to remain at his table, instead of going over and taking her in his arms and covering her face with sweet kisses. Ah, work! how ardently he called on it as his only refuge from torturing thoughts. But for the most part he was unable to work; he was obliged to feign attention, keeping his eyes fixed upon the page, his sorrowful eyes that grew dim with tears, while his mind, confused, distracted, filled always with one image, suffered the pangs of death. Was he then doomed to see work fail now its effect, he who had always considered it of sovereign power, the creator and ruler of the world? Must he then throw away his pen, renounce action, and do nothing in future but exist? And tears would flow down his white beard; and if he heard Clotilde coming upstairs again he would seize his pen quickly, in order that she might find him as she had left him, buried seemingly in profound meditation, when his mind was now only an aching void.

It was now the middle of September; two weeks that had seemed interminable had passed in this distressing condition of things, without bringing any solution, when one morning Clotilde was greatly surprised by seeing her grandmother, Felicite, enter. Pascal had met his mother the day before in the Rue de la Banne, and, impatient to consummate the sacrifice, and not finding in himself the strength to make the rupture, he had confided in her, in spite of his repugnance, and begged her to come on the following day. As it happened, she had just received another letter from Maxime, a despairing and imploring letter.

She began by explaining her presence.

"Yes, it is I, my dear, and you can understand that only very weighty reasons could have induced me to set my foot here again. But, indeed, you are getting crazy; I cannot allow you to ruin your life in this way, without making a last effort to open your eyes."

She then read Maxime's letter in a tearful voice. He was nailed to an armchair. It seemed he was suffering from a form of ataxia, rapid in its progress and very painful. Therefore he requested a decided answer from his sister, hoping still that she would come, and trembling at the thought of being compelled to seek another nurse. This was what he would be obliged to do, however, if they abandoned him in his sad condition. And when she had finished reading the letter she hinted that it would be a great pity to let Maxime's fortune pass into the hands of strangers; but, above all, she spoke of duty; of the assistance one owed to a relation, she, too, affecting to believe that a formal promise had been given.

"Come, my dear, call upon your memory. You told him that if he should ever need you, you would go to him; I can hear you saying it now. Was it not so, my son?"

Pascal, his face pale, his head slightly bent, had kept silence since his mother's entrance, leaving her to act. He answered only by an affirmative nod.

Then Felicite went over all the arguments that he himself had employed to persuade Clotilde — the dreadful scandal, to which insult was now added; impending want, so hard for them both; the impossibility of continuing the life they were leading. What future could they hope for, now that they had been overtaken by poverty? It was stupid and cruel to persist longer in her obstinate refusal.

Clotilde, standing erect and with an impenetrable countenance, remained silent, refusing even to discuss the question. But as her grandmother tormented her to give an answer, she said at last:

"Once more, I have no duty whatever toward my brother; my duty is here. He can dispose of his fortune as he chooses; I want none of it. When we are too poor, master shall send away Martine and keep me as his servant."

Old Mme. Rougon wagged her chin.

"Before being his servant it would be better if you had begun by being his wife. Why have you not got married? It would have been simpler and more proper."

And Felicite reminded her how she had come one day to urge this marriage, in order to put an end to gossip, and how the young girl had seemed greatly surprised, saying that neither she nor the doctor had thought of it, but that, notwithstanding, they would get married later on, if necessary, for there was no hurry.

"Get married; I am quite willing!" cried Clotilde. "You are right, grandmother."

And turning to Pascal:

"You have told me a hundred times that you would do whatever I wished. Marry me; do you hear? I will be your wife, and I will stay here. A wife does not leave her husband."

But he answered only by a gesture, as if he feared that his voice would betray him, and that he should accept, in a cry of gratitude, the eternal bond which she had proposed to him. His gesture might signify a hesitation, a refusal. What was the good of this marriage *in extremis,* when everything was falling to pieces?

"Those are very fine sentiments, no doubt," returned Felicite. "You have settled it all in your own little head. But marriage will not give you an income; and, meantime, you are a great expense to him; you are the heaviest of his burdens."

The effect which these words had upon Clotilde was extraordinary. She turned violently to Pascal, her cheeks crimson, her eyes filled with tears.

"Master, master! is what grandmother has just said true? Has it come to this, that you regret the money I cost you here?"

Pascal grew still paler; he remained motionless, in an attitude of utter dejection. But in a faraway voice, as if he were talking to himself, he murmured:

"I have so much work to do! I should like to go over my envelopes, my manuscripts, my notes, and complete the work of my life. If I were alone perhaps I might be able to arrange everything. I would sell La Souleiade, oh! for a crust of bread, for it is not worth much. I should shut myself and my papers in a little room. I should work from morning till night, and I should try not to be too unhappy."

But he avoided her glance; and, agitated as she was, these painful and stammering utterances were not calculated to satisfy her. She grew every moment more and more terrified, for she felt that the irrevocable word was about to be spoken.

"Look at me, master, look me in the face. And I conjure you, be brave, choose between your work and me, since you say, it seems, that you send me away that you may work the better."

The moment for the heroic falsehood had come. He lifted his head and looked her bravely in the face, and with the smile of a dying man who desires death, recovering his voice of divine goodness, he said:

"How excited you get! Can you not do your duty quietly, like everybody else? I have a great deal of work to do, and I need to be alone; and you, dear, you ought to go to your brother. Go then, everything is ended."

There was a terrible silence for the space of a few seconds. She looked at him earnestly, hoping that he would change his mind. Was he really speaking the truth? was he not sacrificing himself in order that she might be happy? For a moment she had an intuition that this was the case, as if some subtle breath, emanating from him, had warned her of it.

"And you are sending me away forever? You will not permit me to come back tomorrow?"

But he held out bravely; with another smile he seemed to answer that when one went away like this it was not to come back again on the following day. She was now completely bewildered; she knew not what to think. It might be possible that he had chosen work sincerely; that the man of science had gained the victory over the lover. She grew still paler, and she waited a little longer, in the terrible silence; then, slowly, with her air of tender and absolute submission, she said:

"Very well, master, I will go away whenever you wish, and I will not return until you send for me."

The die was cast. The irrevocable was accomplished. Each felt that neither would attempt to recall the decision that had been made; and, from this instant, every minute that passed would bring nearer the separation.

Felicite, surprised at not being obliged to say more, at once desired to fix the time for Clotilde's departure. She applauded herself for her tenacity; she thought she had gained the victory by main force. It was now Friday, and it was settled that Clotilde should leave on the following Sunday. A dispatch was even sent to Maxime.

For the past three days the mistral had been blowing. But on this evening its fury was redoubled, and Martine declared, in accordance with the popular belief, that it would last for three days longer. The winds at the end of September, in the valley of the Viorne, are terrible. So that the servant took care to go into every room in the house to assure herself that the shutters were securely fastened. When the mistral blew it caught La Souleiade slantingly, above the roofs of the houses of Plassans, on the little plateau on which the house was built. And now it raged and beat against the house, shaking it from garret to cellar, day and night, without a moment's cessation. The tiles were blown off, the fastenings of the windows were torn away, while the wind, entering the crevices, moaned and sobbed wildly through the house; and the doors, if they were left open for a moment, through forgetfulness, slammed to with a noise like the report of a cannon. They might have fancied they were sustaining a siege, so great were the noise and the discomfort.

It was in this melancholy house shaken by the storm that Pascal, on the following day, helped Clotilde to make her preparations for her departure. Old Mme. Rougon was not to return until Sunday, to say good-bye. When Martine was informed of the approaching separation, she stood still in dumb amazement, and a flash, quickly extinguished, lighted her eyes; and as they sent her out of the room, saying that they would not require her assistance in packing the trunks, she returned to the kitchen and busied herself in her usual occupations, seeming to ignore the catastrophe which was about to revolutionize their household of three. But at Pascal's slightest call she would run so promptly and with such alacrity, her face so bright and so cheerful, in her zeal to serve him, that she seemed like a young girl. Pascal did not leave Clotilde for a moment, helping her, desiring to assure himself that she was taking with her everything she could need. Two large trunks stood open in the middle of the disordered room; bundles and articles of clothing lay about everywhere; twenty times the drawers and the presses had been visited. And in this work, this anxiety to forget nothing, the painful sinking of the heart which they both felt was in some measure lessened. They forgot for an instant — he watching carefully to see that no space was lost, utilizing the hat-case for the smaller articles of clothing, slipping boxes in between the folds of the linen; while she, taking down the gowns, folded them on the bed, waiting to put them last in the top tray. Then, when a little tired they stood up and found themselves again face to face, they would smile at each other at first; then choke back the sudden tears that started at the recollection of the impending and inevitable misfortune. But though their hearts bled they remained firm. Good God! was it then true that they were to be no longer together? And then they heard the wind, the terrible wind, which threatened to blow down the house.

How many times during this last day did they not go over to the window, attracted by the storm, wishing that it would sweep away the world. During these squalls the sun did not cease to shine, the sky remained constantly blue, but a livid blue, windswept and dusty, and the sun was a yellow sun, pale and cold. They saw in the distance the vast white clouds rising from the roads, the trees bending before the blast, looking as if they were flying all in the same direction, at the same rate of speed; the whole country parched and exhausted by the unvarying violence of the wind that blew ceaselessly, with a roar like thunder. Branches were snapped and whirled out of sight; roofs were lifted up and carried so far away that they were never afterward found. Why could not the mistral take them all up together and carry them off to some unknown land, where they might be happy? The trunks were almost packed when Pascal went to open one of the shutters that the wind had blown to, but so fierce a gust swept in through the half open window that Clotilde had to go to his assistance. Leaning with all their weight, they were able at last to turn the catch. The articles of clothing in the room were blown about, and they gathered up in fragments a little hand mirror which had fallen from a chair. Was this a sign of approaching death, as the women of the faubourg said?

In the evening, after a mournful dinner in the bright dining room, with its great bouquets of flowers, Pascal said he would retire early.

Clotilde was to leave on the following morning by the ten o'clock train, and he feared for her the long journey — twenty hours of railway traveling. But when he had retired he was unable to sleep. At first he thought it was the wind that kept him awake. The sleeping house was full of cries, voices of entreaty and voices of anger, mingled together, accompanied by endless sobbing. Twice he got up and went to listen at Clotilde's door, but he heard nothing. He went downstairs to close a door that banged persistently, like misfortune knocking at the walls. Gusts blew through the dark rooms, and he went to bed again, shivering and haunted by lugubrious visions.

At six o'clock Martine, fancying she heard her master knocking for her on the floor of his room, went upstairs. She entered the room with the alert and excited expression which she had worn for the past two days; but she stood still, astonished and uneasy, when she saw him lying, half-dressed, across his bed, haggard, biting the pillow to stifle his sobs. He got out of bed and tried to finish dressing himself, but a fresh attack seized him, and, his head giddy and his heart palpitating to suffocation, recovering from a momentary faintness, he faltered in agonized tones:

"No, no, I cannot; I suffer too much. I would rather die, die now —"

He recognized Martine, and abandoning himself to his grief, his strength totally gone, he made his confession to her:

"My poor girl, I suffer too much, my heart is breaking. She is taking away my heart with her, she is taking away my whole being. I cannot live without her. I almost died last night. I would be glad to die before her departure, not to have the anguish of seeing her go away. Oh, my God! she is going away, and I shall have her no longer, and I shall be left alone, alone, alone!"

The servant, who had gone upstairs so gaily, turned as pale as wax, and a hard and bitter look came into her face. For a moment she watched him clutching the bedclothes convulsively, uttering hoarse cries of despair, his face pressed against the coverlet. Then, by a violent effort, she seemed to make up her mind.

"But, monsieur, there is no sense in making trouble for yourself in this way. It is ridiculous. Since that is how it is, and you cannot do without mademoiselle, I shall go and tell her what a state you have let yourself get into."

At these words he got up hastily, staggering still, and, leaning for support on the back of a chair, he cried:

"I positively forbid you to do so, Martine!"

"A likely thing that I should listen to you, seeing you like that! To find you some other time half dead, crying your eyes out! No, no! I shall go to mademoiselle and tell her the truth, and compel her to remain with us."

But he caught her angrily by the arm and held her fast.

"I command you to keep quiet, do you hear? Or you shall go with her! Why did you come in? It was this wind that made me ill. That concerns no one."

Then, yielding to a good-natured impulse, with his usual kindness of heart, he smiled.

"My poor girl, see how you vex me? Let me act as I ought, for the happiness of others. And not another word; you would pain me greatly."

Martine's eyes, too, filled with tears. It was just in time that they made peace, for Clotilde entered almost immediately. She had risen early, eager to see Pascal, hoping doubtless, up to the last moment, that he would keep her. Her own eyelids were heavy from want of sleep, and she looked at him steadily as she entered, with her inquiring air. But he was still so discomposed that she began to grow uneasy.

"No, indeed, I assure you, I would even have slept well but for the mistral. I was just telling you so, Martine, was I not?"

The servant confirmed his words by an affirmative nod. And Clotilde, too, submitted, saying nothing of the night of anguish and mental conflict she had spent while he, on his side, had been suffering the pangs of death. Both of the women now docilely obeyed and aided him, in his heroic self-abnegation.

"What," he continued, opening his desk, "I have something here for you. There! there are seven hundred francs in that envelope."

And in spite of her exclamations and protestations he persisted in rendering her an account. Of the six thousand francs obtained by the sale of the jewels two hundred only had been spent, and he had kept one hundred to last till the end of the month, with the strict economy, the penuriousness, which he now displayed. Afterward he would no doubt sell La Souleiade, he would work, he would be able to extricate himself from his difficulties. But he would not touch the five thousand francs which remained, for they were her property, her own, and she would find them again in the drawer.

"Master, master, you are giving me a great deal of pain —"

"I wish it," he interrupted, "and it is you who are trying to break my heart. Come, it is half-past seven, I will go and cord your trunks since they are locked."

When Martine and Clotilde were alone and face to face they looked at each other for a moment in silence. Ever since the commencement of the new situation, they had been fully conscious of their secret antagonism, the open triumph of the young mistress, the half concealed jealousy of the old servant about her adored master. Now it seemed that the victory remained with the servant. But in this final moment their common emotion drew them together.

"Martine, you must not let him eat like a poor man. You promise me that he shall have wine and meat every day?"

"Have no fear, mademoiselle."

"And the five thousand francs lying there, you know belong to him. You are not going to let yourselves starve to death, I suppose, with those there. I want you to treat him very well."

"I tell you that I will make it my business to do so, mademoiselle, and that monsieur shall want for nothing."

There was a moment's silence. They were still regarding each other.

"And watch him, to see that he does not overwork himself. I am going away very uneasy; he has not been well for some time past. Take good care of him."

"Make your mind easy, mademoiselle, I will take care of him."

"Well, I give him into your charge. He will have only you now; and it is some consolation to me to know that you love him dearly. Love him with all your strength. Love him for us both."

"Yes, mademoiselle, as much as I can."

Tears came into their eyes; Clotilde spoke again.

"Will you embrace me, Martine?"

"Oh, mademoiselle, very gladly."

They were in each other's arms when Pascal reentered the room. He pretended not to see them, doubtless afraid of giving way to his emotion. In an unnaturally loud voice he spoke of the final preparations for Clotilde's departure, like a man who had a great deal on his hands and was afraid that the train might be missed. He had corded the trunks, a man had taken them away in a little wagon, and they would find them at the station. But it was only eight o'clock, and they had still two long hours before them. Two hours of mortal anguish, spent in unoccupied and weary waiting, during which they tasted a hundred times over the bitterness of parting. The breakfast took hardly a quarter of an hour. Then they got up, to sit down again. Their eyes never left the clock. The minutes seemed long as those of a death watch, throughout the mournful house.

"How the wind blows!" said Clotilde, as a sudden gust made all the doors creak.

Pascal went over to the window and watched the wild flight of the storm-blown trees.

"It has increased since morning," he said. "Presently I must see to the roof, for some of the tiles have been blown away."

Already they had ceased to be one household. They listened in silence to the furious wind, sweeping everything before it, carrying with it their life.

Finally Pascal looked for a last time at the clock, and said simply:

"It is time, Clotilde."

She rose from the chair on which she had been sitting. She had for an instant forgotten that she was going away, and all at once the dreadful reality came back to her. Once more she looked at him, but he did not open his arms to keep her. It was over; her hope was dead. And from this moment her face was like that of one struck with death.

At first they exchanged the usual commonplaces.

"You will write to me, will you not?"

"Certainly, and you must let me hear from you as often as possible."

"Above all, if you should fall ill, send for me at once."

"I promise you that I will do so. But there is no danger. I am very strong."

Then, when the moment came in which she was to leave this dear house, Clotilde looked around with unsteady gaze; then she threw herself on Pascal's breast, she held him for an instant in her arms, faltering:

"I wish to embrace you here, I wish to thank you. Master, it is you who have made me what I am. As you have often told me, you have corrected my heredity. What should I have become amid the surroundings in which Maxime has grown up? Yes, if I am worth anything, it is to you alone I owe it, you, who transplanted me into this abode of kindness and affection, where you have brought me up worthy of you. Now, after having taken me and overwhelmed me with benefits, you send me away. Be it as you will, you are my master, and I will obey you. I love you, in spite of all, and I shall always love you."

He pressed her to his heart, answering:

"I desire only your good, I am completing my work."

When they reached the station, Clotilde vowed to herself that she would one day come back. Old Mme. Rougon was there, very gay and very brisk, in spite of her eighty-and-odd years. She was triumphant now; she thought she would have her son Pascal at her mercy. When she saw them both stupefied with grief she took charge of everything; got the ticket, registered the baggage, and installed the traveler in a compartment in which there were only ladies. Then she spoke for a long time about Maxime, giving instructions and asking to be kept informed of everything. But the train did not start; there were still five cruel minutes during which they remained face to face, without speaking to each other.

Then came the end, there were embraces, a great noise of wheels, and waving of handkerchiefs.

Suddenly Pascal became aware that he was standing alone upon the platform, while the train was disappearing around a bend in the road. Then, without listening to his mother, he ran furiously up the slope, sprang up the stone steps like a young man, and found himself in three minutes on the terrace of La Souleiade. The mistral was raging there — a fierce squall which bent the secular cypresses like straws. In the colorless sky the sun seemed weary of the violence of the wind, which for six days had been sweeping over its face. And like the wind-blown trees Pascal stood firm, his garments flapping like banners, his beard and hair blown about and lashed by the storm. His breath caught by the wind, his hands pressed upon his heart to quiet its throbbing, he saw the train flying in the distance across the bare plain, a little train which the mistral seemed to sweep before it like a dry branch.

XII

*F*rom the day following Clotilde's departure, Pascal shut himself up in the great empty house. He did not leave it again, ceasing entirely the rare professional visits which he had still continued to make, living there with doors and windows closed, in absolute silence and solitude. Martine had received formal orders to admit no one under any pretext whatever.

"But your mother, monsieur, Mme. Felicite?"

"My mother, less than anyone else; I have my reasons. Tell her that I am working, that I require to concentrate my thoughts, and that I request her to excuse me."

Three times in succession old Mme. Rougon had presented herself. She would storm at the hall door. He would hear her voice rising in anger as she tried in vain to force her way in. Then the noise would be stilled, and there would be only a whisper of complaint and plotting between her and the servant. But not once did he yield, not once did he lean over the banisters and call to her to come up.

One day Martine ventured to say to him:

"It is very hard, all the same, monsieur, to refuse admittance to one's mother. The more so, as Mme. Felicite comes with good intentions, for she knows the straits that monsieur is in, and she insists only in order to offer her services."

"Money!" he cried, exasperated. "I want no money, do you hear? And from her less than anybody. I will work, I will earn my own living; why should I not?"

The question of money, however, began to grow pressing. He obstinately refused to take another sou from the five thousand francs locked up in the desk. Now that he was alone, he was completely indifferent to material things; he would have been satisfied to live on bread and water; and every time the servant asked him for money to buy wine, meat, or sweets, he shrugged his shoulders — what was the use? there remained a crust from the day before, was not that sufficient? But in her affection for her master, whom she felt to be suffering, the old servant was heart-broken at this miserliness which exceeded her own; this utter destitution to which he abandoned himself and the whole house. The workmen of the faubourgs lived better. Thus it was that for a whole day a terrible conflict went on within her. Her doglike love struggled with her love for her money, amassed sou by sou, hidden away, "making more," as she said. She would rather have parted with a piece of her flesh. So long as her master had not suffered alone the idea of touching her treasure had not even occurred to her. And she displayed extraordinary heroism the morning when, driven to extremity, seeing her stove cold and the larder empty, she disappeared for an hour and then returned with provisions and the change of a hundred-franc note.

Pascal, who just then chanced to come downstairs, asked her in astonishment where the money had come from, furious already, and prepared to throw it all into the street, imagining she had applied to his mother.

"Why, no; why, no, monsieur!" she stammered, "it is not that at all."

And she told him the story that she had prepared.

"Imagine, M. Grandguillot's affairs are going to be settled — or at least I think so. It occurred to me this morning to go to the assignee's to inquire, and he told me that you would undoubtedly recover something, and that I might have a hundred francs now. Yes, he was even satisfied with a receipt from me. He knows me, and you can make it all right afterward."

Pascal seemed scarcely surprised. She had calculated correctly that he would not go out to verify her account. She was relieved, however, to see with what easy indifference he accepted her story.

"Ah, so much the better!" he said. "You see now that one must never despair. That will give me time to settle my affairs."

His "affairs" was the sale of La Souleiade, about which he had been thinking vaguely. But what a grief to leave this house in which Clotilde had grown up, where they had lived together for nearly eighteen years! He had taken two or three weeks already to reflect over the matter. Now that he had the hope of getting back a little of the money he had lost through the notary's failure, he ceased to think anymore about it. He relapsed into his former indifference, eating whatever Martine served him, not even noticing the comforts with which she once more surrounded him, in humble adoration, heart-broken at giving her money, but very happy to support him now, without his suspecting that his sustenance came from her.

But Pascal rewarded her very ill. Afterward he would be sorry, and regret his outbursts. But in the state of feverish desperation in which he lived this did not prevent him from again flying into a passion with her, at the slightest cause of dissatisfaction. One evening, after he had been listening to his mother talking for an interminable time with her in the kitchen, he cried in sudden fury:

"Martine, I do not wish her to enter La Souleiade again, do you hear? If you ever let her into the house again I will turn you out!"

She listened to him in surprise. Never, during the thirty-two years in which she had been in his service, had he threatened to dismiss her in this way. Big tears came to her eyes.

"Oh, monsieur! you would not have the courage to do it! And I would not go. I would lie down across the threshold first."

He already regretted his anger, and he said more gently:

"The thing is that I know perfectly well what is going on. She comes to indoctrinate you, to put you against me, is it not so? Yes, she is watching my papers; she wishes to steal and destroy everything up there in the press. I know her; when she wants anything, she never gives up until she gets it. Well, you can tell her that I am on my guard; that while I am alive she shall never even come near the press. And the key is here in my pocket."

In effect, all his former terror — the terror of the scientist who feels himself surrounded by secret enemies, had returned. Ever since he had been living alone in the deserted house he had had a feeling of returning danger, of being constantly watched in secret. The circle had narrowed, and if he showed such anger at these attempts at invasion, if he repulsed his mother's assaults, it was because he did not deceive himself as to her real plans, and he was afraid that he might yield. If she were there she would gradually take possession of him, until she had subjugated him completely. Therefore his former tortures returned, and he passed the days watching; he shut up the house himself in the evening, and he would often rise during the night, to assure himself that the locks were not being forced. What he feared was that the servant, won over by his mother, and believing she was securing his eternal welfare, would open the door to Mme. Felicite. In fancy he saw the papers blazing in the fireplace; he kept constant guard over them, seized again by a morbid love, a torturing affection for this icy heap of papers, these cold pages of manuscript, to which he had sacrificed the love of woman, and which he tried to love sufficiently to be able to forget everything else for them.

Pascal, now that Clotilde was no longer there, threw himself eagerly into work, trying to submerge himself in it, to lose himself in it. If he secluded himself, if he did not set foot even in the garden, if he had had the strength, one day when Martine came up to announce Dr. Ramond, to answer that he would not receive him, he had, in this bitter desire for solitude, no other aim than to kill thought by incessant labor. That poor Ramond, how gladly he would have embraced him! for he divined clearly the delicacy of feeling that had made him hasten to console his old master. But why lose an hour? Why risk emotions and tears which would leave him so weak? From daylight he was at his table, he spent at it his mornings and his afternoons, extended often into the evening after the lamp was lighted, and far into the night. He wished to put his old project into execution — to revise his whole theory of heredity, employing the documents furnished by his own family to establish the laws according to which, in a certain group of human beings, life is distributed and conducted with mathematical precision from one to another, taking into account the environment — a vast bible, the genesis of families, of societies, of all humanity. He hoped that the vastness of such a plan, the effort necessary to develop so colossal an idea, would take complete possession of him, restoring to him his health, his faith, his pride in the supreme joy of the accomplished work. But it was in vain that he threw himself passionately, persistently, without reserve, into his work; he succeeded only in fatiguing his body and his mind, without even being able to fix his thoughts or to put his heart into his work, every day sicker and more despairing. Had work, then, finally lost its power? He whose life had been spent in work, who had regarded it as the sole motor, the benefactor, and the consoler, must he then conclude that to love and to be loved is beyond all else in the world? Occasionally he would have great thoughts, he continued to sketch out his new theory of the equilibrium of forces, demonstrating that what man receives in sensation he should return in action. How natural, full, and happy would life be if it could be lived entire, performing its functions like a well-ordered machine, giving back in power what was consumed in fuel, maintaining itself in vigor and in beauty by the simultaneous and logical play of all its organs. He believed physical and intellectual labor, feeling and reasoning should be in equal proportions, and never excessive, for excess meant disturbance of the equilibrium and, consequently, disease. Yes, yes, to begin life over again and to know how to live it, to dig the earth, to study man, to love woman, to attain to human perfection, the future city of universal happiness, through the harmonious working of the entire being, what a beautiful legacy for a philosophical physician to leave behind him would this be! And this dream of the future, this theory, confusedly perceived, filled him with bitterness at the thought that now his life was a force wasted and lost.

At the very bottom of his grief Pascal had the dominating feeling that for him life was ended. Regret for Clotilde, sorrow at having her no longer beside him, the certainty that he would never see her again, filled him with overwhelming grief. Work had lost its power, and he would sometimes let his head drop on the page he was writing, and weep for hours together, unable to summon courage to take up the pen again. His passion for work, his days of voluntary fatigue, led to terrible nights, nights of feverish sleeplessness, in which he would stuff the bedclothes into his mouth to keep from crying out Clotilde's name. She was everywhere in this mournful house in which he secluded himself. He saw her again, walking through the rooms, sitting on the chairs, standing behind the doors. Downstairs, in the dining room, he could not sit at table, without seeing her opposite him. In the workroom upstairs she was still his constant companion, for she, too, had lived so long secluded in it that her image seemed reflected from everything; he felt her constantly beside him, he could fancy he saw her standing before her desk, straight and slender — her delicate face bent over a pastel. And if he did not leave the house to escape from the dear and torturing memory it was because he had the certainty that he should find her everywhere in the garden, too: dreaming on the terrace; walking with slow steps through the alleys in the pine grove; sitting under the shade of the plane trees; lulled by the eternal song of the fountain; lying in the threshing yard at twilight, her gaze fixed on space, waiting for the stars to come out. But above all, there existed for him a sacred sanctuary which he could not enter without trembling — the chamber where she had confessed her love. He kept the key of it; he had not moved a single object from its place since the sorrowful morning of her departure; and a skirt which she had forgotten lay still upon her armchair. He opened his arms wildly to clasp her shade floating in the soft half light of the room, with its closed shutters and its walls hung with the old faded pink calico, of a dawnlike tint.

In the midst of his unremitting toil Pascal had another melancholy pleasure — Clotilde's letters. She wrote to him regularly twice a week, long letters of eight or ten pages, in which she described to him all her daily life. She did not seem to lead a very happy life in Paris. Maxime, who did not now leave his sick chair, evidently tortured her with the exactions of a spoiled child and an invalid. She spoke as if she lived in complete retirement, always waiting on him, so that she could not even go over to the window to look out on the avenue, along which rolled the fashionable stream of the promenaders of the Bois; and from certain of her expressions it could be divined that her brother, after having entreated her so urgently to go to him, suspected her already, and had begun to regard her with hatred and distrust, as he did everyone who approached him, in his continual fear of being made use of and robbed. He did not give her the keys, treating her like a servant to whom he found it difficult to accustom himself. Twice she had seen her father, who was, as always, very gay, and overwhelmed with business; he had been converted to the Republic, and was at the height of political and financial success. Saccard had even taken her aside, to sympathize with her, saying that poor Maxime was really insupportable, and that she would be truly courageous if she consented to be made his victim. As she could not do everything, he had even had the kindness to send her, on the following day, the niece of his hairdresser, a fair-haired, inno-cent-looking girl of eighteen, named Rose, who was assisting her now to take care of the invalid. But Clotilde made no complaint; she affected, on the contrary, to be perfectly tranquil, contented, and resigned to everything. Her letters were full of courage, showing neither anger nor sorrow at the cruel separation, making no desperate appeal to Pascal's affection to recall her. But between the lines, he could perceive that she trembled with rebellious anger, that her whole being yearned for him, that she was ready to commit the folly of returning to him immediately, at his lightest word.

And this was the one word that Pascal would not write. Everything would be arranged in time. Maxime would become accustomed to his sister; the sacrifice must be completed now that it had been begun. A single line written by him in a moment of weakness, and all the advantage of the effort he had made would be lost, and their misery would begin again. Never had Pascal had greater need of courage than when he was answering Clotilde's letters. At night, burning with fever, he would toss about, calling on her wildly; then he would get up and write to her to come back at once. But when day came, and he had exhausted himself with weeping, his fever abated, and his answer was always very short, almost cold. He studied every sentence, beginning the letter over again when he thought he had forgotten himself. But what a torture, these dreadful letters, so short, so icy, in which he went against his heart, solely in order to wean her from him gradually, to take upon himself all the blame, and to make her believe that she could forget him, since he forgot her. They left him covered with perspiration, and as exhausted as if he had just performed some great act of heroism.

One morning toward the end of October, a month after Clotilde's departure, Pascal had a sudden attack of suffocation. He had had, several times already, slight attacks, which he attributed to overwork. But this time the symptoms were so plain that he could not mistake them — a sharp pain in the region of the heart, extending over the whole chest and along the left arm, and a dreadful sensation of oppression and distress, while cold perspiration broke out upon him. It was an attack of angina pectoris. It lasted hardly more than a minute, and he was at first more surprised than frightened. With that blindness which physicians often show where their own health is concerned, he never suspected that his heart might be affected.

As he was recovering his breath Martine came up to say that Dr. Ramond was downstairs, and again begged the doctor to see him. And Pascal, yielding perhaps to an unconscious desire to know the truth, cried:

"Well, let him come up, since he insists upon it. I will be glad to see him."

The two men embraced each other, and no other allusion was made to the absent one, to her whose departure had left the house empty, than an energetic and sad hand clasp.

"You don't know why I have come?" cried Ramond immediately. "It is about a question of money. Yes, my father-in-law, M. Leveque, the advocate, whom you know, spoke to me yesterday again about the funds which you had with the notary Grandguillot. And he advises you strongly to take some action in the matter, for some persons have succeeded, he says, in recovering something."

"Yes, I know that that business is being settled," said Pascal. "Martine has already got two hundred francs out of it, I believe."

"Martine?" said Ramond, looking greatly surprised, "how could she do that without your intervention? However, will you authorize my father-in-law to undertake your case? He will see the assignee, and sift the whole affair, since you have neither the time nor the inclination to attend to it."

"Certainly, I authorize M. Leveque to do so, and tell him that I thank him a thousand times."

Then this matter being settled, the young man, remarking the doctor's pallor, and questioning him as to its cause, Pascal answered with a smile:

"Imagine, my friend, I have just had an attack of angina pectoris. Oh, it is not imagination, all the symptoms were there. And stay! since you are here you shall sound me."

At first Ramond refused, affecting to turn the consultation into a jest. Could a raw recruit like him venture to pronounce judgment on his general? But he examined him, notwithstanding, seeing that his face looked drawn and pained, with a singular look of fright in the eyes. He ended by auscultating him carefully, keeping his ear pressed closely to his chest for a considerable time. Several minutes passed in profound silence.

"Well?" asked Pascal, when the young physician stood up.

The latter did not answer at once. He felt the doctor's eyes looking straight into his; and as the question had been put to him with quiet courage, he answered in the same way:

"Well, it is true, I think there is some sclerosis."

"Ah! it was kind of you not to attempt to deceive me," returned the doctor, smiling. "I feared for an instant that you would tell me an untruth, and that would have hurt me."

Ramond, listening again, said in an undertone:

"Yes, the beat is strong, the first sound is dull, while the second, on the contrary, is sharp. It is evident that the apex has descended and is turned toward the armpit. There is some sclerosis, at least it is very probable. One may live twenty years with that," he ended, straightening himself.

"No doubt, sometimes," said Pascal. "At least, unless one chances to die of a sudden attack."

They talked for some time longer, discussed a remarkable case of sclerosis of the heart, which they had seen at the hospital at Plassans. And when the young physician went away, he said that he would return as soon as he should have news of the Grandguillot liquidation.

But when he was alone Pascal felt that he was lost. Everything was now explained: his palpitations for some weeks past, his attacks of vertigo and suffocation; above all that weakness of the organ, of his poor heart, overtasked by feeling and by work, that sense of intense fatigue and impending death, regarding which he could no longer deceive himself. It was not as yet fear that he experienced, however. His first thought was that he, too, would have to pay for his heredity, that sclerosis was the species of degeneration which was to be his share of the physiological misery, the inevitable inheritance bequeathed him by his terrible ancestry. In others the neurosis, the original lesion, had turned to vice or virtue, genius, crime, drunkenness, sanctity; others again had died of consumption, of epilepsy, of ataxia; he had lived in his feelings and he would die of an affection of the heart. And he trembled no longer, he rebelled no longer against this manifest heredity, fated and inevitable, no doubt. On the contrary, a feeling of humility took possession of him; the idea that all revolt against natural laws is bad, that wisdom does not consist in holding one's self apart, but in resigning one's self to be only a member of the whole great body. Why, then, was he so unwilling to belong to his family that it filled him with triumph, that his heart beat with joy, when he believed himself different from them, without any community with them? Nothing could be less philosophical. Only monsters grew apart. And to belong to his family seemed to him in the end as good and as fine as to belong to any other family, for did not all families, in the main, resemble one another, was not humanity everywhere identical with the same amount of good and evil? He came at last, humbly and gently, even in the face of impending suffering and death, to accept everything life had to give him.

From this time Pascal lived with the thought that he might die at any moment. And this helped to perfect his character, to elevate him to a complete forgetfulness of self. He did not cease to work, but he had never understood so well how much effort must seek its reward in itself, the work being always transitory, and remaining of necessity incomplete. One evening at dinner Martine informed him that Sarteur, the journeyman hatter, the former inmate of the asylum at the Tulettes, had just hanged himself. All the evening he thought of this strange case, of this man whom he had believed he had cured of homicidal mania by his treatment of hypodermic injections, and who, seized by a fresh attack, had evidently had sufficient lucidity to hang himself, instead of springing at the throat of some passer-by. He again saw him, so gentle, so reasonable, kissing his hands, while he was advising him to return to his life of healthful labor. What then was this destructive and transforming force, the desire to murder, changing to suicide, death performing its task in spite of everything? With the death of this man his last vestige of pride as a healer disappeared; and each day when he returned to his work he felt as if he were only a learner, spelling out his task, constantly seeking the truth, which as constantly receded from him, assuming ever more formidable proportions.

But in the midst of his resignation one thought still troubled him —
what would become of Bonhomme, his old horse, if he himself should
die before him? The poor brute, completely blind and his limbs paralyzed, did not now leave his litter. When his master went to see him,
however, he turned his head, he could feel the two hearty kisses which
were pressed on his nose. All the neighbors shrugged their shoulders
and joked about this old relation whom the doctor would not allow to
be slaughtered. Was he then to be the first to go, with the thought that
the knacker would be called in on the following day. But one morning,
when he entered the stable, Bonhomme did not hear him, did not raise
his head. He was dead; he lay there, with a peaceful expression, as if
relieved that death had come to him so gently. His master knelt beside
him and kissed him again and bade him farewell, while two big tears
rolled down his cheeks.

It was on this day that Pascal saw his neighbor, M. Bellombre, for
the last time. Going over to the window he perceived him in his garden,
in the pale sunshine of early November, taking his accustomed walk;
and the sight of the old professor, living so completely happy in his
solitude, filled him at first with astonishment. He could never have
imagined such a thing possible, as that a man of sixty-nine should live
thus, without wife or child, or even a dog, deriving his selfish happiness
from the joy of living outside of life. Then he recalled his fits of anger
against this man, his sarcasms about his fear of life, the catastrophes
which he had wished might happen to him, the hope that punishment
would come to him, in the shape of some housekeeper, or some female
relation dropping down on him unexpectedly. But no, he was still as
fresh as ever, and Pascal was sure that for a long time to come he would
continue to grow old like this, hard, avaricious, useless, and happy. And
yet he no longer execrated him; he could even have found it in his heart
to pity him, so ridiculous and miserable did he think him for not being
loved. Pascal, who suffered the pangs of death because he was alone! He
whose heart was breaking because he was too full of others. Rather
suffering, suffering only, than this selfishness, this death of all there is
in us of living and human!

In the night which followed Pascal had another attack of angina
pectoris. It lasted for five minutes, and he thought that he would
suffocate without having the strength to call Martine. Then when he
recovered his breath, he did not disturb himself, preferring to speak to
no one of this aggravation of his malady; but he had the certainty that
it was all over with him, that he might not perhaps live a month longer.
His first thought was Clotilde. Should he then never see her again? and
so sharp a pang seized him that he believed another attack was coming

on. Why should he not write to her to come to him? He had received
a letter from her the day before; he would answer it this morning. Then
the thought of the envelopes occurred to him. If he should die suddenly,
his mother would be the mistress and she would destroy them; and not
only the envelopes, but his manuscripts, all his papers, thirty years of
his intelligence and his labor. Thus the crime which he had so greatly
dreaded would be consummated, the crime of which the fear alone,
during his nights of fever, had made him get up out of bed trembling,
his ear on the stretch, listening to hear if they were forcing open the
press. The perspiration broke out upon him, he saw himself dispossessed, outraged, the ashes of his work thrown to the four winds. And
when his thoughts reverted to Clotilde, he told himself that everything
would be satisfactorily arranged, that he had only to call her back — she
would be here, she would close his eyes, she would defend his memory.
And he sat down to write at once to her, so that the letter might go by
the morning mail.

But when Pascal was seated before the white paper, with the pen
between his fingers, a growing doubt, a feeling of dissatisfaction with
himself, took possession of him. Was not this idea of his papers, this
fine project of providing a guardian for them and saving them, a
suggestion of his weakness, an excuse which he gave himself to bring
back Clotilde, and see her again? Selfishness was at the bottom of it. He
was thinking of himself, not of her. He saw her returning to this poor
house, condemned to nurse a sick old man; and he saw her, above all,
in her grief, in her awful agony, when he should terrify her some day
by dropping down dead at her side. No, no! this was the dreadful
moment which he must spare her, those days of cruel adieus and want
afterward, a sad legacy which he could not leave her without thinking
himself a criminal. Her tranquility, her happiness only, were of any
consequence, the rest did not matter. He would die in his hole, then,
abandoned, happy to think her happy, to spare her the cruel blow of
his death. As for saving his manuscripts he would perhaps find a means
of doing so, he would try to have the strength to part from them and
give them to Ramond. But even if all his papers were to perish, this was
less of a sacrifice than to resign himself not to see her again, and he
accepted it, and he was willing that nothing of him should survive, not
even his thoughts, provided only that nothing of him should henceforth
trouble her dear existence.

Pascal accordingly proceeded to write one of his usual answers, which,
by a great effort, he purposely made colorless and almost cold. Clotilde,
in her last letter, without complaining of Maxime, had given it to be
understood that her brother had lost his interest in her, preferring the

society of Rose, the niece of Saccard's hairdresser, the fair-haired young girl with the innocent look. And he suspected strongly some maneuver of the father: a cunning plan to obtain possession of the inheritance of the sick man, whose vices, so precocious formerly, gained new force as his last hour approached. But in spite of his uneasiness he gave Clotilde very good advice, telling her that she must make allowance for Maxime's sufferings, that he had undoubtedly a great deal of affection and gratitude for her, in short that it was her duty to devote herself to him to the end. When he signed the letter tears dimmed his sight. It was his death warrant — a death like that of an old and solitary brute, a death without a kiss, without the touch of a friendly hand — that he was signing. Never again would he embrace her. Then doubts assailed him; was he doing right in leaving her amid such evil surroundings, where he felt that she was in continual contact with every species of wickedness?

The postman brought the letters and newspapers to La Souleiade every morning at about nine o'clock; and Pascal, when he wrote to Clotilde, was accustomed to watch for him, to give him his letter, so as to be certain that his correspondence was not intercepted. But on this morning, when he went downstairs to give him the letter he had just written, he was surprised to receive one from him from Clotilde, although it was not the usual day for her letters. He allowed his own to go, however. Then he went upstairs, resumed his seat at his table, and tore open the envelope.

The letter was short, but its contents filled Pascal with a great joy.

*B*ut the sound of footsteps made him control himself. He turned round and saw Martine, who was saying:

"Dr. Ramond is downstairs."

"Ah! let him come up, let him come up," he said.

It was another piece of good fortune that had come to him. Ramond cried gaily from the door:

"Victory, master! I have brought you your money — not all, but a good sum."

And he told the story — an unexpected piece of good luck which his father-in-law, M. Leveque, had brought to light. The receipts for the hundred and twenty thousand francs, which constituted Pascal the personal creditor of Grandguillot, were valueless, since the latter was insolvent. Salvation was to come from the power of attorney which the doctor had sent him years before, at his request, that he might invest all or part of his money in mortgages. As the name of the proxy was in blank in the document, the notary, as is sometimes done, had made use of the name of one of his clerks, and eighty thousand francs, which had been invested in good mortgages, had thus been recovered through the agency of a worthy man who was not in the secrets of his employer. If Pascal had taken action in the matter, if he had gone to the public prosecutor's office and the chamber of notaries, he would have disentangled the matter long before. However, he had recovered a sure income of four thousand francs.

He seized the young man's hands and pressed them, smiling, his eyes still moist with tears.

"Ah! my friend, if you knew how happy I am! This letter of Clotilde's has brought me a great happiness. Yes, I was going to send for her; but the thought of my poverty, of the privations she would have to endure here, spoiled for me the joy of her return. And now fortune has come back, at least enough to set up my little establishment again!"

In the expansion of his feelings he held out the letter to Ramond, and forced him to read it. Then when the young man gave it back to him, smiling, comprehending the doctor's emotion, and profoundly touched by it, yielding to an overpowering need of affection, he caught him in his arms, like a comrade, a brother. The two men kissed each other vigorously on either cheek.

"Come, since good fortune has sent you, I am going to ask another service from you. You know I distrust everyone around me, even my old housekeeper. Will you take my dispatch to the telegraph office!"

He sat down again at the table, and wrote simply, "I await you; start tonight."

"Let me see," he said, "today is the 6th of November, is it not? It is now near ten o'clock; she will have my dispatch at noon. That will give her time enough to pack her trunks and to take the eight o'clock express this evening, which will bring her to Marseilles in time for breakfast. But as there is no train which connects with it, she cannot be here until tomorrow, the 7th, at five o'clock."

After folding the dispatch he rose:

"My God, at five o'clock tomorrow! How long to wait still! What shall I do with myself until then?"

Then a sudden recollection filled him with anxiety, and he became grave.

"Ramond, my comrade, will you give me a great proof of your friendship by being perfectly frank with me?"

"How so, master?"

"Ah, you understand me very well. The other day you examined me. Do you think I can live another year?"

He fixed his eyes on the young man as he spoke, compelling him to look at him. Ramond evaded a direct answer, however, with a jest — was it really a physician who put such a question?

"Let us be serious, Ramond, I beg of you."

Then Ramond answered in all sincerity that, in his opinion, the doctor might very justly entertain the hope of living another year. He gave his reasons — the comparatively slight progress which the sclerosis had made, and the absolute soundness of the other organs. Of course they must make allowance for what they did not and could not know, for a sudden accident was always possible. And the two men discussed the case as if they been in consultation at the bedside of a patient, weighing the pros and cons, each stating his views and prognosticating a fatal termination, in accordance with the symptoms as defined by the best authorities.

Pascal, as if it were someone else who was in question, had recovered all his composure and his heroic self-forgetfulness.

"Yes," he murmured at last, "you are right; a year of life is still possible. Ah, my friend, how I wish I might live two years; a mad wish, no doubt, an eternity of joy. And yet, two years, that would not be impossible. I had a very curious case once, a wheelwright of the faubourg, who lived for four years, giving the lie to all my prognostications. Two years, two years, I will live two years! I must live two years!"

Ramond sat with bent head, without answering. He was beginning to be uneasy, fearing that he had shown himself too optimistic; and the doctor's joy disquieted and grieved him, as if this very exaltation, this disturbance of a once strong brain, warned him of a secret and imminent danger.

"Did you not wish to send that dispatch at once?" he said.

"Yes, yes, go quickly, my good Ramond, and come back again to see us the day after tomorrow. She will be here then, and I want you to come and embrace us."

The day was long, and the following morning, at about four o'clock, shortly after Pascal had fallen asleep, after a happy vigil filled with hopes and dreams, he was wakened by a dreadful attack. He felt as if an enormous weight, as if the whole house, had fallen down upon his chest, so that the thorax, flattened down, touched the back. He could not breathe; the pain reached the shoulders, then the neck, and paralyzed the left arm. But he was perfectly conscious; he had the feeling that his heart was about to stop, that life was about to leave him, in the dreadful oppression, like that of a vise, which was suffocating him. Before the attack reached its height he had the strength to rise and to knock on the floor with a stick for Martine. Then he fell back on his bed, unable to speak or to move, and covered with a cold sweat.

Martine, fortunately, in the profound silence of the empty house, heard the knock. She dressed herself, wrapped a shawl about her, and went upstairs, carrying her candle. The darkness was still profound; dawn was about to break. And when she perceived her master, whose eyes alone seemed living, looking at her with locked jaws, speechless, his face distorted by pain, she was awed and terrified, and she could only rush toward the bed crying:

"My God! My God! what is the matter, monsieur? Answer me, monsieur, you frighten me!"

For a full minute Pascal struggled in vain to recover his breath. Then, the viselike pressure on his chest relaxing slowly, he murmured in a faint voice:

"The five thousand francs in the desk are Clotilde's. Tell her that the affair of the notary is settled, that she will recover from it enough to live upon."

Then Martine, who had listened to him in open-mouthed wonder, confessed the falsehood she had told him, ignorant of the good news that had been brought by Ramond.

"Monsieur, you must forgive me; I told you an untruth. But it would be wrong to deceive you longer. When I saw you alone and so unhappy, I took some of my own money."

"My poor girl, you did that!"

"Oh, I had some hope that monsieur would return it to me one day."

By this time the attack had passed off, and he was able to turn his head and look at her. He was amazed and moved. What was passing in the heart of this avaricious old maid, who for thirty years had been saving up her treasure painfully, who had never taken a sou from it, either for herself or for anyone else? He did not yet comprehend, but he wished to show himself kind and grateful.

"You are a good woman, Martine. All that will be returned to you. I truly think I am going to die —"

She did not allow him to finish, her whole being rose up in rebellious protest.

"Die; you, monsieur! Die before me! I do not wish it. I will not let you die!"

She threw herself on her knees beside the bed; she caught him wildly in her arms, feeling him, to see if he suffered, holding him as if she thought that death would not dare to take him from her.

"You must tell me what is the matter with you. I will take care of you. I will save you. If it were necessary to give my life for you, I would give it, monsieur. I will sit up day and night with you. I am strong still; I will be stronger than the disease, you shall see. To die! to die! oh, no, it cannot be! The good God cannot wish so great an injustice. I have prayed so much in my life that he ought to listen to me a little now, and he will grant my prayer, monsieur; he will save you."

Pascal looked at her, listened to her, and a sudden light broke in upon his mind. She loved him, this miserable woman; she had always loved him. He thought of her thirty years of blind devotion, her mute adoration, when she had waited upon him, on her knees, as it were, when she was young; her secret jealousy of Clotilde later; what she must have secretly suffered all that time! And she was here on her knees now again, beside his deathbed; her hair grey; her eyes the color of ashes in her pale nunlike face, dulled by her solitary life. And he felt that she was unconscious of it all; that she did not even know with what sort of love she loved him, loving him only for the happiness of loving him: of being with him, and of waiting on him.

Tears rose to Pascal's eyes; a dolorous pity and an infinite human tenderness flowed from his poor, half-broken heart.

"My poor girl," he said, "you are the best of girls. Come, embrace me, as you love me, with all your strength."

She, too, sobbed. She let her grey head, her face worn by her long servitude, fall on her master's breast. Wildly she kissed him, putting all her life into the kiss.

"There, let us not give way to emotion, for you see we can do nothing; this will be the end, just the same. If you wish me to love you, obey me. Now that I am better, that I can breathe easier, do me the favor to run to Dr. Ramond's. Waken him and bring him back with you."

She was leaving the room when he called to her, seized by a sudden fear.

"And remember, I forbid you to go to inform my mother."

She turned back, embarrassed, and in a voice of entreaty, said:

"Oh, monsieur, Mme. Felicite has made me promise so often —"

But he was inflexible. All his life he had treated his mother with deference, and he thought he had acquired the right to defend himself against her in the hour of his death. He would not let the servant go until she had promised him that she would be silent. Then he smiled once more.

"Go quickly. Oh, you will see me again; it will not be yet."

Day broke at last, the melancholy dawn of the pale November day. Pascal had had the shutters opened, and when he was left alone he watched the brightening dawn, doubtless that of his last day of life. It had rained the night before, and the mild sun was still veiled by clouds. From the plane trees came the morning carols of the birds, while far away in the sleeping country a locomotive whistled with a prolonged moan. And he was alone; alone in the great melancholy house, whose emptiness he felt around him, whose silence he heard. The light slowly increased, and he watched the patches it made on the windowpanes broadening and brightening. Then the candle paled in the growing light, and the whole room became visible. And with the dawn, as he had anticipated, came relief. The sight of the familiar objects around him brought him consolation.

But Pascal, although the attack had passed away, still suffered horribly. A sharp pain remained in the hollow of his chest, and his left arm, benumbed, hung from his shoulder like lead. In his long waiting for the help that Martine had gone to bring, he had reflected on the suffering which made the flesh cry out. And he found that he was resigned; he no longer felt the rebelliousness which the mere sight of physical pain had formerly awakened in him. It had exasperated him, as if it had been a monstrous and useless cruelty of nature. In his doubts as a physician, he had attended his patients only to combat it, and to relieve it. If he ended by accepting it, now that he himself suffered its horrible torture, was it that he had risen one degree higher in his faith of life, to that serene height whence life appeared altogether good, even with the fatal condition of suffering attached to it; suffering which is perhaps its spring? Yes, to live all of life, to live it and to suffer it all without rebellion, without believing that it is made better by being made painless, this presented itself clearly to his dying eyes, as the greatest courage and the greatest wisdom. And to cheat pain while he waited, he reviewed his latest theories; he dreamed of a means of utilizing suffering by transforming it into action, into work. If it be true that man feels pain more acutely according as he rises in the scale of civilization, it is also certain that he becomes stronger through it, better armed against it, more capable of resisting it. The organ, the brain which works, develops and grows stronger, provided the equilibrium between the sensations which it receives and the work which it gives back be not broken. Might not one hope, then, for a humanity in which the amount of work accomplished would so exactly equal the sum of sensations received, that suffering would be utilized and, as it were, abolished?

The sun had risen, and Pascal was confusedly revolving these distant hopes in his mind, in the drowsiness produced by his disease, when he felt a new attack coming on. He had a moment of cruel anxiety — was this the end? Was he going to die alone? But at this instant hurried footsteps mounted the stairs, and a moment later Ramond entered, followed by Martine. And the patient had time to say before the attack began:

"Quick! quick! a hypodermic injection of pure water."

Unfortunately the doctor had to look for the little syringe and then to prepare everything. This occupied some minutes, and the attack was terrible. He followed its progress with anxiety — the face becoming distorted, the lips growing livid. Then when he had given the injection, he observed that the phenomena, for a moment stationary, slowly diminished in intensity. Once more the catastrophe was averted.

As soon as he recovered his breath Pascal, glancing at the clock, said in his calm, faint voice:

"My friend, it is seven o'clock — in twelve hours, at seven o'clock tonight, I shall be dead."

And as the young man was about to protest, to argue the question, "No," he resumed, "do not try to deceive me. You have witnessed the attack. You know what it means as well as I do. Everything will now proceed with mathematical exactness; and, hour by hour, I could describe to you the phases of the disease."

He stopped, gasped for breath, and then added:

"And then, all is well; I am content. Clotilde will be here at five; all I ask is to see her and to die in her arms."

A few moments later, however, he experienced a sensible improvement. The effect of the injection seemed truly miraculous; and he was able to sit up in bed, his back resting against the pillows. He spoke clearly, and with more ease, and never had the lucidity of his mind appeared greater.

"You know, master," said, Ramond, "that I will not leave you. I have told my wife, and we will spend the day together; and, whatever you may say to the contrary, I am very confident that it will not be the last. You will let me make myself at home, here, will you not?"

Pascal smiled, and gave orders to Martine to go and prepare breakfast for Ramond, saying that if they needed her they would call her. And the two men remained alone, conversing with friendly intimacy; the one with his white hair and long white beard, lying down, discoursing like a sage, the other sitting at his bedside, listening with the respect of a disciple.

"In truth," murmured the master, as if he were speaking to himself, "the effect of those injections is extraordinary."

Then in a stronger voice, he said almost gaily:

"My friend Ramond, it may not be a very great present that I am giving you, but I am going to leave you my manuscripts. Yes, Clotilde has orders to send them to you when I shall be no more. Look through them, and you will perhaps find among them things that are not so very bad. If you get a good idea from them some day — well, that will be so much the better for the world."

And then he made his scientific testament. He was clearly conscious that he had been himself only a solitary pioneer, a precursor, planning theories which he tried to put in practice, but which failed because of the imperfection of his method. He recalled his enthusiasm when he believed he had discovered, in his injections of nerve substance, the universal panacea, then his disappointments, his fits of despair, the shocking death of Lafouasse, consumption carrying off Valentin in spite of all his efforts, madness again conquering Sarteur and causing him to hang himself. So that he would depart full of doubt, having no longer the confidence necessary to the physician, and so enamored of life that he had ended by putting all his faith in it, certain that it must draw from itself alone its health and strength. But he did not wish to close up the future; he was glad, on the contrary, to bequeath his hypotheses to the younger generation. Every twenty years theories changed; established truths only, on which science continued to build, remained unshaken. Even if he had only the merit of giving to science a momentary hypothesis, his work would not be lost, for progress consisted assuredly in the effort, in the onward march of the intellect.

And then who could say that he had died in vain, troubled and weary, his hopes concerning the injections unrealized — other workers would come, young, ardent, confident, who would take up the idea, elucidate it, expand it. And perhaps a new epoch, a new world would date from this.

"Ah, my dear Ramond," he continued, "if one could only live life over again. Yes, I would take up my idea again, for I have been struck lately by the singular efficacy of injections even of pure water. It is not the liquid, then, that matters, but simply the mechanical action. During the last month I have written a great deal on that subject. You will find some curious notes and observations there. In short, I should be inclined to put all my faith in work, to place health in the harmonious working of all the organs, a sort of dynamic therapeutics, if I may venture to use the expression."

He had gradually grown excited, forgetting his approaching death in his ardent curiosity about life. And he sketched, with broad strokes, his last theory. Man was surrounded by a medium — nature — which irritated by perpetual contact the sensitive extremities of the nerves. Hence the action, not only of the senses, but of the entire surface of the body, external and internal. For it was these sensations which, reverberating in the brain, in the marrow, and in the nervous centers, were there converted into tonicity, movements, and thoughts; and he was convinced that health consisted in the natural progress of this work, in receiving sensations, and in giving them back in thoughts and in actions, the human machine being thus fed by the regular play of the organs. Work thus became the great law, the regulator of the living universe. Hence it became necessary if the equilibrium were broken, if the external excitations ceased to be sufficient, for therapeutics to create artificial excitations, in order to reestablish the tonicity which is the state of perfect health. And he dreamed of a whole new system of treatment — suggestion, the all-powerful authority of the physician, for the senses; electricity, friction, massage for the skin and for the tendons; diet for the stomach; air cures on high plateaus for the lungs, and, finally, transfusion, injections of distilled water, for the circulatory system. It was the undeniable and purely mechanical action of these latter that had put him on the track; all he did now was to extend the hypothesis, impelled by his generalizing spirit; he saw the world saved anew in this perfect equilibrium, as much work given as sensation received, the balance of the world restored by unceasing labor.

Here he burst into a frank laugh.

"There! I have started off again. I, who was firmly convinced that the only wisdom was not to interfere, to let nature take its course. Ah, what an incorrigible old fool I am!"

Ramond caught his hands in an outburst of admiration and affection.

"Master, master! it is of enthusiasm, of folly like yours that genius is made. Have no fear, I have listened to you, I will endeavor to be worthy of the heritage you leave; and I think, with you, that perhaps the great future lies entirely there."

In the sad and quiet room Pascal began to speak again, with the courageous tranquility of a dying philosopher giving his last lesson. He now reviewed his personal observations; he said that he had often cured himself by work, regular and methodical work, not carried to excess. Eleven o'clock struck; he urged Ramond to take his breakfast, and he continued the conversation, soaring to lofty and distant heights, while Martine served the meal. The sun had at last burst through the morning mists, a sun still half-veiled in clouds, and mild, whose golden light warmed the room. Presently, after taking a few sips of milk, Pascal remained silent.

At this moment the young physician was eating a pear.

"Are you in pain again?" he asked.

"No, no; finish."

But he could not deceive Ramond. It was an attack, and a terrible one. The suffocation came with the swiftness of a thunderbolt, and he fell back on the pillow, his face already blue. He clutched at the bedclothes to support himself, to raise the dreadful weight which oppressed his chest. Terrified, livid, he kept his wide open eyes fixed upon the clock, with a dreadful expression of despair and grief; and for ten minutes it seemed as if every moment must be his last.

Ramond had immediately given him a hypodermic injection. The relief was slow to come, the efficacy less than before.

When Pascal revived, large tears stood in his eyes. He did not speak now, he wept. Presently, looking at the clock with his darkening vision, he said:

"My friend, I shall die at four o'clock; I shall not see her."

And as his young colleague, in order to divert his thoughts, declared, in spite of appearances, that the end was not so near, Pascal, again becoming enthusiastic, wished to give him a last lesson, based on direct observation. He had, as it happened, attended several cases similar to his own, and he remembered especially to have dissected at the hospital the heart of a poor old man affected with sclerosis.

"I can see it — my heart. It is the color of a dead leaf; its fibers are brittle, wasted, one would say, although it has augmented slightly in volume. The inflammatory process has hardened it; it would be difficult to cut —"

He continued in a lower voice. A little before, he had felt his heart growing weaker, its contractions becoming feebler and slower. Instead of the normal jet of blood there now issued from the aorta only a red froth. Back of it all the veins were engorged with black blood; the suffocation increased, according as the lift and force pump, the regulator of the whole machine, moved more slowly. And after the injection he had been able to follow in spite of his suffering the gradual reviving of the organ as the stimulus set it beating again, removing the black venous blood, and sending life into it anew, with the red arterial blood. But the attack would return as soon as the mechanical effect of the injection should cease. He could predict it almost within a few minutes. Thanks to the injections he would have three attacks more. The third would carry him off; he would die at four o'clock.

Then, while his voice grew gradually weaker, in a last outburst of enthusiasm, he apostrophized the courage of the heart, that persistent life maker, working ceaselessly, even during sleep, when the other organs rested.

"Ah, brave heart! how heroically you struggle! What faithful, what generous muscles, never wearied! You have loved too much, you have beat too fast in the past months, and that is why you are breaking now, brave heart, who do not wish to die, and who strive rebelliously to beat still!"

But now the first of the attacks which had been announced came on. Pascal came out of this panting, haggard, his speech sibilant and painful. Low moans escaped him, in spite of his courage. Good God! would this torture never end? And yet his most ardent desire was to prolong his agony, to live long enough to embrace Clotilde a last time. If he might only be deceiving himself, as Ramond persisted in declaring. If he might only live until five o'clock. His eyes again turned to the clock, they never now left the hands, every minute seeming an eternity. They marked three o'clock. Then half-past three. Ah, God! only two hours of life, two hours more of life. The sun was already sinking toward the horizon; a great calm descended from the pale winter sky, and he heard at intervals the whistles of the distant locomotives crossing the bare plain. The train that was passing now was the one going to the Tulettes; the other, the one coming from Marseilles, would it never arrive, then!

At twenty minutes to four Pascal signed to Ramond to approach. He could no longer speak loud enough to be heard.

"You see, in order that I might live until six o'clock, the pulse should be stronger. I have still some hope, however, but the second movement is almost imperceptible, the heart will soon cease to beat."

And in faint, despairing accents he called on Clotilde again and again. The immeasurable grief which he felt at not being able to see her again broke forth in this faltering and agonized appeal. Then his anxiety about his manuscripts returned, an ardent entreaty shone in his eyes, until at last he found the strength to falter again:

"Do not leave me; the key is under my pillow; tell Clotilde to take it; she has my directions."

At ten minutes to four another hypodermic injection was given, but without effect. And just as four o'clock was striking, the second attack declared itself. Suddenly, after a fit of suffocation, he threw himself out of bed; he desired to rise, to walk, in a last revival of his strength. A need of space, of light, of air, urged him toward the skies. Then there came to him an irresistible appeal from life, his whole life, from the adjoining workroom, where he had spent his days. And he went there, staggering, suffocating, bending to the left side, supporting himself by the furniture.

Dr. Ramond precipitated himself quickly toward him to stop him, crying:

"Master, master! lie down again, I entreat you!"

But Pascal paid no heed to him, obstinately determined to die on his feet. The desire to live, the heroic idea of work, alone survived in him, carrying him onward bodily. He faltered hoarsely:

"No, no — out there, out there —"

His friend was obliged to support him, and he walked thus, stumbling and haggard, to the end of the workroom, and dropped into his chair beside his table, on which an unfinished page still lay among a confusion of papers and books.

Here he gasped for breath and his eyes closed. After a moment he opened them again, while his hands groped about, seeking his work, no doubt. They encountered the genealogical tree in the midst of other papers scattered about. Only two days before he had corrected some dates in it. He recognized it, and drawing it toward him, spread it out.

"Master, master! you will kill yourself!" cried Ramond, overcome with pity and admiration at this extraordinary spectacle.

Pascal did not listen, did not hear. He felt a pencil under his fingers. He took it and bent over the tree, as if his dying eyes no longer saw. The name of Maxime arrested his attention, and he wrote: "Died of ataxia in 1873," in the certainty that his nephew would not live through the year. Then Clotilde's name, beside it, struck him and he completed the note thus: "Has a son, by her Uncle Pascal, in 1874." But it was his own name that he sought wearily and confusedly. When he at last found it his hand grew firmer, and he finished his note, in upright and bold characters: "Died of heart disease, November 7, 1873." This was the supreme effort, the rattle in his throat increased, everything was fading into nothingness, when he perceived the blank leaf above Clotilde's name. His vision grew dark, his fingers could no longer hold the pencil, but he was still able to add, in unsteady letters, into which passed the tortured tenderness, the wild disorder of his poor heart: "The unknown child, to be born in 1874. What will it be?" Then he swooned, and Martine and Ramond with difficulty carried him back to bed.

The third attack came on about four o'clock. In this last access of suffocation Pascal's countenance expressed excruciating suffering. Death was to be very painful; he must endure to the end his martyrdom, as a man and a scientist. His wandering gaze still seemed to seek the clock, to ascertain the hour. And Ramond, seeing his lips move, bent down and placed his ear to the mouth of the dying man. The latter, in effect, was stammering some vague words, so faint that they scarcely rose above a breath:

"Four o'clock — the heart is stopping; no more red blood in the aorta — the valve relaxes and bursts."

A dreadful spasm shook him; his breathing grew fainter.

"Its progress is too rapid. Do not leave me; the key is under the pillow — Clotilde, Clotilde —"

At the foot of the bed Martine was kneeling, choked with sobs. She saw well that monsieur was dying. She had not dared to go for a priest notwithstanding her great desire to do so; and she was herself reciting the prayers for the dying; she prayed ardently that God would pardon monsieur, and that monsieur might go straight to Paradise.

Pascal was dying. His face was quite blue. After a few seconds of immobility, he tried to breathe: he put out his lips, opened his poor mouth, like a little bird opening its beak to get a last mouthful of air. And he was dead.

XIII

*I*t was not until after breakfast, at about one o'clock, that Clotilde received the dispatch. On this day it had chanced that she had quarreled with her brother Maxime, who, taking advantage of his privileges as an invalid, had tormented her more and more every day by his unreasonable caprices and his outbursts of ill temper. In short, her visit to him had not proved a success. He found that she was too simple and too serious to cheer him; and he had preferred, of late, the society of Rose, the fair-haired young girl, with the innocent look, who amused him. So that when his sister told him that their uncle had sent for her, and that she was going away, he gave his approval at once, and although he asked her to return as soon as she should have settled her affairs at home, he did so only with the desire of showing himself amiable, and he did not press the invitation.

Clotilde spent the afternoon in packing her trunks. In the feverish excitement of so sudden a decision she had thought of nothing but the joy of her return. But after the hurry of dinner was over, after she had said good-bye to her brother, after the interminable drive in a hackney coach along the avenue of the Bois de Boulogne to the Lyons railway station, when she found herself in the ladies' compartment, starting on the long journey on a cold and rainy November night, already rolling away from Paris, her excitement began to abate, and reflections forced their way into her mind and began to trouble her. Why this brief and urgent dispatch: "I await you; start this evening." Doubtless it was the answer to her letter; but she knew how greatly Pascal had desired that she should remain in Paris, where he thought she was happy, and she was astonished at his hasty summons. She had not expected a dispatch, but a letter, arranging for her return a few weeks later. There must be something else, then; perhaps he was ill and felt a desire, a longing to see her again at once. And from this time forward this fear seized her with the force of a presentiment, and grew stronger and stronger, until it soon took complete possession of her.

All night long the rain beat furiously against the windows of the train while they were crossing the plains of Burgundy, and did not cease until they reached Macon. When they had passed Lyons the day broke. Clotilde had Pascal's letters with her, and she had waited impatiently for the daylight that she might read again carefully these letters, the writing of which had seemed changed to her. And noticing the unsteady characters, the breaks in the words, she felt a chill at her heart. He was ill, very ill — she had become certain of this now, by a divination in which there was less of reasoning than of subtle prescience. And the rest of the journey seemed terribly long, for her anguish increased in proportion as she approached its termination. And worse than all, arriving at Marseilles at half-past twelve, there was no train for Plassans until twenty minutes past three. Three long hours of waiting! She breakfasted at the buffet in the railway station, eating hurriedly, as if she was afraid of missing this train; then she dragged herself into the dusty garden, going from bench to bench in the pale, mild sunshine, among omnibuses and hackney coaches. At last she was once more in the train, which stopped at every little way station. When they were approaching Plassans she put her head out of the window eagerly, longing to see the town again after her short absence of two months. It seemed to her as if she had been away for twenty years, and that everything must be changed. When the train was leaving the little station of Sainte-Marthe her emotion reached its height when, leaning out, she saw in the distance La Souleiade with the two secular cypresses on the terrace, which could be seen three leagues off.

It was five o'clock, and twilight was already falling. The train stopped, and Clotilde descended. But it was a surprise and a keen grief to her not to see Pascal waiting for her on the platform. She had been saying to herself since they had left Lyons: "If I do not see him at once, on the arrival of the train, it will be because he is ill." He might be in the waiting-room, however, or with a carriage outside. She hurried forward, but she saw no one but Father Durieu, a driver whom the doctor was in the habit of employing. She questioned him eagerly. The old man, a taciturn Provençal, was in no haste to answer. His wagon was there, and he asked her for the checks for her luggage, wishing to see about the trunks before anything else. In a trembling voice she repeated her question:

"Is everybody well, Father Durieu?"

"Yes, mademoiselle."

And she was obliged to put question after question to him before she succeeded in eliciting the information that it was Martine who had told him, at about six o'clock the day before, to be at the station with his wagon, in time to meet the train. He had not seen the doctor, no one had seen him, for two months past. It might very well be since he was not here that he had been obliged to take to his bed, for there was a report in the town that he was not very well.

"Wait until I get the luggage, mademoiselle," he ended, "there is room for you on the seat."

"No, Father Durieu, it would be too long to wait. I will walk."

She ascended the slope rapidly. Her heart was so tightened that she could scarcely breathe. The sun had sunk behind the hills of Sainte-Marthe, and a fine mist was falling from the chill grey November sky, and as she took the road to Les Fenouilleres she caught another glimpse of La Souleiade, which struck a chill to her heart — the front of the house, with all its shutters closed, and wearing a look of abandonment and desolation in the melancholy twilight.

But Clotilde received the final and terrible blow when she saw Ramond standing at the hall door, apparently waiting for her. He had indeed been watching for her, and had come downstairs to break the dreadful news gently to her. She arrived out of breath; she had crossed the quincunx of plane trees near the fountain to shorten the way, and on seeing the young man there instead of Pascal, whom she had in spite of everything expected to see, she had a presentiment of overwhelming ruin, of irreparable misfortune. Ramond was pale and agitated, notwithstanding the effort he made to control his feelings. At the first moment he could not find a word to say, but waited to be questioned. Clotilde, who was herself suffocating, said nothing. And they entered the house thus; he led her to the dining room, where they remained for a few seconds, face to face, in mute anguish.

"He is ill, is he not?" she at last faltered.

"Yes," he said, "he is ill."

"I knew it at once when I saw you," she replied. "I knew when he was not here that he must be ill. He is very ill, is he not?" she persisted.

As he did not answer but grew still paler, she looked at him fixedly. And on the instant she saw the shadow of death upon him; on his hands that still trembled, that had assisted the dying man; on his sad face; in his troubled eyes, which still retained the reflection of the death agony; in the neglected and disordered appearance of the physician who, for twelve hours, had maintained an unavailing struggle against death.

She gave a loud cry:

"He is dead!"

She tottered, and fell fainting into the arms of Ramond, who with a great sob pressed her in a brotherly embrace. And thus they wept on each other's neck.

When he had seated her in a chair, and she was able to speak, he said:

"It was I who took the dispatch you received to the telegraph office yesterday, at half-past ten o'clock. He was so happy, so full of hope! He was forming plans for the future — a year, two years of life. And this morning, at four o'clock, he had the first attack, and he sent for me. He saw at once that he was doomed, but he expected to last until six o'clock, to live long enough to see you again. But the disease progressed too rapidly. He described its progress to me, minute by minute, like a professor in the dissecting room. He died with your name upon his lips, calm, but full of anguish, like a hero."

Clotilde listened, her eyes drowned in tears which flowed endlessly. Every word of the relation of this piteous and stoical death penetrated her heart and stamped itself there. She reconstructed every hour of the dreadful day. She followed to its close its grand and mournful drama. She would live it over in her thoughts forever.

But her despairing grief overflowed when Martine, who had entered the room a moment before, said in a harsh voice:

"Ah, mademoiselle has good reason to cry! for if monsieur is dead, mademoiselle is to blame for it."

The old servant stood apart, near the door of her kitchen, in such a passion of angry grief, because they had taken her master from her, because they had killed him, that she did not even try to find a word of welcome or consolation for this child whom she had brought up. And without calculating the consequences of her indiscretion, the grief or the joy which she might cause, she relieved herself by telling all she knew.

"Yes, if monsieur has died, it is because mademoiselle went away."

From the depths of her overpowering grief Clotilde protested. She had expected to see Martine weeping with her, like Ramond, and she was surprised to feel that she was an enemy.

"Why, it was he who would not let me stay, who insisted upon my going away," she said.

"Oh, well! mademoiselle must have been willing to go or she would have been more clear-sighted. The night before your departure I found monsieur half-suffocated with grief; and when I wished to inform mademoiselle, he himself prevented me; he had such courage. Then I could see it all, after mademoiselle had gone. Every night it was the same thing over again, and he could hardly keep from writing to you to come back. In short, he died of it, that is the pure truth."

A great light broke in on Clotilde's mind, making her at the same time very happy and very wretched. Good God! what she had suspected for a moment, was then true. Afterward she had been convinced, seeing Pascal's angry persistence, that he was speaking the truth; that between her and work he had chosen work sincerely, like a man of science with whom love of work has gained the victory over the love of woman. And yet he had not spoken the truth; he had carried his devotion, his self-forgetfulness to the point of immolating himself to what he believed to be her happiness. And the misery of things willed that he should have been mistaken, that he should have thus consummated the unhappiness of both.

Clotilde again protested wildly:

"But how could I have known? I obeyed; I put all my love in my obedience."

"Ah," cried Martine again, "it seems to me that I should have guessed."

Ramond interposed gently. He took Clotilde's hands once more in his, and explained to her that grief might indeed have hastened the fatal issue, but that the master had unhappily been doomed for some time past. The affection of the heart from which he had suffered must have been of long standing — a great deal of overwork, a certain part of heredity, and, finally, his late absorbing love, and the poor heart had broken.

"Let us go upstairs," said Clotilde simply. "I wish to see him."

Upstairs in the death-chamber the blinds were closed, shutting out even the melancholy twilight. On a little table at the foot of the bed burned two tapers in two candlesticks. And they cast a pale yellow light on Pascal's form extended on the bed, the feet close together, the hands folded on the breast. The eyes had been piously closed. The face, of a bluish hue still, but already looking calm and peaceful, framed by the flowing white hair and beard, seemed asleep. He had been dead scarcely an hour and a half, yet already infinite serenity, eternal silence, eternal repose, had begun.

Seeing him thus, at the thought that he no longer heard her, that he no longer saw her, that she was alone now, that she was to kiss him for the last time, and then lose him forever, Clotilde, in an outburst of grief, threw herself upon the bed, and in broken accents of passionate tenderness cried:

"Oh, master, master, master —"

She pressed her lips to the dead man's forehead, and, feeling it still warm with life, she had a momentary illusion: she fancied that he felt this last caress, so cruelly awaited. Did he not smile in his immobility, happy at last, and able to die, now that he felt her here beside him? Then, overcome by the dreadful reality, she burst again into wild sobs.

Martine entered, bringing a lamp, which she placed on a corner of the chimneypiece, and she heard Ramond, who was watching Clotilde, disquieted at seeing her passionate grief, say:

"I shall take you away from the room if you give way like this. Consider that you have someone else to think of now."

The servant had been surprised at certain words which she had overheard by chance during the day. Suddenly she understood, and she turned paler even than before, and on her way out of the room, she stopped at the door to hear more.

"The key of the press is under his pillow," said Ramond, lowering his voice; "he told me repeatedly to tell you so. You know what you have to do?"

Clotilde made an effort to remember and to answer.

"What I have to do? About the papers, is it not? Yes, yes, I remember; I am to keep the envelopes and to give you the other manuscripts. Have no fear, I am quite calm, I will be very reasonable. But I will not leave him; I will spend the night here very quietly, I promise you."

She was so unhappy, she seemed so resolved to watch by him, to remain with him, until he should be taken away, that the young physician allowed her to have her way.

"Well, I will leave you now. They will be expecting me at home. Then there are all sorts of formalities to be gone through — to give notice at the mayor's office, the funeral, of which I wish to spare you the details. Trouble yourself about nothing. Everything will be arranged tomorrow when I return."

He embraced her once more and then went away. And it was only then that Martine left the room, behind him, and locking the hall door she ran out into the darkness.

Clotilde was now alone in the chamber; and all around and about her, in the unbroken silence, she felt the emptiness of the house. Clotilde was alone with the dead Pascal. She placed a chair at the head of the bed and sat there motionless, alone. On arriving, she had merely removed her hat: now, perceiving that she still had on her gloves, she took them off also. But she kept on her traveling dress, crumpled and dusty, after twenty hours of railway travel. No doubt Father Durieu had brought the trunks long ago, and left them downstairs. But it did not occur to her, nor had she the strength to wash herself and change her clothes, but remained sitting, overwhelmed with grief, on the chair into which she had dropped. One regret, a great remorse, filled her to the exclusion of all else. Why had she obeyed him? Why had she consented to leave him? If she had remained she had the ardent conviction that he would not have died. She would have lavished so much love, so many caresses upon him, that she would have cured him. If one was anxious to keep a beloved being from dying one should remain with him and, if necessary, give one's heart's blood to keep him alive. It was her own fault if she had lost him, if she could not now with a caress awaken him from his eternal sleep. And she thought herself imbecile not to have understood; cowardly, not to have devoted herself to him; culpable, and to be forever punished for having gone away when plain common sense, in default of feeling, ought to have kept her here, bound, as a submissive and affectionate subject, to the task of watching over her king.

The silence had become so complete, so profound, that Clotilde lifted her eyes for a moment from Pascal's face to look around the room. She saw only vague shadows — the two tapers threw two yellow patches on the high ceiling. At this moment she remembered the letters he had written to her, so short, so cold; and she comprehended his heroic sacrifice, the torture it had been to him to silence his heart, desiring to immolate himself to the end. What strength must he not have required for the accomplishment of the plan of happiness, sublime and disastrous, which he had formed for her. He had resolved to pass out of her life in order to save her from his old age and his poverty; he wished her to be rich and free, to enjoy her youth, far away from him; this indeed was utter self-effacement, complete absorption in the love of another. And she felt a profound gratitude, a sweet solace in the thought, mingled with a sort of angry bitterness against evil fortune. Then, suddenly, the happy years of her childhood and her long youth spent beside him who had always been so kind and so good-humored, rose before her — how he had gradually won her affection, how she had felt that she was his, after the quarrels which had separated them for a time, and with what a transport of joy she had at last given herself to him.

Seven o'clock struck. Clotilde started as the clear tones broke the profound silence. Who was it that had spoken? Then she remembered, and she looked at the clock. And when the last sound of the seven strokes, each of which had fallen like a knell upon her heart, had died away, she turned her eyes again on the motionless face of Pascal, and once more she abandoned herself to her grief.

It was in the midst of this ever-increasing prostration that Clotilde, a few minutes later, heard a sudden sound of sobbing. Someone had rushed into the room; she looked round and saw her Grandmother Felicite. But she did not stir, she did not speak, so benumbed was she with grief. Martine, anticipating the orders which Clotilde would undoubtedly have given her, had hurried to old Mme. Rougon's, to give her the dreadful news; and the latter, dazed at first by the suddenness of the catastrophe, and afterward greatly agitated, had hurried to the house, overflowing with noisy grief. She burst into tears at sight of her son, and then embraced Clotilde, who returned her kiss, as in a dream. And from this instant the latter, without emerging from the overwhelming grief in which she isolated herself, felt that she was no longer alone, hearing a continual stir and bustle going on around her. It was Felicite crying, coming in and going out on tiptoe, setting things in order, spying about, whispering, dropping into a chair, to get up again a moment afterward, after saying that she was going to die in it. At nine o'clock she made a last effort to persuade her granddaughter to eat something. Twice already she had lectured her in a low voice; she came now again to whisper to her:

"Clotilde, my dear, I assure you you are wrong. You must keep up your strength or you will never be able to hold out."

But the young woman, with a shake of her head, again refused.

"Come, you breakfasted at the buffet at Marseilles, I suppose, but you have eaten nothing since. Is that reasonable? I do not wish you to fall ill also. Martine has some broth. I have told her to make a light soup and to roast a chicken. Go down and eat a mouthful, only a mouthful, and I will remain here."

With the same patient gesture Clotilde again refused. At last she faltered:

"Do not ask me, grandmother, I entreat you. I could not; it would choke me."

She did not speak again, falling back into her former state of apathy. She did not sleep, however, her wide open eyes were fixed persistently on Pascal's face. For hours she sat there, motionless, erect, rigid, as if her spirit were far away with the dead. At ten o'clock she heard a noise; it was Martine bringing up the lamp. Toward eleven Felicite, who was sitting watching in an armchair, seemed to grow restless, got up and went out of the room, and came back again. From this forth there was a continual coming and going as of impatient footsteps prowling around the young woman, who was still awake, her large eyes fixed motionless on Pascal. Twelve o'clock struck, and one persistent thought alone pierced her weary brain, like a nail, and prevented sleep — why had she obeyed him? If she had remained she would have revived him with her youth, and he would not have died. And it was not until a little before one that she felt this thought, too, grow confused and lose itself in a nightmare. And she fell into a heavy sleep, worn out with grief and fatigue.

When Martine had announced to Mme. Rougon the unexpected death of her son Pascal, in the shock which she received there was as much of anger as of grief. What! her dying son had not wished to see her; he had made this servant swear not to inform her of his illness! This thought sent the blood coursing swiftly through her veins, as if the struggle between them, which had lasted during his whole life, was to be continued beyond the grave. Then, when after hastily dressing herself she had hurried to La Souleiade, the thought of the terrible envelopes, of all the manuscripts piled up in the press, had filled her with trembling rage. Now that Uncle Macquart and Aunt Dide were dead, she no longer feared what she called the abomination of the Tulettes; and even poor little Charles, in dying, had carried with him one of the most humiliating of the blots on the family. There remained only the envelopes, the abominable envelopes, to menace the glorious Rougon legend which she had spent her whole life in creating, which was the sole thought of her old age, the work to the triumph of which she had persistently devoted the last efforts of her wily and active brain. For long years she had watched these envelopes, never wearying, beginning the struggle over again, when he had thought her beaten, always alert and persistent. Ah! if she could only succeed in obtaining possession of them and destroying them! It would be the execrable past destroyed, effaced; it would be the glory of her family, so hardly won, at last freed from all fear, at last shining untarnished, imposing its lie upon history. And she saw herself traversing the three quarters of Plassans, saluted by everyone, bearing herself as proudly as a queen, mourning nobly for the fallen Empire. So that when Martine informed her that Clotilde had come, she quickened her steps as she approached La Souleiade, spurred by the fear of arriving too late.

But as soon as she was installed in the house, Felicite at once regained her composure. There was no hurry, they had the whole night before them. She wished, however, to win over Martine without delay, and she knew well how to influence this simple creature, bound up in the doctrines of a narrow religion. Going down to the kitchen, then, to see the chicken roasting, she began by affecting to be heartbroken at the thought of her son dying without having made his peace with the Church. She questioned the servant, pressing her for particulars. But the latter shook her head disconsolately — no, no priest had come, monsieur had not even made the sign of the cross. She, only, had knelt down to say the prayers for the dying, which certainly could not be enough for the salvation of a soul. And yet with what fervor she had prayed to the good God that monsieur might go straight to Paradise!

With her eyes fixed on the chicken turning on the spit, before a bright fire, Felicite resumed in a lower voice, with an absorbed air:

"Ah, my poor girl, what will most prevent him from going to Paradise are the abominable papers which the unhappy man has left behind him up there in the press. I cannot understand why it is that lightning from heaven has not struck those papers before this and reduced them to ashes. If they are allowed to leave this house it will be ruin and disgrace and eternal perdition!"

Martine listened, very pale.

"Then madame thinks it would be a good work to destroy them, a work that would assure the repose of monsieur's soul?"

"Great God! Do I believe it! Why, if I had those dreadful papers in my hands, I would throw everyone of them into the fire. Oh, you would not need then to put on anymore sticks; with the manuscripts upstairs alone you would have fuel enough to roast three chickens like that."

The servant took a long spoon and began to baste the fowl. She, too, seemed now to reflect.

"Only we haven't got them. I even overheard some words on the subject, which I may repeat to madame. It was when mademoiselle went upstairs. Dr. Raymond spoke to her about the papers, asking her if she remembered some orders which she had received, before she went away, no doubt; and she answered that she remembered, that she was to keep the envelopes and to give him all the other manuscripts."

Felicite trembled; she could not restrain a terrified movement. Already she saw the papers slipping out of her reach; and it was not the envelopes only which she desired, but all the manuscripts, all that unknown, suspicious, and secret work, from which nothing but scandal could come, according to the obtuse and excitable mind of the proud old *bourgeoise.*

"But we must act!" she cried, "act immediately, this very night! Tomorrow it may be too late."

"I know where the key of the press is," answered Martine in a low voice. "The doctor told mademoiselle."

Felicite immediately pricked up her ears.

"The key; where is it?"

"Under the pillow, under monsieur's head."

In spite of the bright blaze of the fire of vine branches the air seemed to grow suddenly chill, and the two old women were silent. The only sound to be heard was the drip of the chicken juice falling into the pan.

But after Mme. Rougon had eaten a hasty and solitary dinner she went upstairs again with Martine. Without another word being spoken they understood each other, it was decided that they would use all possible means to obtain possession of the papers before daybreak. The simplest was to take the key from under the pillow. Clotilde would no doubt at last fall asleep — she seemed too exhausted not to succumb to fatigue. All they had to do was to wait. They set themselves to watch, then, going back and forth on tiptoe between the study and the bed-room, waiting for the moment when the young woman's large motion-less eyes should close in sleep. One of them would go to see, while the other waited impatiently in the study, where a lamp burned dully on the table. This was repeated every fifteen minutes until midnight. The fathomless eyes, full of gloom and of an immense despair, did not close. A little before midnight Felicite installed herself in an armchair at the foot of the bed, resolved not to leave the spot until her granddaughter should have fallen asleep. From this forth she did not take her eyes off Clotilde, and it filled her with a sort of fear to remark that the girl scarcely moved her eyelids, looking with that inconsolable fixity which defies sleep. Then she herself began to feel sleep stealing over her. Exasperated, trembling with nervous impatience, she could remain where she was no longer. And she went to rejoin the servant, who was watching in the study.

"It is useless; she will not sleep," she said in a stifled and trembling voice. "We must find some other way."

It had indeed occurred to her to break open the press.

But the old oaken boards were strong, the old iron held firmly. How could they break the lock — not to speak of the noise they would make and which would certainly be heard in the adjoining room?

She stood before the thick doors, however, and felt them with her fingers, seeking some weak spot.

"If I only had an instrument," she said.

Martine, less eager, interrupted her, objecting: "Oh, no, no, madame! We might be surprised! Wait, I will go again and see if mademoiselle is asleep now."

She went to the bedroom on tiptoe and returned immediately, saying: "Yes, she is asleep. Her eyes are closed, and she does not stir."

Then both went to look at her, holding their breath and walking with the utmost caution, so that the boards might not creak. Clotilde had indeed just fallen asleep: and her stupor seemed so profound that the two old women grew bold. They feared, however, that they might touch and waken her, for her chair stood close beside the bed. And then, to put one's hand under a dead man's pillow to rob him was a terrible and sacrilegious act, the thought of which filled them with terror. Might it not disturb his repose? Might he not move at the shock? The thought made them turn pale.

Felicite had advanced with outstretched hand, but she drew back, stammering:

"I am too short. You try, Martine."

The servant in her turn approached the bed. But she was seized with such a fit of trembling that she was obliged to retreat lest she should fall.

"No, no, I cannot!" she said. "It seems to me that monsieur is going to open his eyes."

And trembling and awe-struck they remained an instant longer in the lugubrious chamber full of the silence and the majesty of death, facing Pascal, motionless forever, and Clotilde, overwhelmed by the grief of her widowhood. Perhaps they saw, glorifying that mute head, guarding its work with all its weight, the nobility of a life spent in honorable labor. The flame of the tapers burned palely. A sacred awe filled the air, driving them from the chamber.

Felicite, who was so brave, who had never in her life flinched from anything, not even from bloodshed, fled as if she was pursued, saying:

"Come, come, Martine, we will find some other way; we will go look for an instrument."

In the study they drew a breath of relief. Felicite looked in vain among the papers on Pascal's work-table for the genealogical tree, which she knew was usually there. She would so gladly have begun her work of destruction with this. It was there, but in her feverish excitement she did not perceive it.

Her desire drew her back again to the press, and she stood before it, measuring it and examining it with eager and covetous look. In spite of her short stature, in spite of her eighty-odd years, she displayed an activity and an energy that were truly extraordinary.

"Ah!" she repeated, "if I only had an instrument!"

And she again sought the crevice in the colossus, the crack into which she might introduce her fingers, to break it open. She imagined plans of assault, she thought of using force, and then she fell back on stratagem, on some piece of treachery which would open to her the doors, merely by breathing upon them.

Suddenly her glance kindled; she had discovered the means.

"Tell me, Martine; there is a hook fastening one of the doors, is there not?"

"Yes, madame; it catches in a ring above the middle shelf. See, it is about the height of this molding."

Felicite made a triumphant gesture.

"Have you a gimlet — a large gimlet? Give me a gimlet!"

Martine went down into her kitchen and brought back the tool that had been asked.

"In that way, you see, we shall make no noise," resumed the old woman, setting herself to her task.

With a strength which one would not have suspected in her little hands, withered by age, she inserted the gimlet, and made a hole at the height indicated by the servant. But it was too low; she felt the point, after a time, entering the shelf. A second attempt brought the instrument in direct contact with the iron hook. This time the hole was too near. And she multiplied the holes to right and left, until finally she succeeded in pushing the hook out of the ring. The bolt of the lock slipped, and both doors opened.

"At last!" cried Felicite, beside herself.

Then she remained motionless for a moment, her ear turned uneasily toward the bedroom, fearing that she had wakened Clotilde. But silence reigned throughout the dark and sleeping house. There came from the bedroom only the august peace of death; she heard nothing but the clear vibration of the clock; Clotilde fell asleep near one. And the press yawned wide open, displaying the papers with which it overflowed, heaped up on its three shelves. Then she threw herself upon it, and the work of destruction began, in the midst of the sacred obscurity of the infinite repose of this funereal vigil.

"At last!" she repeated, in a low voice, "after thirty years of waiting. Let us hurry — let us hurry. Martine, help me!"

She had already drawn forward the high chair of the desk, and mounted on it at a bound, to take down, first of all, the papers on the top shelf, for she remembered that the envelopes were there. But she was surprised not to see the thick blue paper wrappers; there was nothing there but bulky manuscripts, the doctor's completed but unpublished works, works of inestimable value, all his researches, all his discoveries, the monument of his future fame, which he had left in Ramond's charge. Doubtless, some days before his death, thinking that only the envelopes were in danger, and that no one in the world would be so daring as to destroy his other works, he had begun to classify and arrange the papers anew, and removed the envelopes out of sight.

"Ah, so much the worse!" murmured Felicite; "let us begin anywhere; there are so many of them that if we wish to get through we must hurry. While I am up here, let us clear these away forever. Here, catch Martine!"

And she emptied the shelf, throwing the manuscripts, one by one, into the arms of the servant, who laid them on the table with as little noise as possible. Soon the whole heap was on it, and Felicite sprang down from the chair.

"To the fire! to the fire! We shall lay our hands on the others, and too, by and by, on those I am looking for. These can go into it, meantime. It will be a good riddance, at any rate, a fine clearance, yes, indeed! To the fire, to the fire with them all, even to the smallest scrap of paper, even to the most illegible scrawl, if we wish to be certain of destroying the contamination of evil."

She herself, fanatical and fierce, in her hatred of the truth, in her eagerness to destroy the testimony of science, tore off the first page of one of the manuscripts, lighted it at the lamp, and then threw this burning brand into the great fireplace, in which there had not been a fire for perhaps twenty years, and she fed the fire, continuing to throw on it the rest of the manuscript, piece by piece. The servant, as determined as herself, came to her assistance, taking another enormous notebook, which she tore up leaf by leaf. From this forth the fire did not cease to burn, filling the wide fireplace with a bright blaze, with tongues of flame that seemed to die away from time to time, only to burn up more brightly than ever when fresh fuel fed them. The fire grew larger, the heap of ashes rose higher and higher — a thick bed of blackened leaves among which ran millions of sparks. But it was a long, a never-ending task; for when several pages were thrown on at a time, they would not burn; it was necessary to move them and turn them over with the tongs; the best way was to stir them up and then wait until they were in a blaze, before adding more. The women soon grew skillful at their task, and the work progressed at a rapid rate.

In her haste to get a fresh armful of papers Felicite stumbled against a chair.

"Oh, madame, take care," said Martine. "Someone might come!"

"Come? who should come? Clotilde? She is too sound asleep, poor girl. And even if anyone should come, once it is finished, I don't care; I won't hide myself, you may be sure; I shall leave the empty press standing wide open; I shall say aloud that it is I who have purified the house. When there is not a line of writing left, ah, good heavens! I shall laugh at everything else!"

For almost two hours the fireplace blazed. They went back to the press and emptied the two other shelves, and now there remained only the bottom, which was heaped with a confusion of papers. Little by little, intoxicated by the heat of the bonfire, out of breath and perspiring, they gave themselves up to the savage joy of destruction. They stooped down, they blackened their hands, pushing in the partially consumed fragments, with gestures so violent, so feverishly excited, that their grey locks fell in disorder over their shoulders. It was like a dance of witches, feeding a hellish fire for some abominable act — the martyrdom of a saint, the burning of written thought in the public square; a whole world of truth and hope destroyed. And the blaze of this fire, which at moments made the flame of the lamp grow pale, lighted up the vast apartment, and made the gigantic shadows of the two women dance upon the ceiling.

But as she was emptying the bottom of the press, after having burned, handful by handful, the papers with which it had been filled, Felicite uttered a stifled cry of triumph.

"Ah, here they are! To the fire! to the fire!"

She had at last come upon the envelopes. Far back, behind the rampart formed by the notes, the doctor had hidden the blue paper wrappers. And then began a mad work of havoc, a fury of destruction; the envelopes were gathered up in handfuls and thrown into the flames, filling the fireplace with a roar like that of a conflagration.

"They are burning, they are burning! They are burning at last! Here is another, Martine, here is another. Ah, what a fire, what a glorious fire!"

But the servant was becoming uneasy.

"Take care, madame, you are going to set the house on fire. Don't you hear that roar?"

"Ah! what does that matter? Let it all burn. They are burning, they are burning; what a fine sight! Three more, two more, and, see, now the last is burning!"

She laughed with delight, beside herself, terrible to see, when some fragment of lighted soot fell down. The roar was becoming more and more fierce; the chimney, which was never swept, had caught fire. This seemed to excite her still more, while the servant, losing her head, began to scream and run about the room.

Clotilde slept beside the dead Pascal, in the supreme calm of the bedroom, unbroken save by the light vibration of the clock striking the hours. The tapers burned with a tall, still flame, the air was motionless.

And yet, in the midst of her heavy, dreamless sleep, she heard, as in a nightmare, a tumult, an ever-increasing rush and roar. And when she opened her eyes she could not at first understand. Where was she? Why this enormous weight that crushed her heart? She came back to reality with a start of terror — she saw Pascal, she heard Martine's cries in the adjoining room, and she rushed out, in alarm, to learn their cause.

But at the threshold Clotilde took in the whole scene with cruel distinctness — the press wide open and completely empty; Martine maddened by her fear of fire; Felicite radiant, pushing into the flames with her foot the last fragments of the envelopes. Smoke and flying soot filled the study, where the roaring of the fire sounded like the hoarse gasping of a murdered man — the fierce roar which she had just heard in her sleep.

And the cry which sprang from her lips was the same cry that Pascal himself had uttered on the night of the storm, when he surprised her in the act of stealing his papers.

"Thieves! assassins!"

She precipitated herself toward the fireplace, and, in spite of the dreadful roaring of the flames, in spite of the falling pieces of soot, at the risk of setting her hair on fire, and of burning her hands, she gathered up the leaves which remained yet unconsumed and bravely extinguished them, pressing them against her. But all this was very little, only some *debris*; not a complete page remained, not even a few fragments of the colossal labor, of the vast and patient work of a lifetime, which the fire had destroyed there in two hours. And with growing anger, in a burst of furious indignation, she cried:

"You are thieves, assassins! It is a wicked murder which you have just committed. You have profaned death, you have slain the mind, you have slain genius."

Old Mme. Rougon did not quail. She advanced, on the contrary, feeling no remorse, her head erect, defending the sentence of destruction pronounced and executed by her.

"It is to me you are speaking, to your grandmother. Is there nothing, then, that you respect? I have done what I ought to have done, what you yourself wished to do with us before."

"Before, you had made me mad; but since then I have lived, I have loved, I have understood, and it is life that I defend. Even if it be terrible and cruel, the truth ought to be respected. Besides, it was a sacred legacy bequeathed to my protection, the last thoughts of a dead man, all that remained of a great mind, and which I should have obliged everyone to respect. Yes, you are my grandmother; I am well aware of it, and it is as if you had just burned your son!"

"Burn Pascal because I have burned his papers!" cried Felicite. "Do you not know that I would have burned the town to save the honor of our family!"

She continued to advance, belligerent and victorious; and Clotilde, who had laid on the table the blackened fragments rescued by her from the burning flames, protected them with her body, fearing that her grandmother would throw them back again into the fire. She regarded the two women scornfully; she did not even trouble herself about the fire in the fireplace, which fortunately went out of itself, while Martine extinguished with the shovel the burning soot and the last flames of the smoldering ashes.

"You know very well, however," continued the old woman, whose little figure seemed to grow taller, "that I have had only one ambition, one passion in life — to see our family rich and powerful. I have fought, I have watched all my life, I have lived as long as I have done, only to put down ugly stories and to leave our name a glorious one. Yes, I have never despaired; I have never laid down my arms; I have been continually on the alert, ready to profit by the slightest circumstance. And all I desired to do I have done, because I have known how to wait."

And she waved her hand toward the empty press and the fireplace, where the last sparks were dying out.

"Now it is ended, our honor is safe; those abominable papers will no longer accuse us, and I shall leave behind me nothing to be feared. The Rougons have triumphed."

Clotilde, in a frenzy of grief, raised her arm, as if to drive her out of the room. But she left it of her own accord, and went down to the kitchen to wash her blackened hands and to fasten up her hair. The servant was about to follow her when, turning her head, she saw her young mistress' gesture, and she returned.

"Oh! as for me, mademoiselle, I will go away the day after tomorrow, when monsieur shall be in the cemetery."

There was a moment's silence.

"But I am not sending you away, Martine. I know well that it is not you who are most to blame. You have lived in this house for thirty years. Remain, remain with me."

The old maid shook her grey head, looking very pale and tired.

"No, I have served monsieur; I will serve no one after monsieur."

"But I!"

"You, no!"

Clotilde looked embarrassed, hesitated a moment, and remained silent. But Martine understood; she too seemed to reflect for an instant, and then she said distinctly:

"I know what you would say, but — no!"

And she went on to settle her account, arranging the affair like a practical woman who knew the value of money.

"Since I have the means, I will go and live quietly on my income somewhere. As for you, mademoiselle, I can leave you, for you are not poor. M. Ramond will explain to you tomorrow how an income of four thousand francs was saved for you out of the money at the notary's. Meantime, here is the key of the desk, where you will find the five thousand francs which monsieur left there. Oh? I know that there will be no trouble between us. Monsieur did not pay me for the last three months; I have papers from him which prove it. In addition, I advanced lately almost two hundred francs out of my own pocket, without his knowing where the money came from. It is all written down; I am not at all uneasy; mademoiselle will not wrong me by a centime. The day after tomorrow, when monsieur is no longer here, I will go away."

Then she went down to the kitchen, and Clotilde, in spite of the fanaticism of this woman, which had made her take part in a crime, felt inexpressibly sad at this desertion. When she was gathering up the fragments of the papers, however, before returning to the bedroom, she had a thrill of joy, on suddenly seeing the genealogical tree, which the two women had not perceived, lying unharmed on the table. It was the only entire document saved from the wreck. She took it and locked it, with the half-consumed fragments, in the bureau in the bedroom.

But when she found herself again in this august chamber a great emotion took possession of her. What supreme calm, what immortal peace, reigned here, beside the savage destruction that had filled the adjoining room with smoke and ashes. A sacred serenity pervaded the obscurity; the two tapers burned with a pure, still, unwavering flame. Then she saw that Pascal's face, framed in his flowing white hair and beard, had become very white. He slept with the light falling upon him, surrounded by a halo, supremely beautiful. She bent down, kissed him again, felt on her lips the cold of the marble face, with its closed eyelids, dreaming its dream of eternity. Her grief at not being able to save the work which he had left to her care was so overpowering that she fell on her knees and burst into a passion of sobs. Genius had been violated; it seemed to her as if the world was about to be destroyed in this savage destruction of a whole life of labor.

XIV

*I*n the study Clotilde was buttoning her dress, holding her child, whom she had been nursing, still in her lap. It was after lunch, about three o'clock on a hot sunny day at the end of August, and through the crevices of the carefully closed shutters only a few scattered sunbeams entered, piercing the drowsy and warm obscurity of the vast apartment. The rest and peace of the Sunday seemed to enter and diffuse itself in the room with the last sounds of the distant vesper bell. Profound silence reigned in the empty house in which the mother and child were to remain alone until dinner time, the servant having asked permission to go see a cousin in the faubourg.

For an instant Clotilde looked at her child, now a big boy of three months. She had been wearing mourning for Pascal for almost ten months — a long and simple black gown, in which she looked divinely beautiful, with her tall, slender figure and her sad, youthful face surrounded by its aureole of fair hair. And although she could not smile, it filled her with sweet emotion to see the beautiful child, so plump and rosy, with his mouth still wet with milk, whose gaze had been arrested by the sunbeam full of dancing motes. His eyes were fixed wonderingly on the golden brightness, the dazzling miracle of light. Then sleep came over him, and he let his little, round, bare head, covered thinly with fair hair, fall back on his mother's arm.

Clotilde rose softly and laid him in the cradle, which stood beside the table. She remained leaning over him for an instant to assure herself that he was asleep; then she let down the curtain in the already darkened room. Then she busied herself with supple and noiseless movements, walking with so light a step that she scarcely touched the floor, in putting away some linen which was on the table. Twice she crossed the room in search of a little missing sock. She was very silent, very gentle, and very active. And now, in the solitude of the house, she fell into a reverie and all the past year arose before her.

First, after the dreadful shock of the funeral, came the departure of Martine, who had obstinately kept to her determination of going away at once, not even remaining for the customary week, bringing to replace her the young cousin of a baker in the neighborhood — a stout brunette, who fortunately proved very neat and faithful. Martine herself lived at Sainte-Marthe, in a retired corner, so penuriously that she must be still saving even out of her small income. She was not known to have any heir. Who, then, would profit by this miserliness? In ten months she had not once set foot in La Souleiade — monsieur was not there, and she had not even the desire to see monsieur's son.

Then in Clotilde's reverie rose the figure of her grandmother Felicite. The latter came to see her from time to time with the condescension of a powerful relation who is liberal-minded enough to pardon all faults when they have been cruelly expiated. She would come unexpectedly, kiss the child, moralize, and give advice, and the young mother had adopted toward her the respectful attitude which Pascal had always maintained. Felicite was now wholly absorbed in her triumph. She was at last about to realize a plan that she had long cherished and maturely deliberated, which would perpetuate by an imperishable monument the untarnished glory of the family. The plan was to devote her fortune, which had become considerable, to the construction and endowment of an asylum for the aged, to be called Rougon Asylum. She had already bought the ground, a part of the old mall outside the town, near the railway station; and precisely on this Sunday, at five o'clock, when the heat should have abated a little, the first stone was to be laid, a really solemn ceremony, to be honored by the presence of all the authorities, and of which she was to be the acknowledged queen, before a vast concourse of people.

Clotilde felt, besides, some gratitude toward her grandmother, who had shown perfect disinterestedness on the occasion of the opening of Pascal's will. The latter had constituted the young woman his sole legatee; and the mother, who had a right to a fourth part, after declaring her intention to respect her son's wishes, had simply renounced her right to the succession. She wished, indeed, to disinherit all her family, bequeathing to them glory only, by employing her large fortune in the erection of this asylum, which was to carry down to future ages the revered and glorious name of the Rougons; and after having, for more than half a century, so eagerly striven to acquire money, she now disdained it, moved by a higher and purer ambition. And Clotilde, thanks to this liberality, had no uneasiness regarding the future — the four thousand francs income would be sufficient for her and her child. She would bring him up to be a man. She had sunk the five thousand francs that she had found in the desk in an annuity for him; and she owned, besides, La Souleiade, which everybody advised her to sell. True, it cost but little to keep it up, but what a sad and solitary life she would lead in that great deserted house, much too large for her, where she would be lost. Thus far, however, she had not been able to make up her mind to leave it. Perhaps she would never be able to do so.

Ah, this La Souleiade! all her love, all her life, all her memories were centered in it. It seemed to her at times as if Pascal were living here still, for she had changed nothing of their former manner of living. The furniture remained in the same places, the hours were the same, the habits the same. The only change she had made was to lock his room, into which only she went, as into a sanctuary, to weep when she felt her heart too heavy. And although indeed she felt very lonely, very lost, at each meal in the bright dining room downstairs, in fancy she heard there the echoes of their laughter, she recalled the healthy appetite of her youth; when they two had eaten and drank so gaily, rejoicing in their existence. And the garden, too, the whole place was bound up with the most intimate fibers of her being, for she could not take a step in it that their united images did not appear before her — on the terrace; in the slender shadow of the great secular cypresses, where they had so often contemplated the valley of the Viorne, closed in by the ridges of the Seille and the parched hills of Sainte-Marthe; the stone steps among the puny olive and almond trees, which they had so often challenged each other to run up in a trial of speed, like boys just let loose from school; and there was the pine grove, too, the warm, embalsamed shade, where the needles crackled under their feet; the vast threshing yard, carpeted with soft grass, where they could see the whole sky at night, when the stars were coming out; and above all there were the giant plane trees, whose delightful shade they had enjoyed every day in summer, listening to the soothing song of the fountain, the crystal clear song which it had sung for centuries. Even to the old stones of the house, even to the earth of the grounds, there was not an atom at La Souleiade in which she did not feel a little of their blood warmly throbbing, with which she did not feel a little of their life diffused and mingled.

But she preferred to spend her days in the workroom, and here it was that she lived over again her best hours. There was nothing new in it but the cradle. The doctor's table was in its place before the window to the left — she could fancy him coming in and sitting down at it, for his chair had not even been moved. On the long table in the center, among the old heap of books and papers, there was nothing new but the cheerful note of the little baby linen, which she was looking over. The bookcases displayed the same rows of volumes; the large oaken press seemed to guard within its sides the same treasure, securely shut in. Under the smoky ceiling the room was still redolent of work, with its confusion of chairs, the pleasant disorder of this common workroom, filled with the caprices of the girl and the researches of the scientist. But what most moved her today was the sight of her old pastels hanging against the wall, the copies which she had made of living flowers, scrupulously exact copies, and of dream flowers of an imaginary world, whither her wild fancy sometimes carried her.

Clotilde had just finished arranging the little garments on the table when, lifting her eyes, she perceived before her the pastel of old King David, with his hand resting on the shoulder of Abishag the young Shunammite. And she, who now never smiled, felt her face flush with a thrill of tender and pleasing emotion. How they had loved each other, how they had dreamed of an eternity of love the day on which she had amused herself painting this proud and loving allegory! The old king, sumptuously clad in a robe hanging in straight folds, heavy with precious stones, wore the royal bandeau on his snowy locks; but she was more sumptuous still, with only her tall slender figure, her delicate round throat, and her supple arms, divinely graceful. Now he was gone, he was sleeping under the ground, while she, her pure and triumphant beauty concealed by her black robes, had only her child to express the love she had given him before the assembled people, in the full light of day.

Then Clotilde sat down beside the cradle. The slender sunbeams lengthened, crossing the room from end to end, the heat of the warm afternoon grew oppressive in the drowsy obscurity made by the closed shutters, and the silence of the house seemed more profound than before. She set apart some little waists, she sewed on some tapes with slow-moving needle, and gradually she fell into a reverie in the warm deep peacefulness of the room, in the midst of the glowing heat outside. Her thoughts first turned to her pastels, the exact copies and the fantastic dream flowers; she said to herself now that all her dual nature was to be found in that passion for truth, which had at times kept her a whole day before a flower in order to copy it with exactness, and in her need of the spiritual, which at other times took her outside the real, and carried her in wild dreams to the paradise of flowers such as had never grown on earth. She had always been thus. She felt that she was in reality the same today as she had been yesterday, in the midst of the flow of new life which ceaselessly transformed her. And then she thought of Pascal, full of gratitude that he had made her what she was. In days past when, a little girl, he had removed her from her execrable surroundings and taken her home with him, he had undoubtedly followed the impulses of his good heart, but he had also undoubtedly desired to try an experiment with her, to see how she would grow up in the different environment, in an atmosphere of truthfulness and affection. This had always been an idea of his. It was an old theory of his which he would have liked to test on a large scale: culture through environment, complete regeneration even, the improvement, the salvation of the individual, physically as well as morally. She owed to him undoubtedly the best part of her nature; she guessed how fanciful and violent she might have become, while he had made her only enthusiastic and courageous.

In this retrospection she was clearly conscious of the gradual change that had taken place within her. Pascal had corrected her heredity, and she lived over again the slow evolution, the struggle between the fantastic and the real in her. It had begun with her outbursts of anger as a child, a ferment of rebellion, a want of mental balance that had caused her to indulge in most hurtful reveries. Then came her fits of extreme devotion, the need of illusion and falsehood, of immediate happiness in the thought that the inequalities and injustices of this wicked world would he compensated by the eternal joys of a future paradise. This was the epoch of her struggles with Pascal, of the torture which she had caused him, planning to destroy the work of his genius. And at this point her nature had changed; she had acknowledged him for her master. He had conquered her by the terrible lesson of life which he had given her on the night of the storm. Then, environment had acted upon her, evolution had proceeded rapidly, and she had ended by becoming a well-balanced and rational woman, willing to live life as it ought to be lived, satisfied with doing her work in the hope that the sum of the common labor would one day free the world from evil and pain. She had loved, she was a mother now, and she understood.

Suddenly she remembered the night which they had spent in the threshing yard. She could still hear her lamentation under the stars — the cruelty of nature, the inefficacy of science, the wickedness of humanity, and the need she felt of losing herself in God, in the Unknown. Happiness consisted in self-renunciation. Then she heard him repeat his creed — the progress of reason through science, truths acquired slowly and forever the only possible good, the belief that the sum of these truths, always augmenting, would finally confer upon man incalculable power and peace, if not happiness. All was summed up in his ardent faith in life. As he expressed it, it was necessary to march with life, which marched always. No halt was to be expected, no peace in immobility and renunciation, no consolation in turning back. One must keep a steadfast soul, the only ambition to perform one's work, modestly looking for no other reward of life than to have lived it bravely, accomplishing the task which it imposes. Evil was only an accident not yet explained, humanity appearing from a great height like an immense wheel in action, working ceaselessly for the future. Why should the workman who disappeared, having finished his day's work, abuse the work because he could neither see nor know its end? Even if it were to have no end why should he not enjoy the delight of action, the exhilarating air of the march, the sweetness of sleep after the fatigue of a long and busy day? The children would carry on the task of the parents; they were born and cherished only for this, for the task of life which is transmitted to them, which they in their turn will transmit to others. All that remained, then, was to be courageously resigned to the grand common labor, without the rebellion of the ego, which demands personal happiness, perfect and complete.

She questioned herself, and she found that she did not experience that anguish which had filled her formerly at the thought of what was to follow death. This anxiety about the Beyond no longer haunted her until it became a torture. Formerly she would have liked to wrest by force from heaven the secrets of destiny. It had been a source of infinite grief to her not to know why she existed. Why are we born? What do we come on earth to do? What is the meaning of this execrable existence, without equality, without justice, which seemed to her like a fevered dream? Now her terror was calmed; she could think of these things courageously. Perhaps it was her child, the continuation of herself, which now concealed from her the horror of her end. But her regular life contributed also to this, the thought that it was necessary to live for the effort of living, and that the only peace possible in this world was in the joy of the accomplishment of this effort. She repeated to herself a remark of the doctor, who would often say when he saw a peasant returning home with a contented look after his day's work: "There is a man whom anxiety about the Beyond will not prevent from sleeping." He meant to say that this anxiety troubles and perverts only excitable and idle brains. If all performed their healthful task, all would sleep peacefully at night. She herself had felt the beneficent power of work in the midst of her sufferings and her grief. Since he had taught her to employ everyone of her hours; since she had been a mother, especially, occupied constantly with her child, she no longer felt a chill of horror when she thought of the Unknown. She put aside without an effort disquieting reveries; and if she still felt an occasional fear, if some of her daily griefs made her sick at heart, she found comfort and unfailing strength in the thought that her child was this day a day older, that he would be another day older on the morrow, that day by day, page by page, his work of life was being accomplished. This consoled her delightfully for all her miseries. She had a duty, an object, and she felt

in her happy serenity that she was doing surely what she had been sent
here to do.

Yet, even at this very moment she knew that the mystic was not
entirely dead within her. In the midst of the profound silence she heard
a slight noise, and she raised her head. Who was the divine mediator
that had passed? Perhaps the beloved dead for whom she mourned, and
whose presence near her she fancied she could divine. There must always
be in her something of the childlike believer she had always been,
curious about the Unknown, having an instinctive longing for the
mysterious. She accounted to herself for this longing, she even explained
it scientifically. However far science may extend the limits of human
knowledge, there is undoubtedly a point which it cannot pass; and it
was here precisely that Pascal placed the only interest in life — in the
effort which we ceaselessly make to know more — there was only one
reasonable meaning in life, this continual conquest of the unknown.
Therefore, she admitted the existence of undiscovered forces surrounding the world, an immense and obscure domain, ten times larger than
the domain already won, an infinite and unexplored realm through
which future humanity would endlessly ascend. Here, indeed, was a field
vast enough for the imagination to lose itself in. In her hours of reverie
she satisfied in it the imperious need which man seems to have for the
spiritual, a need of escaping from the visible world, of interrogating the
Unknown, of satisfying in it the dream of absolute justice and of future
happiness. All that remained of her former torture, her last mystic
transports, were there appeased. She satisfied there that hunger for
consoling illusions which suffering humanity must satisfy in order to
live. But in her all was happily balanced. At this crisis, in an epoch
overburdened with science, disquieted at the ruins it has made, and
seized with fright in the face of the new century, wildly desiring to stop
and to return to the past, Clotilde kept the happy mean; in her the
passion for truth was broadened by her eagerness to penetrate the
Unknown. If sectarian scientists shut out the horizon to keep strictly
to the phenomenon, it was permitted to her, a good, simple creature, to
reserve the part that she did not know, that she would never know. And
if Pascal's creed was the logical deduction from the whole work, the
eternal question of the Beyond, which she still continued to put to
heaven, reopened the door of the infinite to humanity marching ever
onward. Since we must always learn, while resigning ourselves never to
know all, was it not to will action, life itself, to reserve the Unknown —
an eternal doubt and an eternal hope?

Another sound, as of a wing passing, the light touch of a kiss upon
her hair, this time made her smile. He was surely here; and her whole

being went out toward him, in the great flood of tenderness with which her heart overflowed. How kind and cheerful he was, and what a love for others underlay his passionate love of life! Perhaps he, too, had been only a dreamer, for he had dreamed the most beautiful of dreams, the final belief in a better world, when science should have bestowed incalculable power upon man — to accept everything, to turn everything to our happiness, to know everything and to foresee everything, to make nature our servant, to live in the tranquility of intelligence satisfied. Meantime faith in life, voluntary and regular labor, would suffice for health. Evil was only the unexplained side of things; suffering would one day be assuredly utilized. And regarding from above the enormous labor of the world, seeing the sum total of humanity, good and bad — admirable, in spite of everything, for their courage and their industry — she now regarded all mankind as united in a common brotherhood, she now felt only boundless indulgence, an infinite pity, and an ardent charity. Love, like the sun, bathes the earth, and goodness is the great river at which all hearts drink.

Clotilde had been plying her needle for two hours, with the same regular movement, while her thoughts wandered away in the profound silence. But the tapes were sewed on the little waists, she had even marked some new wrappers, which she had bought the day before. And, her sewing finished, she rose to put the linen away. Outside the sun was declining, and only slender and oblique sunbeams entered through the crevices of the shutters. She could not see clearly, and she opened one of the shutters, then she forgot herself for a moment, at the sight of the vast horizon suddenly unrolled before her. The intense heat had abated, a delicious breeze was blowing, and the sky was of a cloudless blue. To the left could be distinguished even the smallest clumps of pines, among the blood-colored ravines of the rocks of the Seille, while to the right, beyond the hills of Sainte-Marthe, the valley of the Viorne stretched away in the golden dust of the setting sun. She looked for a moment at the tower of St. Saturnin, all golden also, dominating the rose-colored town; and she was about to leave the window when she saw a sight that drew her back and kept her there, leaning on her elbow for a long time still.

Beyond the railroad a multitude of people were crowded together on the old mall. Clotilde at once remembered the ceremony. She knew that her Grandmother Felicite was going to lay the first stone of the Rougon Asylum, the triumphant monument destined to carry down to future ages the glory of the family. Vast preparations had been going on for a week past. There was talk of a silver hod and trowel, which the old lady was to use herself, determined to figure to triumph, with her eighty-two years. What swelled her heart with regal pride was that on this occasion she made the conquest of Plassans for the third time, for she compelled the whole town, all the three quarters, to range themselves around her, to form an escort for her, and to applaud her as a benefactress. For, of course, there had to be present lady patronesses, chosen from among the noblest ladies of the Quartier St. Marc; a delegation from the societies of working-women of the old quarter, and, finally, the most distinguished residents of the new town, advocates, notaries, physicians, without counting the common people, a stream of people dressed in their Sunday clothes, crowding there eagerly, as to a festival. And in the midst of this supreme triumph she was perhaps most proud — she, one of the queens of the Second Empire, the widow who mourned with so much dignity the fallen government — in having conquered the young republic itself, obliging it, in the person of the sub-prefect, to come and salute her and thank her. At first there had been question only of a discourse of the mayor; but it was known with certainty, since the previous day, that the sub-prefect also would speak. From so great a distance Clotilde could distinguish only a moving crowd of black coats and light dresses, under the scorching sun. Then there was a distant sound of music, the music of the amateur band of the town, the sonorous strains of whose brass instruments were borne to her at intervals on the breeze.

She left the window and went and opened the large oaken press to put away in it the linen that had remained on the table. It was in this press, formerly so full of the doctor's manuscripts, and now empty, that she kept the baby's wardrobe. It yawned open, vast, seemingly bottomless, and on the large bare shelves there was nothing but the baby linen, the little waists, the little caps, the little socks, all the fine clothing, the down of the bird still in the nest. Where so many thoughts had been stored up, where a man's unremitting labor for thirty years had accumulated in an overflowing heap of papers, there was now only a baby's clothing, only the first garments which would protect it for an hour, as it were, and which very soon it could no longer use. The vastness of the antique press seemed brightened and all refreshed by them.

When Clotilde had arranged the wrappers and the waists upon a shelf, she perceived a large envelope containing the fragments of the documents which she had placed there after she had rescued them from the fire. And she remembered a request which Dr. Ramond had come only the day before to make her — that she would see if there remained among this *debris* any fragment of importance having a scientific interest. He was inconsolable for the loss of the precious manuscripts which the master had bequeathed to him. Immediately after the doctor's death he had made an attempt to write from memory his last talk, that summary of vast theories expounded by the dying man with so heroic a serenity; but he could recall only parts of it. He would have needed complete notes, observations made from day to day, the results obtained, and the laws formulated. The loss was irreparable, the task was to be begun over again, and he lamented having only indications; he said that it would be at least twenty years before science could make up the loss, and take up and utilize the ideas of the solitary pioneer whose labors a wicked and imbecile catastrophe had destroyed.

The genealogical tree, the only document that had remained intact, was attached to the envelope, and Clotilde carried the whole to the table beside the cradle. After she had taken out the fragments, one by one, she found, what she had been already almost certain of, that not a single entire page of manuscript remained, not a single complete note having any meaning. There were only fragments of documents, scraps of half-burned and blackened paper, without sequence or connection. But as she examined them, these incomplete phrases, these words half consumed by fire, assumed for her an interest which no one else could have understood. She remembered the night of the storm, and the phrases completed themselves, the beginning of a word evoked before her persons and histories. Thus her eye fell on Maxime's name, and she reviewed the life of this brother who had remained a stranger to her, and whose death, two months before, had left her almost indifferent. Then, a half-burned scrap containing her father's name gave her an uneasy feeling, for she believed that her father had obtained possession of the fortune and the house on the avenue of Bois de Boulogne through the good offices of his hairdresser's niece, the innocent Rose, repaid, no doubt, by a generous percentage. Then she met with other names, that of her uncle Eugene, the former vice emperor, now dead, the cure of Saint-Eutrope, who, she had been told yesterday, was dying of consumption. And each fragment became animated in this way; the execrable family lived again in these scraps, these black ashes, where were now only disconnected words.

Then Clotilde had the curiosity to unfold the genealogical tree and spread it out upon the table. A strong emotion gained on her; she was deeply affected by these relics; and when she read once more the notes added in pencil by Pascal, a few moments before his death, tears rose to her eyes. With what courage he had written down the date of his death! And what despairing regret for life one divined in the trembling words announcing the birth of the child! The tree ascended, spread out its branches, unfolded its leaves, and she remained for a long time contemplating it, saying to herself that all the work of the master was to be found here in the classified records of this family tree. She could still hear certain of his words commenting on each hereditary case, she recalled his lessons. But the children, above all, interested her; she read again and again the notes on the leaves which bore their names. The doctor's colleague in Noumea, to whom he had written for information about the child born of the marriage of the convict Etienne, had at last made up his mind to answer; but the only information he gave was in regard to the sex — it was a girl, he said, and she seemed to be healthy. Octave Mouret had come near losing his daughter, who had always been very frail, while his little boy continued to enjoy superb health. But the chosen abode of vigorous health and of extraordinary fecundity was still the house of Jean, at Valqueyras, whose wife had had two children in three years and was about to have a third. The nestlings throve in the sunshine, in the heart of a fertile country, while the father sang as he guided his plow, and the mother at home cleverly made the soup and kept the children in order. There was enough new vitality and industry there to make another family, a whole race. Clotilde fancied at this moment that she could hear Pascal's cry: "Ah, our family! what is it going to be, in what kind of being will it end?" And she fell again into a reverie, looking at the tree sending its latest branches into the future. Who could tell whence the healthy branch would spring? Perhaps the great and good man so long awaited was germinating there.

A slight cry drew Clotilde from her reflections. The muslin curtain of the cradle seemed to become animate. It was the child who had wakened up and was moving about and calling to her. She at once took him out of the cradle and held him up gaily, that he might bathe in the golden light of the setting sun. But he was insensible to the beauty of the closing day; his little vacant eyes, still full of sleep, turned away from the vast sky, while he opened wide his rosy and ever hungry mouth, like a bird opening its beak. And he cried so loud, he had wakened up so ravenous, that she decided to nurse him again. Besides, it was his hour; it would soon be three hours since she had last nursed him.

Clotilde sat down again beside the table. She took him on her lap, but he was not very good, crying louder and louder, growing more and more impatient; and she looked at him with a smile while she unfastened her dress, showing her round, slender throat. Already the child knew, and raising himself he felt with his lips for the breast. When she placed it in his mouth he gave a little grunt of satisfaction; he threw himself upon her with the fine, voracious appetite of a young gentleman who was determined to live. At first he had clutched the breast with his little free hand, as if to show that it was his, to defend it and to guard it. Then, in the joy of the warm stream that filled his throat he raised his little arm straight up, like a flag. And Clotilde kept her unconscious smile, seeing him so healthy, so rosy, and so plump, thriving so well on the nourishment he drew from her. During the first few weeks she had suffered from a fissure, and even now her breast was sensitive; but she smiled, notwithstanding, with that peaceful look which mothers wear, happy in giving their milk as they would give their blood.

When she had unfastened her dress, showing her bare throat and breast, in the solitude and silence of the study, another of her mysteries, one of her sweetest and most hidden secrets, was revealed at the same time — the slender necklace with the seven pearls, the seven fine, milky stars which the master had put around her neck on a day of misery, in his mania for giving. Since it had been there no one else had seen it. It seemed as if she guarded it with as much modesty as if it were a part of her flesh, so simple, so pure, so childlike. And all the time the child was nursing she alone looked at it in a dreamy reverie, moved by the tender memory of the kisses whose warm perfume it still seemed to keep.

A burst of distant music seemed to surprise Clotilde. She turned her head and looked across the fields gilded by the oblique rays of the sun. Ah, yes! the ceremony, the laying of the corner stone yonder! Then she turned her eyes again on the child, and she gave herself up to the delight of seeing him with so fine an appetite. She had drawn forward a little bench, to raise one of her knees, resting her foot upon it, and she leaned one shoulder against the table, beside the tree and the blackened fragments of the envelopes. Her thoughts wandered away in an infinitely sweet reverie, while she felt the best part of herself, the pure milk, flowing softly, making more and more her own the dear being she had borne. The child had come, the redeemer, perhaps. The bells rang, the three wise men had set out, followed by the people, by rejoicing nature, smiling on the infant in its swaddling clothes. She, the mother, while he drank life in long drafts, was dreaming already of his future. What would he be when she should have made him tall and strong, giving herself to him entirely? A scientist, perhaps, who would reveal to the world something of the eternal truth; or a great captain, who would confer glory on his country; or, still better, one of those shepherds of the people who appease the passions and bring about the reign of justice. She saw him, in fancy, beautiful, good and powerful. Hers was the dream of every mother — the conviction that she had brought the expected Messiah into the world; and there was in this hope, in this obstinate belief, which every mother has in the certain triumph of her child, the hope which itself makes life, the belief which gives humanity the ever renewed strength to live still.

What would the child be? She looked at him, trying to discover whom he resembled. He had certainly his father's brow and eyes, there was something noble and strong in the breadth of the head. She saw a resemblance to herself, too, in his fine mouth and his delicate chin. Then, with secret uneasiness, she sought a resemblance to the others, the terrible ancestors, all those whose names were there inscribed on the tree, unfolding its growth of hereditary leaves. Was it this one, or this, or yet this other, whom he would resemble? She grew calm, however, she could not but hope, her heart swelled with eternal hope. The faith in life which the master had implanted in her kept her brave and steadfast. What did misery, suffering and wickedness matter! Health was in universal labor, in the effort made, in the power which fecundates and which produces. The work was good when the child blessed love. Then hope bloomed anew, in spite of the open wounds, the dark picture of human shame. It was life perpetuated, tried anew, life which we can never weary of believing good, since we live it so eagerly, with all its injustice and suffering.

Clotilde had glanced involuntarily at the ancestral tree spread out beside her. Yes, the menace was there — so many crimes, so much filth, side by side with so many tears, and so much patient goodness; so extraordinary a mixture of the best and the most vile, a humanity in little, with all its defects and all its struggles. It was a question whether it would not be better that a thunderbolt should come and destroy all this corrupt and miserable anthill. And after so many terrible Rougons, so many vile Macquarts, still another had been born. Life did not fear to create another of them, in the brave defiance of its eternity. It continued its work, propagated itself according to its laws, indifferent to theories, marching on in its endless labor. Even at the risk of making monsters, it must of necessity create, since, in spite of all it creates, it never wearies of creating in the hope, no doubt, that the healthy and the good will one day come. Life, life, which flows like a torrent, which continues its work, beginning it over and over again, without pause, to the unknown end! life in which we bathe, life with its infinity of contrary currents, always in motion, and vast as a boundless sea!

A transport of maternal fervor thrilled Clotilde's heart, and she smiled, seeing the little voracious mouth drinking her life. It was a prayer, an invocation, to the unknown child, as to the unknown God! To the child of the future, to the genius, perhaps, that was to be, to the Messiah that the coming century awaited, who would deliver the people from their doubt and their suffering! Since the nation was to be regenerated, had he not come for this work? He would make the experiment anew, he would raise up walls, give certainty to those who were in doubt, he would build the city of justice, where the sole law of labor would insure happiness. In troublous times prophets were to be expected — at least let him not be the Antichrist, the destroyer, the beast foretold in the Apocalypse — who would purge the earth of its wickedness, when this should become too great. And life would go on in spite of everything, only it would be necessary to wait for other myriads of years before the other unknown child, the benefactor, should appear.

But the child had drained her right breast, and, as he was growing angry, Clotilde turned him round and gave him the left. Then she began to smile, feeling the caress of his greedy little lips. At all events she herself was hope. A mother nursing, was she not the image of the world continued and saved? She bent over, she looked into his limpid eyes, which opened joyously, eager for the light. What did the child say to her that she felt her heart beat more quickly under the breast which he was draining? To what cause would he give his blood when he should be a man, strong with all the milk which he would have drunk? Perhaps he said nothing to her, perhaps he already deceived her, and yet she was so happy, so full of perfect confidence in him.

Again there was a distant burst of music. This must be the apotheosis, the moment when Grandmother Felicite, with her silver trowel, laid the first stone of the monument to the glory of the Rougons. The vast blue sky, gladdened by the Sunday festivities, rejoiced. And in the warm silence, in the solitary peace of the workroom, Clotilde smiled at the child, who was still nursing, his little arm held straight up in the air, like a signal flag of life.

Printed in the United States
67662LVS00008B/1-18